MONTAUK TRILOGY

MONTAUK TRILOGY

Smew: The Dawn of an Epidemic

A Cast of Shadows: An Immigrant's Story

Tempered Steel: The Folly of Revenge

John M. Aronian III MD

MONTAUK TRILOGY

Edited by Bennett Creative Services

Printed in the United States of America

ACKNOWLEDGEMENTS

Death sometimes comes like a lightening strike, shocking and terminal.

So it was with my husband, John Aronian. Though we seemed unprepared for his demise, I want to thank him for leaving behind a legacy of physical reminders: this book (over which he struggled for many years) in need of editing and publication, and his beloved vegetable garden which I now maintain. These have brought me closer to his spirit and to nature with its renewal of life. I also want to thank Laurel Aronian, my patient and literate grandchild who helped me, as only a thirteen-year old can, use the computer for editing. Thanks to Ruby Allen, my artistic grand daughter for much of the fanciful art work. And thanks to Sebastian Roldan, my Ecuadorian friend who supplied insight into "the Arduous Passage" and colloquial Spanish language,to my friend Andi Simon who made me realize that writing is a form of therapy. Especially to my wonderful son and daughter who have supported me through this difficult time. And lastly to my editor, Nicole Bennett for her sensible suggestions and timely work, thank you.

Dianne Aronian

To Peri and JM
In Remembrance of Grampus

Table of Contents

Smew

The Dawn of an Epidemic

The East End of Long Island

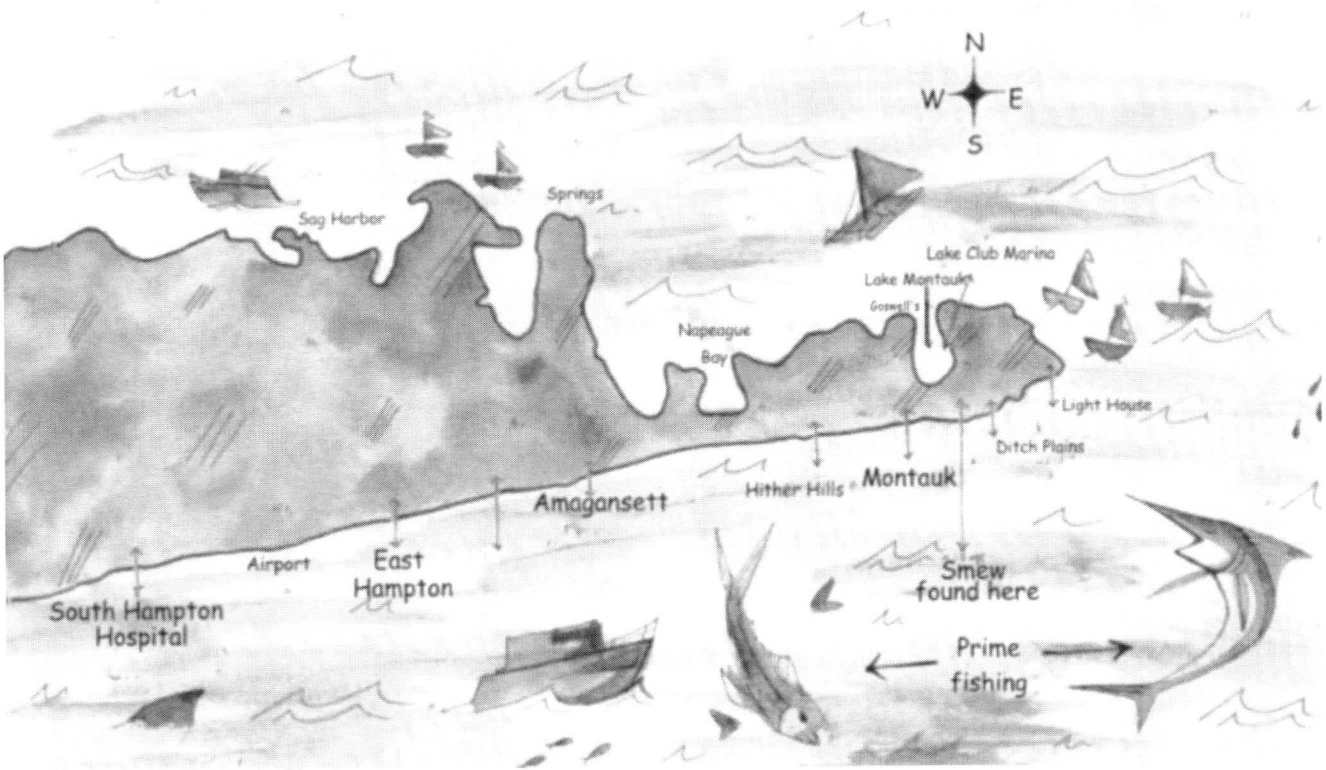

1

Wednesday, August 30th 2006

JACK MARTIN WALKED toward his daughter's laptop with his well-worn *Peterson's* in hand. The DSL connection was slow but finally the Google page appeared and he typed in "SMEW, *Merges albellus.*" He read again from the *Peterson*:

"Field marks of the Eurasian strays listed below can be found in *A Field Guide to the Birds of Britain and Europe* (No.8 in the series). Some strays have been substantiated by specimens or photographs in areas outside of the British Isles, where they are indigenous; others are convincing sight records. Some sightings of European waterfowl are suspect and could be aviary or zoo escapees."

The photographs and information displayed on the screen confirmed Jack's initial impression of the bird he had seen earlier that morning. He dialed the Suffolk County Audubon office.

<<<>>>

It was a late August morning in Montauk and it looked and felt like fall. The break in the weather had come none too soon, for the mid-nineties heat of the last seven days had begun to frazzle the residents and make them feel as incendiary as the dry scrub pine forest of the eastern tip of Long Island. Salvation in the form of thunderstorms had lasted two days and returned calm to that community. Everyone was gearing up for the last holiday weekend and, after it, the slow return to a normal life on the East End. It had been a busy and profitable summer for the merchants, but for those who lived in Montauk the great increase in tourists, or "seasonal residents," if you chose to be polite, was a bit intimidating. This summer the lines at the Montauk Bakery were longer than they had been during previous high seasons and persisted for most of the day. The IGA parking lot was always filled and the shoppers who parked along the beach road ignored the temporary "No Parking" signs placed by the East Hampton Police and rarely bothered to pay the fines they incurred for their violations. Simply getting in or out of town for work or a medical visit became a time-consuming chore. And restaurants! Forget about having a peaceful meal away from home and kids. Any meal would be quieter at home, with fewer children, and certainly more reliable food. For the residents of Montauk, life would be much improved in one week, and the rain had greatly helped their waiting.

There was ground fog as Jack drove south on Essex and turned east on Route 27 to meet T.C. at the Gone

Fishing Marina. As he kept an eye out for rabbits and deer, Jack watched the first light of dawn creep onto the horizon. He hoped the cool night and rains would have enlivened the recently dour game fish on the southside. He could hear the fog horn sounding from the Montauk Lighthouse as he continued east and then north onto East Lake Drive. The fog had not looked that thick when Jack started out that morning and he had paused to take a peek at the sea at the foot of Essex Street. But the horn was on for a reason. Jack pulled into the parking area near the docks and saw T.C. walking down the three steps onto the pier where the *Ruby-Belle* was moored.

Tiziano Corporale was the son of a mid-island commercial fisherman, craftsman, and self-taught artist who had loved Italian renaissance art. He had burdened his son by naming him after the man who, in his opinion, was one of the greatest artists of all time: Titian. By junior high school it was clear to Tiziano Corporale that he needed a nick name other than "Tits." But his sisters loved the name given their brother by their schoolmates and as soon as they were old enough to know what tits were, they teased him mercilessly. The girls even offered him their cast-off bras. It must certainly have been much like growing up as a "boy named Sue." Notwithstanding, T.C. survived and became a sport fishing guide and water fowler and a decoy carver of considerable fame. Any serious collector of contemporary decoys had more than one "Corporale" in his possession.

A wiry and well-tattooed five foot five, he looked the part of a seaman. An aggressive lacrosse player in college, he remained nimble and facile, moving about a boat in the roughest of seas. Soft grey-blue eyes, a mischievous smile, and a small "flavor-saver" lower-lip moustache gave him a Puckish appearance. He had a reputation for guiding his clients to the fish even when the weather would have kept most captains off the water. If a sport wanted to fish and T.C. thought it could be done safely, even if not comfortably, they would fish, a truth to which Jack could attest with an occasional bruise or two to show for his effort.

He and Jack had been fishing together for a number of years and enjoyed being on the water more as a team than as captain and client. This morning they had planned to first look along the South Side for the school-sized bluefin tuna that had appeared inshore two weeks earlier and had provided light tackle sport and superb eating for those who knew what they were and how to catch them. Jack had added a heavier fly rod to his arsenal: a twelve weight with a large capacity fly reel—he and T.C. meant to hook and land a tuna on the long rod.

Hearing a horn, T.C. turned around and walked back to Jack's car, taking the last bites of his egg whites on a roll and washing it down with a Diet Coke. As he stood by the open window, Jack reached out, tapped the can in his captain's hand and quipped, "Takes the rust off chrome bumpers. If you can find any chrome these days."

"Cleans out my colon pretty good, Doc."

"That, my friend, is more information than I need."

The flags at the marina hung limp in the air, auguring a calm morning on the water. Only leftover swells might make it other than a perfect morning to fish but because Jack wanted to avoid any possibility of being queasy on the water, he reached into his shirt pocket and popped the Bonine he'd stashed there.

Even if a trip was planned as a fly-fishing outing, Tits always insisted on having tackle available for any and all possibilities, so in addition to Jack's three fly rods there was spinning, trolling, and live-lining tackle to be taken on board. Jack and T.C. found a relatively clean and almost odorless marina cart and loading their gear into it, then started down the pier to the *Ruby-Belle*.

This was the second year that Jack's son-in-law, Arden Alden, had a boat moored in the marina. This new boat was special, one of a handful of truly beautiful, mid-sized, center consoles at Gone Fishing Marina.

Arden and Jack's daughter, Pericole, had been married a short month after 9/11 and the all too vivid memory of that event had certainly tempered the spirit of the wedding. Five years later the couple had two lovely daughters and Arden had developed the prospering landscape business that had permitted him to buy a mist green Contender christened after the babies: *Ruby-Belle*. This morning Arden could not get onto the water and insisted that Jack and T.C. take the *Ruby-Belle* and enjoy themselves.

T.C. and Jack cast off the mooring lines and headed out of Lake Montauk toward the inlet and then Block Island Sound. Every time he went out to fish, Jack wondered at the foresight of Carl Fisher, the man who had built Montauk and had connected the freshwater Lake Montauk to the sea, thus creating one of America's great pleasure boating and sport fishing harbors. As they passed the Coast Guard base and approached the eastern breakwater, they saw the pair of king eiders that in May, after wintering in Montauk, had taken up residence on a small strip of sand. Why the two birds had not migrated north to the subarctic in March puzzled Jack. T.C. suggested it was simply that they liked Montauk. "Lots of food and no Eskimos," he had said. The pair of fishermen always watched the birdlife in and around Montauk but rarely spotted a new species neither of them could identify. That would change this day.

As they turned east onto the glassy water of the north side's Gin Beach, T.C. throttled up to thirty knots. This was still a relatively conservative speed, for gas was nearing four dollars a gallon at the marina and in the spirit of conserving gas there was no reason to run any faster for the short six miles to the Point. Jack turned ninety degrees and looked back at the twin 225 Yamaha four strokes that were pushing them almost noiselessly along the shoreline.

"You can hear yourself think these days," Jack noted sleepily.

"Yup, they're quieter than an inboard and damned cheap to run."

They passed Shag, Stepping Stones, and, finally, the North Bar with no additional conversation. It was still too early in the morning for idle banter. The rips were just beginning to build as Jack and T.C. turned west around the Point. It was clear that they would have a good incoming tide on which to drift whenever they stopped to fish the South Side. The dictum had always been "an outgoing tide fishes the north and an incoming fishes the south."

Jack leaned back against the seat next to T.C. and pointed toward Block Island. "Nobody headed out. We'll be alone anywhere we fish."

Jack thought about the coincidences that had brought him, a fresh water fisherman and fly tyer, to the salt. First it was the home that he and his wife, Dina, had built on the beach in Belize and, second, it was his daughter falling in love with Montauk and chucking a life on Seventh Avenue to open a B&B there. Both events abruptly placed him into regions of the world where salt water fly fishing was, an exciting new game.

As Jack and T.C. turned the corner at the lighthouse in clear weather, the foghorn was still sounding. Maybe it was foggy off shore, but not here.

As the *Ruby-Belle* slowed, T.C. turned his hat around, peak now to the front, and wiped a few drops of salt spray off his dark glasses in anticipation of needing them.

"You're quiet this morning, Doc," he said as a way of breaking the silence.

"Just enjoying the ride, the solitude, and just waking up. These wild nights out here get to me, T.C."

"There will be no solitude come Saturday, Doc. Two or three hundred boats will be all over the place, getting in each other's way and putting down any fish that might show."

T.C. and Jack stayed about a quarter mile off the beach until they came to Ditch Plains. They had seen no sign of feeding tuna, and except for an occasional mild swell the sea was calm. T.C. looked at the sky and water and then over to Jack's tackle and asked, "Are you rigged on all three rods? Those few birds back at The Cottages were working something and we've seen schools of baitfish on the depth display, so I'll bet there are bass in there. Let's check your tackle before we begin a fishing drift."

T.C. felt the various flies were appropriate so he and Jack continued west toward town. After another mile or so they reversed direction and motored slowly east again, looking for either working birds or the tell-tale bathtub-sized swirls of feeding tuna.

The sun, which was at last showing as a pink crescent above the cloud-line on the horizon, would soon be creeping upward in the otherwise clear morning sky. As they approached the Warhol estate, known as "The Cottages", a group of gulls were still rafted up and a few common terns were talking noisily and diving toward the surface. There were no cormorants visible for the terns to be pestering, so they must have been watching baitfish beneath the surface. As T.C. and

Jack watched and waited for the predators to push the helpless baitfish to the surface and begin the feast, T.C. took the *Ruby-Belle* just up to the rafted gulls, within a hundred yards of the shore.

Why did terns so despise cormorants? Jack had observed the phenomenon. Whenever the two species coexisted, terns would dive fiercely into feeding cormorants, hitting them and bothering them until they up and flew away. He'd come to the conclusion that he was witnessing an evolutionary phenomenon: a species set on removing the competition. Near the herring gulls, Jack caught sight of a sea duck that looked a bit like a male common merganser in breeding plumage but was much whiter and smaller in size. The bird occasionally dove and resurfaced nearby. Jack was surprised and intrigued that he couldn't identify the sea duck. He was making note of the color of its eye and its bill when he realized that T.C. had been talking to him.

"Sixteen feet. I'd put the sinking line and squid fly out there, Doc. Daaahktah Jaack," he sang trying to get Jack's attention.

"T.C. what's that duck? Just beyond the gulls." Jack pointed toward eleven o'clock and said, "He'll resurface in a minute. Now he's up again. See?"

"I've no idea. Certainly is a beautiful little guy. Take the wheel," T.C. directed as he went around the console and into the anterior hold of the boat, rummaged through his duffel, and returned with his binoculars. They were new and gyro-stabilizing.

em to look for the tuna, anyway," T.C. said ined the little duck and then passed the glasses to Jack.

"Neat, they hold the frame steady, no motion at all. I won't ask!" Jack had seen the Sworovska logo as he held the glass in his hand and thought that this was something for the MOMA catalogue and too precious to be on the water. "Awfully heavy, T.C."

"That's all the stabilizing mechanics and, no, you don't want to know what they cost."

Jack looked at T.C. and then back at the duck, which had resurfaced closer to them. "Any ideas?" he asked the captain.

"Dunno, Doc. Some migrant come down here early, maybe? We'll look it up later. Right now, you got to get that squid fly out there. We need a fish in the boat."

The water off this piece of beach was very special, not just because it was in front of a fifty-million-dollar property but because it was strewn with boulders and was usually inordinately clear. The rocks ran out from the beach for almost fifty yards and the bottom, in sixteen feet of water, was prime fishing area. Baitfish hid in the structure and big stripers loved to feed there. Trespassing nighttime surfcasters were known to walk over a mile to sneak onto the beach and they always returned home with monster bass that feasted on the live eels that swam as bait among the rocks.

His 350-grain Airflow line would sink about five inches a second and Jack wanted the fly to be well down in the water column, so after putting it seventy feet closer to the shore he counted to ten before starting his retrieve. On the third strip of the line a fish hit the fly and soon he and T.C. brought a twenty-four-inch striper to the boat. "Sammidge size fish. Jeez, I wish we could keep these. They are sooo delicious," Jack said as he caught his third one. He was obliged to release several more fish because not one of them was a twenty-nine-inch keeper.

"Doc," T.C. advised, "let that fly sink deeper. Get under those schoolies, your sammidge fish, and closer to the bottom. You have sixteen feet here."

On the next cast Jack counted to twenty and began his retrieve. Almost at once there was a solid strike and this fish headed away from the boat into deeper water.

"Daaahktah Jaack," chimed T.C. as he swung the boat to face the moving fish and to let Jack stay in the bow. After a few minutes battle Jack brought the fish to the boat and T.C. lifted it out with the BogaGrip and slid all thirty-two inches into the live well.

"Sushi, T.C. The lady will make some tasty treats tonight if you can stop by," Jack said, anticipating the beautiful plate Dina would present.

Jack then caught and released another bass, a cookie-cutter copy of the one in the well, and then watched as the gulls awakened and dove with the now much larger and noisier group of terns. Sizable swirls appeared on the water's surface, with baitfish showering into the air to escape being devoured by the feeding striped bass. T.C. turned to Jack, handing him the gurgler, and said, "Use your surface lure."

T.C. switched rods with Jack and watched while Jack cast the strange surface lure into the mayhem and a huge mouth immediately engulfed it. This fish came out of the water more like a snook than a striper. For Jack, surface action was always exciting because fish became so athletic. Over the next half-hour the two men caught and released a number of fish but none as large as the one in the well. When T.C. wasn't assisting Jack, he scanned the sea for any sign of a school of tuna, and finally he saw what he was looking for. Pointing to an area in the water that was unusually nervous, T.C. called to Jack, "Doc, look out there behind us a few hundred yards. Those are not bass."

Before the *Ruby-Belle* set out in a new direction Jack looked back at the little duck and painted a mental picture of the arcing black line made by the bill, the eye, the feathers at the back of the head and shoulders. The remainder of the bird was almost white. *Who is that pretty creature and why is it here?* Jack wondered. He made a note to himself to check *Peterson's* that afternoon and then tried to calm himself in anticipation of possibly catching tuna.

Perhaps a quarter of a mile away and a bit farther from shore, a group of birds was diving to the surface, and occasionally there was a large boil beneath them. If these were bass or blues, they were huge. As Jack looked back for a last time at the strange little duck, T.C. started the motors. They headed east to get ahead of the feeding school and then away from the beach to be in line with it. Cutting the motors, T.C. and Jack drifted quietly and watched the feeding fish approach. Jack had switched to the heavy rod and had carefully stripped some sixty feet of line onto the floor of the boat. T.C. reminded Jack that they were drifting in only thirty-five feet of water, so a hooked tuna would have to swim away from the boat and would not be able to dive deeper in the water.

"If they stay on top as they go by, start your retrieve at once," he instructed Jack. "If they are down, let it sink ten feet or so."

Moments later T.C. pointed excitedly off the starboard side of the boat. "There's one out of the water! Not very big, he might be maybe thirty or forty pounds."

Jack had seen most of the fish as it porpoised out of the water in chase of what looked like peanut bunker. T.C. kept turning the silent motors, rotating the boat in the current so that Jack was in a position to cast either right or left in front of the approaching fish. A boil appeared on the surface not fifty feet away from them.

"Here they are! Get that anchovy out there and strip! They're still on top. Daaahktah Jaack!"

Jack made one false cast and shot the heavy line beyond but well ahead of the last surface boil.

"What's your leader, how heavy?"

"Fifteen pounds, Tiziano. Heavy enough?" Jack saw T.C.'s face drop and he quickly added, "Forty, Captain, Forty pounds!"

The fish hit the fly halfway to the boat. Jack responded forcefully, strip setting twice, and looking down to make sure he was not standing on the line piled like spaghetti on the floor of the boat.

"Small fish, Doc. Saw him take. Hold on." Jack saw the pile disappear and felt the fish moving rapidly away from them and noticed that they were well into the backing in literally the blink of an eye. Thirty miles per hour translates to fifty feet a second so standing on the line meant losing a fish, holding the line meant burnt fingers, and touching the reel handle could break a bone in the hand or fingers. T.C. started the engines and they were in hot pursuit of the tuna. T.C. shouted to Jack, "I'll just keep you close until he stops the first run and then you have some work to do."

In about fifteen minutes the fish was next to the boat and T.C. reached down, grabbed the wrist of the tuna's large tail and lifted the tired fish out of the water. It was a small fish, probably only twenty pounds, but it was all muscle. Jack slipped the hook out of the corner of its mouth, felt its quivering flank, and watched as T.C. lowered it headfirst into the sea. The tail began working as soon as the head was submerged, and they watched it disappear into the depths. Jack held out his hand to his friend. He was pumped, no other word for it, but he was also a bit arm weary and wanted a time out so offered to take the wheel.

But before Jack and T.C. had time to switch places, the rest of the tuna had vanished and T.C. had to settle for a keeper bass. They bled and filleted the two bass and headed for home and a late breakfast. Enough was enough, Jack thought, and anyway he had a bird to identify.

<<<>>>

When Jack was back at his daughter's house on Essex Street, he put the fillets into the garage fridge, walked into the kitchen and called to Dina. Soon his wife and two granddaughters came into the room.

"Grampus is home! Say 'Hi', Ruby, Belle," Dina lovingly instructed her granddaughters.

"Hi Gramputh," Ruby said. "Where the fish?"

"The striped bass is in the fridge, Ruby." He lifted a girl in each arm and gave them a spin. "Let me wash my hands and I'll show you."

Ruby loved to see and touch any fish that came into the house and both children ate all sea creatures with great relish.

As Jack was displaying the filleted bass to the girls, he asked Dina to bring him the *Peterson's* from the living room. He explained that he wanted to identify the puzzling sea duck.

It was not until he had reached the last pages of colored prints, the ones listed as "Accidentals from Eurasia" that he saw the odd little bird. "Look at this, Dina," he called out to his wife while he was tapping at the field guide. "This is what we saw. A smew." There was the little duck, exactly as they had seen it just hours ago, as if Jack had taken a digital image when he was on the water. "A sighting has not been reported in America for decades and never below Rhode Island. I wonder why it's here?" he asked, half to himself. After returning the fish to the frig he walked over to his daughter's laptop to Google more information about the smew.

While he waited for the computer to boot, Jack dialed T.C., gave him the information on the bird, and they agreed that Jack should call the Audubon Society. Before Jack hung up, he confirmed with T.C. that they'd meet tomorrow, same time.

<<<>>>

Back in the kitchen, Jack called the local Audubon chapter.

"Suffolk Audubon, Cindy speaking."

"Cindy, this is Jack Martin. Is Frank Vogelslieder around?"

As he waited for his friend to come on the line Jack took a bottle of cold water from the fridge and poured a glass. Then he sat on one of the stools next to the center island.

"Jack? How are you? How are the babies?" asked Frank in his loud, always energetic voice. Frank was a friend from New York City. They had met at one of the bandings of the peregrine chicks born atop New York Hospital. In those days Jack had been the caretaker of the parent birds which had nested on a ledge on the building's twenty-fifth floor. After some brief catching up, Jack explained that he was fishing on the South Side with T.C. and saw a smew off of the Warhol estate.

"Did you take a photo of it?"

"No, but I Googled it. T.C. had fancy glasses, plus, we were close to it. There's no question what I saw,

Frank, but I'll have a camera when we're out tomorrow morning. Some very nice fish, if you want to join with us."

"Love to Jack but I can't. Our fall fund raiser is soon and I'm buried at the office."

"We'll be out at five and back by ten. And the tuna are around," Jack added, in an attempt to lure his old friend. Frank was a wade fisherman and an excellent fly caster, one of the best on the beaches of the East End with a two-handed rod.

"Jack, I have to say no. But get me a close up shot of that smew."

While they spoke, Dina started planning for the next family meal. With about two days of lunch and dinner bass on hand, she selected red and yellow peppers, green jalapeño, scallions and a plump lime and began prep for a ceviche lunch to be served on Jack's fresh mesclun. The other meals were yet to be decided. She handed the platter of fillets to Jack. "Give me about a pound, from the tail end of two fillets, and also cut two pieces for the girls."

Jack chatted happily with Dina as he worked on the bass fillet, alternating that with large bites of a sinfully succulent melon. He walked over to his wife with a generous spoonful of the Cranshaw. "Here, open wide, it is fabulous." Dina smiled at the melon's sweetness and wiped a drop of its liquor from her chin.

"Dina, I'll bet that we hear back from Frank before dinner. I wouldn't be surprised if as we speak people were up on the bluffs glassing that bird and confirming my sighting. Just makes sense. 'Nother bite of melon?"

"No thanks, I've been nibbling on the bass and veggies."

Half an hour later the large bowl of ceviche was curing in the fridge, awaiting the arrival of the luncheon participants, and next to it sat pieces of fillet sized for the babies. Jack had inspected the wine cooler and found the last bottle of a local tocai waiting there. Lunch would be wonderful.

No matter where the Martins were, at home in Westchester, in the Bahamas with the kids, in Belize, or in Montauk, Jack would say his favorite meals were eaten at "Spa Dina," where nutritious food was nearly fat free but sumptuous. Dina had a knack for taking most any recipe, decreasing the fat content, and making the meal fabulous and free of any caloric guilt. The exceptions were the occasional desserts: fruit pies in summer and tropical cakes in Belize Today would be by the book, ceviche for lunch for whoever showed and tonight it would be sushi, sashimi, and a piece of grilled bass with local fresh veggies. Jack saw a pile of ripe peaches in a colander on the drain board. That meant a peach pie with either frangipane or slivered almonds.

<<<>>>

Everyone arrived for lunch. The babies had their cooked fresh fish and the adults had a colorful and piquant ceviche. After eating, the children and Jack took naps. He'd had a second glass of the Channing Daughters Tocai which, adding to the early morning on the water, guaranteed Jack would doze peacefully. Arden went back to work and Pericole sorted a few piles of laundry. It was a quiet and cool afternoon, at least for a few hours.

But sooner than anyone had anticipated it was five-thirty and all had reassembled in the kitchen: the babies clean from the tub, Arden back from the job, Pericole prepping bass for the little ones, Dina cutting fish for sushi, and Jack coming up from the wine cellar with a pinot for dinner.

<<<>>>

The phone rang at six on the nose.

"I know who that is," Jack said as he headed for the phone, dragging with him Ruby who was clamped to his leg like a great gall on a tree trunk.

"Hi, Frank!"

Silence for a moment and then, "You must have caller ID, Jack."

"Nope. Psychics ID. It just had to be you with a confirmation from someone else who spotted the duck."

"You have it, three of them in fact. The bird was up at Caswell's a while ago but it was acting very strange, they said: swimming in circles, disoriented. Jack, get a photo in the morning and call me." Frank gave Jack his cell phone number.

"It might be early, Frank, but I'll call you. Is six OK?"

"What was that about, Dad?" Arden asked as soon as Jack had hung up the phone.

"Tits and I saw a duck from northern Europe this morning, Arden, a smew. You missed a good fishing morning. I landed my first tuna on the fly; sadly, they disappeared before T.C. had a shot at them. Oh, by the way, did T.C. tell you we got stuck on a rock near The Cottages, but we rocked the boat off. Don't think we did any damage."

Arden went pale. He'd been sitting with Baby Belle on his lap and both had been smiling happily. The smile was gone and his brow furrowed as he stood up very quickly. He threw Jack the bird and sat back down. "That's just bullshit, Doc. But just you wait until Saturday and I'll show you how to catch tuna."

"Wid you an haf de worhl muckin up ahlz de waatah? No lee chanz fu dot, bwoy, you no kech nuttin, nuh?" Jack goaded him in Belizian Creole.

Everyone had a good laugh at Arden's expense while Jack refilled the glasses with the remains of the tocai from lunch. Jack picked out four place settings—mats, napkins, and flatware—and started toward the door leading to the terrace and the outdoor table.

2

Thursday, August 31st 2006

THE EASEL WAS next to the door of the new terrarium on the north side of the house. Once a greenhouse the room had become a crafts center for the Vogelslieders. The wide yard and the scrub oak beyond assured wonderful light in the space all year round.

Frank Vogelslieder was a retired graphic designer. Now in his sixties, he'd sold a lucrative business and his uptown Park Avenue apartment, and he and his wife, Callie, had moved to a home in Hither Hills. He had been a member of the Manhattan Audubon chapter and had known the peregrine people in the city from the earliest restoration efforts of Tom Cade and Marty Gilroy, the moving forces from the Sapsucker Facility at Cornell University. He had first met Jack Martin at the banding ceremony of one of Red-Red's early clutches of falconettes: three, big, noisy, female chicks temporarily removed for banding from their eyrie atop the New York Hospital. Frank and Jack had kept in touch, and when Jack's daughter bought in Montauk the two men had much opportunity to exchange notes.

Frank was an affable mesomorph who loved his retirement. His great shock of unruly, white hair gave him the look of an eccentric artist, a Reuben Nakian look-alike, while his watercolor scenes of the East End were very like an unsophisticated Wyeth—more N.C. actually than Andrew; and certainly more art nouveau than the older representative artists. He and Callie had agreed to run the local Audubon chapter when it had begun to falter and clearly needed new blood and new approaches to fundraising. Frank brought them into the twenty-first century. He had a website built and in no time had a "hot sightings" page up and running. He put the chapter's life list on the site after composing it from the records of almost thirty years. His posters asking people to log-on had brought new species every season and e-mail sales of T-shirts and life list books became brisk. The chapter was once again solvent and was seeking projects around the county.

Early Thursday morning, Frank's phone rang. It was Jack.

"Frank, T.C. and I went out this morning and found the smew. It's on the beach at Turtle Cove so you can get close-up and personal. But the poor creature doesn't look well."

"Thanks, I'll get over to Turtle before some dog spooks it," Frank replied sleepily.

He dressed, picked up a small cage, and went out to his pickup. If the bird was sick, he'd get it to the two young vets in Amagansett. They both dealt with the exotics: weird pets of the rich and famous summer residents of the Hamptons. The gal of the couple, who Frank thought was extraordinarily beautiful, was, in fact, a Bonacker, descended from an 18th century, East End fishing family. Sheila McCorkle had been born in Amagansett, raised in Springs, gone to St. John's and then Cornell Vet where she met her husband to be. They both had interned at New York City's Animal Medical Center. She and her husband, Tim Morrissey, had anguished over leaving New York but they didn't want to raise children in Manhattan. While they were at the Center, a client with an ill parrot had told her that there were many city folks who summered on the Island and brought their unusual pets with them. She convinced the couple that they could and would make a comfortable life for themselves on the East End. So, Drs. McCorkle and Morrissey opened the East End Veterinary Clinic in the northeastern part of Amagansett not far from the IGA. Their life was good and baby number one was finally on the way.

Frank pulled off the approach road to the Montauk Lighthouse and walked to the edge of the bluff above Turtle Cove. Other than one surfcaster, the bird was alone on the beach. He put an "official business" sign on his dash, picked up the cage, and followed the path down to the beach. He'd made this walk frequently because the calm waters of the Cove almost always held baitfish and food meant predators, stripers and blues. The pebbly bottom made for easy wading and there was plenty of room for a back cast with his two-handed fly rod. Frank loved this spot.

The smew was standing on one leg, its head tucked onto its opposite shoulder in a yoga position, and its eyes were closed. Frank squatted next to the pretty little bird, talked quietly to it, then quacked softly.

"You don't know if they quack. They might have a soft whistle, a smew's mew," he mused.

The bird looked at Frank with mucous-coated eyes and did not move. There were crystals, probably salt, on its beak and in its nostrils.

"Sick little guy. It's a road trip for you. Let's get you in this cage," he said as he opened the little carrier door and quickly settled the pliant bird into it.

"Damn! I should have worn gloves," he said to no one, making a mental note to put a pair in each empty cage so he wouldn't be unprepared next time.

Stepping to the water's edge, Frank rinsed his hands in the surf and looked out toward the sea where he saw Jack and T.C. headed toward him.

Boy, that really is some beautiful boat, he thought. He was happy for the young couple with their great house, good babies, and for Arden with his talent as a first-rate landscaper.

Waving, he lifted the cage, gave Jack and T.C. a thumb up, and headed back up the bluff toward his truck and the ride to the vet's office.

<<<>>>

Jack always enjoyed the sea birds. Whether he was on the water here, on the Cape, or in Belize, pelagics were intriguing and, theoretically, they never went to land except for breeding. Shearwaters, boobies, storm petrels and gannets always were exciting to watch because of their grace and beauty and because their presence usually meant baitfish were near. Autumn, already in the air, would bring migratory species from as far away as the Arctic Circle to winter around Montauk or at least to stop there on their way further south. Feeding in the food-rich waters of Eastern Long Island before continuing a much longer journey, they would follow the baitfish and receding warm waters, many species traveling the length of the globe. Some peregrine falcons from the sub-arctic tundra traveled as far as the Andes while others of their species went no further than the Mayan ruins of Guatemala. But migration was essential to very many of the western hemisphere species and Montauk was one of the best places to see them.

As they ran west to re-enact yesterday morning's tuna quest, T.C. kept a course to the west about a mile off shore and they were now passing Montauk town proper and headed to Hither Hills. They'd seen a few surfers in their wet suits at the Ditch. Neoprene-clad, they appeared at first as if they were black seals lolling in the calm sea, young bulls gathered and waiting for the arrival of the cows, but waiting, actually, only for a seemingly non-existent wave. It was still not six a.m. and Jack guessed most of them would soon be off their boards, out of the water, and in trucks headed to a local job. Jack's musing was interrupted when he noticed T.C. staring at him with an amused smirk. He looked the doctor up and down and finally said, "How long have we been fishing together? Five years isn't it? And I don't really know the first thing about you."

"Six, actually, we met at the Boys and Girls Harbor Charity fishing event in two-thousand. You know the family and that I love to fish, that now it controls my brain."

"That's what I mean. I only know the fisherman."

Jack stood, bowed deeply, hat in hand, and replied, "Good sir, you are looking at none other than—are you ready for this—The Lone Surgeon. With my robotic nurse companion, Tontonita Esquisita, we go about in our silver Mercedes from one operating room another, helping the undermanned and bailing out the under talented. You must have heard of me or seen me on TV. Few people have ever seen behind my mask of sanity. You are among the privileged few, T.C. Now, any questions?" Jack sat down next to his bewildered captain and poked him with his elbow until he finally laughed.

"How long has it been since you were in the OR?"

"Persistent, aren't you!" Jack looked at T.C. as he tried to remember a past life, largely, but not completely forgotten. It still haunted some of his dreams, though fewer and fewer with time. Images of young surfer girls were supplanting those from the operating room and they were certainly better.

"Eight years since New York Hospital," he finally said. "It has been eight years since I did the last kidney transplant and, interestingly, those last few were as adjuncts to a kidney/pancreas combined procedure. Thank God the younger surgeons did the difficult pancreas part of it and then did all of the post-op care. I was very happy just to be a convenient but skilled technician."

"How many of those operations did you do? Must have been quite a few."

"I never counted, but it must have been close to five hundred over a period of almost twenty some years. That's a close guess I'd say."

"Was it always exciting to give someone a new kidney?"

"For the recipient it was, but as the surgeon, I preferred it to be routine."

"There's always excitement on the medical TV shows—hollering, shootings, blood, sex."

Jack laughed and pulled the brim of T.C.'s hat down over his friend's eyes. "Once I did eight transplants over a summer holiday weekend. My senior partner was on vacation and a flood of organs came into the region from drownings, suicides, highway deaths, you name it. We matched better than the rest of the city. Most were away for the weekend so we did the work. It was heady and I ran on adrenalin for almost seventy-two hours."

"You were some kind of freakin' Iron Man, Doc."

Jack shook his head no and flexed his tanned, minimalist biceps and tweaking his pecs said, "I was much younger then, probably in my early forties. Wore out several assistants that weekend, I did. But my most memorable operation was not my most athletic."

They had reached Hither Hills and saw no fish action so T.C. began to turn back east. He called out to Jack, "You got ten minutes to tell me about it, Doc. Then we'll be back at The Cottages and you'll have to do some fishing."

"I haven't purposefully thought about this or any of that part of my life for what, a decade almost? This happened in the late seventies when transplantation was a primitive science and it was mostly kids who were dying of kidney failure. It was very emotional for both families and physicians. These kids were chronically ill for years and were dwarfed in many ways, physically, emotionally, and sexually. They were short, partly crippled youths with lousy teeth and bones. They were tragic and transplant was supposed to give them a new lease on life, let them live.

"Jimmy Scanlon was maybe fourteen but looked about eight. He walked funny because of hip problems and wouldn't smile. There wasn't much to smile about. He had rejected and lost a kidney from his father and now was rejecting a second transplant, this time from his mother. In those days we didn't have availability of good drugs to stop rejection so mostly we used large doses of steroids, cortisone, to blunt the immune system. That caused problems in itself, giving all those steroids. We also tried to use organs from close family members so there was some commonality and less chance for rejection.

"Jimmy's transplanted kidney was huge, swollen from the body's attempt to reject it, filling it full of lymphocytes and other immune debris. You could see it bulge out on his little abdomen. We'd look at it with ultrasound or with a scan that let radio-isotopes light it up so that we could get a look at its size, the blood flow into it and some other things. I remember looking at the new scan and seeing isotope outside of the kidney, suggesting a leak, bleeding, as it were. We thought the thing had split open like an over ripe fruit. That was the consensus. We talked to his parents and told them what we'd found. They understood that it meant the kidney would have to come out, and they were devastated. They held each other tearfully because they understood that this would mean Jimmy would not have long to live. He simply could not survive on dialysis. You could see in their faces and then hear them talk of how they had both failed their son and that these rejections were their own fault because they did not have better kidneys to give to him. Tough stuff, T.C."

Jack paused and looked into his coffee cup and, finding it empty, stashed it in the trash bag. "I took him to the OR presumably to remove it and hoped to get him in and out alive. He was that sick. T.C., it looked like a big mushy eggplant when I got down to it. It was at least three times normal size and had a split in the upper half that went almost through the kidney. It was oozing blood and not pumping like you expect arteries to do. I knew that if I took it out—it would only take five minutes to do so—I was signing his death warrant. I did something that my team had never done before. Probably no one had ever done it. I packed the fracture, the split, with a material that helps blood to coagulate and put some large sutures with bolsters, cushions on them, around the entire upper half of the kidney and gently snugged it together. It was like bailing it, I guess. We watched for a while and didn't see bleeding so we washed the wound with antibiotics and somehow got him back together again.

"I'm not a religious man but something was at work that night, with us in the OR and with Jimmy afterwards. His parents were delighted, though I made clear to them that we might have just postponed the inevitable for a day or so. They did not care because as long as the kidney was inside Jimmy, they had hope and prayer. And their prayers were answered. His rejection was controlled and he walked clumsily out of the hospital with a functioning transplant. I don't remember his long-term follow-up but I do remember that night."

Jack and T.C. looked at each other and saw that they both had tears forming. Jack reached into his trousers and pulled out two tissues and they had a good blow and then shared an embarrassing moment of silence. They were now back at Ditch Plains and the last two surfers were in the parking lot, tan bodies and white butts partially hidden by sheltering doors, they were toweling and changing into work clothes and would soon be heading off to their employ. It was all predictable behavior for that indigenous, non-migrating species, Homo-surfiens.

T.C. broke the mood by saying, "Doc, it's not happening yet. Let's go back to Warhol's and see if the bass are still there. We have good tide running and the drift will be perfect. Stay with the sinker. I'll cast a teaser and see if I can get them up."

As they neared The Cottages, T.C. rigged a hookless surface lure to a spinning rod. They slowed as the boat's power was turned off and then began to drift parallel to the estate.

Jack looked toward the cluster of Cotswold-like buildings on the dune and said, "I hear that Warhol had some kind of parties at this place, lots of New York celebs and jetsetters. Wild times if you believe the stories. Have you seen the photos on the wall at the Shagwong?"

"You mean Jackie-O sun bathing in the nude? You can't tell who it is, just some skinny lady getting a tan."

"It makes a good story and people are always staring at those pictures. But let's fish."

T.C. kept the boat positioned to Jack's best advantage for a forehand cast toward the beach and then he cast the surface plug into the white water. The retrieve caused a great deal of surface disturbance meant to imitate a baitfish in distress, an easy target. A hungry bass usually was tempted to rise in the water column and attack the harmless lure. If a pass was made at the teaser, Jack would immediately cast to the spot and retrieve a large fly away from the plug. Very often the fish would switch to the fly and a hook-up occurred. Seeing that large mouth open and engulf, suck in the fly in the vacuum created by its opening, was simply amazing. You could actually hear the fish strike.

They had drifted almost a quarter of a mile without touching a fish when Jack's line stopped in the water. He strip set twice but nothing happened.

"Hit it again, Doc. Sink it in good! You're tipped with forty pounds and it won't break."

"T.C. that's the bottom, not a fish. It is not moving. Just our drift is taking line from my hand," Jack called from over his shoulder.

The drift of the boat had cleared the line from the floor and it did feel like the bottom. No dash away and no head shaking, just a slow steady removal of line from the reel. But T.C. knew better and said, "Lines coming off faster than we're drifting. Daaahtah Jaack has a big one."

"You've been peeking when I was peeing over the gunwale! Are you jealous?"

The men exchanged smiles as T.C. started the motors and held the boat still in the current. Line, now the gelspun backing, continued to peel off the reel.

"Rock's still moving west and even faster. Get to the stern until I can turn us, Doc."

"OH! My goodness, golly, goshes! Vee are catching very great bigness of a fish, Sahib Titties," Jack Jaipured at T.C.

Motors in reverse, T.C. turned the boat backwards toward the fish, rotating the stern seaward. Jack was then able to move up the portside to the bow. Slowly and steadily T.C. brought them closer to the creature and soon the fly line began to appear on the reel.

T.C. nodded at Jack's taught line in the water and said, "Twenty pounds at least, and around here could be thirty. More. She's going to move faster when she sees the boat. We're still shallow so it won't be down, just away. Keep steady pressure. How's your drag?"

Jack had loosened the resistance of the reel when he stripped line for casting, so he reached across his left hand and the rod and turned the drag a bit. As they regained line and control, Jack looked down. He could see sandy bottom between the rocks and weed and then the colored twenty-foot tip of the fly line and he tried to visualize the fish, which was now just some thirty-five feet away. Judging from the angle of the line in the water, the fish was only three or four feet from the surface and it would soon see the boat. She probably did not yet realize that she was in trouble. She, because any fish this size was a "she". The morning light reflected off her flanks as she turned left to head out to sea and the safety of deeper water. In moments she was more than two hundred feet away and just beginning to slow down. Big stripers may not be fast but, at the end of a battle, they become doggedly stubborn and resist coming to boat. She came to the surface and wallowed there the way a big striper is likely to do.

"Did you see the size of that tail?" T.C. asked in amazement.

Jack had, and they both knew that this was a very special fish but it was not until fifteen minutes later when T.C. slipped a Boga on her lower jaw and lifted that they both realized how special.

Jack put on his glasses and read the scale. "Scale's bouncing just over thirty, Captain! Let her go easy!" Jack slipped the hook from her jaw and T.C. held her head under water with the BogaGrip while Jack held his friend's belt lest he be pulled into the water if the fish bolted. In a moment her tail and gills began to work simultaneously and he released her. As they watched her swim slowly and strongly away from the boat T.C. said, "That's a lovely fish and she was caught the right way. That squid fly is a mess. Better change it. Anyway, I smell tuna."

3

FRANK PULLED UP in front of the East End Veterinary Clinic on Town Lane, just east of the Windmill. It was only seven o'clock, so he walked around to the house next to the work office and rang the bell.

The newly cedar-shaked seven room Cape with its guest cottage turned office was in a mixed commercial zone, too near the railroad, Route 27, and the IGA strip mall to be prime residential real estate. Had it been on Jessup Street in Quogue or off Georgica in East Hampton, the young couple would not have been able to consider it. But here the mature and exemplary landscaping, the raised-bed veggie patch, the tailored beds of perennials, and the secluding privet hedge made it a dream house for the young veterinarians.

Frank had phoned ahead and knew that Tim Morrissey, DVM, would be up and would meet him. Sheila Morrisey, under doctor's orders, was not working for the last month of her pregnancy, so her husband Tim was carrying the workload. With his right hand, Tim opened the front door while with his left he held the collar of Midgebil, the almost seated year-old otter hound. Frank spent the next minute scratching and talking to the gregarious and appreciative pup.

"Enough, Midge, inside," ordered Tim. The dog disappeared and Tim greeted his friend. "Where is this smew you've brought me?"

Tim was a very handsome man who stood a head taller than Frank and as they moved away from the door, the morning breeze ruffled his bright red hair. Even though he'd played ball, three sports in fact, at a small upstate school, he moved gracefully, not with a stocky jock's swagger. He'd been taught to appreciate the great fortune of a good wife and a comfortable lifestyle. Closing the door against Midge's escape, they walked to Frank's pickup and found the bird agonal. Before Frank could reach into the cage, Tim stopped him and said, "Wait, Frank, just in case." Tim paused, watching the bird's last movements. "You said this bird is from northern Europe and that his gyroscope wasn't working last evening?"

"That's right. He was swimming in circles and no longer feeding."

"He's dying as we watch him so we need to take precautions. When avian flu comes to our shores it will more likely arrive from a migrant bird than from some smuggled aliens or illegal Chinese feathers in a pillow or a coat. I'll get cultures, and then double bag him for the freezer, and then call the authorities. Did you handle him?"

"Just to put him in the cage. And I washed in the surf."

"Let's do this out back."

Tim put on mask and gloves and took the cage to a table behind the office. Then he went inside and came out with culture swabs, tubes, and a syringe with a fine long needle, betadine and more gloves, and a mask for Frank. The duck now appeared to be dead. He handed Frank the protective items, shrugged, and said, "Who knows."

He removed the limp creature from the cage and after taking culture samples from eyes, beak, and cloaca, he positioned it carefully on its back and poured some Betadine onto the breast feathers. He picked up the syringe, had Frank pull the guard off the needle, and, after some brief palpation, went into the chest with the long needle.

"It's small, but, there, blood. OK, that's it. Frank, hold that isolation bag open for me."

They double-bagged the bird and then put gloves, masks, and cage into a small incinerator that Tim was licensed to use. After they cleaned up, Tim said to Frank, "Not sure where to send all this but we'll find out fast enough."

The two men said goodbye, and Tim promised to keep Frank posted.

<<<>>>

Going back into the office, Tim put the specimens into the isolation refrigerator and the bird into the freezer. Then he washed thoroughly. He looked at his watch and knew that Farley Maniskjevic would be in his office at the Animal Medical Center in Manhattan.

Sheila sat in the kitchen pretending to be interested in her breakfast. Tim looked at his wife and marveled how beautiful she looked eight and a half-months pregnant.

"What are you wearing?" he said to her jokingly. "I don't recognize the dress."

"You're not supposed to." Sheila struggled to her feet and did a halting pirouette for her husband. She wore a simple dress with a pinafore cut made from Laura Ashley fabric. It was flattering and certainly comfortable.

"Something from Ma Ternity Boutique?" he quipped.

"Nope, it's an original."

"An original what? Have you been splurging?"

"No, honey, it's an original 'Lanie'. Ole's daughter made it." Sheila sat back down heavily. "You remember the little summer dresses I bought last year? Well I asked her to do something similar that would fit me now. I stopped in earlier this month for some measurements and Ole dropped it off the other day when he came to work." She stood and tried to twirl again but grabbed a chair back when she teetered slightly. After she steadied herself, she continued, "You should see the design studio she's set up in the house. The girl is really talented. She's paid for her surfing and is saving for college."

Tim poured himself a fresh cup of coffee and took the last bite of a sliced tomato on whole wheat toast that was his breakfast. Looking at his wristwatch, he picked up the phone and sat across from his wife.

"Sounds like a great kid but right now I have to call Farley." As he picked up the phone he said, "How the hell did his Polish immigrant parents come up with the name Farley?"

His wife laughed at him and dipped her low-sodium toast into her fat free yogurt. "Yummy, honey, want to try some? OUCH!" Sheila pushed at her huge belly and muttered, "Damn this little guy anyway." She hurriedly looked at Tim to see if it had registered. It had.

"OH, SHIT, Oh, oh, oh shit!"

Almost in tears, Sheila struggled up and went over to her flabbergasted husband. She rested her head on his shoulder and said, "I'm sorry dear. The girls didn't have the screen turned away during my sonogram and I saw. Actually, the new tech turned the screen toward me and said, 'Look, there's his little pee-pee'. When she saw my face, she realized her mistake. I thought I could keep it from you but I blew it on the very first day." Stamping a swollen ankle, she swore quietly at herself.

Giving her a kiss and a big hug, Tim managed to laugh. "I'll pretend to be surprised at the appropriate time." He took a sip of the black coffee and punched Farley's number into the portable phone.

"Maneskjevic."

"So how the heck did they pick Farley? Granger? FDR's old Postmaster? The college?"

"That's Farleigh, Farleigh Dickenson University, you illiterate. I don't know. I never asked. How does Granger suit you, good looks and all that? And Mom was a movie fan. What's up, Doc? When's the day?"

Tim had gotten up and was walking around the kitchen as they spoke. He approached the sink to deposit his cup. "Soon, I expect. Sheila is spending a few weeks on the sofa with her legs elevated. Pretty funny when you realize that's how she got this way."

Tim ducked when the yogurt-covered toast flew past his head and then continued in a more serious tone, "Another week or so and they plan to induce her or tickle it out of her." Then Tim explained to his friend the reason for his call—the dead smew.

In the following moments of silence Tim could hear Farley thinking. Probably having the same thoughts Tim had tossed around for the last hour.

"Any human contact?" Farley finally asked.

"Just Frank, and he washed up right after touching it. So did I."

"I'll get a courier out to you this morning to pick up the cultures. Just keep them iced." Changing his tone to soothe his friend, Farley said, "I can read your mind, buddy, and my worries are the same as yours. But chances are it's nothing. By the way, is it a boy or a girl?"

"We don't know the sex." He turned to his wife and gave a thumb's up. "*We* want it to be a surprise. But don't expect 'Farley' to be on any shortlist."

"Thanks, Tim. I'll keep you posted...get it? Posted? Postmaster General? Tim?"

"Bye, Farley."

Tim looked at Sheila, a Cheshire grin on her face as she said, "Farley McCorkle Morrissey. Not bad actually. Not bad at all."

<<<>>>

Thursday morning Tim only had four clients to see and was able to shut his office by midday and then spend the afternoon with Sheila planning and re-planning their new life with baby. They'd not done any baby shopping since they wanted the gender to be a surprise, but now that they knew they talked about how a boy's room should be decorated. Sheila suggested that they hang the walls with Tim's old team pictures and maybe even a coveted letter sweater he still kept in mothballs. They knew that décor might not make a jock of him but his genetics sure could and they both seemed to enjoy a few hours of daydreaming together that afternoon.

The messenger Farley sent had arrived at three and took the culture back to the lab but left the smew with Tim.

That evening, after an early dinner, they watched *Capote* and marveled at the acting performance of the lead. Tim couldn't get his mind off that pretty little duck in his freezer. He did not sleep easily and when he finally drifted off it was to transient images of what-ifs and hypothetical scenarios of an avian flu epidemic tormenting his first hours.

4

Friday, September 1st 2006

When she noticed her rapid weight gain and that her blood pressure had inched up from her usual 120/60 of her first seven months of pregnancy to 135/80, Sheila had called Dr. Savony. That had been two weeks ago and she was now at least thirty-eight weeks and was still worried. Sheila knew Dr. Katya Savony would make herself available if a patient needed her, and the information about the jump in weight and blood pressure brought the doctor to the phone.

"Sheila, come in to see me today, please. Now if you can."

"Sure, is forty-five minutes all right?"

"I'll want a urine specimen, so don't pee."

Sheila laughed at the thought of a car ride on a full bladder and said to her doctor, "Well, I may leave part of it in the truck, but I'll try."

Tim was too busy caring for neighborhood pets to leave the office and accompany Sheila to the doctor, so she gave her husband a hug and waddled to her Chevy four-door pickup. Using all her strength and the overhead handle, she struggled into the high front seat, all the while swearing at the East End working mother's Rolls Royce. But how else could you move children, the essential big dog, groceries and beach stuff without a pickup? SUVs belonged to the seasonal folks, but natives drove pickups!

Once in the doctor's office, Sheila submitted her urine and blood samples. As they waited for the lab results, Dr. Savony explained her concerns about Pregnancy Induced Hypertension (PIH). While they chatted, Katya repeated a check on Sheila's blood pressure; it was 145/80. With an announcing knock on the door, a nurse entered and handed Katya a computer printout.

The doctor looked at the lab results on the printout and then spoke to Sheila. "You are spilling a very small amount of protein in your urine, which might be from the higher blood pressure and its effect on your kidneys. But it may not be." She came out from behind her desk and walked around to where Sheila sat and pulled up a chair so she could face her friend. She took her hand. "Your workup looks fine. But, to play it safe, I'm going to see if Ed Handley is in his office. He deals with our high-risk pregnancies, and even though I don't expect your blood pressure will be an issue I want to do another fetal and placental Doppler and ultrasound. I think your baby is ready to pop out healthy but let's go ahead and gather one more piece of fresh information for Ed."

Katya then called both destinations to make sure they were ready to greet the VIP patient she was sending them. Sheila tried to protest the wheelchair, but her doctor's face told her not to try. In less than half an hour she was being pushed through Dr. Handley's door, her labs and ultrasound in hand.

Dr. Handley issued Sheila toward a large leather sofa as soon as she entered his office. He sat next to her. Sheila had the sense that Handley had slept many a night right here.

"While you were being wheeled and poked and studied, I had a chance to talk to Katya," he began. "With all your lab work in good order, the liver functions, the coagulation studies, the renal function and," he paused to look at the Doppler study she'd brought him, "a great looking baby on sono, we have a very good margin of safety for both of you.

"What we worry about early on in pregnancy with PIH is a compromised, constricted, and reduced blood flow through the placenta that creates a potential for fetal injury. Close to term as we are, we worry about injury to the mother from the high blood pressure. Your ultrasound and placental Doppler were fine and we could go ahead today, if we had the indication to do so, and plan a C-section and deliver a fine and healthy baby, but I don't think that we need to do that. Not based on what I see today. Let's do this…" He rose and went to his desk where he began to write as he talked to her.

The doctor went on to give Sheila an in-depth description of PIH. As Sheila listened, she anticipated explaining it to Tim. She asked questions where appropriate and Dr. Handley answered them for her. By the end of their discussion, she felt comfortable with her knowledge and with their decision and with the safety of herself and their baby.

"I'm quite happy with all of this, but if I have any trouble selling it to Tim can I have him call you?"

"Of course, anytime."

Sheila went back to thank Katya and then trundled out to her truck for the ride home and the talk with Tim.

Tim wasn't always a good listener because he was too fast a thinker; with his mind racing ahead he did not always pay close attention to a conversation. He was just closing up shop, spraying and wiping down the examination rooms. This was a job Ole should have been doing but he was once again a no-show and he would probably have a bona fide excuse. "That man simply has too many pots on too many stoves," he complained to himself. Glancing up he saw that it was exactly three pm. He heard Sheila drive into the yard so he dropped his spray bottle and paper towels, washed his hands, and went out to meet his wife.

Sheila was still sitting in the cab with the door open and she appeared to be crying.

"Hey, what's this all about?" Tim stepped up onto the running board and gave his wife a kiss. "Something I need to know? You're here so it can't be so very bad! Come on down, your sofa has been lonesome."

He helped her out of the truck and they walked toward the house. She thought, *He is dear and I have no reason to be crying. I'm fine and so is Farley. Damn that tech. No, it's not her fault.*

Sheila stopped, turned toward her husband and put her arms around his neck and kissed him warmly.

"I'm OK. In fact, we're both fine. I think I'm just very tired. Come on in and I'll tell you about my day."

They walked into the house and Sheila plopped down on the sofa, resting her ankles on the arm.

"Short version or long?"

"Just tell me what went on. Want a glass of cold tea?"

"Yes, that would be lovely." She wriggled to get more comfortable and sighed. "Better. All the tests were perfect. The baby and I are fine but if anything changes, he may decide to go ahead with a C-section." Slowly and carefully Sheila told him of her discussion with Handley.

Tim's mind was on caution—actually it was on stop—sorting information and trying to formulate questions. As he sat watching Sheila and listening to her relate the day's events, he realized that Sheila and Dr. Handley were in control of the situation and he would have to be a by-stander, a helpful and concerned onlooker. Until he was needed, anyway.

He finally said, "It is all very interesting, honey."

She scrunched a pillow behind her, so she was facing Tim.

"I guess I don't have any questions. Do you believe that? As long as you two are fine I'm OK with waiting the next week. But tell me once more that both of you are fine!"

Sheila reached over and took Tim's hand and pulled him toward her, kissed him and put his hand on her belly.

"We're fine, both of us. And as long as nothing changes, we're a go for launch. I have a short tether; I'm attached to Dr. Handley at the hip for the next few days. Now I, rather, we, are hungry." She offered a hand so Tim could help her up and said, "Let's see if there is something in the fridge or if we have to go to town for dinner."

<<<>>>

Jack's wife and daughter and Ruby had left for a stroll in East Hampton before they had to extract Baby Belle from daycare, and Jack had a quiet house to himself. Tackle tinkering and changing of leaders and flies completed, he glanced at the kitchen clock and saw that the financial markets would be open for another hour and he wanted an idea of how the week was going to end, an interest from their past life when assets were not mostly fixed income. Waiting for Google to upload he picked up the phone and called the Audubon.

"Vogelslieder here."

"It's Jack.

"I was going to call you after talking to the vet. The bird died en route. He took cultures."

"For bird flu?"

Frank didn't have any details and suggested Jack call Tim.

Jack made the call as he scrolled down the financial updates. *The ride continues,* he thought as he noted the up tickers.

"Morrissey."

"It's Jack Martin."

"Aha, the famous Dr. Martin. Or do we now say infamous? It's good to talk to you. I'm just finishing here so let me pull up a chair." Jack heard a pause, then Tim continued. "Let me bring you up to date. Yesterday I called an old friend at the Animal Medical Center."

"I know them well; we know each other well, I should say," Jack said. "I took two peregrine fledglings there after first flight mishaps. One of the girls actually went down the incinerator chimney when she tried to land atop it and she was retrieved from the ash box looking like a crow. Thank God it was not running and was cold and the vets were able to pull her through. You were probably there after I left."

"Yes, you're right, but we used to watch the youngsters from the hospital observation decks in June when the parents were teaching them to catch prey. Anyway, getting back to the smew—Farley did the lab work on West Nile so he was the man to check on this bird. The darn thing is still in my freezer and that bothers me a bit. But I guess it's safe there. What do you know about H5N1, Jack?"

"Not a great deal more than we read or hear about on TV. Everyone knows it has been a problem in the Far East in poultry. Migrants are another story and we anecdotally hear about Eastern European and Baltic migrants which test positive. That's the concern with the smew isn't it? Why did it die and from what?"

"We should have an answer tomorrow, if Farley can gear up fast."

Jack said he'd be at home in Westchester for the weekend; he and Dina were expecting to have Labor Day festivities with a group of good friends. He asked Tim to contact him as soon as he learned anything.

5

IT WAS SATURDAY morning, Labor Day weekend, in Amagansett. Everyone had shopped on either Thursday or Friday and the townsfolk were preparing to hunker down until the following Tuesday when life would return to normal. School was set to reopen, shopping lines would disappear, gas prices might begin to ease and the idiots on jet skis would disappear until the next season's Memorial Day weekend. Sheila's weight and blood pressure were down, and she looked and felt better. She was determined to make it to term and a spontaneous delivery.

In the early afternoon Tim poured himself a tumbler of unsweetened iced tea and walked into the living room where Sheila was in her usual spot on the sofa, looking regally plump. He held out a hand to her and with Tim's help she stood and stretched. Tim invited his wife to take a short stroll with him.

On the way out through the kitchen, Tim filled a second glass of tea and pushed open the sliding door onto the patio. As he held it open for his wife he said,

"You'll have a few months to be outside with the baby before it gets cold."

"I know, and when we finally have a frost, I'll miss my flowers." She stopped and fondled one of the dahlias that stood aside her hip. "Just look at them, Tim. They certainly have been wonderful this year."

Sheila and Tim took a turn around the yard, looking at all the still-colorful flower beds, and then headed toward the office building. They were surprised to see Ole Johnson's battered red pickup parked alongside the office. He wasn't scheduled to be at Tim and Shelia's and Ole was so busy with his many jobs that he rarely came by for a social visit. Besides cleaning Tim's office, he was sometimes pressed into a role as OR assistant when things were very busy. He also cleaned the Audubon office once a week.

Ole was part of the skilled trades' community of Montauk and Amagansett. Tall, blond, and pale-skinned where not tanned, he looked as if he'd stepped off of the Norwegian biathlon team in the last Winter Olympics. Taciturn to a fault, fine featured, a Norseman described him best. He had married well, or so everyone thought when he wedded Christina Sondgaard. But soon after their daughter Lanie was born, Christina began to find motherhood and marriage stifling. She took to wandering, disregarding her family. As their marriage spiraled downward in Christina's morass of drink and infidelity, Ole fell into a depression. He became a no-show at work and thus a poor provider in the deteriorating home. When Christina finally abandoned him and their daughter, Ole collected himself and fought his way back to being a father and a hard worker. He found a series of part-time jobs that allowed him to keep himself and Lanie dry, fed, and almost a family.

Ole was also an avid fly tier, and Tim always kept the feathers dropped or molted from the many exotics, which he and Sheila treated in the office. Mostly parrots. They were pets of the summer folk on the East End, birds who vacationed with their owners rather than being left alone in the city. What Ole did with the bright feathers Tim did not know. The saltwater patterns Ole tied and showed to Tim looked like food, baitfish or squid, not parrots.

Tim and Sheila went into the office and found Ole next to the freezer, the smew in hand. Tim rarely used profanity but it flowed easily at this moment.

"God damn it, Ole. Bag that fucking bird. And do it fast!" he shouted.

Tim turned on the exhaust fan and then took out another isolation bag. He held the bag open and said, "Put those bags inside this one and open the freezer!" Glaring at Ole he continued, "Explain while you wash and disinfect the counter."

"I heard about the duck and wanted to see if the feathers were useful. That's all, Doc."

Tim cut him short, turned toward Sheila, and with his heart racing said, "Oh, my God honey, get out of here please, now!"

He whisked his wife out the door and turned back to Ole. "You're a damn feather freak. Clean all the surfaces with Clorox, wash up well, and then wait for me."

Tim went into the house and found Sheila at the sink, washing her hands. She turned and spoke softly to Tim. "I wish Farley had taken that bird on Friday when they took the cultures and blood. Now we have to worry about Ole. As if Frank wasn't enough."

"It's also you I now have to worry about, you and the baby."

Tim knew that he had to talk to someone at South Hampton Hospital and yet he did not want to start a panic. He rubbed his wife's shoulders and said, "Handley carries a beeper. Would you mind calling him for me? I think I need his help."

The phone rang only a few minutes after Sheila had punched in her number for a call back.

"Sheila? Any problem, dear?"

"Sorry to bother you on the weekend, Dr. Handley. No, I'm just fine. Tim, my husband, needs to talk to you about a problem we might have here."

Tim told Handley about the events of the last few days, and about Frank and Ole's direct contact with the bird.

"This may be nothing but I'd like to talk to someone in Infectious Diseases to get some guidelines and to see if they want Frank and Ole to come in for cultures or monitoring."

"Tim, the chief of the Medical Service, Irv Pender, is a neighbor. He's also Head of Infectious Diseases.

I saw him come in from Maidstone a while ago, so let me walk over there and chat with him and then have him call you. I'll give him this number."

Tim went back to the office and found a chastened Ole sitting at the doctors' desk and for several minutes, they chatted about his mistake. Ole told Tim that he was going to the Canyon on a tuna trip and would bring Tim a loin, a kind of apology gift, and that he'd be in on Tuesday to help Tim in the office.

Back in the house, Tim waited for a call from Dr. Pender and did a little prep work for a dinner of salad and a piece of striper fillet. While he puttered, he opened a bottle of Osprey's Domain chardonnay. Wanting to share, he called to Sheila. "Do you want your sip now or with dinner, honey?"

"Sip!? Yesterday it was four ounces! What's with a sip?"

"That was before I knew it was a boy, my love."

There was no immediate reply but Tim soon heard her bare feet on the random width pine of the dining room floor and Sheila appeared, arms on hips, at the kitchen door. "So, it's OK for me to have wine if it's a girl? No brain to hurt there, huh, buster? And who was summa cum laude anyway? Just who!"

The phone rang as he was handing her a glass.

"Dr. Morrissey, Tim? This is Irv Pender. I'm sitting here with Ed Handley. Do you really think that this could be H5N1?"

"Dr. Pender, with what they call a European erratic, there is a chance. We should have an answer at latest tomorrow, more likely today. I sent samples to the Animal Medical Center. My concern is the two people with unprotected exposure. Frank will keep in touch, but that idiot Ole might not. He knows I'm mad at him."

"Tim, those two need to come see me in my office tomorrow a.m. Let's hope it turns out to be nothing—it would be one hell of an introduction to the disease. We don't have a lot of baseline information that's solid because almost all of our data comes from under-diagnosed and under-reported areas and sources, mostly from the third world. And Tim, thanks for the heads up."

Tim had hung up the phone. He heard Sheila call to him from the sofa. "Oh, honey, I forgot to tell you. When you were with Ole, Frank called. He wants you to call him. He's at home.'

Tim set his glass of wine on the counter next to the phone, found Frank Vogelslieder's number in the call list, and pushed the autodial. On the second ring Frank answered.

"I think I'm crazy, and it's probably nothing, but I'm feeling as if a cold's coming on. I'm achy and logy. What do we do?" Tim heard the anxiety in Frank's voice.

"No fever or chills or cough?"

"Nope, just coldish."

"I've just spoken to the head of Infectious Diseases at South Hampton Hospital. He wants you in his office tomorrow morning at ten a.m."

"His office, huh, makes me feel kind of special, as if he's going out of his way."

"Frank, if this is nothing there is no reason to make a fuss. Dr, Pender wants to keep a lid on it until we know what's going on. I should have those test results in the next twelve. Just take some Tylenol if you need it. When I know anything, you'll hear from me."

Tim refilled his glass and called Ole. Lanie answered the phone and told Tim that her father was with some friends on an overnight tuna trip to the canyon and that he'd be home again on Sunday or more likely Monday. Tim left his number with the girl and asked that Ole call him whenever he came home. He stressed the "whenever".

Sheila called to Tim from her place on the sofa, "Honey, there's a new recipe I want to try for the bass. Would you crush some garlic for me? I'll be right there. And set the oven to four-fifty, please."

Tim had cut two pieces of bass from a fillet a friend had dropped off that morning. He was going to sauté them in some herbs and butter, a simple but delicious preparation. He also had some wonderful greens and tomatoes from Vickie's stand up the road and there were plenty of herbs in Sheila's garden area. But if she wanted to try something else, he was happy that she felt up to the task.

"Three nice cloves enough?" Knowing how his wife loved garlic, he minced four.

Among the pantry's emergency rations were instant mashed potatoes, and it was a surprisingly useful box in times of hurry and need. Sheila mixed a cup of the soft white flakes with a small amount of skimmed milk, some olive oil, salt, and the crushed garlic, making it into a light paste. Then she coated the top of each piece of fish with a one-half inch thick layer of the redolent mix. When the oven was at 450 degrees, she heated a stick-free skillet on top of the stove, added some olive oil, and when the pan was very hot, she added the fillets and quickly browned the fish. Peeking to see they were nice and crispy brown but not fully cooked, and with great difficulty bent and put the pan into the oven on a rack near the broiler.

"There. Nothing to it; a husband could do this. Six minutes, Emeril, then plate it out. I'm going back to my book. Do you think you might see your way clear to give a bit more wine to your long-suffering wife?"

It was a perfect end of summer dinner. Tim had set the table on the veranda and cut a large bouquet of the last of Sheila's dahlias and the huge pink, coral, and orange blooms were the perfect centerpiece. The recipe was a "keeper" just as Sheila had thought it would be. Much easier than jacketing the fillet in thin par-boiled slices of russets and trying to brown all sides, this new treatment was delicious and, if you cheated and used the flakes, a snap to prepare.

"Tim, I don't think we'll be doing this a week from now. Or even six months from now. You won't be unhappy when little Farley intrudes on our life, will you?"

Her husband smiled at her, shook his head and reached over and took both her hands, "Not at all. Not one bit."

<<<>>>

Farley Maniskjevic wore many hats at Manhattan's Animal Medical Center. He was on the Medical Board, the Peer Review Committee, did some arcane viral research in his labs, and now was in charge of the Avian Influenza Unit—he was the "Bird Flu Man."

The New York City health officials had designated regional facilities to be in charge of setting up bird flu testing centers and the Center had been given the nod. It was a logical choice since they had done the same thing with the West Nile epidemic. Setting up the lab for testing had not been difficult. It only took a bit of money and the center had plenty of that. They were well endowed and their wealthy East Side neighbors and clients gave generously at any of their fundraising events. The research labs were easily outfitted to do DNA studies, and the technique of polymerase chain reaction was now commonly performed. Farley had a first-class lab and his team had proven that while testing the birds sent to them during the four years of the West Nile outbreak. When Farley got the call from Tim, he was delighted to get the lab up and running again.

Sitting at an outdoor cafe in Manhattan, Farley and his wife were a striking couple, both were tall, blond, and regal. They looked more like touring European royalty than first generation New Yorkers Claudette's pageboy was severe and she dressed like Uma Thurman. Crisp linen blouse and slacks in complimentary pastels made her a showstopper and only the casually wrapped silk scarf entwining her long neck softened the cameo. Farley was a Polish prince in every aspect of his life except with friends. With them, he was easygoing, quick with a quip, and didn't have any affectation at all. Ordinarily he refused to carry a cell phone but today he was on call, and a call came. Without setting down his sandwich, he reached across his chest with his left hand, pushed the phone up and out of the pocket and flipped it open. He recognized Tim Morrissey's number so he answered the call.

"Hi, Tim. At least it's not the Center. What's going on?"

"Well, probably nothing but Frank Vogelslieder, the Audubon guy who rescued the smew, called and is feeling prodromal. Nothing specific, just malaise and he's feeling a bit achy. And also, I found my janitor fondling the bird and ready to steal feathers. When do you expect results on those cultures?"

"Soon, Tim. We don't have a formal protocol set up so it takes a bit longer than if we did. Stony Brook is your center on the Island that would have the CDC connections. I'll see if I can reach them in the morning. And your local hospital, South Hampton isn't it? We should have something set up with them also. For cases like this I'm sure they'll want cultures and titers now and in the convalescent phase. Standard stuff if the bird is positive. Just like we did with West Nile. Monitor those two and keep in touch. Don't go fishing."

"Gotcha. Not much chance of fishing when I'm covering office hours for two for the next few weeks."

Tim walked over and sat next to his wife, gave her a kiss on the forehead and soulfully lamented, "I hate to think about what is going to happen if that bird has H5N1 titers and was culture positive. Can you imagine how many dead birds will wind up on our doorstep? And it won't just be crows like the last time. They'll drag in gulls that are mummified, road kill, anything that doesn't fly away. Damn. Double damn. How's little Farley's pee-pee today?"

Tim was ready to duck but nothing flew his way.

<<<>>>

Almost any living organism can be identified by its DNA sequences. In humans, forensic scientists usually examine thirteen DNA segments or regions that will vary in all persons. Put together these pieces of genetic material make a DNA fingerprint that is almost unique to a given person. The same essentially holds true for animals, insects, bacteria, viruses, even wine. These techniques are used in criminal investigation, after a catastrophe like 9/11, in questions of paternity, in transplantation matching, and also in issues of infection or contamination.

Scientists can, in the lab, create small fragments of DNA-like material they call probes, which will combine or bind to the DNA they are trying to identify. By elucidating the pattern of binding, they can identify the DNA in question, matching it to a person or a virus.

By using a process called polymerase chain reaction, or PCR, scientists replicate millions of times the DNA sample they wish to study, thus giving enough material for analysis and identification. This PCR process followed by use of DNA probe (or in the case of some viruses, an RNA probe) was what might permit Farley Maneskjevic's lab at the Animal Medical Center or the labs at Stony Brook to identify the Avian Influenza Virus *if* it existed in the samples sent to them.

At eight that evening, Farley called Tim from his lab. "It's H5N1, no question about it. I ran the PCRs myself, in fact, twice."

So, there it was. Bird flu was here on the East End. So far it existed only in one bird, one lost soul from Northern Europe. Had he cuddled with anyone in Montauk, other than Frank and Ole, that is? Tim pushed his fears to the back of his mind and rejoined his wife.

In the living room, Sheila was on her left side on the sofa reading Patterson's *Beach Road.* When she saw her husband enter the room, she waved the book at him and said, "Nothing like this really ever happens out here. Life is too sedate. When I read *Amagansett* two years ago, I could believe the story because it happened in a different time and the actions, even the people seemed appropriate. But I couldn't see myself living in this story. Everyone on drugs, a racial hate crime and people who just seem unreal makes it hard to believe. I just can't—what is it you're supposed to do? Suspend —disbelief? —yes, so it doesn't work for me." He had sat down next to her and was stroking her hair. "Well, kid, there's a new story that will need to be written. And it will be even harder to believe. That was Farley who just called. That smew had H5N1. Want to write the novel we're going to be living?"

Sheila closed the book and looked at her husband. He looked tired, really tired. Only after an all-nighter at the Animal Center, or in bed when they were first married, had he ever looked this way. She tenderly rested her hand on Tim's and said, "Get a notepad and sit down. You need to make a list for tomorrow."

Tim walked to the desk, picked up a small spiral notebook and pulled a chair up next to the sofa. "OK, Number one: I have to call Pender tonight. Number Two: Frank, ditto. Number Three: Ole, he's out in the Canyon."

That left only Jack Martin, and Tim would call him first thing in the morning.

Frank was home and told Tim that he felt better. His symptoms were improved and his wife was fine.

"Frank, the cultures on the bird were positive, he had H5N1. You may well have it in a very mild form. I'm sure Dr. Pender will fill you in on details and set up a schedule for you to be tested and monitored. He'll want to follow your body's response, your immunity and do some data collecting for a better understanding of the disease. My guess is that in the morning you will be fine, just as you say. But keep me informed."

"Sure, Tim, and thanks very much. I'll see Pender at ten."

Tim then called Ole's house and once again spoke with his daughter who said she didn't expect to hear from her dad before Monday.

"Please have him call me *as soon as* he gets home. Tell him it is very important," Tim instructed Lanie.

Dr. Pender was next and when his service answered they patched Tim through almost immediately.

"Tim, What's the matter? Or shouldn't I guess?"

"No need to guess. The bird had H5N1, that's confirmed. Frank feels better but he'll be in your office in the morning. I think that does it for tonight, sir."

"Thanks for the help, young man. How does it go? May you live in interesting times? Just get Ole Johnson to me when you can. Good night."

<<<>>>

Not since mid-July had there been surf enough to warrant biking a board to Ditch or Caswell's, and Lanie had spent those hours in which she might have been on the water sewing her school wardrobe and the few "on the side" contracts she had with people like Sheila. Since the dissolution of her parents' marriage Lanie had become steadily more scholarly and domestic because she recognized that, try as her father might, a well-run house needed to be a joint effort.

Lanie had always been a water rat but had been forced to leave the swim team when she needed to be at home during practice hours. She did continue to look longingly at the sea and the surfers she saw there. It became a siren call to her.

She was a combination of her parents, both of whom were handsome. Her face, broad with a prominently sculpted nose, might have been mistaken for that of a young Ingrid Bergman. But her physique was that of a swimmer and surfer, with well-muscled broad shoulders and a slim and trim body. Because she biked her board to the beach, her legs were also muscled and attractive. She listened longingly to the conversations of the men with boards, begged old magazines from them, and watched *Blue Crush* countless times. When profit from her industry permitted and her father blessed the expense, she went to Main Beach to be outfitted, and the Garrys who ran the shop kindly saw to it that her dollars were well spent. And so Lanie began to balance school, home-making, a cottage industry, and time on the water.

For the last two summers she had worked in a small boutique in Amagansett, an elegant little store where the owner, Francine, designed and manufactured the clothes she sold. Even though Lanie had never used a sewing machine she was facile and with an expert teacher she was soon patching together functional school clothes from the excess materials around the work shop area in the rear of the store. Her mentor recognized a talent and cultivated it, showing Lanie how to sketch and how to make a pattern.

Francine's small store catered to the wealthy young women who summered on the East End and whose social calendar demanded that they dress for lunch or dinner several times a week. Life was not just tennis dresses and bathing suits. These women loved the light, airy, and sexy designs that were available at Froufrou and kept Francine at her machine most evenings. Although most of her business was seasonal, it was, as Lanie saw, very lucrative.

That first summer Francine presented Lanie with what looked like a large, old-fashioned scrapbook, which she called a croqui. It was meant to hold all of Lanie's designs and sketches along with swatches and patterns, thus creating a record of the young woman's talent. A year later, because she added her work from home, the volume was full, and Lanie had begun a second. Francine had generously helped Lanie acquire a good used sewing machine and set her up at home with a makeshift workshop of her own.

Francine frequently made sourcing trips into Manhattan and one day informed Lanie that she'd like to take the two volumes of the croqui with her to show to a friend. Not too many years after her graduation from Parsons and her rapid successes in the fashion industry, Francine had joined the part-time faculty of the school and had taught alongside Karan and other industry colleagues. This day she took Lanie's work to a friend on the admissions committee and they examined it carefully as they lunched together. Francine explained the social and financial issues swirling around the young woman but there was no question that if Lanie was interested in a Parsons education it would be offered to her. Francine decided to keep the decision a secret until she was certain that her apt pupil would be able to make the commitment emotionally and financially.

Academics weren't an issue—Lanie was an honor student. Her father had wraparound bumper stickers attesting to that fact. But money might be a large issue.

6

Sunday, September 3rd 2006

FRANK VOGELSLIEDER WALKED up to the front desk of South Hampton Hospital and introduced himself to the security guard.

"We were expecting you, sir," the guard said. "Dr. Pender is in his office."

Three hallway turns later he saw the door to the Division of Infectious Diseases, knocked, walked in, and did a quick double take when he saw Irv Pender.

"Frank? Good to meet you. The clothes? I managed nine holes with a six-thirty tee," Dr. Pender chuckled as he shook Frank's hand and gestured for him to sit.

Frank did some quick math and decided that Pender was a near par golfer and that if he had been with a foursome it must have been a quartet of top-flight players. No other way he could have arrived here before Frank.

Pender was about Frank's height and weight, and he looked to be in his mid-sixties. Tanned and curly haired, his nose and eyebrows suggested an eastern European, probably Semitic origin. Frank, himself a first generation American born of European escapees was very accurate in his guessing. The progeny of most of his parents' friends, his contemporaries, had physiognomy he had learned to recognize. He was betting Magyar for Pender, probably Pandar or something close, and he took a try. "Hojh vojh, Pandar," it came out Paaandaaarrrr, elongated "ah's" and rolled "r."

The doctor stopped, took off his half-glasses and answered Frank in Magyar, "How did you know?"

"Parents probably came over on the same boat, but mine were from Czechoslovakia. My name is probably no more 'Birdsong' than yours is Pender."

The men shook hands again warmly. The physician looked at his patient and softly said, "And still we haven't learned. It's as if the world learned nothing. But that's for another time. This morning it's a different story for our grandchildren."

In an examination room, he asked Frank to strip to his skivvies and then did a careful physical examination. With a small light focused on Frank's oropharynx he said, "I want to get an X-ray and some blood work. We are not equipped here to do the definitive testing so that will have to be done at Stony Brook. Your chest is clear as a bell so I doubt anything will show on your film. But we need to gather as much data on you as we can. You don't mind being our guinea pig, do you?"

"Not at all, Doc. If you can be here on a Sunday, so can I."

After Frank dressed, he followed the sound of Pender's golf shoe cleats to the ER where blood samples and nose and throat cultures were taken. Then Pender walked Frank to the radiology suite in the ER and waited while his film was taken and developed.

"As predicted, Frank, you have a clear chest x-ray. You're free to go home. Incidentally, your wife is fine, isn't she?"

"Yes, she is."

"We'll want to test all the contacts, her included. Thank you again for coming in to see me."

Frank drove home and stopped on the way to see Tim and Sheila. They were sitting outside having lunch when he arrived, and Tim invited him to join them.

"Thanks, but Callie has luncheon guests and I'm sure they are waiting for me so they can begin. Just wanted you to know all went well. Dr. Pender said he'll be contacting Stony Brook and that they may want me in again. Will you let me know when you hear from Ole?"

"Sure, Frank, please say hello to Callie."

"Will do. You look ready to pop, Sheila. Keep us in the loop, kids."

He left, and Sheila snorted. "Kids! He's such a delight. But I feel like an old woman and it's time for a change. Maybe a ride on a bumpy road or across the golf course will give Farley an incentive." She reached for the sliced tomatoes. "Gotta feed the boy."

<<<>>>

In Yorktown, back in Westchester, Jack had managed to get out of bed at six-thirty without waking Dina, slip into T-shirt and shorts, and, walking only on the quiet floorboards, sneak out of their bedroom. Closing the barn siding and stained-glass door of their inner sanctum behind him, he semi-belayed himself down the normally creaky spiral metal stairway to the first floor. He made himself a cup of half-caff and began washing the wine glasses. They had had a fun filled relaxing dinner party with good friends. Food and wine were served generously attesting to the empty bottles of the night before which were overflowing in the recycle pail. Jack made a mental note to bundle them out when his wife was awake. While the glasses dried, Jack had some shredded wheat and berries and finished his reheated cup of coffee. Walking to the living room windows he looked at the thermometer affixed to the outside. Their little microclimate was always a bit cooler than the surrounding woods and as it read fifty-six degrees Fahrenheit, he quietly slid open all the first-floor doors, went back into the kitchen, and checked the time. *Five of eight, let her sleep,* he thought.

Jack picked up a pruner and a gardener's shear and went out onto the screened porch where he gathered two wicker baskets and then went across the lawn and into his garden. He harvested a few ripe tomatoes and two long oriental cukes and then filled the basket with a mixture of herbs, heavy on the parsley. He would make an "herby egg" for his wife, almost coddling it with a cup of a chiffonade of fresh mixed herbs. More than enough green goodness to balance the yolk, he thought, but now eggs were on the ten best foods list.

What, Jack thought, happened to the odious half your daily cholesterol allowance tag that an egg once carried? As he squatted to look at the new crop of tiny haricot verts on the just knee-high viney plants, he heard the phone ring. He'd forgotten to bring the portable outside with him and that meant Dina had answered. Walking back inside he picked up the phone extension and heard his wife's voice, "Here he is now, Tim."

"Jack, your bird, the smew, tested positive for H5N1."

Jack laughed. "Would you please stop calling it 'your smew'? I don't want this thing to implode on me so that I have my tail between my legs."

"How about 'our smew', does that work for you?" Tim said. "I'll keep you up to date, though if this baby drops down on us it may change that PDQ."

"You can't begin to imagine, Tim."

The sound of Dina descending drew Jack into the hall. "So it's 'your smew' is it! Poor Dad, poor Grampus. Did you eat? I can't believe I'm hungry after that dinner but the coffee smelled so very good."

"You were awake?" Jack started to sing his favorite Puccini aria, "Nessun dorma, nessun dorma, la pricipessa isa up anda dressda," not that he was an operatic tenor.

"Enough Pavarotti, I was just resting my eyes until you washed the glasses. Wazzin dot bakskit, hubbin?" she asked when she saw Jack's harvest. "Are you making me an herby egg?"

After Jack poured Dina a cup of tea, he began to mince a large handful of the mixed herbs. He heated a non-stick omelet pan, added a tablespoon of good Sicilian olive oil, and dumped in the herbs. When the chiffonade was seared and starting to crisp, he broke two large, cage-free brown eggs on top of it, salted and peppered it lightly, covered the pan, and lowered the heat. Then he put a generous chunk of Terranova pizza bread into the toaster oven. When the yolks of the smothered eggs were just clouded over and beginning to set, he slid the contents of the pan onto a large warm plate and drizzled the now brilliant green olive oil over them.

"Well, you heard him. 'Bird Flu Martin', is at your service, ma'am. Do you think it was a coincidence that Frank was sick? Knowing so little about the disease, it's difficult to make an educated guess." He took the embellished eggs out of the pan.

Dina sipped her tea and walked toward the table. "Less than two days after handling the bird seems fast, but you know we often have a cold a day or two after being in the airport or on a plane. I think he'll test positive."

"Is that your woman's intuition or a sententious declaration from the Oracle of Yorktown? Your eggs are ready, Pandora."

Jack presented the plate with a flourish and backed away as his wife squealed, "Not two! I didn't ask for two. You'll have to help me."

"Glad to assist, but just a nibble or two."

All Jack managed to pilfer were two bites and a bite of yolky bread. After he'd cleared the mess he'd made, he went to the computer to check the mail and learn more about bird flu. He planned to call Frank later in the day, after he was sure that Frank was back home from the doctor visit.

Just before dinner he made that call and was delighted to find his friend completely well. But until the test results were complete no one would rest easily.

<<<>>>

After Sheila had gone to bed, Tim sat in the kitchen with his spiral notebook open. Someone, he decided, needed to document what was happening, and he knew enough of the players that he was confident he could keep an accurate record. But he wondered how long it would be before his world was completely transformed. Between avian flu and a new baby, Tim knew he was living the last chapter of their first life, his and Sheila's. He jotted down his costive thoughts for about an hour, and when he was so tired he could no longer think, he and his seemingly recalcitrant muse went up to bed convinced that this writing would be best left to someone else.

7

THE HUDSON CANYON is a trough that leads from the mouth of the Hudson River as an extension of New York Bay and runs some 400 miles, southeasterly, until it drops off of the continental shelf into the depths of the Atlantic. Most likely created by the flow of the great river into the sea, the "Canyon" as it is generally called, is an off-shore destination for game fishermen seeking species in the normally much cooler waters of the north Atlantic. The Gulf Stream, that great northerly flowing current of warm water from the south Atlantic that eventually turns east across the ocean and permits palm trees to grow on the shore of Scotland, is responsible for attracting marlin, mahi-mahi, wahoo, and other warm water species as far north as New England. The food-rich waters off Long Island and northern New Jersey, which send schools of baitfish into the Canyon's waters, are a great attraction to the warm water species. And those fishes hold great attraction for big game fishermen.

A trip to the Canyon usually means up to an eighty mile, four to five-hour trip in a seaworthy boat. Since the best fishing is always at first light or even at night, charter and private craft leave in the late afternoon, planning to fish most of the night, or at midnight, planning to fish the morning bite. Usually, if the weather and seas prove hospitable enough, it is a day and a half adventure, and some fishermen devote two days to the trip. If the weather changes and a sea comes up, any amount of time spent out there is intolerable. Perhaps that is why to date no effort has been made to reach and tap the apparently huge stores of natural gas lying frozen a mile under water in the floor of the canyon. The fisherman's rewards can be great. Several species of tuna, with always the chance of a giant bluefin worth tens of thousands of dollars, sometimes two species of billfish, along with the other table-worthy species make the strong of heart and stomach risk fickle weather and seas. But it is not a place for everyone.

Ole and four charter captains saw the forecast for superb weather, had a free two days without work scheduled, and had the choice of boats, all of which were veterans of fishing the Canyon. They chose the *Joycie*, a broad-beamed, red-hulled veteran, because there was more room aft and, if they needed it, a tuna door. This hinged section of the stern's transom could swing open and allow a large fish to be slid into the boat at what was almost sea level. It obviated the almost impossible task of lifting as much as 700 pounds over the gunwale. Since a giant bluefin could be worth as much as $25,000, you did not want to drag it home tied alongside the boat. A trophy of that magnitude needed to be properly cared for.

As they loaded pails of saltwater ice, bait, food and drink, the friends joked about the past trips that were now ancient history.

"Levitan, hey Jim, you remember those twins we brought with us once?"

"Every good boat needs twin screws to keep things going," came the reply, "in case one motor gives out or needs a rest. Where are they now, Cap Malensone? But this is a fishing trip and I don't think at my age I'd be up for much more. Up's the operative word here, Cap."

And so, the banter went for the three and a half-hour run out to the area of blue water they wanted to fish. The ride gave them plenty of time to thaw butterfish and bunker and cut them— "chunks", the pieces were called—and to thaw and rig whole squid. The plan was to find fish feeding on the surface and either drift through them or troll around the edges of the activity. Otherwise they'd drift in the strong current and toss out a steady stream of chunks until tuna were attracted to the free meal, and then they would add hooks to some of the chunks.

At five p.m. the autopilot had brought them to the area they had designated, but there were no birds visible or detected on the radar so they began to chunk. It was almost six o'clock when Captain Chuck Malensone called down from the bridge. "Fish busting one hundred yards out."

There were five heavy spinning rods fitted with Stella reels in a rocket launcher under the bridge and they were already baited, three with chunks and two with squid. The five spread themselves around the stern of the boat and tossed the baits out and into the now black waters of the Canyon.

Both squid were eaten almost at once, and two seventy-pound yellowfin tuna were expertly gaffed near the eye and swung aboard. The fish were stunned and then split from vent to gills and all innards removed and tossed overboard, adding to the chum. The carcasses were packed with saltwater ice and put in a huge cooler. Tuna were a warm-blooded fish and heated up during battle, so it was important to bring the temperature down rapidly to preserve the best marketable flesh. The action continued for an hour and then it simply stopped, but they had put six fish on ice.

As it became dark, Captain Chuck turned on the deck lights and brought out two roasted chickens, which he cut up and passed around on melamine plates. Ice cold beer washed the meal down easily.

The men began chunking again at nine, and at eleven they all heard the sound of feeding fish just as Captain Chuck saw them on the lookdown Doppler display. This time they were big eye tuna mixed with albacore, and the team put six more fish on ice. At midnight Fritz Manning and Jack Aiello took a nap, leaving the other three men sitting in the stern and stargazing.

"Ole, I'm tired but too wired to sleep," Chuck said. "I might be the youngest of the captains, but I keep thinking I'm getting too old for these trips."

Ole reached into his pocket, pulled out a handkerchief and wiped off his face. "Guess I worked up a sweat on that last fish. Kind of achy and tired but no way I could sleep either." His host went into the hold and came out with a thermos of coffee and some sandwiches, and the three men talked until four-thirty in the morning when they started chunking again.

At first light they began to hear birds and then saw them, the pelagic shearwaters, petrels, and even a few early season gannets, diving over fish that were breaking quite close to the boat. Captain Chuck turned off the lighting and called down into the hold, "Breakfast is being served on the poop deck and the tuna have arrived."

Once again, the men spread out around the boat and began to catch fish. After Ole had landed a very nice hundred-pound yellowfin, he racked his rod and collapsed in a fighting chair. The bite lasted almost an hour and ended as quickly as it had begun. The fish, now either well fed or finally boat shy, dove and vanished. But six more yellowfin were on ice. Fritz turned, looked at Ole and said, "You OK? You look pale and sweaty."

"Just a bit queasy. Too much coffee or maybe getting old like you guys. I'm happy with three fish on ice, two and a half for Goswell's, and a half for me and Doctor Morrissey."

Chuck tried to lighten the mood for Ole and handed him a Coke as he said, "Just one more chum line and we'll head home."

They chunked uneventfully for three more hours, all the while eating and enjoying a very calm sea. Then Chuck turned the *Joycie* toward home, setting the auto-pilot before joining the others on the deck. He looked over to his friend again and said, "Ole, why don't you take a nap? Grab three or four before we hit the inlet."

"I'd rather sleep right here if it's OK with you guys. I don't like it inside."

Leaving Ole nodding off in the fighting chair, the other men climbed up onto the bridge and jockeyed for a comfortable spot for the ride home.

They had caught fish and had a good time. The weather could not have been better and the sea was as calm as any could remember it. The tuna they sold commercially in the Montauk Market more than made up for the fact they had not booked charters those days. They had noticed a drop in the number of charters for the spring and summer of this season, and even though the fall was fairly well booked, they all had free days. This was unusual—in the past they never had a day free after the middle of August. Maybe it was the gas prices. Maybe it was fiscal restraint. Only time would tell.

8

Monday, September 4th 2006

Tim lay in bed watching Sheila as she slept. He marveled at the almost nine-month growth of their son within his private water-world. For almost a year his fetal mind, heart, limbs and intestinal and urinary tracts, his little pee-pee, all of him had been growing, living, working and swimming in the safety of his mother's womb. Any day now he'd make the greatest transition of his life. No matter what he accomplished after his birth, that event, the moment he entered the world, would surely be miraculous.

The nights were noticeably longer now and Tim, who in summer liked to rise at dawn, was going to have to switch life-modes. Soon the alarm clock would have to return, unless their new alarm clock, Little Farley, or whoever he might become, would do the job for them.

Now in the kitchen, Tim brewed a small pot of coffee and then sat out on the terrace to enjoy the first cup.

"Brisk. I love this weather," he said to no one while blowing on and sipping from his cup. There was a definite nip in the early morning air and he guessed that soon the migrating flocks of geese and ducks would be passing overhead at night, sounding almost like a pack of hounds at chase. And with those flocks would come the distant early morning sound of shotguns resounding in the marshes. As he thought about walking on the empty beaches with his wife and newborn son, the phone rang, pulling him back into the reality of the last five days.

"Hey, Tim, I have some work for you today, you slacker. My contact at Stony Brook just called and they want to run some definitive tests on your Audubon buddy. Get him down there this morning."

Farley told Tim where to send Frank, and Ole when he heard from him, and wished him a happy birthing day.

<<<>>>

Frank was home setting up his easel in the yard, readying for a day of plein-air painting. Watercolors offered little flexibility other than stylistically and he wanted to try overlaying thick white paint as mixing media to achieve striking contrast. Unlike working with oils where one worked from shadows, painting in the darkest portions of the canvas, toward the light and reflections by adding layers of lighter and brighter colors, with watercolors you traditionally created your light or white areas and then worked away from the 'light' to the darkest parts of the paper. Frank wasn't sure it would work but it would be fun to try and if successful, well, he'd just wait and see. When the phone rang, he was not surprised that it was Tim.

<<<>>>

Tuesday, September 5th 2006

An early morning call interrupted Tim's pre breakfast coffee.

"Doc, Ole here."

The voice was thick and somewhat nasal, as if he'd been drinking. But when Tim heard the cough and sounds of expectoration, he became worried.

"We were in the Canyon overnight, two nights actually. You know the routine. Took some bigeye and yellowfin to Goswell's, and we got top dollar. I saved some nice loin for you."

"What's with the cough?"

"Just a cold, might have a bit of a fever. I didn't sleep for two nights. Too much of a good time is all it is. I'll be in later to clean up for you and get things ready for Tuesday."

When Tim told him he had set up a doctor's appointment for him, Ole protested loudly, "I'm not seeing anybody for a damn cold. It's no damn problem." Ole rarely cursed. He was church-going Norwegian Lutheran and his outburst increased Tim's concern.

"Ole, that bird, the smew, had bird flu. We think Frank had a mild case. He went to South Hampton Hospital and was tested." He paused, looked for cogency in his choice of words to Ole.

"Hearing you're sick so soon after handling that bird makes me worried you might have it as well, and you absolutely must see the doctor. This morning. And Ole, I need to know who was on the boat with you on the Canyon trip."

"No way! I'm fine and you aren't gonna scare those boys with some bird flu story. I'll see you later after I get some sleep."

"Ole, either you get over here right now or I call the police to get you. There are your choices. Which will it be?"

Ole was silent. Tim thought he might have hung up on him until he heard him cough again.

"No police. I'll be there."

"Pack a bag, just in case. And be here in half an hour."

Tim heard the pickup pull into the driveway and he walked out to see Ole. He looked haggard, unshaven, and grungy. Two days on the water will do that to you. On closer inspection Ole appeared diaphoretic, sweaty, and he just sat in the cab, not getting out. He nodded toward the truck bed and a cooler there.

"Your loin, Doc, and it's a beauty."

Tim reached over the side of the truck and lifted one end of the red and white container and was surprised at its weight.

"Hope, that's mostly ice."

"Close to a twenty-pound loin of yellowfin."

"Thanks, you can be sure it won't go wanting."

Tim slid the cooler backward and then off the tailgate and went inside to call Pender. His service answered, said he should be in his office, found him, and patched Tim through.

"Dr. Pender, Tim here. I have Ole Johnson with me and he's sick. Productive cough, probably a fever, and he looks like shit. Sorry, but that does describe him. What next, sir?"

"I'll get our isolation room set up for him and then meet him at the door to the ER. Just have him drive up and we'll take care of the car for him. Thanks for all the work, Tim."

Tim went back outside just in time to see Ole turn the corner, headed for Route 27 and, presumably, home. He went back inside and called Pender again.

"He's flown home, I guess. I'll get him to you as soon as I can."

Tim woke Sheila, told her what had happened and then drove to Ole's house in Hither Hills. A lovely young woman who Tim had never met let him in the front door. He assumed she was Ole's daughter, the girl whom Sheila had talked about.

Ole was sitting at the kitchen table in a space that looked more like the backroom of a fashion designer's studio than a handyman's home. There were two mannequins draped with partially sewn dresses and next to them what looked like half of a ping-pong table spread with the patterns, pins, and paraphernalia of dressmaking. The walls were hung with pages from fashion magazines and free-style sketches of ideas from the girl's mind. Lanie, she had introduced herself, appeared distraught, struggling to maintain her composure.

"I was just getting some things together, Doc. Here is the list of people who were on the boat with me—names and numbers. Don't scare them, if you can help it." He lifted his bag, kissed his daughter and told her he'd call her later.

Lanie looked at Tim with tear-filled eyes, and said "Dr. Morrissey, *what* is going on? Is Dad really sick?"

Tim briefly explained, telling her that Frank was already better and that the disease rarely went from person to person. Then he assured her that he'd be back later to drive her to SHH so she could see her father and get herself tested as well.

"I know now why my wife speaks so highly of you, Lanie. This is quite a shop you have here, and I love what you have made for Sheila."

With his hand on the front door Tim turned to Ole and said, "We're going to be all right my friend."

9

On Tuesday September 5th, much to the delight of all parents and even some of the students, school began promptly at eight a.m. Cars and busses were filled with the tanned youth of South Hampton and the neighboring towns of the East End. New clothes, book bags and haircuts were the order of the day. Those teens who had not been employed over the summer and were not used to the early wakeup call slept in whatever transport they found themselves until disgorged at the school door. Although football practice had begun in August for a few dozen young men, for the vast majority, school, its classrooms and sports fields seemed a novelty.

There was a lot to talk about that first day—trips, new students, summer romances—and teachers were more tolerant than usual of chatter after starting bells. At lunchtime, the cafeteria was a beehive of sound and motion. In the computer labs the young hackers could both complete assignments and simultaneously carry on encrypted and clandestine live chats across the room and even in other schools. It went on uninterrupted because none of the instructors could match their students' facility with the computer or texted cell phone.

When the last class of the day ended, no one could guess what would transpire on the local TV news broadcast that evening and how it would affect their lives for another few weeks.

<<<>>>

As soon as he had finished talking to Tim, Irv Pender called Dr. Raju Gupta, the acting head of the Medical Board of SHH.

"Raju, it's Irv. I need you to meet me in my office in ten minutes, sooner if possible."

"I have a full office in half an hour. What's wrong?"

"Dr. Gupta, unless I am mistaken, which I doubt, as we speak you have an almost certain H5N1 case headed to your ER."

It took a moment for a reply which, by its syncopation, suggested disbelief. "My God! Are you sure? *Here?* On the East End?"

"Here! Get the group to cover you and free up your morning. I'll need you in the ER with me."

Irving Pender was standing outside the ER as Ole pulled up. He walked to Ole's pickup and handed him a mask.

"Put this on Mr. Johnson, and leave the keys. Security will take care of the truck for you."

He led Ole to the isolation room in the rear of the ER where they met the intensivist and his nurse.

"Ole Johnson, this is Dr. Matt Colicchio and this is Nurse Eliza Dooley. They'll get things going for you. Until we know if you have bird flu, we plan to keep you in an isolation situation, for your own safety as well as that of others. Hopefully you will just be our guest for a day or two, but while you are here, I would ask you to please consider all the rules we have set up as necessary. Right now, we need to take some cultures, blood tests, and do a chest X-ray." He turned to his intensivist, "Matt, he's all yours."

Pender walked out of the ER and started to cut across the hospital's grounds toward his office. He looked around for Gupta and began to muse about the events of the last two days when his reverie was broken by the sound of Gupta calling his name.

He looked back to see Raju, waving his long arms in the air, almost sprinting to catch up to him. Gupta was young enough and fit enough to catch him, but Irv stopped and waited for the windmill to reach him.

Raju was a first-generation American, but he had assimilated some of his parent's charming Indian affectations of speech and body language, it was always a delight to talk to him. Pender almost expected him to have an accent when he nodded slowly or waggled his head from side to side in a cultural gesture of affirmation. Catching up with his colleague, Raju stopped and spoke somewhat breathlessly, "As my Dad would say, 'My goodness gracious, what a fine messing up of things we seem to have'."

"Seem to have, Raju. Hang on to that '*seem*' for a while. I'll give you the details as we walk."

In the five minutes or so that it took to get to Pender's office he distilled the events of the last few days. Raju was quiet while he listened but at last, he spoke. "We have one sick man and one on the mend. Neither yet confirmed as avian influenza. We have five—seven exposures if we count Morrissey and the wives. We can take care of that many but not more. The bigger problem is that we cannot do the testing in our laboratories. And we might not have, or readily be able to get, the necessary drugs, at least not as quickly as Stony Brook. They are the tertiary care facility for both Nassau and Suffolk and..." He paused for a moment and then continued. "I will need pencil and paper and also I need a cup of tea."

Irv and Raju passed through the waiting area, skirted around the secretarial desk, and went into Pender's office. Once inside, he pointed to a large easel with a pad of newsprint, which he used for didactic sessions or review or hypothetical exercises with the infectious disease staff. He flipped to a clean page and handed Raju a pack of colored, felt-tip magic markers. As Raju thought aloud, Pender went to the window area where a well-used hot-and-cold water dispenser sat at the ready. Next to it were a selection of coffees and teas.

"Gunpowder, green, or Darjeeling?" he asked his colleague as he looked over the selection.

"Darjeeling, please, strong, two bags, and nothing else in it."

Raju set about sketching a decision pathway starting with a yes/no on Vogelslieder's and Johnson's illnesses being H5N1 and carried it to the ultimate point of small epidemic proportions. On a second page he listed whom the hospital would need to contact if the tests were positive.

"Who has the blood and cultures on Frank Vogelslieder? Raju asked Irv.

Irv explained that the samples were at the lab at Stony Brook and that Frank went there himself for additional samples. "I haven't been contacted with results yet but I'm good friends with my counterpart there, Sanford Miller. I'll call him now and see what he knows."

He went to his desk, opened his phone file, and found the direct number for Dr. Sanford Miller. Miller surprised him by saying, "Is that you Irv," as soon as he picked up.

"You 'Up Islanders' don't know many folks with a 631 exchange. It's all Manhasset and Oyster Bay for you. Have you even seen the Hamptons, Sandy?"

"Wouldn't have wanted to this past weekend. What can you do for me?"

It was the banter of friends who had known each other for the decades since their residency training. Irv knew that if at any point they had to bail, Sandy would be there to help. He visualized Miller at his desk, half-glasses precariously perched on the end of his nose, almost a mirror-image of himself, brothers certainly, pressed from the same mold and family history. Strange, he thought, how very much we are alike in every aspect of ourselves.

"Well, I can suggest you sit down. And I can suggest you not travel east for a few days. I thought that tomorrow would be the start of the quiet fall season out here but we may have a tiger by the tail … or, more appropriately, a smew by the tail feathers."

Miller listened quietly while Pender related once again the events of the last days and then he said softly, "Irv, I'm putting you on hold."

When Sandy came back on the line his voice was clearly that of an annoyed chief of service.

"The lab will have the results for us in an hour. The samples came in and someone didn't consider them a priority. A weekend warrior, I presume. Anyway, it's handled. I'll call the lab in fifteen minutes and hold until the results are read to me. Screw their damn hour. Welcome back to the real world where there are bosses. I'll call you right back."

Irv turned to his friend, his boss, who was still struggling with his diagrams.

"We'll have our answer. *Soon*. Sandy is riding the lab."

Just then, Dr. Pender's secretary knocked, came in with a Starbuck's latte, and pointed to the blinking light on one of Pender's in-house extensions.

"Dr. Colicchio from the ER. Anything you need, sir?"

"Yes, please, holler when Sandy Miller calls. Right after that get me Dr. Tim Morrissey, the vet. And thanks for the coffee." Pender pressed the phone extension and spoke to his intensivist, "Matt? What you got?"

Matt Colicchio had heard rales, fine crackling sounds, when he'd ausculted Ole's chest, listening carefully to the sounds of his breathing. "The sounds of a hand wrinkling the cellophane from a cigarette package" was how his elderly physical diagnosis professor had described it, so he wasn't surprised when he saw the chest X-ray. Both lung fields had small areas of splotchy whiteness, almost as if some ornamentation, perhaps snow-flake tattoos across his thorax, had shown up on the film.

"Boss, he has bilateral patchy infiltrates on his chest film. It's completely compatible with a viral pneumonia. Physical exam corroborates it. Most everything else is OK. A mild leukocytosis with a shift is about the only abnormality. Temp 101.3 and he is wiped! His IV is in and cultures are ready to go. What do you want me to do next?"

"Start him on antibiotics and antivirals and I'll get to you shortly. Hang onto those cultures until we speak. They, with others, may be going to Stony Brook by courier."

Pender walked over to where Raju was looking at his diagram and said, "If Frank comes back positive and has already recovered, what do you think we have waiting for us in the ER? The chest film is compatible with a viral pneumonia. Would you want to bet lunch on this one? It may mean we eat right here."

"I'll bet 'yes'. Not that I want H5N1 but because it would be good to rattle the bars a bit. Just the way Miller is doing right now. Nothing's happened since

9/11 and the anthrax days, and we need to know if the system changes we made will work."

The intercom suddenly interrupted their conversation and the secretary's voice announced Sandy Miller on line two.

Irv looked at his CEO and walked back to his desk. "Still want to bet 'yes'?"

Raju nodded; it was almost a wobble but not quite.

"It's positive," Sandy said. "Vogelslieder had bird flu, good old H5N1. I will want follow up titers and cultures, let's say in two weeks and again in a month after that. Collect them there and send them here. I assume you have the specimens on Johnson ready to go?" Sandy asked Irv also to send all the specimens from Lanie, the fishermen, the vet and all the wives directly to his office. A moment later, he asked the million-dollar question: "How is Ole Johnson? Just how sick is he?"

"He has a bilateral viral pneumonia, but other than being exhausted from a two-day trip out to the Canyon he's OK. He's in our isolation unit in the ER. I'm expecting his daughter and the others for testing later today. Do you want me to set up a road trip for him?"

"No, let's wait until we have results on his tests and see how he does. I'll talk to administration to find out exactly what they want to do in preparation for a possible outbreak and we really ought to get our catastrophe plans in place. But let's stay cool headed and under the radar. At this point we don't need the police involved and the media breathing down our necks. Best-case scenario would be to have the one or two that have been infected get well without the public knowing about the flu and then release the information after it's all over. Let's play it close to the vest for now, OK?"

"You bet. I'll have a courier on the way as soon as I can. Thanks, Sandy."

Pender got Matt on the phone and relaying the facts of his conversation, told him to get the cultures together as they were taken, and then prepare to send them by hospital vehicle directly to Dr. Sanford Miller. He also wanted to know if Ole had given them the contact information for the four fishermen.

Colicchio called back after a few minutes and said, "Ole gave the info to Tim Morrissey, who was going to reach them. But I have the information in duplicate, four names and two cell numbers."

"Good, get them up to my office, would you?" Moments later he heard his fax ring.

Next, he called Tim Morrissey and asked him to bring Johnson's daughter over for cultures.

<<<>>>

Tim had two more clients to see, both short post-op visits, then he could clean up and check on Sheila. But first he dialed the Johnson house and told Lanie that her father had pneumonia and was being treated. "Lanie, he's going to be fine," Tim said reassuringly.

"How can you say that, Dr. Morrissey? If he has bird flu, he's going to die just like they do in China."

"Lanie, most people who get medical care recover. That's what we expect will happen with your father, *if* it's bird flu, and we don't even know that yet."

Lanie remained quiet, waiting for Tim to continue. He thought he heard her crying.

"Have you tried to reach your mom?"

"What for? I don't even know where the hell she is or who she's with. Forget her."

Tim dropped the painful subject and gently said, "We're going to need to do cultures on you today and send them to the lab. As soon as I can locate them, your dad's fishing friends will also get tested. And I expect more tests will be performed in a week or so. I'll come by and pick you up in an hour. OK?"

She sniffled her acquiescence.

<<<>>>

"Can I see Dad?" were the first words out of Lanie's mouth. She had seen Tim pull up in front of their saltbox and had come running out to his truck.

"Sure, but they will make you put on a gown and a mask. He's being treated as if he had bird flu and also for other causes of pneumonia. I'm sure he'll be fine in a day or so. Hop in."

Tim wondered why he did not have full confidence in that statement. They were not in an Indonesian or Sumatran village but in New York and they had the world's best medical care right at SHH and Stony Brook. But it was the unknown that made him unsure. To date there had been no American experience with H5N1. To date! But he knew that was changing as he drove west toward the hospital. SHH would begin to write the American text on avian influenza and Tim hoped it would be a very short book with a happy ending.

When they arrived at the hospital, Tim saw two men he recognized as charter captains walking toward the ER. He did the same math that Pender had done when he'd heard that the other two captains, possibly infected with the H5N1 virus, were out that morning on charters, possibly exposing as many as a dozen more people. But he doubled and then redoubled the numbers and then he had the human vectors spread all over Queens, the Bronx, Manhattan, and Westchester, the entire drainage basin for folks who chartered boats out of Montauk. He shuddered at the implications. It was too much to hope that none of the four had been out working the waters off Montauk and the fact that the two were already here at the hospital was good, very good. Pender had said results of all tests could be known by tonight and if the other two fishermen came in promptly for testing, maybe by tomorrow this whole episode could be put to rest. Fervently, he hoped that would be the case.

They met in a room in the ER that Dr. Matt Colicchio had set aside for his personal use. Matt made the introductions.

"This is my nurse practitioner, Eliza Dooly. You probably know her uncle, Captain Chuck Malensone He rescued a number of the *Pelican* passengers. Captain Jim Levitan, this is Dr. Tim Morrissey and the young lady is Lanie Johnson. Her dad is in our isolation room just around the corner. As you may or may not know, Frank Vogelslieder of the Audubon office has been diagnosed as having had avian influenza, what you call 'bird flu'. Frank is fine and Ole is being treated for what we presume is the same illness; we will have his test results back today. This afternoon we want blood samples and nose and throat swabs from both of you. Those cultures will go to Stony Brook for analysis and we should have answers tonight. I fully expect you to be negative. We'll test you again in two weeks and probably a month after that. If you develop any cold or flu-like symptoms, please call me at once and we will check you again. We believe that if you test negative today it is very unlikely that you would change and become positive. Any questions?"

Matt took Lanie to the isolation room and gave her a gown and a mask and let her in to see her father. Ole had shaved and cleaned up nicely. He was sitting up in bed and had an IV attached to his left forearm.

"Hi, kid. They don't think I'll be here very long. You holding up?"

"Dad, I'm scared. What, what if…" She trailed off into tears and collapsed on her father's bed. Ole immediately realized Lanie feared for his life, feared that she would be alone if he died. But he didn't know what to say to his daughter and he looked over at Matt, his eyes begging for help, for rescue from his inadequacy.

Matt saw the problem at once and came immediately to the rescue of both father and daughter.

"Lanie, you can spend as much time with your father as you like. And if you want to you can sleep at my house tonight and come back with me in the morning."

"Thanks, Dr. Colicchio, I'd like that. But there are some chores at home that I have to take care of, so I'd so appreciate it if tomorrow I can see Dad and then get home."

Dr. Pender came into the ER and motioned to Matt through the window. Then he gowned and went into the isolation room as he put on a mask. He introduced himself to Lanie and walked over to the bed.

"Ole, let me take a listen to your chest. I have to make sure my staff knows what they're hearing." He winked at Ole as he sat on the edge of the bed and put the stethoscope on his back. "Just as you described Matt. Ole, I know I'm probably repeating what Dr. Colicchio said, but it bears repeating." After a brief summation he gave Ole a pat on the shoulder. "If your buddies all test negative and I expect they will, the rest will be easy. And that goes for you, too, young lady."

Pender went out of the isolation room, put his mask and gown and gloves in a hamper, and motioned to the two fishing captains. "Walk with me, gentlemen, I've got to get to my office. We should have your test results tonight but it might not be until morning. *Until* we know you are negative, I want you to stay at home. Is that clear?"

Jim Levitan stopped in his tracks and spoke up almost at once. "Doc, I have a photo shoot in the morning. We'll be chasing albies for an article in *Salt Water Fly Fishing* magazine."

Hardly a month went by without one of Jim's superb photographs of the eyes and mouths of voraciously feeding game fish or of victoriously happy fishermen gracing the pages of one of the fine magazines now devoted to saltwater fly fishing. Sometimes the same picture appeared in more than one journal, but that was show-biz.

Pender stopped and taking off his glasses he rubbed his eyes, looked at Levitan and began slowly and forcefully.

"Only if you're cleared, Captain, only if you're cleared," he said.

"But I feel fine and..."

"Up to now we have not had to involve the police." Pender used his glasses to punctuate his words with gentle taps on Levitan's chest. "If your tests are negative you can fish. If not, you are grounded. And if I have to lock you in your house until then, I will. And if you're positive, no matter how you feel, you stay at home. Got it?"

"Yup, I got it, Doc. You call the shots."

Pender looked at his lenses, polished them quickly and put them back on.

"Where are the other two from the boat?" he asked Levitan.

"They said they'd be here and I'm sure they will. They had morning charters. I'll call them again as soon as you finish with us."

As Pender turned again toward the ER exit, he saw Frank Vogelslieder walk into the ER with a woman he assumed to be his wife Callie. He walked over and introduced himself to her.

"I guess Frank brought you in to be tested."

"Yes. In fact, I gave him a scare this morning because I woke up a bit achy."

Pender looked at Callie and as he put a hand on her forehead he said, "My portable thermometer. I forget they have digitals just as fast. Talk to me."

"Well, just achy and a bit stuffy and congested," Callie said. "But considering the change in the weather and that I got drenched last week, the chances are it's just a cold."

"Well, let's just check on your diagnosis, shall we?" Irv led her to Matt's office and then said goodbye.

Callie's chest X-ray was clear and blood count was normal, so Frank and his wife had a pleasant drive back to Montauk.

<<<>>>

Captain Levitan left the ER, went to his pickup, and retrieved his cell phone from the center console. He called his two friends and found that they were together at the marina in Montauk. They both were just in from half-day trips for blues and would be on their way to the hospital after they cleaned up. He told them he'd wait for them outside the ER then he found Matt and told him that the last two captains were on their way.

Levitan walked out to the front of the ER, lit a cigarette, then looked at it. He ground it out and threw the pack into the garbage. *New life as of now, if I test clean. I needed to get rid of those things anyway,* he thought. He considered that the events of the last days might make a good photo essay and made a note to himself to ask Colicchio, later when his pals got to the hospital for tests, if he could take photos.

In half an hour Matt Colicchio had the cultures from everyone from the first group who were even tangentially exposed to the smew, himself and Callie Vogelslieder included. He packed them in a cold unit and was ready to pass them to the courier. When the driver arrived in the ER, Matt reiterated his instructions that the specimens were to go to no one but Dr. Miller.

Then at almost five the last two captains came into the ER with Levitan. Fortunately, they had kept excellent records so Matt got from them contact numbers for their morning charter guests. He took cultures and asked them not to charter again until they were cleared. They had been prepped by Levitan so they quickly agreed and by six o'clock a second courier left for Stony Brook and Miller's office. When Levitan asked Matt about a photo essay of the bird flu scare, Matt told him that maybe after all test results were in and everything had settled down it could be arranged.

Now that they could confirm that they were dealing with H5N1, avian flu, Irv Pender asked Sandy Miller to make the appropriate contacts in Albany. That would cover the obligations for all reportable diseases. Town, county, and state would have been notified and that left only the CDC.

10

Sandy Miller had friends in Atlanta, very good friends who had been in his wedding party. What a day that had been. The wedding and reception were on his in-law's waterfront estate on the North Shore in Manhasset. He remembered losing count of how many people went swimming but he remembered no one had a suit and he'd wondered how many families were started that night. The next morning guests were still cuddling on the dock or in his father-in-law's sailboat.

Harvey Damrosh had been among those revelers and he was now a division head at the CDC, so Sandy called him immediately.

"Sandy? Good to hear from you. Everything all right?"

Miller kicked off his shoes and rubbed his ankles, one vexation, one irritation eliminated. "I need your help. Have a seat and be surprised."

Five minutes later Sandy Miller heard his friend chuckle softly and say, "Dr. Miller, you folks have just helped me win a sizable bet, one big enough to put some fancy Syrahs in my cellar. I was sure it would happen this way and was willing to bet on it. My team here has been compiling a lot of data from our people in the field. We even have H5N1 growing in culture. But we will want that bird for a lot of reasons. Our guess, call it a hunch, is that this virus may not have the pandemic capabilities many people suggest. Third World peoples sleeping amidst a flock of infected ducks might have a catastrophic effect on the community but what you folks have found will offer a more realistic understanding of this virus's virulence in the conditions we face in this country. I'll have someone there tomorrow and it will probably our epidemiologist He's done a lot of data collecting already and is in town. He'll bring a coffin for the deceased."

"What do we tell the police when this story is made public and people start calling them with reports of sick or dead birds?" Miller asked.

"He will answer all of your questions. But Sandy, if, just if, this thing spreads, do you have quarantine plans and capabilities? Would you need help?"

"We have everything we need. We have a large police force and there is an Air National Guard station just outside Quogue. We could marshal enough bodies to do just about anything we need to do, if and when we needed it. But I hope this is just the proverbial tempest in a teapot. As long as the community stays calm, we'll be fine. And as long as the media stay calm, the people will follow suit. We'll look for your man tomorrow."

Sanford Miller then made a quick and calculated decision to complete the testing quietly and try to avoid any undue concern among his staff. He'd called the virology lab and spoke to the director, asking him to keep these tests as quiet as he could even if it meant he had to run them himself. Until they had confirmed the diagnoses, neither of them wanted to have rumor spread throughout the hospital

The virology director did run the tests himself and the first two—the two Johnsons—proved positive for H5N1 but the other four were negative. He then called Sandy Miller to give him the results and to find when he might receive the final two specimens.

Knowing it would be a while before those PCR results were available, Miller had gone home early. He'd spent an hour with the president of Stoney Brook Hospital reviewing their emergency protocols and then had left the grounds content that they were as prepared as one could be.

<<<>>>

When the phone rang in his office, Irv Pender was sitting with Gupta. The two men had been reviewing the SHH catastrophe plans, just in case. The test results at once presented a "good news/bad news" dilemma: relief that the four were negative but concern about the Johnsons. Pender immediately called Matt Colicchio and the pressing issue at once became Lanie. It was clear that transmission from bird to human had occurred. But in Lanie's case she could only have contracted the H5N1 from her father, human to human transfer. This gave the potential for epidemic very real.

The young woman was asymptomatic and looked and felt fine. Was she going to be another Frank Vogelslieder or another Ole? Either would be acceptable to them and that went into the equation of their decision making. Did it make sense to hospitalize her as a precaution? Wasn't it almost as safe having her with Matt and on precautionary oral antivirals? What was Gupta's take on the situation?

The three professionals agreed to keep to their earlier plan and let the young woman have a short but controlled leash, at least for the next twelve hours. They also agreed that it was time to contact the local constabulary and bring them up to speed on the events of the last week.

Raju Gupta picked up the telephone for the in-house lines. The hospital's operator came on the line and he greeted her with warm familiarity, "Mildred, Gupta here. Please connect me with the chief of the South Hampton police, not the village police."

After what seemed an interminable amount of time, the phone was answered by someone with a deep voice who said, "South Hampton Police. Officer Stansik speaking. May I help you?"

"Officer Stansik, this is Dr. Gupta at the SHH. May I please speak to Chief Tavaris?"

"Chief is in a meeting. Can someone else help you, sir?"

"No, I need to speak to him at once."

"Sir, the meeting will be over in about a half hour and I'll have him call you then."

"Stansik, unless you want to be back at the Academy for a refresher course you will connect me to the chief. Is that clear?"

"One minute, Dr. Gupta."

When Tavaris came on the line, Gupta apologized for extracting his friend from a meeting. Then he explained the events of the last now seven days and suggested that Tavaris speak with Dr. Miller before he decided how he would handle the dissemination of information about the smew and the three people who had contracted the illness. Gupta stressed that SHH wanted the police "in the loop" and prepared for any eventuality.

Then, Raju forced himself up and out of the comfortable chair and started for the door. His hand on the knob, he turned back toward Pender.

"I'll be in the administrative office for a while."

Back in his own cloister Raju immediately called Tim Morrissey.

Tim was in the kitchen when the phone rang. "Stork watch, Morrissey speaking," the expectant father answered.

"Hah, good, very good. Gupta, here. You got me to laugh. We have positive tests on Ole and his daughter so now I need a favor from you."

Tim readily agreed to visit the local police barracks, and after checking on Sheila he snuck past a dozing Midgebil and out the door. He then drove east along the Napeague Stretch toward Montauk.

As he dropped down out of Amagansett leaving behind the lush tailored landscape of expensive living and drove onto the "stretch", the scenery became a sea level pine barren much of which was in preserve, too fragile an environment to sustain development. Occasional dirt roads led to grandfathered homes in the dunes. The occasional osprey nests sat atop the taller snags off to the north on the horizon. It wasn't until Tim reached the upgrade into Montauk that the scenery completely changed. He passed several large seaside motels, the Lobster Pot, the Clam Bar, Cyril's, and finally a few seven to eight figure homes. The speed limit dropped to forty and then thirty as Tim slowed, knowing that a radar trap always awaited the speeders. It was here to the south that the first awe-inspiring wide-angle view of the ocean rewarded the driver. Sometimes calm, without swells, sometimes white capped and turbulent, it served as a forecast for aspiring fisherman. Tim passed Empire Gas, John's Pancake House, and the florist, then he turned left off of Route 27. Just past Phil's Garage sat the one story pre-fab structure, vinyl sided and asphalt shingled, that was the Montauk Police Barracks. He pulled into the restrictively small parking lot and found a spot between cruisers, his pickup dwarfing all other vehicles there. Tim looked at the fragile building and wondered how it could withstand the storms that swept across the town most of the fall and winter. The wooden steps and ramp to the front door seemed an afterthought to the building's construct, pushed against the foundation for access.

He nodded to the receptionist/secretary and queried of her, "Eckard?" She pointed her pen to a door to her right, at the end of a short corridor. Captain Rolf Eckard was in his office and he greeted Tim from across his neat desk. When Tim had finished his briefing, it was quiet for a moment. Eckard looked up at the wall. Five p.m. Finally, he spoke.

"I assume you'll get us guidelines, Tim, that we'll have some more information by tomorrow.".

"That's my understanding and I'm sure you will hear from everyone on a regular basis. Right now I have to catch your buddies in Amagansett before they close shop."

"Wait a moment, Tim." Eckard picked up his cell phone and pushed the speaker button.

"Charlie, you in the office?"

"Yup" the voice came back.

"Stay there. Doc Morrissey's on his way over. He's leaving here now."

"But..."

"Stay there, Ace, just stay there."

Tim smiled, rapped Eckard's desk twice, gave a salute, and hurried out the door.

11

WORD OF A potential epidemic began to spread through the hospital staff. The clerk in a gynecologist's office called her friend, a nurse in 'labor and delivery.' And so the word was out that a patient suspected of having bird flu was in isolation in the ER. As soon as she had a free moment, that nurse called her cousin, Francis Tarker, the news anchor at the local TV station. Now the news was really out.

<<<>>>

Frances Tarker, the six p.m. news anchor person at the major Long Island TV station, pointed the remote at the sixty-inch plasma screen and mashed the power button under her well-manicured thumb and ended her view of the blond, multi-million-dollar anchor babe.

"Skinny, tight-assed bitch just reads and smiles and shakes back her hair. Her 'bio' can't touch mine but there she is in New York City and here am I in a pissant town on a pissant channel!"

Reaching down she added a bit more resistance to her "Bow-flex abs" workout and resumed her exercising, always with an eye on the mirrored wall of the spacious bedroom. A cross between Jane Russell and Demi Moore, she was statuesque but not top heavy and as long as she exercised in or out of bed and counted calories, she would not be Rubenesque. She was bright, well-educated and aggressive but somehow, she was stuck, mired in what she considered a back-water scenario. Only thirty-five she still had time to break into the world of seven figure salaries. All she needed was a chance to be seen, a chance to be heard, a chance to be noticed as what she needed to be, a superstar. Looking again in the mirror she decided- if her brains didn't get her there, she'd use her body.

12

AT FIVE O'CLOCK, a call came to Doctor Gupta from the Channel 21 newsroom. His secretary identified the caller and then buzzed her boss. "Frances Tarker's on the line," she said. "She's the six o'clock anchorperson. Somehow, she knows about your patient in the ER. Want to talk to her?"

"I'll pick up in two minutes. First I want to talk to Pender." Had it been his style Raju would have kicked something but he only wrinkled his eyes and massaged his graying temples. As his father would have said, he was greatly vexed.

Pender's counsel was succinct and to the point. He said "Raju tell her as much of the truth as you want to. This isn't damage control, but it's your chance to prevent having to do just that. Tell her to speak with you daily and you'll keep her informed. You don't want her on the air saying we would not talk."

Raju sat and sipped his tea for the thirty seconds he still had left of the "two minutes" and then picked up the phone.

"This is Dr. Raju Gupta. How can I help you?"

"Dr. Gupta, an hour ago we received a call from a source who told us that you have diagnosed two cases of bird flu at SHH, and that many others are potentially infected. Can you confirm that?"

"Ms. Tarker, part of your information is correct. We do have test results that indicate that two people who handled an infected bird contracted the disease. One is fine and the other should be so also, in a day or so. We are testing several other people who had contact with the two original cases and so far, four of the six are negative. The results on the others will be in later tonight. We know that person-to-person, human-to-human shall we say, transfer of this virus is rare in the literature that we have access to, so it is *very* unlikely that anyone else will have contracted the illness."

Gupta knew his numbers didn't quite jive but he hoped he had given information enough.

"Have the police been notified?" Tarker asked.

"Yes, and the authorities at Stony Brook as well."

"Is there a reason you have kept this a secret?"

He let her question slide unanswered and countered, "Ms. Tarker, if you contact me regularly, daily, I assure you, you will be kept fully informed. What I've told you is on the record, and which, I will add, is all we know at this time. Tomorrow, I believe, we will know more."

"But Dr. Gupta, the implications of this are..." She had paused and Gupta stepped into her thoughts.

"What do you see as the implications?" He felt himself now greatly vexed by the insinuation of her questions.

"Well, I'm not sure. But there must be implications!"

"When you decide what they are, jot them down and give me a call. We'll discuss them together. I'll expect to hear from you tomorrow."

Raju returned the phone to its cradle, turned off the phone recorder, and sat back in his ordinarily very comfortable chair. He was not happy with Frances Tarker's abrasiveness. But then, since she was an anchor, and he tried to assure himself that she was just a face who was scripted, she didn't pose a threat. Why, he wondered, was his seat suddenly uncomfortable?

Raju then called Irv Pender. As soon as his colleague picked up the phone, Raju said, "She wanted to discuss the 'implications' of this event but when I asked her 'which implications' she flummoxed with, 'well, there must be some'."

Pender tried to make light of Gupta's concern and the two doctors, at Raju's invitation, decided to watch the news together in the administrative office. Raju tried to regain his composure while he was waiting for Pender, and as he poured the hot water for tea, he spoke to himself. "Too bad there are no leaves to read. Certainly, none with these damned bags."

<<<>>>

At six p.m. Drs. Gupta and Pender sat down in Raju's office to watch the local news broadcast, while some thirty miles to the west, Dr. Miller and two hospital administrators did the same.

Frances Tarker looked tense. She was sitting straighter than usual and was repeatedly gripping and releasing the pen in her right hand. Her Chanel suit was impeccably tailored and what appeared to be a Hermes scarf completed her evening's attire. To say she was stunning was not an overstatement. However, she was not chatting with her co-host, Dan Fleisher, as was her usual lead-in demeanor, and when they cut to her in a close-up for her opening statements, she switched the pen to her left hand and seemed to be waiting for something to happen. She was still not in control.

Trying to maintain a visage more serious, more concerned than usual she began, "Good Evening. This is not a typical evening here on Long Island but rather an historic and potentially catastrophic one."

"Catastrophic?" Raju murmured. "Who wrote that copy?"

"Yes, I said catastrophic because two confirmed cases of avian influenza, bird flu, were just diagnosed in Suffolk County, and health officials, rather than activate a plan to safeguard the communities, have chosen to hide the truth from us. Why they have done so is a mystery to this reporter, but we will, in the next half hour, look at the implications of both this breaking story and the inactivity, even deception, of the people who are responsible for protecting the people of Long Island: the health and police officials."

As Raju reached for the ringing phone, his secretary beat him to it and then announced Dr. Miller on the line.

"Sandy, what is she doing?"

"Just keep watching. We'll talk later. I didn't mention it to you but I did call a friend at CDC to cover our backsides. He said he'd get someone up here in the morning and to keep going as we were. Later."

Tarker had left her desk and walked to a projection of a large map of eastern Long Island. There were large red circles around Montauk and Amagansett and also around Southampton Hospital and the facility at Stony Brook. She began again.

"We don't know how this started but we know where it started. The infected men live in Montauk and Amagansett. So, it appears that the East End is contaminated. Since one of the victims is being treated at Southampton Hospital, that facility and its employees are also at risk. The other man is walking the streets as I report to you. Can you imagine? Walking the streets! Let's look at what we know about bird flu."

Frances walked back to her desk and tried to sit down gracefully but her hands were shaking. She quickly placed them in her lap, out of sight.

"Dan, please tell us about H5, umm, H5N1, the avian influenza bacteria…virus."

"Thanks, Frances. We first heard about this disease when it began to attack poultry flocks in the Far East. In the past, we have seen assaults by influenza viruses on other populations—pigs, and of course, humans.

With vaccines, we have made the human populations relatively safe and vaccines are being prepared for avian flu to safeguard poultry stocks worldwide. But the problem is that this variety of avian influenza, called H5N1, has spread to humans in many places. In China, Indonesia, and Sarawak, people have contracted the disease and succumbed. It has not reached epidemic proportions but most experts fear it could. Some say it will. They fear the virus will mutate, much like the AIDS virus is able to do, making transfer of the virus from human to human easier and possibly leading to an epidemic. Even a pandemic is possible."

"Dan, isn't the problem that here, in Suffolk, we don't know if this is the old H5N1 or a newer, mutated form, a much more dangerous form, and that a pandemic might just be starting here?"

Someone cut the news to a commercial break, and Raju turned and looked at Irv Pender. Shaking his head, he said, "What she means is pandemonium, not a pandemic. Some heads should roll there tomorrow!"

When the commercial break ended, Frances Tarker returned to the screen and began again. "We have asked an epidemiological scientist to give us an expert opinion of the worst-case scenario for what is going on at this moment in Suffolk. Dr. Leopold Storch is a virologist and epidemiologist at SUNY Albany." Because they hadn't time to set up a remote feed from his offices, a picture of the man appeared behind Tarker. "Dr. Storch, good evening."

"Good evening, Frances." The voice was calm and betrayed no quaver of anxiety as did Tarker's.

"Dr. Storch, our audience hopes and assumes, and probably prays, that the medical knowledge and expertise available on Long Island will control this outbreak. But what if it can't? What could possibly happen and how would it happen? Give us the worst-case scenario." Her anxiety seemed to spread from her nervous hands and she seemed almost breathless and the two doctors watched her anxiously.

"Frances, I don't know that such a description is possible or appropriate at this time. We have no reason to assume a worst-case scenario."

"Is that because it is so very bad that you don't want to discuss it? Because it means quarantines, roadblocks, the National Guard, loss of lives, even children's lives?" Tarker gestured behind her to the projection of the map and the man and continued. "The thought of a new plague there, sweeping across Long Island, is just too frightening. But Dr. Storch, isn't it your job to do just that, what I'm asking you to do? You construct worst-case scenarios. You did it for the Anthrax scare and for a 'dirty bomb' after the horrors of 9/11. And the numbers of deaths from a pandemic here could exceed those of 9/11, could they not, Dr. Storch?"

"Miss Tarker, my job is not to create havoc or a scenario when it is not justified."

The engineers in the control room at some unseen signal cut abruptly from the Albany voice feed, and on the TV screen Frances Tarker's hands were seen to be clenching and unclenching repeatedly. The camera switched to Dan Fleischer, and her co-anchor rescued her as best he could.

"Frances, I've just received some information from the newsroom. It seems that proper authorities had been contacted by Stoney Brook and they, along with the Communicable Disease Center in Atlanta, have approved all activity to the present time and will have consulting people here tomorrow morning. And so, ladies and gentlemen, perhaps we don't need Dr. Storch's scenario after all. At least the CDC doesn't seem to think we do and that makes at least this man very happy. It's time for traffic and weather with Jacquelin Frost."

The cameras cut to Jackie and when they finally returned to the anchor desk Dan Fleisher was seated there without Frances Tarker, and he finished the broadcast alone.

Raju looked at Pender who was slumped in the big leather chair. He had his glasses set on the arm and was massaging his temples. Neither man spoke, each waiting for the other to begin. Gupta finally got up, stretched, and stood between his friend and his view of the now blank TV screen. "That was reality TV at its worst. My guess is she won't be on tomorrow. Let's hope not, anyway."

The phone rang. Raju spoke briefly to Sandy Miller and turned back to Pender. They marveled at Miller's timely intervention and the difference it had made in the end of the broadcast, and then they both moved slowly toward the door, tacitly acknowledging that their spouses were holding dinner in anticipation of their arrival. Gupta put a long arm across Pender's shoulders as they moved through the outer office. There was fatigue in his voice.

"Tomorrow is going to be a busy day. Will you call me in the morning as soon as you see our patient?"

"Of course, and I'll let you know the other test results as soon as I've got them."

13

AT SIX-THIRTY P.M. that Tuesday, just after the news, the long shadows of the late afternoon were disappearing and twilight of an autumn evening was just descending on the East End, but the communications system of the towns there was coming alive. Phones rang, neighbors met in the backyard, and the bakeries and ice cream parlors became information exchange centers.

Frances Tarker's dramatic news report was on the lips of a very large segment of the population. Word spread almost as rapidly as it had that September morning five years ago and people, as if following Tarker's lead, began to confuse and even equate the two events.

They knew nothing about the smew and those that had handled the bird. They did not know how or when the virus had come to the East End but they all heard first- or second-hand of Tarker's broadcast. Fortunately, anticipation of another work or school day sent most people home and to sleep. But more than a few had already decided upon what seemed to them an appropriate isolation to protect themselves from the rest of the community until they had more information. They had made plans to keep children inside, eat what food they had in the house, and to go to work only if they had to and could not find an excuse for absenteeism. A lot of heads would stay in the sand until six o'clock the next afternoon when they would once again emerge to view the evening news.

<<<>>>

Ole was holding his own or on the mend and it was with some degree of satisfaction that Matt Colicchio left the hospital, Lanie in tow, and headed home for the night. They stopped and did some shopping so Matt could fix dinner for the two of them—fresh corn and big hamburgers on the grill and some local tomatoes with good olive oil, all served with a crusty loaf of Tuscan bread. They both ate with gusto, chatting about work, school, anything but the obvious, and by eight-thirty Lanie was falling asleep on her feet. Matt showed her the guest room and shower, gave her two of the antiviral capsules, and sent her off to bed. Even though she had tested positive and was infected with the virus, Lanie looked and acted like a healthy teen. Unable to sleep himself, Matt sat with a book and a beer but he spent most of the next hour or two thinking about what the morning might bring. At eleven he got the call from Dr. Pender that the last two fishermen were clear; they had tested negative.

It was now very likely that the contagion, this H5N1 virus, had left their small community.

<<<>>>

Francis Tarker could not fall asleep. She had sat up watching and re-watching her CD copy of her evening's performance. She had driven and controlled the broadcast as she had wanted to, as she had planned. An Oscar winning performance? Perhaps not because of the ending but damn close. She was sure she'd held the attention of the citizenry of the East End but she could only hope that it was seen "down island" in New York. Perhaps it had been picked up and relayed onto a national broadcast.

She looked at the notes on the legal pad, items on which she would query Gupta, and hoped he would be a source of ammunition for the fire she planned to ignite, a fire that would light up around Frances Tarker, sending her like a phoenix into prominence, recognition and a big fat salary.

It was almost one a.m. when she walked into the bedroom and slipped out of her peignoir and stood before her dressing mirror.

"God, what a great body to go with this brain." Her voice had roused her fiancé from his semi-sleep and he rolled to face her.

"Think we might just turn off the brain for a while and turn on the body?"

It was three a.m. when they finally slid moistly apart, agreeing that it was time to sleep.

14

Wednesday, September 6th 2006

During the night Matt thought he heard Lanie get up and walk around and maybe even cough, but he was not sure. He guessed she was just using the bathroom and he had no trouble going back to sleep.

At five-thirty, before first light, his internal alarm went off and Matt got out of bed and rolled onto a yoga mat where he endured twenty minutes of lumbo-sacral stretching and strengthening exercises, and then he showered. Standing in the relaxing pulse of the hot water, Matt was able to reflect on the last day and speculate on this new one. Lanie was his major concern. Instead of being able to go home to her chores she would need a chest X-ray and additional testing.

He had watched only part of the six o'clock news while still in the ER, but seeing Tarker lose control bothered him greatly. He wondered if this was going to be the typical reaction of many folks on the East

End. He wondered if people here were so very irrational or if it was the mishegoss, he loved that word, of Ms. Tarker.

As he toweled and then shaved that portion of his face that did not have a neat and very flattering beard, he heard Lanie cough—a dry, tight cough of early tracheo-pulmonary irritation. He couldn't remember when flu victims were most infectious and when that infectivity tapered off, and he would research that as soon as he got to the hospital.

As he dressed, he hollered down the hall to Lanie and asked her if she was hungry. "I usually have cereal and berries, but I have eggs if you want them."

"Anything is fine. Cereal," she said and coughed again. *Well,* he thought, *she did have the most intimate contact with her father, closed in the house as they were.*

Lanie came into the kitchen and Matt roughed her curly blond hair and slid a hand onto her cheek. At least she did not feel febrile. He surreptitiously washed his hands and said, "Help yourself. Cereals are over there. Also berries. Milk's in the fridge, sorry, but it's two percent," he said.

On the counter were boxes of Kashi Nuggets and Autumn Wheat, as well as blueberries and raspberries. Lanie poured some of the Kashi Nuggets and added fruit. Into a half cup of coffee went two spoons of sugar and half a cup of milk. She ate the cereal and berries dry. Reaching into her shirt pocket she removed the envelope of capsules and popped two into her mouth.

"When did the cough start, Lanie?"

"This morning. Well, during the night. These things aren't working, are they?"

Matt avoided her remark. "Feel OK, otherwise?"

"Just tired. And a bit achy, I guess. Think I've got it?"

"It's very possible, but remember, Frank never was sicker than you are now. We'll check you over when we get to the horse-pistol."

Lanie laughed at the corruption of the word, and Matt was pleased to see her smile, the first one he'd noticed that morning. But he was justifiably worried about the cough and was almost certain what the chest X-ray would show.

<<<>>>

On her third stop of the morning, Pat Hannon's suspicions were realized. There was something very wrong. Her bus was very quiet. She looked into her rearview mirror and then did a head count. Ordinarily at this point she'd have fourteen students on the bus but even a recount showed only eight nodding bodies. One body short for each of the first stops? Well, that happened, but there were four missing at this one.

"What's up guys? Where is everyone?" she asked of the awake few.

Shrugs greeted her query but finally Frankie D'Angelo, sitting in the second row, volunteered. "Their moms were afraid of the bird flu, Ms. Hannon."

Pat was sixty so she could remember chicken pox and measles outbreaks which shrunk her own grammar school classes, but these days only during very, very bad weather, like that of two winters ago when schools were closed until the severe cold abated, did she see her bus with only half its riders. By the time she reached school she was still only at fifty percent occupancy. When she chatted with the three other drivers who were standing together in front of the brick upper-school, she found their numbers were down as well, again almost half empty.

Pat sat down on the edge of the sidewalk and nudged the drowsy driver next to her. "What do the parents think they are going to avoid Jim?"

Jimmy Beggs sipped his cold coffee and tried to make some sense of the absenteeism. He turned toward Pat and set his empty cup on the curb. "They're scared and don't know the right thing to do so they panic and hole up at home. There has been no health advisory, no advice at all. They've all invested a great deal in these kids and don't want to see anything happen to them. I'll bet you the buses will be full again by Friday, after this all blows over."

Heads nodded in agreement, but Pat spoke as she stood up, a skeptic minority of one. "I hope you're right, guys, but if they let that lady loose on TV again tonight, I think you'd lose that bet Jimmy."

Pat waved to her friends as she went back to her bus and headed to the barn and her own vehicle and then her daily few hours of helping her husband at their stationery store. She thought it might be her imagination but it sure seemed easier to find a parking space as she pulled up in front of the shop, and the beach breakfast establishment across the street had an unusual number of empty tables available, as well as counter space. *This is crazy,* she thought as she went into their shop.

<<<>>>

When Matt and Lanie arrived at the ER, they were hailed by Drs. Pender and Gupta who Matt had seen drive in behind them. Matt did not like to arrive at the same time as his bosses but a glance at his watch showed that even he himself was earlier than usual.

The four walked in lock-step toward the ER entry, and Matt broke the tension that surrounded them, "Morning X-ray should be up and waiting for us, gentlemen. I hope you two slept as well as we did. I'd forgotten how much teenagers can eat but this gal reminded me." As they walked through the automatic door, Matt caught Pender's eye and slowed his pace. While Gupta and Lanie proceeded toward Ole's bed, Matt told Irv about Lanie's cough and malaise.

Pender patted the younger physician on the back and said, "That's still only three and there shouldn't be any more."

Raju Gupta walked toward the viewing panel where Ole's films were displayed. Matt and Pender were only a few steps behind him. The CEO spoke as he reviewed the X-rays.

"I spent much of the time last night worrying about the loose cannon, Tarker, and what she might do today! I can't wait for her call. Would you like to field it today, Irv?"

Pender chuckled at the suggestion. "Hah, she's your kitten, Raju. I don't even want to think about the calls you're going to get today." He looked at the films and nodded appreciatively. Turning to Gupta he continued. "Certainly Sandy will call when this CDC fellow flies in and as CEO you should greet him; but if he wants to consult with me, I'm available at his convenience."

Matt and Lanie headed to Ole's room. Ole's morning film was much improved and the man himself was attacking a breakfast tray.

Lanie walked over to her father and gave him a kiss. "Hi, Dad. I think my X-ray is going to look like yours did yesterday. I'm sorry, Dad!"

Once again Lanie burst into tears and fell into her father's arms, upsetting the tray onto the bed. Her father took her in his arms and hugged her tightly. "You sorry? I'm the jerk who had to see the bird and try to get some feathers. If it weren't for me this whole deal would be over with. I'm the one to say 'I'm sorry', kiddo. And if you need this bed for a day or so, that's OK. I'm ready to share it."

Colicchio looked toward the other physicians and gave an unhappy raise of his Casanova eyebrows and a shake of his head. Then he gave Lanie a mask and escorted her to the small X-ray room adjacent to the isolation room. Since the tech was off working the unit, Matt took the film himself. He'd learned long ago that as an ER specialist you had to function in any capacity, including X-ray tech.

He led Lanie to the frame. Holding the film cassette and moving her chest up and against it, he said, "Put your chin on this rest. Hands on hip and elbows back, shoulders also."

Through the opening in the back of the gown he noticed the young woman's muscular back and deep tan and then he remembered seeing her on the beach on those few occasions he'd been able to get there.

"Still surfing, Lanie?"

"I try to get out, when I can. How'd you know?"

"I've seen you at the Ditch."

"Yeah, great surfing there but too many old men who think they're hot stuff and try to hit on you. Some are older than Dad."

"Deep breath and hold it," he said. The machine buzzed and then Matt told Lanie to breathe normally. "We don't need a lateral view. This will tell the whole story. Hey, you can't blame them for trying. Just brush them off."

"I do, don't worry."

Matt stepped into the backroom and put the film into the automatic developer.

"Five minutes at most. Let's go back to your Dad."

Shortly, Matt came back with Lanie's film.

"Care to join us for a day or two, Lanie?"

Matt put the film up next to her father's and pointed out the few white patchy areas he said, "We'll treat you like we did your Dad. It seemed to have worked very well for him and it will for you. Your test was positive, Lanie, but I'm not worried about you. You'll be fine." He looked at his colleagues and said, "Drs. Gupta and Pender, can we chat?"

Matt walked into his office in the ER and closed the door behind them.

"Where do you want to put her, Dr. Pender, in an ID isolation bed? Then if we have to move her, it could be tough. After last night's TV melodrama, the quieter we are and the less moving we do the better." He shrugged unhappily and continued, "And someone seems inclined to let the press know what's going on. But you call the shots."

"Matt, she'd be best served in the pulmonary ICU, in an isolation room."

The others agreed, and both the admitting office and the P-ICU were called.

Dr. Gupta told Matt and Pender that he planned to have a series of staff meetings, one for each shift of workers, to fully inform them and explain in detail the events of the last week. He knew it would be better to arm everyone who worked in the hospital with facts before the rumors got out of hand. After last night's Tarker-rama he was sure the fringe, the bottom feeders of the world, would start feasting, even here at the hospital. They needed to be prepared for any eventuality.

With the paperwork completed, Lanie was escorted to the Pulmonary ICU's step-down unit. It was here that people, no longer respirator-dependent, were kept until they could move into the regular hospital facilities. It was frightening for Lanie to see elderly pulmonary cripples and other patients who, still requiring supplementary oxygen, had masks or nasal prongs delivering the needed oxygen. Of course, she feared the worst and once again broke into tears. The staff did the best they could to comfort her, considering her circumstances, her age, and her father in bed downstairs. They took extra care when starting her intravenous line, numbing the site with buffered xylocaine before inserting a needle and using only a small 22-gauge infuser. It was only to be used for antiviral and antibiotic administration and, for the time being, she was not at risk. They could always add a large line when, and if, it was needed. Everyone expected her stay to be of short duration. Even a TV was jerry-rigged into her room by one of the savvy techs in the unit and Lanie settled in as best as her anxiety would allow.

15

SEPTEMBER WAS THE month that everyone at the East End loved. The summer residents were gone and the morning temperatures were in the fifties. Fall flowers, the Montauk daisies, crepe myrtle, and phlox were in bloom, and chard and new potatoes and other fall veggies were found in abundance at the farm stands. The once crowded beaches were empty and both bluefish and striped bass were beginning to prowl the surf making dawn excursions a must for the fisherman. That is how it should have stayed, but by nine o'clock the phones had begun to ring in the normally quiet offices of the East Hampton, Amagansett, and Montauk Police barracks. Bizarre bird behavior on the beach, in parks and on every roadway was being reported. Several carcasses in varying states of decay and desiccation were found along Route 27 and the high-tide line of the beach. The desk sergeants duly recorded names and numbers and detailed locations of the deceased and assured the callers that they "would take care of it." Road kill, though, was not to be touched until there was an executive order for it to be collected.

Captain Rolf Eckerd called Tim Morrissey to see if anyone in authority had, as yet, any idea which carcasses might be of value. Tim had promised to relay such information when he had it but Eckerd wanted it sooner, now.

Tim listened sympathetically to the litany: the abuse of the cell phone, the aggressive behavior of terns, the horny gulls, the trade parade and surf-fisher folk calling in aberrant behavior. He wanted guidelines and he wanted them soon. All Tim could do was assure him that the information would be forthcoming from the CDC that day and ask him to hang loose.

Tim poured himself another half cup of coffee and then he called Farley. He relayed what Eckerd had said to him about the barrage of phone calls, summarized the test results of folks who were in contact with the smew, and he told his friend that he'd expected this community hysteria.

"Farley, with West Nile we knew that the disease could be spread to humans from the viral pool in blackbirds or crows by a vector, the mosquito, which fed on infected birds and then on people. But we don't know much about this virus. For example, is there a vector?"

Farley's answer was Socratic but indefinite. "As far as we know it has always been spread by direct contact with infected birds, but with Lanie it is behaving like an ordinary influenza, spread by cough or sneeze droplets, human to human. We have no idea how long the virus will live in a dead bird, if at all. Your carcasses on the roads are probably old, birds that never had contact with our little duck. Hopefully, no one will get near any dead bird so we'll be OK for now. The CDC are the guys to call the shots."

"We're expecting a visitor from Atlanta and I'm sure he'll give us parameters for road kill and retesting everyone. If we have to screen birds, can you guys do it?"

"Sure, buddy. And just how is Sheila?"

"She's fine. Her PIH seems not to be an issue at this point and the last chat was about doing another sono and inducing her early next week. The tech blew it during the last sono, pointed out his little 'pee-pee.'"

"Sorry, buddy, but that means you have to work on a girl the next time. Try a different position."

"Smew-style perhaps? Goodbye, you pervert."

Tim then called Dr. Pender and learned that they were waiting for the arrival of the CDC, and Pender promised to find out about the screening of dead birds—if and how they might want it done.

"Tim, I'll make you any sized wager you want that we will not find a single domestic bird that's infected. Our smew was a spook who flew in on us. I just wish he'd stopped on the Cape. I'll call you when I have an answer for you."

<<<>>>

Farley had made Tim think once again about his wife. Not that there were many moments of the day when he didn't worry about her. But he was certainly glad he'd tested negative and had not possibly jeopardized his wife or their baby. After Sheila had told him about the conversations with Handley, Tim had Googled PIH just to make sure that Sheila had not left out any details. Interestingly, one of the references was an article in one of the July *New Yorker* magazines. He pulled it up and read it, fascinated by the amount of scientific information in a magazine best noted for its cartoons and Bush-bashing. Clearly, Handley had told Sheila what she needed to know and she had accurately relayed that same information to her husband. Tim found it amazing that the fetus and its placenta could actually behave as if it was a unit that could think and act on its own behalf, even to the detriment of the mother. He found most interesting the origin of the term "eclampsia." It came from the Greek and meant "bright flashings." It was thought that the ancient physicians knew of some of the visual auras that women had during hypertension-induced seizures and had so named the entity. By the end of the article he was satisfied that Sheila was safe and in good hands. If all went smoothly with the induction, she'd be allowed a vaginal delivery, but if her pressure went up or the baby's monitors were showing undue stress, she would have an immediate section. When Tim had asked her why they just didn't plan for a C-section, which seemed the safest approach, she gave him the answer he had hoped to hear.

His wife assured him that the doctor told her, "There is absolutely no reason to take that approach. I expect this to be a routine delivery."

16

THE CALL FROM Sandy Miller came at ten o'clock while Raju was in the staff auditorium addressing the service heads and the charge nurses of the hospital. His call was routed to the phone on the podium. After a few words with Sandy, he redirected his attention to the full auditorium and said, "That was Dr. Sanford Miller, Chief of ID at Stony Brook, with a heads-up to expect a CDC rep here by noon. CDC is, of course, fascinated by our experience of the last week and is anxious to offer any assistance. In my experience, they will not be coming in like the FBI or CIA to take over. They are not the front-line like we are, so do not worry about this visit. Just continue with your usual degree of excellence and expertise. Again, I emphasize that these two patients, the Johnsons, are two of only three who have contracted H5N1. I know that you have heard Ms. Tarker announce that hospital employees are at risk for the flu. But, as you know, we are always at risk. That has been our fate since we chose our present employment. Every time we treat an acute situation in an HIV-positive patient we are at risk. When we handle major trauma or operate electively on anyone, we put ourselves at risk. We know that and yet we carry on. We perform our duties day by day and we take what precautions we can to protect ourselves as mandated by OSHA and common sense.

"Our two patients are in isolation rooms, the safest place for all concerned. Those who are caring for them do so because they know that the risk is minimalized by the isolation systems and regulations. And they *know* that the patients are part of our greater community, part of our extended family. Most importantly, you must remember that we are treating two patients with influenza and not Ebola or Hanta or some other lethal disease. We hospitalize a number of flu victims every fall and winter and we do so without fear. I myself truly believe that these patients pose no more risk to our staff, to you, than any flu patient we will admit in the months ahead.

"Thank you all for meeting with me. Any questions?"

Fred Cleary, a cardiologist, stood and asked, "Raju, do you expect more of the kind of bull crap from Tarker?"

"Fred, I expect a call from Ms. Tarker today. She was invited to be given a daily update, but I'm not sure she'll be allowed by her network to do investigative reporting after last night's debacle. However, I'm prepared to talk to her. We should all maintain our reserve if approached by any of the media, and please refer them to me. Is there anything else?" Gupta paused and waited a moment. "If not, thanks again for your time."

When Dr. Gupta reached his office, he was greeted by the most attractive Constance Streive, a reporter from the Southampton newspaper, and another handsome woman whom he didn't recognize. Connie covered the hospital's social functions and did a monthly piece on summer celebs who used the SHH.

"Dr. Gupta, this is Estancia Bethany of *Long Island Newsday*. She is a very good friend of mine and she and Max have been staying with Jason and me for a week. If you could spare us a few moments, I think we could help to balance last night's Channel 21 news report."

"Of course, ladies, come in. We could use the help."

Raju offered them coffee and sat down at his desk. He explained in careful detail exactly what had happened from the day the smew was found until Lanie's admission this morning. They learned that Stony Brook was on standby and the CDC was coming to collect data that day. Things were under control and there was no epidemic.

"Dr. Gupta, if that bird hadn't been 'rescued', might it not have perished and been washed out to sea? Then none of this would have happened. Is that about right?"

"Estancia, that is possibly correct. But if it had died on the beach and a vulture or a black-backed gull had eaten it we might have begun a wild, endemic viral pool—what we call a sylvatic pool—on the island. Then who knows what might have happened. We know that sylvatic viral pools of H5N1 exist in the Baltic and Eastern European regions and that, to date, they have not caused problems with either the human population or the poultry stocks. But they could and may yet do so. Think of what might happen to our duck farms! The scenario as it occurred might have been the best for all concerned; that is, of course, as long as Lanie gets well quickly."

Connie leaned forward in her chair, and sliding a bit closer to the desk she looked first toward Estancia and then perhaps even a bit sultrily back at Raju. "Dr. Gupta, could we see her and perhaps get a photo for a story?"

Gupta realized he was being played by eyes and thighs but did not mind the slight flirtation. Business was, after all, business. He smiled and hesitated as if debating and then clapped his hands, finalizing the decision.

"If the head of the unit approves and both Lanie and her dad agree, I see no reason not to let you see her. It would certainly be easier to see Ole, but I understand your interest in Lanie. Just five minutes, though. You will have to wear a mask and gown, and I can't guarantee one hundred percent safety. But I think you will have very little risk to yourselves."

"We'll only take photos with her consent. We'll use a sketch instead."

The visit was arranged. The journalists were true to their word, stayed only five minutes, and took photos of Lanie who was happy to pose for the front page.

The press, in fact all the media, would want access to the hospital and patients, but Raju knew he would have to be stingy with that access. If Constance and Estancia did their job well, he'd be able to restrict the others. He had legitimate reasons to keep people away from the patents and could cite risk or requests for privacy. Both would be honored. He had felt confident that these two women had the hospital's best interest at heart.

The next call, however, was from a notorious tabloid scandal sheet, the *Enquirer*'s main competition. His secretary kept the reporter on hold as she walked into her boss's office.

"*The Celestial*," she quipped, "shall I tell them you will send them copies of the daily progress bulletins?"

"Yes, tell them we'll overnight them a package of goodies. But don't remind me to compile it if I forget and, Francine, thanks for all the help the last few days."

<<<>>>

An hour before noon Raju was sitting quietly in his office, worrying about the teenager in his P-ICU. He hoped that in the next few hours her antiviral medications would begin to improve her clinical state but, for some reason, he started to doubt his abilities, his knowledge and expertise.

And yet, he knew not to second guess himself. Time, and not worrying, would determine events That had been his father's philosophic attitude, which was inherited by his physician son. He made himself another cup of tea and looked out onto the manicured grounds of the SHH. He was amazed that the beauty of the day and the scene could be so disrupted by the illness of one young woman. But that was medicine for you.

Francine knocked and came into his office. "She's baaaack!" she said in imitation of the movie *Poltergeist*. "Our anchor-demon is on the line."

"Tell her I'll be with her directly but give me two minutes—I need some tea—before connecting us."

Raju sat, sipped, and watched the clock. When two minutes were up, he picked up the phone.

"Dr. Gupta here."

"This is Frances Tarker. I trust things are going well."

Raju had decided not to mention her meltdown of the night before. He'd simply provide her with the current facts.

"Well, yes, things are as follows: Our first patient, Ole Johnson, is on the mend and he will be discharged soon. His daughter tested positive for the same illness and has been admitted to our Pulmonary ICU as a precaution. We will have a better idea of her progress by tomorrow. The tests on the four fishermen are negative, as are those on the other two men exposed and the wife of the first infected man. When the young woman recovers, as I have no doubts she will, this episode will be over."

"Dr. Gupta, how can you say that when you have no idea how many others have contracted this illness? And what if the girl does not recover? What then? What plans do you have to safeguard the rest of the community? Are you prepared for mass inoculations?

Are you going to offer Tamiflu to the residents of the East End? Have you made plans for a quarantine of the county? There are so many questions that need answers, Dr. Gupta."

"Miss Tarker, there are plans in place both with the police and at the hospital to safeguard the community when and if, and I emphasize when and if, it might become necessary, *BUT,* it is not necessary at the present time. We have had only three cases of avian influenza and two of them have recovered completely. There not an epidemic." Raju sensed Tarker was not through with her interrogation. He heard her take a deep breath, anticipating her turn to speak.

"What about inoculations with a vaccine?"

"There is no avian flu vaccine, as yet, available for public use."

"And quarantine, Doctor? Are plans in place for such measures?"

"Yes, as I've said, the police and hospital are prepared to do what is needed when it is needed. But that time is not now."

Her response was terse and her sign-off clipped. "Thank you, Dr. Gupta. Thank you indeed."

Gupta sat back and wondered what he had said that so irritated the woman and prompted such an abrupt signoff. Had he said something he ought not to have said? Not as he could remember.

17

THE HELICOPTER, ADORNED with CDC and US government logo, landed at the EMS Air-Evac site for SHH.Epidemiologist, Avery Whistler stepped cautiously out and, crouching, hurried from beneath the machines still whirling blades. He had little enough hair as it was and he didn't want to lose any more to an incautious, potentially decapitating, step. A member of the flight crew, probably the co-pilot, stepped out of the chopper, opened a hatch door and removed a medium-sized red and white Thermos cooler and carried it to Dr. Whistler.

He approached Whistler's side, cupped his hands around his mouth and spoke over the noise of the rotors, "Give us an hour's head's up, and we'll be back for you."

He ducked back into his seat in the cramped cockpit and the turbo-shaft engines increased their already deafening whine and began to pivot the helicopter and then it took off, pitched slightly nose down, a huge colorful, metallic dragonfly headed toward a home base somewhere to the west.

The short flight along the Long Island coastline from LaGuardia had been spectacular. The clear skies, blue ocean and almost empty beaches looked very inviting from his view a few thousand feet above. Whistler had seen the barrier islands of Georgia and the Carolinas, but he was unprepared for the majesty of some of the homes along the sound and the ocean.

Raju Gupta greeted him and they chatted amicably as they walked the short distance to the hospital and Gupta's office. They carried the empty cooler between them. "Dr. Gupta, my visit is in no way meant to intrude on the work you are doing," Whistler said.

He spoke with a determination that gave Gupta the sense that this man meant every word of this statement. He continued. "This is a new experience for all of us and I want only to collect some data and take some samples back with me to be studied. I believe Sandy Miller has most of your PCR results and some are at the Animal Medical Center. We'd like to have samples from them as well. And then there is the smew. If someone could take this cooler and retrieve the bird for me it would save lots of time. The isolation precautions are inside in a plastic folder."

"That is easily done, and please, it is Raju. I believe that only Miss Johnson, Lanie, will be culture positive. But I'll give you the whole story in a moment." They entered Gupta's office, and Raju set the cooler beside his secretary's desk and made introductions. "It is really a fascinating story, Avery, would you like coffee or tea?"

They sat in the relative luxury and comfort of the hospital's executive office. Raju spoke for almost an hour, interrupted only occasionally by a question from Whistler.

"I see why you said fascinating. We need to rethink surveillance protocols as we did after 9/11. After Sandy Miller first called us about the infected smew, Harvey Damrosh and I did some rapid calculations. That of course was before we had the negative test results of the captains and the others. One of our demographic statisticians helped us come up with the numbers—twenty-four on the charters, each with an average of four to a family, two from each family in school, classes of thirty, each child going home to a family of four, parents to work, teachers into other classes—Bronx, Queens, Manhattan and New Jersey would have viral pools of considerable magnitude. But this experience of yours has taught us a great deal and the information and specimens I gather today will be invaluable. This virus has not behaved like that one in the last great pandemic, at least not this time.

"Now I'd like to get some cultures from the sick patient, get copies of your laboratory data, and arrange with Sandy and the vets to share material with me." He paused and turned toward Gupta, "Are you a fisherman, Raju?"

"No, why do you ask?"

"Well, as we came across the Island and then along the Atlantic beaches, just before landing here, I saw fish chasing bait, perhaps a quarter of a mile off shore. Big fish, judging by the splashes."

"The retired surgeon who spotted the smew is an avid fisherman. If he's at his daughter's house in Montauk I'm sure he'd be glad to talk to you. Shall I check?"

"You're busy. But I just might have to make a re-visit to him to collect more data." He smiled at Raju. "What do you think?"

"Jack Martin would love to take you out and show you our fishery and if you talk to him, you will be back."

Raju called his clinical pathology office and asked them to copy all the lab work on Frank Vogelslieder and the two Johnsons, and he asked his secretary to tell Tim Morrissey to expect a courier to pick up the smew. Then he took Whistler to the ICU and Lanie's isolation room. He introduced Whistler to Lanie and to Nurse Evangeline Yancy, who was by the young woman's side.

After dressing in isolation garb, Whistler gently swabbed the patient's nose and throat and put the cultures into a small portable cooler.

Raju asked Yancy to make copies of Lanie's films for the CDC, and as Raju and Whistler left the isolation room, they deposited their protective clothing in a yellow hamper marked *Basura Peligrosa,* a monolingual sign of the times.

As they walked back to Gupta's office Whistler asked a probing question, "Have you had any problems with the media?"

Raju told him about Tarker and offered to send him a copy of the broadcast. "But we do need some help with guidelines for the police. What do they do with dead birds? Who can test them and how many and will they find live virus?"

Whistler paused outside Gupta's office and leaned against the wall. "Probably not live virus but surely we could detect antibodies, evidence of infection. The best bet would be to test fresh bodies for a short time and if they are all negative for a week or so, just stop. The labs that did the West Nile testing can do it and I'll get up the information. I'd suggest you incinerate the older bodies, 'out of sight' and all that, and simply using gloves should be adequate protection. Rising, Whistler opened the door to Gupta's office, "Now, if I can use your phone, we have some work to do."

<<<>>>

On their way back to Montauk, Jack had stopped at a small farm stand near Bridge Hampton and bought a peck of tomatoes and two bunches of huge, colorful zinnias. The farmer, recognizing Jack from previous visits, kindly wrapped the flower stems in wet paper toweling and then bagged them, ensuring their survival during the remaining trip. Re-entering their car, her husband handed Dina a quart of raspberries and said, "Lunch, babe. Feed me, Seymour!" By the time he turned north off Route 27 toward the Audubon office she had fed both of them well, and fingers and lips were sweetly stained.

Frank met them at the door and gave a quick tour of the facility: spiffy new logo everywhere and bright, fresh paint showing everything to advantage. Jack stopped in front of the colorful T-shirts and laughed.

He held up a shirt with two blue-footed boobies on the front, their Latin names beneath the colorful feet… Sula…Sula. "These are great. Dina had one I bought her thirty years ago, up at Cornell's Sapsucker bookstore. I doubt she'd wear it now."

Dina took the shirt, folded it and put it back on the pile.

Frank's smile faded as he spoke to Jack, "You know Ole's better but his daughter is sick. Jack, that means..."

"Human to human transmission," Jack interrupted. "I don't know where that leaves us Frank, not sure anyone does." He changed the subject almost at once. "Are you free in the morning, fisherman?"

"Jack, ask me again in a week, but here is an invite to the fete. All donations are gratefully accepted."

As they left the building Jack embraced his friend. "I'm glad you're fine. I really hate having all this on my conscience."

Fifteen minutes later, Jack pulled up to the Morrissey home and office. There were no cars parked by the clinic but Jack drove up to the office door. Leaving Dina in the car he knocked. Tim opened the door almost at once.

"Jack, welcome," Tim said, shaking the older man's hand. "I'm expecting someone from CDC to pick up your feathered friend. I mean that damned bird."

Tim invited Jack to get Dina from the car and come in the house to say hello to Sheila. The Martins walked toward the patio and then in through the door Tim had just entered.

"The Doctors Martin, Dina, Jack. This is my wife Sheila and our son-to-be." Sheila was wearing her Lanie original and Dina immediately complemented her on it.

A taupe blur came out of the kitchen skidding across the floor and bump-stopped against the sofa.

"And this is Midgebil," Sheila said. After further introductions, and once the pup had settled down next to the sofa, Sheila could continue.

"This dress was made by the girl who is in the ICU, Lanie Johnson. She's terrific. You will have to meet her when she's well."

"The person she needs to meet is my daughter who went to Parsons and was in the fashion business," Dina said. "Young people don't design for grandmothers."

The two women were at once comfortable with each other and as Dina followed Sheila back to her recambier sofa and recumbent lifestyle, Midge came and put her head on Dina's feet but kept her eyes on Sheila. Their animated chatter was audible from the kitchen.

Tim spent a few minutes telling Jack about the CDC and last night's Tarkercast but before he could go into detail, the hospital van pulled noisily into the driveway next to the office. Tim would have to get the smew ready for transport so he said his goodbyes. Jack went into the living room to extract his wife, motioning to Sheila to stay put. "Doan kaff, gyal, dat ting dere he only nee wan lee push an he scape he ness."

Seeing Sheila's look of puzzlement, Dina laughed and translated, "Jack's Creole. He said 'Don't cough, that thing only needs a little push to be out of his nest,' or something akin to that." Then Dina took Sheila's hand and said, "It was great meeting you. And good luck, you're going to love being a mother!"

In their car again, Dina enthusiastically told Jack some of the details of her chat with Sheila, most of which was about Lanie, her past and present life situation. She was sure that their daughter Pericole would be glad to act in some stewardship role helping Lanie with her work. Twenty minutes later they pulled into the Alden driveway in Montauk.

18

AT A LATE lunch, after what had been a hectic morning and mid-day, Raju met with Irv Pender and the two shared a quiet moment. His secretary had sent for sandwiches and iced tea and for half an hour she kept the office undisturbed. When they had finished eating, the two men made rounds on their important patients.

Lanie was coughing more and now had a low-grade fever. With the exception of her white blood count, which showed signs of stress and infection, all her blood tests were normal. Her pulse oximeter, measuring the oxygen saturation of her red blood cells, read a very satisfactory 98%.

But both doctors knew that this could at any time change rapidly if the amount of her lung involved in the infection increased. That was why Dr. Colicchio had wanted her in the P-ICU, and as the two left the unit, Raju collared the head nurse. "Babysit her, Yancy," he said. "If her O2 sat drops below ninety-five or even ninety-six percent, everyone needs to know. Please have a repeat X-ray done at two p.m. and send it to Dr. Pender's office. It will be eight hours since her first one and we need to know if there is any change." His expression became more serious. "I'm sure you saw the TV last night."

"Yes, sir, we all did."

"You can guess what they'd do if they even thought we'd dropped the ball on this kid. The good surfing is yet to come this fall, so she gets well, Yancy, she gets well."

"She's my charge from this moment, sir. Flagg will take over the rest of the unit and we won't drop anything, Dr. Gupta."

Ole was out of bed and on the phone when the two physicians walked into his room. When he saw them, he cut his call short and said, "Just on the phone with the boys. Everyone is fine but I was just reminding them to check in with you. I don't want my stupidity causing any more problems."

Raju took Ole's offered hand and gave him a warm handshake.

"I don't think that you need to worry. No one else will get sick. We are keeping a very close eye on Lanie for you and so far, so good."

"What do you mean 'so far', Doctor?"

Raju sat on the edge of Ole's bed and spoke softly to him, "She's holding her own. But as might have happened with you, she might get worse before she gets better. Any change at all and we'll let you know."

"Can I see her?"

Gupta looked at Pender who nodded affirmatively.

'The 'old man' says yes. I'll arrange a road trip for you with the escort service."

An hour later, Lanie was delighted to see her father hop out of the wheelchair and push his portable IV pole into her room, but she noticed that sitting up and swinging her feet over the side of the bed made her feel woozy and a bit short of breath. Almost immediately, an alarm sounded in her room and at the nursing station and seconds later Yancy appeared at her door and asked Lanie how she felt. Yancy noticed that the O2 sat had dropped and was holding at a markedly decreased 92%, and she went back to her desk and called Dr. Pender's office. He came on the line immediately and asked, "Evangeline, what's going on with our girl?"

"Dr. Pender, she dropped her sat to 92%. Did her new film get to you? It left here ten minutes ago."

"I think he just arrived at my door. Call you back in a minute."

Dr. Pender went into his reception area and motioned to the radiology tech standing at Lindsay's desk to bring the film into his office. He flipped a lighting switch on his viewing panel and slid the new film up next to the one taken earlier that day.

"Lindsay, get me Gupta," he called out the door.

He looked at the now diffuse blotchy white areas on Lanie's X-ray, graphic evidence that the virus was multiplying rapidly within her lungs and that as yet their therapeutic measures had accomplished nothing. Discouraged he sat down and stared at the X-ray. "What do we do next?" he wondered. Startled by the phone's intercom buzzer, he reached behind him. He was glad it was Gupta.

"She's worse," he said in an exasperated voice. "I'll alert anesthesia to stand by and I'll make sure Yancy can convert the room for a ventilator if and when we need it. And Colicchio needs to see the new film."

<<<>>>

Escort had wheeled Ole back to the ER, and as he stepped out and began to move toward a chair in his room, he saw someone talking to Dr. Colicchio. He poured himself a glass of water from the carafe and suddenly turned back to look at the woman again. The height, the hair, the motion of her hands, which were exquisite, gave rise to a sinking feeling in Ole's stomach and he sat down quickly. He took a sip from the glass. "Why is she here?" he asked himself. He looked at the woman again, scanning all the way to her feet which were moving the way Christina moved when she was nervous, a little dance she did, as if she had to pee and there was a long line for the toilet. He saw Matt nod toward him and he watched as she turned in the indicated direction. Even from thirty feet away Ole could see that her eyes were red and her mascara had run onto her cheeks. But she looked lovely. Ole caught himself admiring her and was suddenly angry that he would do so. Why was Christina here where she had no right to be. He realized that in fact she had every right even though she had once abrogated them.

It was also her child who was sick. Ole vacated the chair and as a gesture moved to the edge of his bed. She walked slowly to the vacated seat.

"May I?" she asked as she reached for the Kleenex box on his bedside table. Ole nodded. "I'm sorry to show up like this but I heard, on the news. I stopped by the house before coming here. Is that all about Lanie?"

Ole nodded. "I must look a mess."

Surprising himself he said, "No, you look fine."

"How is she?"

"Worse, I think." Ole reached for a tissue. "And it's my fault. All my fault."

"I'd like to see her but I couldn't right now. Can I come back? Tomorrow?"

"I guess, sure."

Christina stood and took one step toward Ole, shook her hands, brought her Kleenex to her eyes, and then hurried out of the ER.

Matt came over and sat down next to Ole. "It took courage for her to come here," he said, patting Ole on the shoulder. Then the doctor informed Ole about his daughter's latest test results.

"Doc, what can I do?'

"We need to do what we're doing. You just keep her spirits up when you visit."

<<<>>>

The breakup of the Johnson marriage came as a surprise to no one, except perhaps to Lanie. At the age of twelve she did not realize what had been going on when her mother would come home late at night, or sometimes not at all. On those occasions she relied on her father to feed her and get her off to school. She didn't recognize the hangovers and her mother's disregard for her appearance as part of a problem.

Ole had done what he could. He'd tried to get his wife to AA or at least to some kind of counseling, but she'd always refused. He'd heard rumors about the nights away though no one ever would say anything to him directly. Fortunately, Lanie's classmates were too young to bait her and make her life even less happy than it was.

When finally Christina came to Ole and said she needed an abortion, he fell apart. He realized that it was not, could not be his child. The procedure ultimately resulted in his filing for divorce and custody and neither was contested.

19

IT WAS SIX O'clock and Frances Tarker stood in front of the large map projection of Suffolk County. She drew a wide red line from north to south across the map in its mid-portion. She was a bit more flamboyantly dressed tonight, having exchanged her Chanel look-alike suit for an aquamarine, figure-hugging knit dress. Frances had a Victoria's Secret figure, which was one of the reasons she was the anchor and tonight there was no visible panty line under the tight skirt.

Poor Dan, thought Raju as he and Irv Pender sat in the CEO's office.

"Good evening, ladies and gentlemen. I was just drawing the battle line."

Quarter-facing the camera, her ample bosom obliterating a good portion of Amagansett, with her right hand Frances Tarker traced a line from the middle of Sag Harbor southward to just west of Wainscott.

"This line divides East Hampton town from South Hampton town and it divides police jurisdictions." She turned full face to the cameras.

"For it was in East Hampton township that the now three confirmed cases of Avian Influenza, bird flu, have occurred. Yes, now it is three cases. An innocent teenager lies gravely ill in the Southampton Hospital." She paused, punctuating with a raised eyebrow. "How many cases will there be tomorrow? No one can say, but we can say that here, where town lines meet is where the East Hampton police will draw the line of quarantine. As far as we know, not one of those either exposed or ill has traveled across this line except to be tested or admitted to the hospital."

Frances Tarker walked toward the anchor desk where Dan Fleisher sat frowning, looking down at his folded hands.

She continued, "It means Steven, that your party scheduled for next weekend on millionaires' row in East Hampton, that big birthday bash, is off. Awww, too bad, Steven. And Renee! It will have to be Citarella on the East Side instead of the East End. And Martha, Oh, Martha, it's at home alone."

The engineers cut to a commercial and a somewhat chubby and smiling, curly haired physician began to talk about Fosamax-D, "Tell me about your GI problems, and..."

Raju and Pender looked at each other and broke into thigh-slapping laughter. There was nothing else to do. It was clear that Frances Tarker had imploded, and having left her script from the onset of the broadcast, it was clear that she would not be back on camera.

"She's gone, Irv. Did you see Fleisher's face? My God, the poor man. I'll bet she's out of the building already. That was a Morton Downey redux."

"I'm sure you're right, Raju, but she has unwittingly made a problem for us. No, I'm wrong, I'm sure this was planned. You know what comes next, don't you? Calls from lawyers for Spielberg, Zellweger, and Stewart. The police will want to know what the 'eff' that was all about."

After the Fosamax sixty seconds, the traffic and weather came on and, finally, Fleisher appeared on the screen and in a dignified voice he said, "Good evening and welcome back to the Channel 21 evening news. We'll return to our planned programming. Frances, for some reason, left our scripted broadcast and presented highly speculative information of her own creation.

"The facts, as we know them to be, are as follows: Two adult males appear to have fully recovered from avian influenza. A third person, the daughter of Mr. Ole Johnson, is still being treated. We know that the four fishermen exposed to Mr. Johnson have all tested negative. None was symptomatic. It seems highly unlikely that a quarantine of any fashion will be necessary but, yes, that is the line of demarcation between jurisdictions which Frances had drawn on our map. It might well have been a line for quarantine *if* such an action was needed. We will have more news on our 'mini-outbreak' as it presents itself and we will give you a complete summary again tomorrow. And now for the rest of the news."

Raju turned off the TV and slapped Pender on the shoulder. "Irv, I need a drink, and not tea."

As Raju and Pender started out of the hospital, they saw the TV remote trucks parked on the street. Suddenly, from their left, appeared two female reporters and their cameramen.

One of the women called out, "Dr. Gupta, can you give us a minute of your time? What do you have to say about the quarantine that Frances Tarker described?"

Raju looked at Irv who made a gracious sweep of his arm toward Raju and stepped aside. "It's your stage Raju," he quipped.

"Dr. Pender and I watched her performance with great interest. Ms. Tarker is quite a showman. But, ladies, all kidding aside, I think she did herself, and each and every one of us involved a great injustice. Dan Fleisher reported the facts as we know them. We have provided Channel 21 with all, I repeat, all the information we have at hand. Why such fabrication was necessary, I have no idea. It can only have created unneeded concern in the community. We saw firsthand, both here in our ER and in the private offices of physicians on the East End, what that kind of hysteria and bad journalism can create. Everyone with a cough or cold or a headache went to see a doctor today. Perfectly understandable when they are made to fear for their lives. They were all seen and cared for and none was suspected of having bird flu." He paused momentarily and looked directly at the cameras. "*Thankfully* no major emergency arose in our area that would have brought a number of gravely ill to our ER. That would have been a problem under the circumstances that Tarker created. What is important is that we have gained firsthand knowledge about avian flu and to date it has not been a major problem for us. If our young patient rebounds as quickly as the other two have, this incident would prove to have been a minor one. I can tell you that as of this evening any quarantine of the East End is not in the offing. Have you anything to add, Dr. Pender?"

Raju walked over to Irv and smiled victoriously at having managed to pull Dr. Pender onto camera.

"No, I think you have said it all. Now, if you could excuse us, Doctor Gupta and I have a date with a cold beer—somewhere cool, dark and quiet."

The crews were delighted that they were given the first face-to-face with the men running the show.

20

HE WAS TIRED of sitting, of writing, and of worrying, so Matt Colicchio left his office and went up to the P-ICU. He could not get his mind off Lanie Johnson. He had great empathy for her, finding herself as she did in such an inhuman and frightening environment. He'd been through it himself as a lad of twelve when he'd fallen out of a tree and hit his head on a limb in mid-fall. For two days he'd lain unconscious in the hospital with a severe concussion and when he finally awoke, he was disoriented, frightened, and alone. But until now Matt hadn't had a moment to go and see Lanie. He closed his office, waved to his assistant, walked into the hospital proper, and climbed the stairs following a path into the P-ICU.

Yancy was at Lanie's bedside and was talking on the phone. There were nasal prongs on Lanie's face, which were delivering oxygen at a flow of about six liters a minute. Her pulse oximeter now read only 86% saturation. A mechanical ventilator was against the wall to the right of the head of the bed. An X-ray hung on the view box just outside her room.

"Anesthesia?" he asked.

Yancy nodded and hung up the phone.

"Her latest film?" Again, the nurse nodded.

"Get me some Versed, Yancy, and bring in the cart."

Rejecting the proffered mask and gown, Matt sat on the edge of Lanie's bed and took her hand in his.

"Frightened?" he asked her. "I was when I was your age and something like this happened to me. You need help breathing for a while. You'll poop out if we don't help you. You need to save your strength and we need to do the work for you until the infection clears up."

"You mean a machine?"

She looked terrified and tears rolled down her cheeks. Matt wiped away the tear drops and nodded.

"Yes, but we will sedate you first."

'Then it will be like being dead!" she said, and beginning to tremble, she fell against Matt.

"No, Lanie, not at all. Just asleep for a while and when you don't need the help you'll wake up and walk out of here."

He hoped he was right and that the antivirals were doing their job to control the infection. But just in case, after they'd intubated Lanie, Matt wanted to call Dr. Pender and ask him if he might find some newer, front line drugs for her.

When the chief of anesthesia appeared, he held up a syringe and said, "Versed." The chief nodded and Matt spoke softly to Lanie.

"You're going to get very drowsy very quickly. I'll be right here and you can hold my hand as you do." Then turning to Yancy he said, "Give her half of it, IV."

Yancy swabbed the port in the IV line and gave half of the contents of the syringe and then flushed the line with the saline which was hanging.

"Ohh, I'm getting so…" were Lanie's final words as her eyes closed and her head relaxed on the bed.

Putting on a mask, gown, and sterile gloves, the anesthesiologist rotated the bed to free up space and set his tray alongside Lanie's head. He removed a laryngoscope and an appropriate endotracheal tube and carefully checked the cuff on the tube. He turned to Yancy and said, "No sense having her wake up. Give her the rest of the Versed and then this Anectine."

When she was fully paralyzed by the second drug, he quickly went about his work of intubating Lanie. With his left hand as a fulcrum, he spread apart the young woman's jaws and carefully slid the laryngoscope past her lips and perfect teeth. Moments later he deftly slid the tube into Lanie's trachea and taped it in place while Matt attached it to the preset ventilator. Then they watched Lanie's O2 sat go up to 94%.

"Not good enough, Matt. Set a low-level PEEP for her," the anesthesiologist said.

Positive End-Expiratory Pressure, or PEEP would keep an extra amount of pressure, and an increased volume of inspired air, in the lungs' small air sacs, the alveoli. It would leave the oxygen in them for a longer period of time and would also push against the walls of the air sacs, moving fluid from between them. Hopefully it would let the capillaries get more blood to the alveoli and thus would permit more oxygen to get into her red blood cells.

The sat jumped to 96%. Watching the monitors, the chief summarized as he prepared to leave.

"Better, but not great. Have Irv try a different antiviral. And add more PEEP if she needs it. That's about all we can do. Just keep her well sedated. No need for her to fight us or remember any of this."

21

THE TWO DOCTORS were sitting in Sligo, a small pub in an out-of-the-way corner of Southampton. they were the only customers in the bar, which had become a hangout for hospital employees who enjoyed good beers and no noise. Franny Ryan, the proprietor, didn't know Gupta and Pender. As they sipped a micro-brew from Franny's hometown, Raju shelled warm, fresh roasted peanuts, a Sligo house-specialty. Just how Franny managed this touch they weren't sure but they certainly were enjoying them. Tossing a trio of shelled but not hulled kernels to his friend, Raju began.

"These, you know, are not nuts at all, they are legumes. They were called 'ground nuts' in Africa and were part of cuisine worldwide before they ever came to America with the slaves. Much like okra, which was gambo in Guinea, and now here gumbo. Gambo became gumbo."

Pender looked at his CEO and just shook his head while Raju continued. "As children, my sister Sari and I grew up in the kitchen: we ate in the kitchen and we did our homework in the kitchen." He paused and pushed more ground nuts toward Pender. "We were always involved with food. During the week my mother had a Bengali woman who cooked for us but on weekends Mom was in the kitchen. My sister and I shared the prep work and the clean-up, especially when we had guests—and that was most of the time. I still cook, but the boys are not fans yet. Just Amalia enjoys it." He put a hand on Pender's forearm and gave it a friendly pat. "You know, I must make rogan josh for you some time. Just how spicy do you like your food?"

Franny had the TV on and was watching the local news broadcast while he was polishing glasses, something he didn't need to do since his new dishwasher spit them out gleaning. But what else was a bartender to do at seven-thirty in the evening except prep for the evening rush? Franny suddenly looked at the men and then back at the screen.

"Well I'll be damned if I don't have celebrities in me bar tonight," he said.

Picking up the remote and turning up the volume, Franny set one of the glasses firmly and loudly down on the bar, snapping them to attention. The physicians suddenly heard Dr. Raju Gupta addressing the news media.

"Jesus, Mary and Joseph! Can I have your autographs, doctors? TV celebs and here, in Sligo."

Raju stopped shelling and watched the screen. Irv Pender took full advantage of the moment.

"Raju, it's a good thing your wife picks your clothes carefully. You look damn natty, and what a commanding voice and manner. Permanent CEO material, I'd say."

Gupta probably blushed but with his natural color and the dim light, Pender couldn't tell.

"Well, Irv, let's wait for your lines."

Just then Pender's cell phone vibrated against his belly.

"Pender," he said.

"It's Matt. We just intubated Lanie. She's on a bit of PEEP and may need more. I wondered if your buddies down island had any next-generation anti-virals in reserve."

"I'll be back in my office in fifteen minutes. Meet me there."

Pender put a ten on the bar and motioned "out" to Raju. Franny pushed the ten back toward him.

"Never charge celebs, friend."

'Take it, Franny, please. We may be no one's friend tomorrow. And light a candle for a little girl in the hospital, will you?"

"We'll do better than a candle, sirs. We'll do much better than that."

As they left Sligo, Pender explained the call to his friend. When they parted, Irv Pender headed back to the hospital. He parked illegally just outside of his building, waved to security, and walked briskly inside. He had Sandy Miller's home number saved in his phone, and punched it in. Miller's wife answered.

In the background he could hear animated conversation. The Millers had dinner guests.

When he came to the phone, Pender told Sandy that Lanie had deteriorated and had been placed on a ventilator. Then he asked if Miller had a new generation anti-viral. The reply came at once.

"In fact, we do. I have one which we received for compassionate use in a patient. I can get it to you tonight, in an hour or two. Is she in the P-ICU?"

"Yes. Have any other suggestions?'

"If the anti-viral doesn't improve her condition in twelve hours, I'd try a bolus of high dose steroids. It might suppress her inflammatory response."

"We were hoping we wouldn't have to do that, but now it looks like we might."

Matt Colicchio walked into the office and sat down next to Pender's desk. "What do we have coming?"

Pender closed his phone. "It's a next generation drug like Rimantidine. It's about to get FDA approval but right now it's still at level three testing. It's safe for us to use it."

Irv told Matt that he'd clear the use with Gupta but that he ought to do so with Ole. "Try not to frighten him," Pender instructed Matt. "He's still kicking himself hard, very hard."

Raju gave Irv his blessing to use the new drug. He also advised that they not wait too long to use the steroids. He favored using them first thing in the morning if she hadn't improved by either X-ray or ventilation criteria.

Matt walked into Ole's room and looked up at the TV screen. Ole was animated and spoke rapidly, "Hey, I just saw your bosses on TV. Good job. Why are you still here doc? Not Lanie I hope."

"Yes, Ole, it's Lanie." He sat next to Ole and explained the details of the evening's events to the worried father.

"Doc, whatever you need to do. It's my fault she's sick so how could I tell you no? Just fix her Doc. And can I see her in the morning?"

"Sure Ole, and we'll let you stay around here until she's out of the woods. And I promise you we'll fix her."

As Matt walked into his office, he saw Ole reach for his cell phone.

<<<>>>

Tim was sitting in the kitchen when Ole's call came in. He recognized the number and answered at once.

"Doc, she's worse," Ole told his employer. "They put her on a machine, a ventilator."

"When?"

"Couple of hours ago. They have some new drug, experimental I think, and they said they wanted to use it. I said OK. Was I right?"

"Absolutely right. I'm glad you called. I'll come to the hospital tomorrow. We're all praying for her Ole, you know that."

"Thanks. I'll be glad to see you."

Tim leaned back in his chair and rubbed his face vigorously. *Stay awake, you dumb redhead. Maybe, just maybe, you can help*. Looking at the clock of the laptop he saw it was eight-thirty. He picked up the phone and called the Alden house. Just after the recorder came on a sleepy woman answered.

"I'm sorry to call at this hour. It's Tim Morrissey. I was hoping to speak to Jack Martin."

"Sure, just a moment." He heard a door open and Pericole call out, "Dad, phone for you. It's Dr. Morrissey."

A moment later he heard the extension lift.

"Sorry to wake you, Jack."

"Just the kids are asleep. The girl?"

"Yes, she's on a vent." He heard Jack curse under his breath. "Ole called me and said they'd gotten a newer drug from down island."

"Good. The science of anti-viral medications was given the fast track by the HIV lobby. All other bugs just came along for the ride." Jack then told Tim that Ole needed his support and that he would ask him to OK all of his decisions. He'd rely on Tim as his good counsel. When Jack asked if there were anything new in the baby business Tim laughed.

"No, not as of an hour ago, but talk to me tomorrow."

<<<>>>

Jack played with his cup of chamomile tea and reached for his wife's hand. "The kid's on a vent. Why? What are we missing here? Tim did say that they are adding a third-generation antiviral tonight but there is a piece missing here, damn it!"

He got up and walked around the granite center island, stopping when he got back to his chair. His wife pushed him toward it.

"Jack, honey, we're both too many years away from it but I know what you're feeling. She's just so young, too young to be so ill. You know she'll get the best that medicine has to offer and that just has to be enough."

"But I just get the sense that I'm missing something. An old brain is a slow brain, Dee. Just like the other parts." He laughed and kissed his wife. "But not always too slow. Come on, I have to get up early. There are fish to chase."

<<<>>>

Sheila was asleep, the kitchen was clean, and Tim was sitting at the computer with a short glass of Wolffer chard, the last of the half-bottle he'd opened at dinner. After his last phone calls Tim decided he wanted to know a little more about avian flu and influenza in general. Specifically, he wanted to know why Lanie was so ill and why Frank had not been.

He opened Google and went to CDC.gov. He scrolled through the options until he found "Influenza." He again scrolled through a list of topics until he found, under "History", an article about reconstruction of the virus that had caused the 1918 pandemic. What he gleaned fascinated him.

Science had enabled the refashioning of the viral DNA much the way the Jurassic Park folks had spawned dinosaurs from DNA extracted from blood in insects preserved in amber. They knew that the viral particle they formed was a different animal from those influenza viruses of today but did not know why. For almost a century now, the annual flu season has always taken its toll on the immunologically weakened: the very young and the very old and infirm. The healthy ten to sixty-year olds were rarely at risk for overwhelming pneumonitis and death. Not so with the pandemics of the late nineteenth and early twentieth centuries, for they struck mightily upon the most immunological competent population, the very group the disease now seems to spare. This historical form of the virus triggered such an immune response that inflammation in the lungs killed the victims. The interstitial pneumonia, occurring in the space between air cells, the alveoli, and amongst the blood vessels, initiated so vigorous a response to the virus that the influx of white blood cells, lymphocytes and fluid accumulating there compressed those elements essential for oxygen exchange to the point that victims literally suffocated or drowned in the accumulated fluid.

The typical flu viruses seen today, those named Hong Kong or after the country of first recognition, didn't normally trigger such a reaction in the healthy. Also, doctors now could treat persons more at risk with antiviral medication and could even for the most part prevent the illness with a vaccine.

The article discussed only briefly the role which high doses of intravenous steroids might have played in the 1918 scenario had they been available at the time. Their ability to block an inflammatory response would theoretically have prevented death while it permitted the body's own immune response to deal with the virus. Today this application of steroids would be available.

Tim drained the last drops from his glass and leaned back in his chair, ruminating.

22

THE COURIER FROM Stony Brook had arrived just after nine-thirty p.m., and by ten Matt had read the protocol for use of the new drug, made an appropriate entry on Lanie's chart, and then mixed and hung the IV preparation.

"I hope you're not planning to stay all night. We can get coverage for her. I'll pull someone from the ER," Matt said to Yancy when he noticed her seemingly settling in at Lanie's bedside.

"Dr Colicchio, I'd prefer to stay. I'll take short naps in the call room and I'll be fine. I can see that you plan to stay so we can spell each other."

Acknowledging that he'd be happy to have the company, he said, "OK, but you grab forty while I do some more work on her chart."

Matt wanted to write a detailed summary of the day's events on Lanie's chart. If she did not survive and became the first American to succumb to avian flu, he wanted to be sure that anyone looking at the record would find all the facts properly recorded. He wanted no holes, no omissions. He was tired but he had already outlined his work in his mind and it had only to be put on paper.

Malpractice wasn't what concerned him, some unjustified suit made by a relative, surely not by Ole, but he remembered the in-service programs run by the hospital's insurance carriers and how at every meeting they stressed documentation. The battle cry was "Document, Document, and Document."

Two hours later he was ready for a nap. He went to awaken Yancy who was in the call room just behind the nursing station. He opened the door quietly and looked down at her lying there in her scrubs on top of the bed sheets.

What he saw was a beautiful woman who must have been almost his age. The absence of a ring on either hand suggested she was unattached, alone in life. At that moment, his aloneness felt poignant to him and briefly it extracted him from the reality of his immediate existence. Yancy must have sensed something because she opened her eyes and sat up. "Matt? I'm sorry," she said embarrassed at the informality. "Dr. Colicchio, do you need me?"

"Indeed. I need a couple of hours sleep so I hope you're ready to take over. And, what does the 'E' stand for?"

"I'm afraid it's Evangeline."

"Well, Evangeline, your 'forest prime-evil' awaits you in Room Two. Just let me get two hours, no more."

Matt tossed her a chilled bottle of spring water and collapsed on the bed she had just relinquished. He was asleep in minutes.

As she walked towards the bathroom on the opposite side of the nursing station, Yancy twisted the top off the bottle of water and drank thirstily. *Hydrate if you want to stay awake and functional,* she thought, remembering how well it had worked when she was in school and had to stay awake studying. She washed her face and neck and dried them vigorously. Finally, she did some stretching. She put on gown, mask, and gloves and went back into Lanie's room.

She gazed at Lanie and said a brief, quiet prayer, a heartfelt request for help. It was one-thirty a.m. and the next doses of the antivirals and antibiotics were due at about two and then the new protocol drug again at four a.m. She'd wake Matt after that was hanging. As long as Lanie was stable she'd let him sleep.

As she sat watching the monitors, she thought about Matt watching her sleep and her sudden awareness of it. How long had he been standing there? She'd sensed his presence, felt a connection to him, to his thoughts perhaps, and it had awakened her. "Good doctor, that one," Yancy said to herself. "Good person and a good man. Enough!" It was time to make notes of Lanie's vital signs.

While Lanie had lain deeply sedated and still paralyzed, the anesthesiologist had placed an arterial monitoring line in her left radial artery at the wrist. He didn't want to have to do it as an emergency if this girl began to crump. Yancy flushed and recalibrated that line, then changed all of the EKG electrodes and finally checked to see that the ventilatory PEEP was holding steady. Her O2 sat was 96%. She was holding her own.

At four a.m. Yancy hung the protocol medication, wiped Lanie's face and smoothed her hair, and then she sat down for a few more minutes, letting Dr. Colicchio sleep a while longer. She wondered if he snored. Her fiancé of those few short weeks certainly did. That engagement ended abruptly enough when she returned to her apartment after a hard day's work to find him in bed with her roommate. The ring had hit him right between the eyes. That was almost two years ago and she was still angry.

Yancy walked to the call room and raised her hand to knock but instead she opened the door quietly. Matt was on his stomach and he was not snoring. She laughed at herself, walked over to the bed, and kicked the mattress briskly.

"I got tired of knocking, Doctor."

Matt sat up and looked at his wristwatch. "My turn, I guess. Four-thirty! You're very generous, but where's my bottle of water?"

Matt tugged the nurse's ponytail gently and went back to Lanie's room.

23

Thursday, September 7th 2006

SOMEWHERE IN THE depth of his sleep, Tim felt the bed move as Sheila struggled to roll over. It was a chore for her to change position but something had awakened her, prompting her to turn. Now awake, she grunted and snuggled her belly against her husband's back and shook him gently. Whispering in his ear she said, "Tell me if you feel anything different, Tim. Not just his moving."

He rolled to face his wife and put his two hands on her distended abdomen.

"There, now! What did you feel?"

"A contraction? I guess that's what it was. But aren't you a week early?"

"Dr. Handley said that the baby looked full term and that I could go into labor any day. I think I just jumped the gun on him."

Tim craned to see the face of the radio. "Four-thirty, it won't be light for over an hour. Do you want me to call?"

"No not yet. But I don't think I'll sleep anymore, honey. Maybe I'll pack a suitcase, something I should have done weeks ago."

Tim went to the hall closet, took the carry-on bag from the top shelf, brought it into the bedroom, and set it on a table next to Sheila's wardrobe. She puttered from drawer to drawer, adding and removing items, and then went to her closet. Tim got back into bed and watched as she pushed the hangers around, searching. Sheila turned and spoke to him, "Not packing for a romantic weekend, am I, honey? What to take?"

By six-thirty the contractions were stronger and regular at about twenty minutes. Sheila took her blood pressure and was pleased to see it was unchanged from the previous night. Wishing herself calm and normotensive seemed to be working for her. It was mind over body, or perhaps mind over her blood pressure.

Sheila watched Tim make coffee and then put some berries and shredded wheat into a bowl for himself but when he offered some, she shook her head.

"No, none for us, we'll just watch this morning."

When Tim came down again, shaved and dressed for work, Sheila pointed to the phone, grunted and said, "Call Handley."

The service answered and said they would find him for her. Five minutes later the phone rang and Sheila said, "I'm in labor," and she gave him the details of the last few hours.

"Get Tim to drive you to the hospital and I'll meet you in Labor. They'll be expecting you at the front door."

Tim briefly walked Midge and gave her food and water and then he helped Sheila into the truck. He could not believe that after a nine month-wait he was finally driving his wife to the hospital.

<<<>>>

It was six-thirty in the morning when Raju Gupta walked briskly into the hospital and turned right, walking past the darkened gift shop. A stack of *Newsday*'s early edition lay on the floor partially blocking the door. The bold headline caught his eye and he grabbed quickly for a copy.

A Bird Flew in from Europe! Strange Duck Not What It's Quacked Up to Be.

He put two dollars in the cash box and walked toward his office.

Raju sat down with a large cup of tea and read Estancia Bethany's lead article. It was more than he could have hoped for. The facts as he had given them to the women were presented precisely and accurately, there was no speculation, no hyperbole and there was, right on the lower half of the front page, a picture of Lanie giving a thumb's up. He wondered how she was this morning and before reading on he called the P-ICU. Nurse Yancy answered.

"Yancy! Are you here already?"

"Yes, I pulled an all-nighter with Dr. Colicchio, sir."

"How is she?"

"We started the new drug last night and she has had two doses. Her O2 sat is holding at ninety-six percent on four millimeters of PEEP. This a.m.'s film is no better, possibly worse than yesterday's. I think Dr. Colicchio's on his way down to the ER and you can catch him there. Sir, I know Ole Johnson wants to come up here this morning to see her."

Raju took the paper and almost jogged to the ER. He was not a religious man. He had slowly grown away from his family's Hindu beliefs and when he married an American woman of Quaker origins, they had found a religious middle ground of self-introspection with a smattering of good old Judeo-Christian ethics tossed in. It was easier for their children to be ecumenical than to grow up completely without religious grounding so they celebrated Hindu, Jewish, and Christian holidays. But today he was finding himself lacking in conviction, coming up short on self-reliance and he was considering having a chat with the hospital chaplain.

Raju found Matt talking to Ole and explaining the events of the past night. He stood by until Matt had finished. Ole looked absolutely crestfallen.

"Mr. Johnson, Ole, look at this morning's newspaper," Raju said enthusiastically. "That girl in the picture is why we have to work even harder. I'll get transport to take you up to see her. Nurse Yancy expects you."

Matt motioned Gupta into his office.

"Sir, the way she looks this morning sucks! I'm sorry, but there's no other word for it. She'll require more PEEP within the hour. We need to talk to Pender and ask him to pull something, a rabbit, I don't care what, but something out of his hat. This isn't a third-world country and this shouldn't be happening."

As Raju was reaching for his phone Pender walked into the ER. "A little bird told me you might need me. But perhaps that was a poor choice of words, sorry."

He pulled up a chair and looked at Matt whose usually neat hair looked slept on and he had obviously not shaved. Add the wrinkled shirt and red eyes and Pender had the diagnosis.

"All-nighter, doctor? That's why you're here, you're young. So where are we gentlemen?"

Matt filled them in on the events of the past night and described this morning's chest X-ray.

Pender stood and began to pace. "You recall our conversation after I spoke to Sandy Miller last night. We should try the solumedrol. It's a powerful steroid. If we can reduce the inflammatory response in the interstitium, just being able to ventilate her more easily will be a help until we lick this thing. We could talk to Jason Phillips in rheumatology, his thoughts on the immune response might just add something to this conversation, but if her PEEP requirements go up, I don't think you have a choice. I wouldn't wait any longer. Giving it now would be my vote. By the way, I saw Tim Morrissey, the vet, bringing in his wife this morning. Looks like Doctor Handley has a busy day for himself." He looked at them both as he started out the door, "I'm here if you need me."

24

PAT HANNON ARRIVED at the bus barn a few minutes earlier than usual because this morning there was no wait line at her local Starbuck's. Several other drivers sat outside the office looking at a newspaper, and she walked over to join them. Discussion was about the upcoming high school football season and the major league playoffs. Consensus favored the Mets and the Bridgehampton Killer Bees. Not a word was spoken about yesterday's half-empty buses or the headlines of the paper, the article Gupta had just read. Pat and her husband had read several other articles earlier that morning and found that they offered little information.

The local community was advised to get a flu shot and see a physician when feeling ill. There was no warning to avoid crowds, to wear a mask, or to stay at home. Not a word that warned of a pandemic and not a word about Frances Tarker.

Pat walked back to her bus, a spiffy new vehicle that carried forty when full. She carefully checked the windshields, rearview mirrors and rear safety door and found they were all clean, up to her standards. Then to complete her pre-flight walk around she tested the turn signals, hazard and stoplights and signs, which swung out from the sides of the bus. Her checks completed she climbed into the driver's seat, fastened her safety belt and started Beelzebub's engine. She'd chosen the name in jest because she considered many of her early-teens passengers the devil's spawn. An hour later when she finally reached the South Hampton Upper School, she had twenty-two students on board, two less than the day before. Unless things changed overnight, Jim Beggs was going to lose his bet.

<<<>>>

At six a.m., through the common wall of their rooms, Jack heard the chirps and gurgles of a baby amusing herself in the near dark. Moments later, he heard Ruby patter across the hall going to where Belle was now awake. "Hi, Baby Belle. Are you awake?" the older girl called out. Then Ruby screamed loudly from the top of the stairs, "Mommie, Baby Belle is awake."

Fortunately, Ruby could operate neither the crib nor the stair-gate mechanisms or she would have had her little sister on the way downstairs. For a few months more both of them were still safe from a potential tumble.

The first response to Ruby's call was the muffled house-shaking bark from Sirus. Moments later the phone rang downstairs. "I'm out of here," Dina laughed, and rolled across the king-sized bed, slipped on a shift, and went out to the children.

Jack heard Ruby's reaction to seeing Dina, "Baby Belle, look it's Grande. Look Grande, Baby Belle is awake."

Then he heard another voice. "Dad!" It was his daughter calling up to him and for a moment he was afraid of what she might say. "T.C. is sick. Call him when you get up."

Pericole ran up the stairs calling to her children, and picking them both up said, "Are my monkeys awake? Are my monkeys all wet, my pissy monkeys?"

"Not me, Mommy," came the pronouncement from Ruby, "just Baby Belle."

Three generations of women moved down to the kitchen for their tumultuous breakfast and prep for preschool and daycare. Jack got up and stretched on the yoga mat, took a quick shower and dressed. He was still bothered by something he couldn't put a finger on, couldn't remember, a sequestrum of knowledge, and a few kb at most. It had again twisted his dreams into undesirable vignettes of forgetfulness, lost keys, lost locker and finally a lost automobile. Very Freudian, yes, but the human computer, his brain, just needed a kick-start. Maybe some coffee would help. The Alden house morning coffee was an ass-kicker. Even diluted with hot water and a generous amount of milk, it was potent stuff, capable of inducing a tremor or even gastric reflux a few hours later.

Jack climbed over the gate at the foot of the stairs, then paused to watch the local weather forecast. It would have been a good morning on the water, cool, little wind and a good tide. He hoped T.C. was OK. Arden came through the living room on his way out for his six-mile morning run with the dog. Sirus would only dignify him with his company if the temperature was at or below 55 degrees Fahrenheit. This morning he was a go.

Arden said, "Maybe late this afternoon we can fish, Grampus. I'm pretty sure I can shake loose then. Gustavo and the men can finish the cleanup on the job without me. I'll let you know at lunch."

The two men walked into the kitchen together to view the spectacle of the morning. Sirus sat by the door whining and stomping his feet in anticipation, Ruby ran around the center island chasing Frick, or was it Frack, one of the black-and-white kittens, and Belle was refusing anything placed on her food tray. Whenever Ruby went by them, either her mother or Dina would pop something into her mouth, egg sandwich or a strawberry morsel. Arden gave his wife a peck and went out the door with Sirus.

"Go ahead, chicken, escape your fatherly duties, seek solitude on the backroads," Jack called after his son-in-law.

"Up yours, Grampus," came the reply, just audible over the crunch of six feet on gravel.

Jack called T.C. who felt his dinner had made him ill but said he was already feeling better. The men agreed that he'd call Arden later and set up fishing for the afternoon. At eight-thirty Jack and Dina walked Ruby the few blocks to the preschool in the Community Catholic Church on the southwest corner of Essex and Route 27 and then walked to the Montauk Bakery where they were to meet Pericole and Belle. After a tasty bite and more coffee, the three ladies would drive to East Hampton. With Belle safely deposited at day care the mother and daughter would have their day on the town.

While Dina was chatting with an acquaintance, Jack snuck into the bakery and peeked into the kitchen, having been lured by the mouthwatering fragrance of yeast, butter, and fresh baking. Alan Van Staal, the owner, saw Jack and came over for a floury handshake and said, "Notice the short line?"

Jack peeked back into the shop and replied, "No line right now!"

"It'll blow over, it always does," Alan said. Then he handed Jack the fresh croissant he'd been holding and said, "Here, careful it's hot."

"Bird flu hysteria?"

"Yup. Insanity."

Jack filled a small cup with decaf, put two dollars on the counter, and waved goodbye to the young women behind the counter who were patiently waiting for customers.

Outside the shop Dina gave him a "how could you" look when she saw the calories in his hand.

"Hey, I didn't buy it, he gave it to me, shoved it in my hand. Can't sell it when it's used," he said playfully to his wife. He bit into the buttery puff of a confection and bit his lip. "Ouch! Damn that's hot."

"Serves you right, Grampus. You don't need that thing, give it to me!"

"Only half" Breaking it in two he watched the steam escape as he handed the bigger piece to Dina. "Bite the tongue and jar the brain! Hah! Double Hah!"

"What did you say?"

"You heard me, bite the tongue and jar the brain. That's what it took, kid!"

"Will you please explain yourself?"

Jack plopped down on one of the benches outside the bakery. "Dina, I just remembered what I've been trying to think of for the last day or two. Sit down for a minute. And have a sip, its decaf."

<<<>>>

As a crisis was being addressed in the PICU and life was being renewed at the Alden residence, Tim Morrissey had pulled up at the front door of SHH and waved to the security officer standing there.

"Good morning, this is a patient of Dr. Handley. Do you have a wheelchair?" he said pointing to his wife.

"Yes sir. If that's Dr. McCorkle we've been expecting her."

Tim helped his wife down from the high front seat and they loaded Sheila and her bag into a wheelchair. As she disappeared into the building, Tim went to park the pickup. On his return to the front door he was directed to the labor area and just as he entered through automatic doors he saw nurses wheeling Sheila into a room. She'd been changed into a gown and had an IV running. As he reached the room he was greeted by a handsome, graying man who introduced himself as Ed Handley.

Handley was in scrubs and wore disposable paper hat and shoe covers—his OR-ready uniform. He sat down next to Sheila, who was already in bed. He opened a pair of sterile size-eight gloves and as he carefully put them on, he said, "What are you timing now, Sheila?"

"Less than five minutes, and they're stronger, with a lot more pelvic pressure."

"Not a lot of pain?"

"Not too much."

"Good. Nurse, some betadine."

The nurse lifted the sheet and helped Sheila position her legs and then poured some betadine on her labia. Handley cautiously examined her and said, "Your cervix is fully effaced and you are about three or four centimeters dilated. I'm amazed you're moving along so fast but I think you have a few hours to go." He tossed his gloves into the trash and turning toward Tim he said, "If she slows down, we'll help a little. We don't want this labor to last too long, so if we need pitocin we'll use it. We've been very lucky the last week or so and I don't want to push it. Doctor, if you have clients, go see them, but see to it your back by noon. Sheila, I'll be around."

Then Handley went off to do a C-section on another patient.

Tim sat next to his wife and gave her a kiss. He held her hand as he said, "I only have two or three animals coming in. I'll be back well before noon. OK, baby?"

"Drive carefully, father Timothy," Sheila said.

<<<>>>

Together, as a transport team, Drs. Gupta and Colicchio wheeled Ole up to the P-ICU and to the entry of Lanie's room. They passed the larger four-bedded unit with all the patients on some form of respiratory support. Ole shook his head and looked up at Matt. Then he looked down and said, "Doc, I can't do this. I won't be able to look at Lanie, not with her like this."

"Ole, we need to put that newspaper photo of her on her wall. Think how excited she'll be when she wakes up and sees it. And you need to sit with her and talk to her."

"But you said she was asleep."

"She is, but you need to tell her you are here with her and that you'll be back again later today, and every day."

Yancy met them at the door and looked toward the arterial line. Both it and the pulse oximeter now read an O2 sat of 88%. Her pulmonary status was deteriorating. Gupta nodded to Matt.

Matt looked at Yancy and said, "Two more millimeters of PEEP. And then get us some tape." She made the adjustment on the ventilator and reached up onto one of the shelves above the bed. Matt and

Yancy taped Lanie's picture to the wall to the right of the young woman's bed, where if—*WHEN*—she opened her eyes she would be sure to see it.

Ole got out of his wheelchair, walked over to Lanie, and kissed her on the forehead, pulled over a chair, and sat beside her bed. He held his daughter's hand and then he spoke to her, whispered actually, so Matt, Gupta, and Yancy could not hear what he said. For the few moments that Ole had his head next to his daughter's ear, Lanie's pulse quickened and then, as Ole rose from her side, it slowed again. The two physicians looked at each other. Matt told Ole that Dr. Gupta would return him to his room. And turning to Nurse Yancy, Matt said, "Draw up two grams of Solumedrol."

It isn't often that the CEO wheels a patient through the corridors of his hospital and a lot of heads turned and wondered who was in the chair, but most people figured it out quickly enough.

<<<>>>

Occasionally she had a sense of what might be called self, of being someone. Who it was wasn't clear, but at times, perhaps when her sedation was wearing off, Lanie could almost feel herself think. Had it actually been her father's voice that seemed to echo around her, so loudly that it seemed amplified, amphoric, like a voice in a large barrel? Unable to turn toward it or away from it she was acutely aware of its commencing and then its cessation.

Then the self would be gone, replaced by nothing she was aware of or recognized. There was just a rhythmic surround. Her heart beat? Her respiration? A steady wing beat?

25

TIM LEFT THE office at eleven-thirty. He had called his clients of the next six days and pushed them into the following week and none had objected when he told them why. An associate had agreed to cover for emergencies and Tim had put a message on his phone explaining his absence. All the bases were covered and it was time to get back to his wife.

When Tim entered Sheila's room, Handley was in the middle of another examination. He looked over his shoulder at Tim, nodded a greeting, and said, "She's making good progress, young man. I just stripped her membranes to hurry things along. She's five centimeters and I can feel a head in there so we'll give her a little Pitocin and pop this puppy out." Handley reached to the ceiling to stretch his back and announced he'd be back shortly, after getting a bite to eat. "Can I bring you a sandwich Doc?"

Tim shook his head no but thanked Handley as he watched the nurse hang the Pitocin drip.

<<<>>>

Raju Gupta sat in his office, emotionally exhausted. The events of the last week had contained the potential for disaster, especially if there had been mass hysteria fueled by Frances Tarker. Again, he wondered at her behavior, her push for sensationalism in her broadcast. Why? What drove her to seemingly self-destruct?

On an easel were the diagrams Raju had drawn that first morning in Irv Pender's office. *Funny,* he thought, *but I have never looked at them again*. Events had dictated actions or a response as they occurred and there had been no way to predict what had occurred, at least not this time. One had to be ready for anything and everything and, perhaps, that was the lesson to be learned. What was the Boy Scout Motto? "Semper Paratus, Always Prepared," wasn't it? Well, it applied to medicine for certain." Raju's thoughts turned to Lanie. By now Colicchio has given her the steroids and their efforts and hard work had to be rewarded. *She simply must get well,* Raju thought.

His secretary knocked on the door and entered his office. "There's a Dr. Jack Martin to see you," she said. Noticing in Raju's expression that the name didn't immediately compute she continued. "He's the surgeon who originally saw the smew in Montauk and he'd like to talk to you about Lanie."

Gupta greeted the man who was, in some sense, responsible for the events of this last week Each man thought he saw in the other signs of fatigue and concern, an unnatural furrow of the brow, a hesitancy to smile at greeting one another.

"Dr. Martin, do come in please." Raju motioned to his leather sofa as he closed the door behind them. Jack leaned back and rested his head comfortably for a moment, sighed and then sat upright and turned toward Gupta.

"Isn't it amazing how events shape our lives?" Jack said. "Our meeting today is a perfect example." He paused, "It's Jack, please. If I hadn't seen that damn bird and called Frank Vogelslieder that young woman might not be on a ventilator, perhaps even dying, and we would not be sitting here talking."

Raju raised his right hand, his bony index finger alone raised in a cautionary gesture. "Do you believe that if that bird had stopped at Point Judith, not even thirty miles from where you found it, things would have been different? I do not. My father would have said, 'this, all of it, was karma.' Not bad or good, just destined to be. Someone would have seen it, it would have been rescued, and then who knows."

Jack had to smile at this sage philosopher. He scratched the back of his neck, pensive, and finally replied, "I'm not sure I can answer that. I have been following what has happened as closely as I could and yesterday when I learned how sick Lanie was, felt I had to something. I sensed that I knew something of import and needed to talk to you.

But it would not compute, I simply couldn't recall what I needed to and it was driving me crazy. You can understand that?" Jack scratched his neck again.

"This morning I was planning on going fishing but my guide called in sick, food poisoning he thought, so I had time to tinker and molder and something clicked in the memory bank. Actually, it was when I bit my tongue while eating a forbidden croissant." Jack laughed and shook his head. "I ate of the forbidden fruit from the tree of knowledge. I know, it's bizarre, but it happened that way. You could say it was always right on the tip of my tongue.

"Well, after that, this morning I called to talk to some friends who work in New York Hospital where I was a transplant surgeon for twenty-five years. CMV, cyto-megalo virus, recrudescence or super-infection was, for a period of time, a huge problem for us in post-trans-plant patients. The dormant virus was awakened by the immunosuppressive drugs we'd administer and it threatened the lives of the post-operative patients. We would lose grafts when we stopped immuno-sup-pression or we'd lose patients when we continued it. I'm sure you're familiar with the phenomenon. It's not unlike all the overwhelming infections we see in other immune-deficient people. HIV is a perfect example.

"But when our research laboratories began to retrieve, harvest I guess, hyper-immune gamma globulin from people who had successfully recovered from CMV infection, we thought we might have a new tool to work with, and it did prove invaluable. We could give it in CMV-positive recipients before transplant and then after surgery, and could prevent a lot of problems. In effect we bolstered the body's ability to fight off the virus or to keep it suppressed."

He leaned forward. "Raju, you have two patients here who have recovered from H5N1 infection and who could be a source of immune gamma globulin. You could plasmapherese them and probably harvest H5N1 immune globulins."

Gupta's mind had picked up Jack's train of thought and was fast-forwarding even as Jack continued, and he raised a hand, interrupting his guest. "Jack, do you believe the technique is applicable in this situation?"

"Will it be the answer? One can't be sure before trying it, but when I talked this morning to the folks in the labs at Robsin Institute, they said it might very well work. You can pherese Frank and Ole, obtain their immune globulins, and fractionate them to extract the specific portion you want to use and then administer it. You could even see if it bound to the viral particles and test it in PCR prep. You don't know if it would be killing to the virus; that would take more time, which is something you don't have. What do you have to lose? I am sure both men would be willing."

Gupta stood, took a few steps, and then returned to the sofa and stood before Jack. "Do you see a downside?"

Jack rose from his seat and gestured uncertainly, "There might be, but if her present downside is her demise, I personally can't see any harm at all in trying this. Yes, HIV or Hep C could be an issue if Frank or Ole have those diseases but we can test for those easily and quickly and neither man fits the profile for either disease. Sure, there might even be some Mad Cow-like prion we don't know about or can't presently detect or cure, but I don't think I'd worry about her succumbing to something twenty years from now if this could save her life today. If this were my child or grandchild, Raju, I would not hesitate."

Gupta became almost animated with a new-found energy. "Jack, you don't need to say another word. I wholeheartedly agree with you. Tell me who can do this for us and we'll do it today."

"I know that they can do it at Stony Brook. Their transplant labs have everything you need. If there is any problem, you could get it done at Cornell."

With his long arm on Jack's shoulders, Gupta walked with Jack out of his office, Raju promising to keep Jack fully informed.

<<<>>>

Raju went to the P-ICU and found Matt and Yancy in Lanie's room. Her latest film showed nearly a white-out of her lung fields. They had given her the large, IV bolus of Solumedrol in an effort to reduce the inflammation in her lungs, but even with the increased PEEP they were having a hard time keeping her O2 saturation at an acceptable level. The girl was continuing to deteriorate.

From the nurses' station Raju called Sandy Miller at Stony Brook and found he also was agreeable to the suggestion by Jack Martin. They had the capacity in their research labs associated with their transplant services, and Sandy immediately wanted to get the needed staff and services ready to help. Raju had then motioned to Matt Colicchio to join him and pointed to a chair across the table.

Quietly, he told Matt of his meeting with Jack Martin and asked his young intensivist for his opinion. Matt brushed away some invisible crumbs and pulled Lanie's chart toward himself. Then he looked across at his boss.

"Raju, we've nothing to lose at this point and I'm certain both men would agree. We've hit her hard with the steroids and now can only watch and hope. So far, she's stable on the increased PEEP but I don't know for how long. As you can see, her latest film stinks. Let's talk to Ole and I'll call Frank."

It was arranged rapidly. Ole understood the gravity of his daughter's situation and Frank Vogelslieder said he'd be at SHH in an hour. With a Southampton police escort the hospital would provide the men with rapid transport to Stony Brook, and security there would be waiting to take them to the pheresis unit.

Plasmapheresis was a lot like hemodialysis. Large volumes of blood would be passed through a system that would remove the plasma and then return the blood cells to the body. It didn't need to clean out toxins, just remove the plasma and replace it, temporarily, with a balanced electrolyte solution, an IV fluid. The removed plasma would then be divided into fractions and the one with the antibodies to the H5N1 virus could be selected out and then transfused into another person, in this case, Lanie.

Raju and Ole were waiting outside the hospital when Frank arrived at the main entry. A hospital transport van sat just a few feet away, its driver standing by, finishing a cup of coffee. Not far beyond was a patrol car, its lights flashing. Frank came up to the men, shook hands with them, and spoke to Ole, "It's much too nice a day for this not to work, Ole. Not a cloud in the sky and that must mean something good is going to happen. I have no doubts about it."

Ole looked at Frank and started to speak but said nothing. Raju walked them to the waiting van and then watched them pull away from the building following the police vehicle onto the street.

On arrival at Stoney Brook they were taken to the pheresis unit, explained the procedure, asked to sign a permit, and then they were seated in Barker loungers. A large needle with two openings was placed in a big vein near the elbow and attached with tubing to the pheresis machine. For several hours Ole and Frank watched blood being removed, processed and returned to their bodies. Finally, the procedure was completed, the needles were removed, dressings applied, and the men ferried back to SHH. Everyone in the labs understood the gravity of the situation and they were prepared to work as long as they were needed. Knowing that they were all a part of the first experiences with H5N1 in America, they all deeply cared that their efforts be successful.

By morning, the hyper-immune globulin fraction would be isolated, packed in a dispensing format and in the refrigerator, awaiting transport to SHH.

26

SEVERAL YOUNG WOMEN among Sheila's friends had delivered babies in the last two years and some of them had used a doula referred by their obstetricians. Half mid-wife and half, what? — witch, oracle, massage therapist? —these women had guided and assisted the labor and answered nursing issues. Sheila hadn't either the time or the inclination to get so involved pre-natally; she thought that when she went into labor she'd deliver and then she'd go home and care for her baby. It would be that simple.

Now in labor she'd begun to second guess that decision and thought it might be helpful to have someone at bedside other than her husband. Just as she was going to ask Tim to get her some ice chips, an attractive young woman came into her room and in an upbeat voice said, "Hi, I'm Cincy DeVoe, one of the doulas at SHH. Nurse Flaherty asked me to come to see you. Since you folks didn't attend any of the pre-birth classes, let's go over some of what was covered in them right now."

Cincy began with the Lamaze breathing techniques and then went on to talk about concentration, blocking out extraneous stimuli and working with the contractions. She kept one hand on Sheila's belly and as soon as she felt a contraction begin, she'd say softly, "Forget about me. Work with the contraction, breathe deeply, and push slowly and steadily when it comes. Distract yourself from the pain by focusing on some detail in the distance. That picture there on the wall is a good focal point."

Then she adjusted Sheila's bed to a near sitting position and watched her during the contractions. Tim was amazed how relaxed yet focused Sheila had become.

Dr. Handley came in and examined her briefly.

"It's witchcraft but it works," he said to Tim. As he walked out the door the doctor added, "I'm going to recovery and then I'll be back."

Sheila looked over at Tim and said, "Graceful, isn't it! Arrgh, it hurts! Supposed to though I suspect." She went right into her breathing routine while Tim watched her face turn crimson and Cincy quietly praised and encouraged her. Minutes later Handley returned and looked at all the monitors. He went through the glove and betadine routine again and when he slipped a hand under her bent legs he looked up, smiled, and said, "Your baby is ready to join the world. I feel nothing but head and hair. One or two more good pushes will do it. Tim, pull up a chair and sit down."

That was an order, not a request.

Flaherty and Handley quickly added a sterile bed-cover and drape and adjusted the bed so that Handley could sit at her feet. It was now as if Sheila were sitting in a chair, albeit more comfortable than the birthing chairs of the early twentieth century.

Sheila looked at the doctor in wonder. "What happened to my C-section?" she asked. Then she felt a major contraction and gritted her teeth, muffling her voice, "Oh, here it goes. This feels like it, Doctor."

Cincy talked quietly to Sheila and pushed down on her belly with both hands as the next contraction began and the head of the baby exited the birth canal.

"His head is out, Sheila, and that was the hardest part of this whole affair," Cincy told her.

From out of nowhere appeared one of the staff pediatricians who stood at Handley's side. As Handley delivered shoulders and then body and legs, Sheila felt a relief of the pressure. Handley put clamps on the cord and divided it and then rubbed the baby briskly. Sheila heard their son begin to cry.

"He's fine, looks like an Apgar ten," announced Handley.

Flaherty and the pediatrician took the bloody and pelose newborn to a nearby bassinet, suctioned his mouth and throat, and then rapidly cleaned and swathed him. Cincy continued to massage Sheila's belly until the uterus expelled the placenta and began to contract down, constricting all blood vessels and stopping any bleeding that occurred with placental separation.

Handley said. "Good work. What do we call this guy anyway? "

Sheila looked over at her husband who was now standing in awe next to the bassinet. She called, "Come here Morrissey and give me a kiss before I fall asleep."

Tim, in a state of shock and wonder, quickly obeyed, then Sheila said, "I don't know yet. The only thing we've called him is Farley. Do we have to decide now?"

"Not at all, you can sleep on it," Handley said.

Sheila's bed was again leveled, sheets were changed and "Baby Boy Morrissey" soon fell asleep next to his dozing mother.

27

JACK HAD LEFT the hospital hopeful that his contribution might just make a difference. Driving back to Montauk he remembered that earlier in the day he had made plans to fish this evening's tide with Arden and T.C. and he found himself reluctantly headed for the marina to meet them.

It was a wonderfully soft fall evening and Jack admitted to himself that the outing might be a mood elevator. The men were already aboard and had the motors idling, waiting for Jack to join them. Jack still felt emotionally a bit detached but he began to relax as they approached the lighthouse. As a concession to his son-in-law they trolled from the Point to Hither Hills and back again. There were no tuna evident but they caught several large bluefish, which they released. It was just over a week since Jack and T.C. had been on the water and seen the smew, and Jack was still greatly distressed by the results of that sighting. As beautiful as the evening was, as much as he loved being on the water with these two men, he was uneasy and sad at heart. More than once during the day Jack had felt tears begin to well up but he fought them off. His visit with Gupta had helped but right now he needed a chance to try to explain to someone else his difficulty with what was happening around them.

"T.C. please shut off the motors. I need to sit here a moment and rest and have you listen to me." Jack took his favorite seat on the gunwale. "You two guys don't realize how hard it is to be a physician, even a retired one, and feel so helpless. That young girl may die because we saw that smew, because birds fascinate me, because I called Frank when we saw it on the beach, because of so very many coincidences subsequent to that event. I thought I'd left this responsibility behind me six years ago when I retired." He stood, took off his hat, and ran his fingers through his hair. "Have you got a beer in the cooler?" he asked T.C.

But they found only bottled water and passed one to Jack who took it back to his seat. He continued, "I can't even imagine Lanie's not getting well. I guess as a physician you think of any sick child as an extension of your own children, you understand the anguish felt by the parent almost as if it were happening to you. You just can't detach yourself. You can't hide in objectivity. At least this man can't."

Jack paused, opened the bottle that Arden had handed him, and took a long drink. Then he splashed some on his face, took another drink and tentatively shook the shoulders of Arden and T.C., both of whom had remained silent.

"But I'm supposed to be fishing this evening, am I not? I'm sorry to burden you with my own issues, gentlemen. Arden, hand me my fly box, that big black one."

Arden picked up the box, flipped the two plastic latches up, and unfolded the box like a book. The inside was like two pages of an illuminated manuscript: large, colorful flies capitalizing row after row of poetry or scripture. A long black exclamation point lay at the far right-hand side. He passed the open book to Jack, marveling at his father-in-law's creations. "Yes, that's it, thanks."

As they drifted toward Caswell's Point Jack pulled out the exclamation point and tied the large yak hair eel pattern of his own design onto the leader and then trailed all ten inches of it in the water alongside the boat. The three of them leaned over the gunwale, watching the creation undulate tantalizingly a foot under the surface of the sea.

"My, my but doesn't that look yummy good." Jack worked the fly in the water, pulsing it along in erratic fashion. "Big fish food, super-sized from Micky D's. No squid tonight, Mama Bass, just eel on the menu."

T.C. straightened up and looked at Jack.

"Won't that tangle when you cast it, Doc?"

"Nope. Here, look at it." Jack lifted it carefully out of the water and swung it slowly toward T.C., who caught it cautiously to avoid getting jabbed by the sharp hook. As T.C. fingered it, he found that the front half and the head had silicone worked into it, shaping it and holding it in that eel shape. Only the tail portion, the last five or six inches wiggled. T.C. flipped the fly back into the water and gave Jack a thumb's up. "Be less erratic with the retrieve Doc. Eels swim more evenly, steadily."

The sea was very calm and Arden was able to maneuver his boat in close to the rocky shallower water along the beach. Jack sent the slinky, sexy fly almost sixty feet toward the shore, let it sink a few seconds and began a slow retrieve. On the third cast he felt resistance and turned his back to his audience.

In an instinctive reflex Jack strip set on the fly but when there was no immediate response, he chimed his usual, "Bottom, guys."

T.C. walked up the port side of the *Ruby-Belle* to where Jack stood in the bow, and hands on hips looked at Jack. "You and your 'bottom', guys. Not with that fly and not in mid retrieve. It's not weighted and you're throwing only three hundred and fifty grains, so once again Doc, you were well up in the column. That ain't bottom. You better set up on that fish before it spits that thing out on you."

While T.C. was jabbering, Jack again strip set twice vigorously and as if on signal the bottom quickly moved eastward fifty feet up the beach and turned right toward open water.

"Damn fast-moving bottom, Dad," Arden said. Jack liked that the young man called him "Dad", and they exchanged smiles.

When he saw Arden move up into the bow with Jack to be in position to ride him a little, T.C. moved quickly to the helm. He steered the boat out into deeper water and as usual he kept the bow positioned to Jack's advantage.

Jack moved to the starboard gunwale and braced against it. He supported the rod above the reel with his left hand, increasing the pressure against the fish. He heard the lyric from the helm. Forty-pound leader, Doc? Daaahkter Jaaaack." T.C. was singing again.

"Always, Captain."

"Then let's tighten that drag and get that fish in the boat while we can still see what we're doing."

In about ten minutes Jack saw the fish come to the surface, her flanks reflecting violet in the twilight. Soon she was beside the boat. About thirty-six inches of tired, hen striper lay on her side next to the boat, her ordinarily Prussian blue back turned black in the dimming light. T.C. looked at her, Boga in hand. "Has to be twenty, Doc. Let her go?"

"Yup, let me try to release her."

Jack moved to the stern where the gunwale was lowest and reached for his leader. Seeing she was too tired to bolt he wrapped it repeatedly around his right hand, working it closer to the fish. Setting down his rod, with his left hand he followed the last two feet of leader down to the corner of the fish's mouth and grabbing hold of her lower lip he lifted her head out of the water. He released the leader and, with his now free hand, he deftly slipped the barbless hook out of her jaw.

"No picture tonight, ma'am. Goodbye."

He righted her in the water and pushed her head toward the bottom. The tail gave one flick, splashing Jack and Arden, and she was gone.

"Home, James. Arden, you'll do for a James."

On the ride home T.C. told Jack about the Frances Tarker debacle and the *Long Island Newsday* counter. Jack found the story hard to believe and said, "Not unlike that aging big blond in the Sandra Bullock movie, *Miss Congeniality*. She imploded because she was getting older and afraid of losing her job. How old is Tarker, T.C.?"

"No idea, Doc, I never paid attention to that."

"Said like a man who has a very, very young girl friend. Have you stopped looking?"

"Me Stop looking?" T.C. joked.

Arden said that he was not surprised at what happened. "She's certainly a good-looking woman but one who's looking to move up and out of Long Island. I'll bet she saw bird flu as an opportunity to shine. All those New York City anchors in their late forties and even fifties are demanding seven figure incomes. Tarker has their looks, and a better body. She sees herself as another Viera or Couric or whoever. But she made a freaking disaster of her life, is what she did."

"Sure sounds that way, Arden."

As they rounded the point and came onto the north side, Jack nudged Arden aside and took over the helm. He pushed upward on the throttle and felt the *Ruby-*

Belle accelerate smoothly, following his urging. "Like glass out here guys, perfect for an amateur."

28

Friday, Septemer 8th 2006

THE STONY BROOK courier with his state police escort arrived at the front door of SHH at nine-thirty a.m. and met by security. His refrigerated parcel was signed over to an officer who took it at once to the P-ICU where Matt Colicchio was extremely happy to see him enter.

Earlier, Sandy Miller had called Irv Pender and expressed concern over the amount of material they were able to send. They'd had only two men to phereses, and he hoped that their contributions would be adequate.

"Irv, if it helps, we can run them again in forty-eight hours and get a bit more. Let me know how it goes. I hope this does the trick for her."

"No more than I do, my friend. Thanks to you."

"Call me and keep me posted."

Pender had then talked to Dr. Gupta and relayed Miller's concerns.

"Irv, this isn't a transplant situation with CMV in every organ of the body," Raju said. "We're just treating the lungs, but we can't rationalize away the fact that it is a small volume. It just has to make the difference."

Before the officer left the P-ICU he went to Lanie's room, said a rosary, and added a Mass card to the growing pile.

"Thanks, Flack, we can sure use the help," Matt said.

"You've got it. More than you can know. She's going to get better."

It had been twelve hours since the steroid dose and there had been no change in either Lanie's PEEP requirements or her X-ray. Matt was hoping that either this immune globulin or all those prayer cards would have made a difference. He looked at Yancy and spoke quietly to her, "I only wish I had his faith. Either this or the steroids will have to work in our favor if she's going to get well, but why not both for good measure? Yancy, let's hang this stuff. I think it is miracle time in the P-ICU."

<<<>>>

The day in the P-ICU had been one of hopeful anticipation, which at least temporarily relieved some of the anxiety-produced fatigue of the staff. They had perfunctorily hung Lanie's medications, each in its time, and noted that her afternoon X-ray looked much like that from the morning. It would have been difficult for it to look any worse but at least her PEEP requirements had not increased.

All agreed that the next twelve hours would be critical and if either the immune globulin or the steroids were having an effect, it would have to be manifest in that time frame.

Ole had heard about Sheila's baby and had called Tim, summoning the will to congratulate the new father. Not much of a philosopher, he still was aware of the balances of life, the give and take, the birth on the one hand and then his daughter, perhaps near death, on the other.

Tim had passed quietly through the unit, waved to Matt, added his prayer for the girl, and then continued on home to make ready for his family's arrival the next day.

<<<>>>

Eight hours had passed since the administration of the immune gamma globulin and they had continued to give Lanie the antivirals and antibiotics, hoping to both treat the infection and prevent any secondary bacterial pneumonia in her lungs.

Yancy and Matt Colicchio were tired after a second all-nighter but they were able to grab naps intermittently throughout the day. Fortunately, Matt was able to have someone cover for him for the ER and he could stay in the P-ICU. Either Raju Gupta or Irv Pender came into the unit every few hours and tried to bolster morale. Ole had been there in the morning and had just arrived for an evening visit.

He sat by Lanie's bed and held her hand. He talked to her in a whisper and once again, as he spoke, they noted her pulse quicken. When he could bear no more, Ole stood up and walked over to the windows that looked out. He could not believe what he saw.

"Doc, Yancy, come over here and look at this."

<<<>>>

They had begun to arrive at dusk. At first it was a few at a time and then larger groups came walking toward the hospital. They were silent but each person carried a candle. Passing cars stopped, the occupants inquiring what was happening. Many parked their vehicles and joined the procession, taking candles offered by someone in the group. As the hospital's evening staff watched from inside the building, the patients who were able joined them at the windows, and though it was nightfall, it was no longer dark on the grass outside the east wing of the building. The assembly of loving and concerned citizens of South Hampton stayed there quietly, silhouetted in the warm glow of candlelight while in front of them a kneeling Father Colgin led the group in silent prayer. After a few minutes he stood, turned, and blessed the gathering, and then, as quietly as they had arrived, they dispersed. Except, that is, for one woman at whom Ole stared, and who stayed, looking at the hospital until finally her taper extinguished itself in its holder.

The next day the media estimated that between one and two thousand men, women, and children had gathered on the hospital lawn to keep vigil.

29

Saturday, September 9th

One might have expected and looked for an epi-phenomenon but none occurred, at least not that Friday night. It had, in fact, been a quiet night for most of SHH, but in the P-ICU the vigil had continued. Yancy and Matt were pulling yet another all-nighter, alternating periods of fitful sleep in the call room. Lanie's late p.m. film might have shown some improvement but no one dared say so. However, during the night her O2 sat had crept to 94% and Matt began to hope things were turning in their favor.

At six a.m. he called a local deli and ordered breakfast, two egg, cheese and bacon sandwiches on rolls, and two large coffees. When he gave his name and the hospital as the delivery address, the voice on the other end changed dramatically. "We were there last night, on the lawn," the woman said with hushed respect. "We'll get these to you in ten minutes. See you soon, Doc."

Fifteen minutes later the security guard brought up the order. He was smiling and gave Matt a pat on the shoulder. "You've made a lot of friends. Everyone at the hospital has the last few days."

"Clarke, who paid for this?" Matt queried.

"Here's the bill that came with it."

On the light green of the standard order pad was one word written in bold capitals, *THANKS.*

Matt took the bag and, nearing tears, walked to the table in the nursing station. He put the bag and note in front of Yancy and watched her as she began to sob. Matt turned to look at Lanie through the glass partition. They sat and ate while the early arrivers for the day shift helped the radiology tech take Lanie's first X-ray of the new day.

There was no question on this film. There was improvement and as a result it was a much happier P-ICU staff that gave its report that morning.

By noon they'd cut the PEEP in half and even with less residual volume in the lungs, Lanie's mid-day film showed further resolution of the pneumonia. She was mobilizing the fluid out of her inflamed lungs and by all parameters she was improving.

When Ole was told of the change of events he was visibly delighted. Exhausted by his concern and refusal to sleep, Lanie's hopeful father at last lay down and closed his eyes for the first time in two days.

Raju's statement to the media in front of the hospital that morning had been that Lanie's physicians were "cautiously optimistic." The TV stations all showed

Gupta's statement and the candlelight vigil of the night before. Finally, at noon, Irv Pender called Sandy Miller and he asked, "Did you have your radio or TV turned on this morning? We are over the hump! It's clear sailing, or surfing when it comes to that young women!"

30

LATE THAT SATURDAY afternoon of the 9th, Dr. Raju Gupta sat at home relaxing at last. He had arrived back in time for a late lunch and then needed to take a walk on the beach with his wife. "I want to talk to you. It's almost five o'clock, the perfect time for the beach." He stood up and gave her a side to side wobble of his head and spoke in perfect imitation of his father, "Vaat-iz-it vit you, voman? You-arr husband vants valking, you must valk. Is it not so?" He started out of the room to her peals of laughter.

Hand in hand they walked the five or so blocks to the ocean, occasionally nodding or waving to a neighbor or acquaintance. There they took off their shoes and headed through the public access lane to the South Hampton Beach. The last of the bitter-end bathers and sun-worshippers were folding their blankets and chairs and heading home. The lifeguard stands were pulled up close to either the dune grass or the snow fences. Soon they would have the beach to themselves.

At the water's edge Raju rolled up the cuffs of his neatly pressed chinos and Amelia tied up her long cotton print skirt between her legs somehow creating billowing pantaloons. The water was still warm enough to be comfortable on their feet and the surf at low tide was only gently caressing the fine pebbles of the beach sand. There would be no need for an intermittent rapid escape from the assault of the incoming waves.

"Listen. Close your eyes and listen to the water my dear," he said reaching for Amelia's hand, and for a few moments they walked blind to anything but the susurration of water on sand.

A group of a dozen sanderlings kept well ahead of them as the couple strolled eastward. Raju pointed to the little birds and put his arm around his wife.

"Remember when I used to read you Elizabeth Bishop's poems? I think I still remember 'The Sandpiper', most of it certainly." He closed his eyes, tilted his head upward toward his memory, and recited it.

He finished and faced his wife, took her hands in his and fought back tears as he said,

"Our world was shaken this past week and a half. How much we were like those little creatures in front of us, or like that one sandpiper. How much we were looking for something, something to turn the tide, something to change what was happening. But what else have we but an obsession when a child is so sick and might die. Medicine must always be an obsession or else we fail. I worry where the next generation of good doctors will come from if they don't have that obsession. And I hope our own boys find an obsession, a passion in their lives, and not just settle for a job, a living."

Amelia swung their joined hands left and right between them. "Raju, if they are inspired, they will find a passion and you do inspire them daily. You make our dinner times exciting for them. We are just two of their teachers and if they can find the same excitement during the day, well, then we will be lucky, and so will they."

The sanderlings were still keeping a safe distance ahead when suddenly they all lifted in flight and in a knot swung out over the sea and sped to the west. Amelia saw a large, grey-black blur fall out of the sky into their midst, scattering all but one of them. It arced low over the water clutching that one small bird in its talons and then, rising, turned toward the land. She marveled at the peregrines speed and agility.

"My god, Raju. Did you see that falcon?"

"Don't. I cannot look at a strange bird."

"Oh, you silly, where is your passion now?"

She wrapped both arms around her husband and they walked on until it became too cool to continue and then they turned back west, walking home in the soft colors of a September evening.

Postscript

Tom and Sheila Morrissey named their new son Colin and continued living the good life in Amagansett as successful veterinarians.

Frances Tarker was noticed by a large New York City news outlet. Because of her assertive performance in South Hampton, she was hired as anchor for a major TV station.

Lanie recovered fully and was able to maintain a somewhat shaky relationship with her mother. She continued to live at home with her father Ole who gave up feather collecting!

Matt and Yancy were married in the Spring of 2007.

Dr Ragu Gupta was approved by the hospital board for the appointment of CEO.

Dr Irv Pender retired and wrote a book: A story about an epidemic.

Dr Jack gets the last word; "All's well that ends well!"

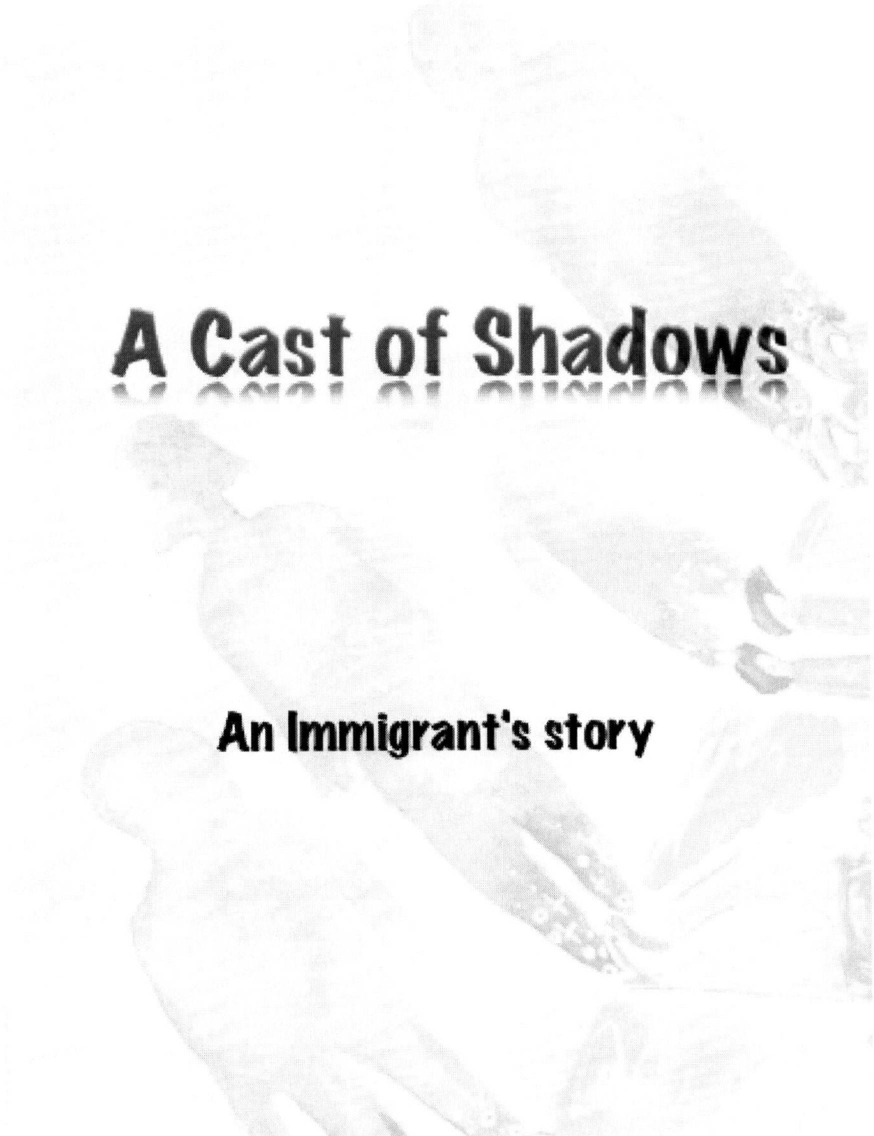

A Cast of Shadows

An Immigrant's story

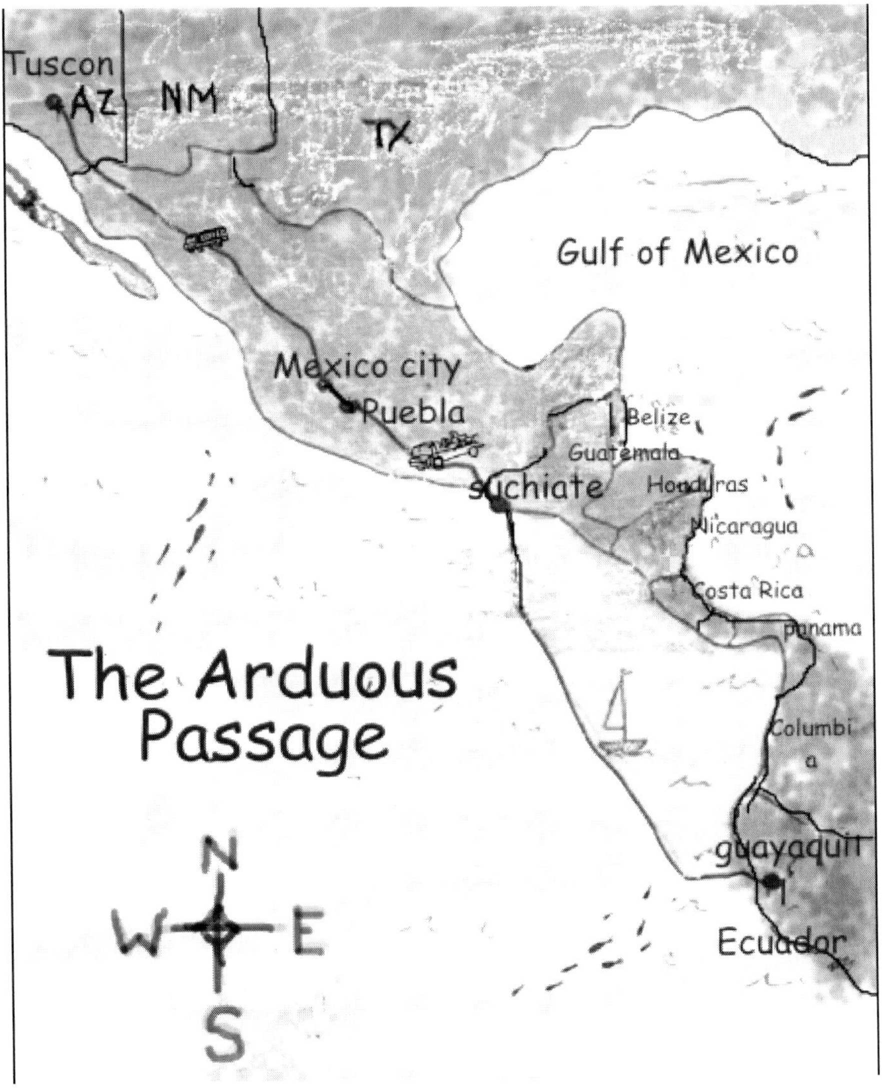

Tuscon
AZ
NM
TX
Gulf of Mexico
Mexico city
Puebla
Belize
Guatemala
suchiate
Honduras
Nicaragua
Costa Rica
panama
Columbi
a
guayaquil
Ecuador
The Arduous
Passage
N
W
E
S

1

A WALK AS A tourist through the streets of Santa Ana de los Cuatro Rios, Ecuador is as beautiful as in any city in the Southern Hemisphere of the New World. Cobbled streets and ornate tiled sidewalks lead you past classic Spanish cathedrals and through the bustling plazas of eight universities. The flower market in the Plazalita del Carmen is a sensuously breathtaking and psychedelic explosion of color, shape and fragrance. But sitting as it does atop the sierra at 8,200 feet, a newcomer to the city must walk slowly and hydrate continuously or succumb as one would in Santa Fe or Gunnison to the headache and malaise of altitude sickness. Life at lower altitude may be easier but it is never as full of contrasts.

Where the city begins to blend into countryside you can picnic above the banks of the Rio Tomebamba, the free and ever flowing laundromat for a large part of the city's nearly one half million population. It needs to be free because as in most of Central and South America, in Ecuador a true class or caste system exists among the populations. Most cannot afford the luxury of a washing machine. If you could earn twenty US dollars a day, life in Cuenca would be very good. Food and fuel are very inexpensive, higher education is readily available, children can learn ballet or become musicians and, most importantly, quality medical care is readily available. But if you earn only the eight US dollars average wage each day as do the great majority of Cuencanos, life is not so easy or inspiring. Children must work and help either at home or on a family farm, and the privileges of health and plenty are not always available.

Cuencanos are Incan stock and therefore not tall people. The men tend to be slender and have stronger Indian facial features. You rarely see a paunch on a man under fifty and even less commonly among the elderly. The ladies are softer and more rounded and feminine but not like the chubby or even fat Hispanic women of Central America or the Caribbean.

<<<>>>

With dark sparkling eyes, ebony hair and an olive complexion, Maritza Ponson-Sucreno was a tiny woman but beautiful. Her husband, Ignacio Jose Sucreno, was taller than most of his contemporaries. His prominent cheekbones, aquiline nose, and pointed chin left little doubt of his ancestry.

They were an intelligent and handsome couple and deserved to have their gene-line perpetuated by many offspring. But it was into the lower-class life of

Cuenca that Maritza and Ignacio finally brought a son, Mundin. He was the joy and fulfillment of their lives and he rolled through the first years of his life like a little brown bowling ball, with nothing to deter him or his progress. His short black hair began just above his brow and covered an inordinate portion of his very round head. Strong, short limbs aided his toddler aims and ambitions. Chattering seemingly wisely and with purpose he had entertained his extended family daily until one day he stopped talking.

Ignacio worked for an uncle on a cacao plantation and also cared for the family garden. His wife did occasional menial domestic work and tended to the home, the few chickens, the veggie patch, and most importantly Mundin. As a family they did not want and had no luxuries. Maritza sewed and mended almost nightly and because they had enough to eat, they stayed healthy. The family's income was occasionally bolstered by cash: US dollars sent from Ignacio's brother in Arizona. So many such dollars in the form of remittances came into Ecuador that the government yielded to pressures, both economic and political, and made those dollars the coin of the realm, replacing the sucre.

Although the population of Cuenca was slowly increasing, its growth would have been much larger if not for the great American magnet that constantly pulled thousands of its people northward. The stories and pictures of life in "el Norte" were such that emigration was an attraction difficult to resist.

Medical care in Ecuador was available to all but was delivered in three distinct tiers. The wealthy had first rate private hospitals whose physicians were well trained in 21st[st] century medicine. A small step below in quality of service was the military's hospitals which served the large army and its veterans. But the government-run clinics which served the populous at large were at best functional but often ineffectual and at times derelict. Understaffed and undersupplied, they were always oversubscribed. Crowds of all ages filled waiting and triage areas and the grave or emergent cases might or might not be promptly recognized and addressed. If medical supplies did not trickle down beyond the military institutions; drugs, especially anti-convulsants, antibiotics, and analgesics, ended up in short supply or even unavailable. Many of the tragedies of Cuencano life occurred in this third world setting, the government hospitals.

Mundin developed a cough, something that he and his playmates often passed among themselves as do children the world over. But then he became febrile and lethargic and his parents took him to the neighborhood clinic. After a long wait his ears and throat received a perfunctory examination and the doctor gave the Sucrenos medication for the fever and the cough. The next day the fever worsened. Mundin became more lethargic and would not eat or drink. That night as his parents dutifully sponged his hot little body, Mundin had a seizure. At the hospital they treated the seizure but did not recognize the opisthotony, the cardinal sign of meningitis, and failed to administer the proper antibiotics. Two days later Mundin was dead.

For Maritza and Ignacio, the decision to go to the US was suddenly a very easy one. Relatives there had urged the move, and it would extract them from the daily expectation of seeing Mundin suddenly appear from another room or from behind a tree in the yard. They hoped it would mean a new beginning and a new happiness for their marriage and their lives. The journey however would not fully safeguard them from a series of tragedies that had, with Mundin's death, begun to haunt their lives.

<<<>>>

If you could obtain a visitor's visa, you could go to Quito, board an AA or LAN airplane, fly to the US and disappear into the crowd. But neither the US nor Ecuador was issuing visas: the former because of 9/11 and the latter because it didn't want to lose a young workforce. Out of this loggerhead that now existed in all of Central and South America arose the Coyote network, the entrepreneurs who could cobble together an illicit voyage of subterfuge and danger, but a voyage that inexorably led to the US borders.

Ignacio needed almost $20,000 US if the Coyotes were to guarantee guided passage for himself and his wife. That money, a huge sum for most seeking the new middle passage to America, would be meted out time and time again during the journey but first it had to be raised. Many would mortgage homes and possessions and pay exorbitant interest rates to send someone north. The lucky had money sent to them from family waiting to receive them upon arrival. Half of the Sucreno's money came from sale of their lands and home and the remainder from Ignacio's brother in Tempe and an uncle on Long Island.

Less than a month after the loss of Mundin a defeated Ignacio walked to the farm village of Ingapirca in search of Dona Inez. In a rural setting of Incan ruins and tourist attractions, of share cropped farms and modest farmers' homes was one property that seemed to be flourishing. Ignacio spied Dona Inez sitting on her veranda. She was dressed in colorful and traditional Indian garments seldom worn by anyone living so close to Cuenca. She sat like as a bright flower imposed upon the dull stone façade of her home. No one knew her age but she claimed to have many great-grandchildren. She held a long clay pipe in the pruned paw of her hand, occasionally bringing the stem to her thin lips. Ignacio guessed that because the pipe remained always in her hand that she did not have the opposing molars to hold it in her mouth. Her few remaining teeth which revealed themselves only rarely were stained from tobacco and yerba mata tea. She inhaled smoke from a draw on the pipe and released slowly from her broad nose with three subsequent breaths. He became aware of the exhaled smoke's unusual and strangely floral aroma. It was like nothing he'd smelled before and the old woman's calm and equanimity of pose suggested the pipe's contents if not cannabis-based was something its equal.

Ignacio sat on the only other available chair opposite her. Between them stood a small square table of unfinished mahogany, its flat surface a hieroglyph of burns and stains.

He waited dutifully, and after some minutes she pointed the pipe stem at Ignacio.

"You have brought me something. Do we need to examine it?"

Ignacio shook his head "no" and put the small parcel on the table. "There is no need Dona Inez."

"A pipe then, Señor Sucreno? It is very good."

Ignacio smiled but declined and stood to leave. From inside her quilted jacket she pulled an envelope and gave it to him. "All you need to know is here."

Ignacio put the letter in his vest, nodded adios and stepped from the veranda. He had just exchanged their entire lives—his, Maritza's and that of Mundin's memory—for a piece of paper inscribed with a name, an address, and a date and time. In exchange for freedom they now had indebtedness. But such was life.

They could have departed from Mantas, Salinas, or as it happened, Guayaquil. It mattered not and their fate would probably been the same. Looking back at that journey many, many years later, Maritza was certain of the fact that the Fates had always measured their lives and here or there snipped parts and pieces away, lengthening some and shortening others. Mundin's death had been proof enough for her.

For the two weeks before their departure they went through the motions of living but, in truth, they no longer had a life in Cuenca. At five a.m. on that last morning they boarded the bus for Guayaquil and the meeting with the first coyote. In the city they made their way from the bus depot to the harbor, stopping only to buy food from a street vendor. The expectant and agitated crowds around one or two of the older fishing vessels meant that they were close to meeting their man. When they found the *San Pietro,* he was there, list in hand, waiting for them.

No one ever wrote home to Cuenca about the details of their trip so Ignacio and Maritza had not anticipated or known that the trip at sea would be so arduous or that it would take six days to get from the Guayaquil harbor to the Guatemalan town a few miles below the Mexican border. One hundred and twenty men, women and children had packed themselves onto the deck and into the small cabin of the craft meant to accommodate no more than a working crew of six with their supplies and catch. With no functioning head facility and little to eat, all soon welcomed the nightly showers that washed vomit and excrement off body, clothes and the deck. During the third night their number decreased to 119 when an elderly man was buried unceremoniously at sea. Few spoke but many cried for days on end. Everyone succumbed to either upper respiratory or gastro-intestinal viral illnesses. Many suffered both and looked desperately to the blessing of landfall and ground beneath their feet.

When they reached northern Guatemala, the vessel stopped about a mile or so offshore, waiting. For what they waited no one knew, but anxiety increased as concerns of "a problem" arose. Most of all, everyone feared that their journey might end in a jail in Guatemala or Mexico. Having bankrupted themselves to make this journey, its disruption most certainly meant for many abject poverty, starvation and probable demise.

Finally, the radio crackled and the captain spoke. Soon a series of smaller launches appeared and began to ferry the people ashore. They stumbled from the docks through the streets of the fishing village like a group of space aliens on parade, on display before an audience of watching citizens. Paul asked himself what portion of the Coyote fee bought the cooperation of this town and the blank faces looking out from doorways and windows. A procession of 119 weary souls shuffled toward the promise of a rest and sustenance.

On a rise in the middle of town they came to an old baronial estate where they were divided into groups and led to rooms, toilets, showers and beds. By the end of the second day there, most of the group were recovered and anxious to move on. On the afternoon of the third day they all assembled in the yard and the coyote gave details of the next day's journey.

The following morning, they walked north out of town and finally came to a river, the border with Mexico, which some called it the Suchiate They all stripped naked, clothes went on top of heads, children perched on men's shoulders and the group waded chest-deep through the water into Mexico. All modesty had been lost during the boat journey and no one was afraid to proceed "desnudo".

Again dry and clothed, they walked at least two hours until they came to a town where three buses were waiting. Money was again exchanged; the group was divided and they proceeded further into Mexico. Most of the travelers had Ecuadorian documents, passports or social security papers which could be used as identification. if Mexican police stopped them. The rule seemed to be tacitly understood between Coyote and Mexican authorities that only undocumented people could be hassled and off-loaded or threatened. In this setting bribes were extracted and the profits for the Coyotes were thinned so refugees without paper were hidden in the buses designed for that purpose. Several hours later and without incident they arrived at a huge banana plantation. The plantation was a city unto itself with housing, shopping and primitive medical and dental care available to the hundreds of workers employed there. In the morning children lined the road as they walked to the local school and mothers hung laundry on lines strung between trees. Roused from their sleeping quarters the coyotes led the travelers led past processing sheds where bunches of bananas were sorted and boxed. They finally arrived at the trucking area and met with another coyote. Ignacio saw the auto-mechanics hauling a motor out of a huge diesel cab and other men working on farm equipment. This was big business farming unlike anything he'd seen.

The coyote told the assembly that there would be no space for superfluous items and any extra clothing or baggage would have to be left behind. They were all going to ride in the false bed of the shipping trucks covered by planking and boxes of bananas. This part of the trip required this subterfuge because it was the part of Mexico patrolled by officials the Coyotes could not bribe.

Like corpses in a large coffin they lay down and were covered and buried. For the children it was horrifying and for the adults simply frightening. Fortunately, the ride took only eight hours and in the evening they arrived at their destination, Puebla, a town nearly mid-Mexico. Extracted from their entombment, the group was led to an unfinished cement structure which had neither plumbing nor electricity. The week they spent there was again horrific because although there were provided ample food, there was no sanitation. Plates could not be washed. Toilets consisted of trench latrines. The confinement once again resulted in general, widespread viral illness.

At last they were divided into groups of five to six people and given written instructions on how to find specific bus drivers who were in Coyote employ. They also received maps to use as guides for the rest of the journey. They were instructed to act like Mexicans and to not look like the foreigners they were.

"This is essential for now you will be traveling among the people, the Mexican people, and you must be a part of them. We will be with you but cannot always help."

It sounded easy enough. They all looked much like Mexicans and they spoke the same language. A group leader was designated and given pesos to purchase bus tickets and give a fee to the drivers. As they began the twelve-hour ride Ignacio noticed a coyote had seated himself unobtrusively in the rear of the bus. He was there in case the police stopped and searched the bus, which might require a bribe.

Halfway through the trip the coyote approached Ignacio and instructed him carefully on what should happen in Mexico City.

"Take your group off at Station Five and look for a man wearing a black jacket and green hat. Do not talk to him. Just watch him and follow him when he leaves. Always be vigilant and act like Mexicans. These are imperative instructions you must follow."

They disembarked as directed and saw the man leaning against a building across the street. He ignored Ignacio's nod but soon sauntered away, as if he expected them to follow. They tailed him at a distance like sheep behind a Judas goat, unaware of destination or fate. After an hour they arrived at a large house where they spent four more days. It was the most comfortable stop of their entire journey.

When it came time to leave, they joined a number of other small groups and boarded a large truck which would carry fifty of them northward for twelve hours. They arrived at a horse and cattle ranch not far from the US border and were taken to dormitory housing. The coyote explained that the group would be here until "arrangements" had been made for the crossing and that might take several days. All knew that they were very near to the crossing and it was difficult to be idle day after day when they wanted to finish the trip. Impatiently they waited but at least they were well fed and comfortable. The evening of the fourth day the coyote came and told them, "Tonight we go."

They were again divided into small groups. The Sucrenos found themselves with strangers, non-Ecuadorians. The small pickup drove over little more than paths through the desert until it drew near to the border. It was dark as they left the pickup.

Before starting out each person was given a gallon of water, a sandwich and a candy bar. The coyote then gave his final instructions:

"Do not touch wires. Conserve your water in case you get lost. If you get lost, stay in the shade until you see or hear someone else. If you wander in the heat your bones will join those of others. Always walk single-file in the dark, hand and hand with the person in front or behind. Always help the ladies and children. Be silent, especially keep the children quiet."

The three coyotes led them to the border and the way across it, one of them leading, one mid-group, and the last at the rear. Just before dawn the three left the group. Again, they advised the refugees to continue north while it was dark but to rest when day came. By the end of the next night they should be approaching Tucson. Each of the travelers seemed to know what they were going to do after that. Each seemed to have some family arranged contact waiting for them in Arizona.

As dawn crept onto the horizon and the desert air began to lose some of its chill, Ignacio led his wife to the south side of a small rise crowned by an ancient saguaro cactus and prepared to settle in for the day. In spite of the coyote's warnings and the crude graves and fragments of bone they passed during the night, the other four in their small group decided to take the chance and continue north, this after heated debate. They welcomed the warming sun. From their vantage point they could see miles of desert in every direction. The couple shared one of their sandwiches and lay sleepily on the hard desert sand. As they nodded off into slumber a harsh siren startled them. It was nowhere near them but it was disconcerting. Then they heard amplified voices and distant shouting and they at once knew that their decision to rest had been the proper one.

As he rested Ignacio filled Maritza's water bottle from his own. The night walk had not been that difficult. The coyote had shown them how to pick the Big Dipper from the millions of stars and then to follow the line of its bowl to the North Star. "Siempre norte," he had said again and again. "Y solamente durante la noche." Travel only by night and at the end of the second night they would see Tempe. It was to be easy. Or so he said.

Most importantly, by that next dawn they would be well beyond most American patrols. When they reached the roads, friendly and understanding people would usually offer them a ride to Tempe. "Vaya con Dios" had been the coyote's last words when he left them at the border and vanished in the darkness.

At dusk they shared their other sandwich and waited to see the sky guide appear. Soon they were once again walking northward. Several hours into the night Ignacio almost stepped on an obstacle he could barely see in their path. Without thinking he kicked it and it reacted violently and rapidly struck him in the calf, holding on in spite of his efforts to kick it free. Only after he had freed himself of the creature did it give a warning rattle and slither off the trail. He pulled Maritza aside and led her safely around where the snake had been. Their first conversation of the night was to shortly become their last together.

Maritza clutched her husband with trembling hands, afraid of what had happened.

"Que ha pasado, mi amor?"

"Serpente."

"Venenoso?" her voice quavered as she whispered.

"Quien sabe? Who knows?"

But he did know. He'd pulled up his pant leg and fingered the already swelling puncture sites. The bloody fang holes were almost two inches apart and he knew the answer to her query. It had been a very large snake and it had held onto him long enough to inject a very large amount of its poisonous venom.

An hour later a tearful Maritza finally left her husband and continued north. As he slipped into unconsciousness Ignacio knew that soon his bones would be picked clean and bleached, a brutal reminder of the dangers of the Arduous Passage.

2

WITH THOSE SMALL blessings and fortuitous events that God sometimes bestows on his wronged children, let it suffice to say that Maritza arrived safely in Tempe and began her mourning and an attempt at recovery. The Ecuadorian community sheltered her, nourished her, and started her on her Americanization. A year later when she finally planned her move to Montauk, New York, she spoke reasonably good English, had acquired an Arizona driver's license, and had a small but much needed savings account. She could clean a home in six hours or work a checkout counter in a grocery chain store. When she boarded the Greyhound bus, she was deemed ready to start a new life.

In Montauk, Ignacio's uncle welcomed Maritza into his home. Carlos Sucreno had a prospering landscaping business and owned several apartment buildings on the East End of Long Island. He knew everyone of import in the Ecuadorian community and introduced Maritza to the people she needed to meet. Soon she was working at the Independent Grocer's Alliance and was able to live on her own in one of Carlos's boarding houses. A few months later he introduced her to one of his workers, a crew chief named Paul Hermanos. Paul had lost a young wife in Cuenca, had endured his own Arduous Passage, and Carlos felt that it was appropriate that the two adults should meet. They were still young enough to begin a new life together. Simpatico they surely were. Sympathetic they naturally were. The few years difference in their ages meant nothing to either of them and after a short courtship they were married.

To Maritza, a new life meant a new family and a new family meant babies. But she was worried. Only a few years ago she had no problem getting pregnant. Getting it to stick had been another matter until Mundin. Now for almost six months she and Paul had tried and so far their efforts were a failure. A friend at work had suggested the free clinic in East Hampton so she made an appointment at the Women's Clinic. The facility had been established by the wealthy and concerned of the Hamptons as a charitable gesture to the growing immigrant work force on the East End. It was staffed for most of the year on a volunteer basis by vacationing NYC physicians, a few retired doctors and a group of nurse practitioners who became the permanent staff.

The NP who interviewed Maritza came to a reasonable and cost-effective first step for her. She concluded that at the age of thirty-five she should be fertile. Two miscarriages and then a term birth just six years ago strengthened that fact. She told Maritza about ovulation and her most fertile period for conception. They talked about abstinence before "O Day", saving the maximum number of sperm for the best time for fertilization. The NP added that perhaps the problem was with her new husband. It would be quicker and cheaper to test Paul first rather than try to do unwarranted fertility studies on Maritza.

For three more ovulatory cycles Maritza followed the nurse's instruction and although one period was almost two weeks late, she was not pregnant. Finally, she decided to talk to Paul.

At first, he laughed at the suggestion and responded with typical male macho braggadocio. "Men never have a problem. Yo soy siempre duro. Always!"

"Yes, you are my tiger, my toro, but we need to know. If it is me it will be very expensive."

They compromised and continued to try the "O Day" technique but when three months later it had failed, Paul relented and agreed to go to the clinic with Maritza.

After a brief discussion with the NP he was given a specimen bottle and told how to proceed. Once again, he balked, but the women cajoled and Maritza even offered a helping hand. Paul took the container and went alone to the toilet room.

When the lab results were made available it was not sanguine information for the Hermanoses. Paul's ejaculate showed very few viable spermatozoa. Most were deformed and had poor motility. To Maritza it was a great disappointment.

Paul began to withdraw from any intimacy even when Maritza would initiate it. Soon he began to come home inebriated and would fall asleep on the sofa. Occasionally he would not come home at all.

One night, Paul stopped at Quito-Quito, a bar favored by Ecuadorians on the East End, and sat alone. After two tequila shots and beer chasers he felt confident enough to go home and face Maritza. He was, politely put, besotted. Singing crudely, he came into the house and found Maritza preparing dinner.

"I am sorry my love. I didn't know I could not make babies for you."

Maritza remained silent and continued her cooking.

"You want niños?" He stood over her and grabbed his crotch. "Not from here, Mama. Tengo una pistola muerta! No bullets, Mama."

He walked around the kitchen, watching his wife who remained silent. Then he continued, "But there are many pistolas around. Good ones. Ones with real bullets." Paul moved toward the door and called back to Maritza. "Go get your niños, chica. Wiggle your tetas and coulu and get your niños!"

Maritza did not know whether or not to laugh at his antics so she cried, for hours she cried. Paul arrived in the morning apologetic and apparently embarrassed by his outbreak but Maritza had been frightened and remained aloof, safe she told herself.

Maritza worked one of the registers at the very busy Amagansett IGA. Most of her co-workers were Hispanics and several were Cuencanos. Her boss, who owned the store, quickly realized that this employee was special. She worked harder, pleased the customers, always had a smile or a laugh for them, and was punctual. Maritza never was late nor had she missed a day of work. Her English was excellent and he trusted her implicitly. Within a few months he had her opening the store and not long afterward she was shutting down as well. This gave him a couple of hours a day to be with his family. When she arrived at work the morning after Paul's antics, she was visibly ill at ease. Candy, the co-worker who had suggested the clinic visit, came up to her and tried to chat.

"A problem from the doctors, Ritza?"

"Yes."

"A problem with you?"

"No. Paul can't have babies."

"Is that why you are upset?"

"Yes. He was saying terrible things and said I should go get my babies from someone else. He said he was a pistola muerta and…oh, I only know that he frightened me."

"But he was drunk. That is not the Paul Hermanos we know."

"But he has been this way since the doctor told us."

"Ritza, he thinks if it works there is nothing wrong, just like all men. You know in Cuenca we say a man's brain is attached to his pee-pee. So, if his pee-pee, his chulo, is no good…well then his brain is no good."

Candy had managed to get Maritza to smile but over the course of the day Candy could see her friend was not herself.

Paul continued to sit in Quito-Quito bemoaning his fate. The tequila had loosened his tongue and he told Tivo Vega about the clinic visit.

"Tivo my friend, how can the damn thing work and be no good? Mumps from those fucking kids crossing the border with us. And now I have a pistola muerta. My new name, Tivo, La Pistola Muerta."

After finishing his beer, the dead gun left for home but that night his new name began to spread through the bar crowd and then through the community.

Naturally Maritza was tormented by what she saw as a deteriorating marriage, a process initiated by Paul's diagnosis and hastened by his behavior. She loved him. Of that she was certain, and she hated to see him punishing himself. But she had no idea of how to change things. Many times since his first outburst, when he was stone sober, he had urged her to "find a gun with bullets". It was as if he had resigned himself to the idea and was trying to win her over, to convince her of the merits of doing so. Slowly and inexorably Maritza began to convince herself that it was Paul's kindness and understanding, his own desire for a family that made him continually suggest she find a sperm donor. She knew Paul would be a wonderful father and the logical sequitur would be to follow his suggestion. But the word "adultery" always came to mind whenever she thought about it. But how she longed to have babies!

3

MARITZA NOTICED THE young man the first time he came through her checkout line at the IGA. She had said hello and an additional nicety just as she did with every customer. But then she looked up at him. He was very young and very handsome. *Almost beautiful,* she thought. Shyly, almost embarrassed to speak to her, he politely replied with a hello and an answer to whatever it was she had said. He paid and then he was gone.

From his Spanish she knew he was Ecuadorian, probably even Cuencano. Almost at once during that brief initial meeting she found herself strangely elated. Even with the next customer, a woman with a week's worth of groceries, she was still buzzing with excitement.

Candy Lopes suddenly appeared behind her.

"Ritza," she whispered. "Did you see that man, that boy? Es un Adonis, no? Could you imagine..." And she broke off with a giggle.

"Candy, I could be his mother. He has chicas chasing him. Young chicas, not old hens like us!"

"But could you imagine?" Then she went back to her register and the next customer.

Several days later their Adonis reappeared. It was late in the day. Probably he was on his way home from work. He had picked up a few items obviously intended for a quick meal. But he had come to Maritza's lane. He could have gone elsewhere, another store or another lane. It happened again two days later and then the following day. Always he appeared at the end of the day and always for a few incidental items. It seemed as though…*But that's nonsense,* she thought, until he spoke and addressed her by her name.

"Buenas tardes, Maritza." The surprise on her face made him laugh. His teeth were white and perfect and his smile was lovely. Still laughing he pointed to her name tag.

Blushing she spoke to him. "Sí, Maritza. Y usted?"

"Osvaldo, Osvaldo Omaya."

He bagged his few items himself, paid and then he left.

When he did not return to the store during the next week, Maritza felt almost lonely, neglected. She chastised herself, calling her feelings nonsense. But she realized that she was more than attracted to this handsome boy. She seemed to have lost Paul, at least for the time being, and all that she had in her life was her job. And when she thought about Osvaldo, she felt that strange warmness a woman feels, a feeling she thought she'd lost for good.

The next week he was back. Almost daily he'd appear close to closing time with some trivial item he'd bring to her register. It began innocently enough. Osvaldo lingered while Maritza prepared to close the store. They chatted about his work, her job, life on the East End. They would leave the store and then each go their own way. But one evening the following week Maritza could not stop herself. She took Osvaldo's hand and led him to her boss's office in the back of the store.

During their lovemaking over the next three months Osvaldo learned intimate details of Maritza's life. Then one day she ran his hand over her belly and spoke quietly, "Uno niño. Uno pequeño Osvaldo."

It was not what he'd expected to happen. It never is in such a situation where a young man is not thinking about the consequences of his actions. He did not know what to say or what to do.

At home Maritza was once again happy. Even Paul, during their infrequent encounters, noticed the smile, the singing, the cleaner house and meals waiting for him when and if he arrived at dinner time. To her husband she looked healthy and perhaps a bit plump but he thought little of it. He was glad that Maritza seemed herself. If she could accept her fate, their fate, perhaps even he could try to do so.

When she began to look pregnant, Paul said nothing but he began once again to withdraw from her and their home. Often he was gone for days. He spent more time at Quito-Quito drinking and talking and again agonizing over his fate as what he now knew was that of a cuckold. He would stagger around the bar, talking and crying to the other men there.

"Mira, amigos. La Pistola Muerta." He would hold his crotch and chant, "Zorro es duro. Siempre duro. Pero yo soy La Pistola Muerta. Y un cornudo. Uno Cachudo."

He would hold his hands and fingers in the universal gesture of cuckoldry and dance singing, "Cachudo, cornudo. Cachudo, cornudo" Dangerously drunk he would proffer imaginary breasts and rub his thighs. "Tetas y culo, amigos, hombres. Ven aqui. Yo soy un falso amor de Maritza."

At some point his friend, Tivo Vega, would rescue Paul and take him to his home to sleep off his indiscretion and embarrassment. But no counsel could keep Paul from repeating his act almost nightly. To his great misfortune one night while he was bemoaning his upcoming fatherhood, Osvaldo was witness to Paul's performance. Names, faces, events and revelation melded into a dangerous confrontation begun by an inebriated Osvaldo's hubris, youthful bravado and taunt.

"Hola, Pistola Muerta. Viejo gallo, viejo toro." He moved toward Paul on tip toe as if a toreador with a cape.

"Venga! Venga! I am good at sticking, Cachudo. Ask her how good I am, Señor Cornudo. I am Zorro."

The crowd who had been laughing at Paul suddenly became deathly silent, shocked by the youth's accusations and taunting. Both matador and ox became a frieze in the center of the bar, a picture in suspended animation. But the foolish Osvaldo resumed his provocation, daring Paul to charge him.

Paul stood, stunned. His mind was a blurred image of the boy in front of him and of Osvaldo coupled with Maritza. Puta! She was old enough to be his mother. This thing taunting him: goading him was a boy, young enough certainly to be his own child. It was too much for a besotted mind to comprehend.

Paul felt a hand dig into his shoulder, turning and pulling him out of the drama, off the stage. Tivo Vega continued moving Paul toward the door, his strong thumb digging into Paul's supraspinatus and making him wince in pain. He continued talking softly to his friend as he led Paul out of the bar.

"Silencio, amigo. Basta. Vamanos muchacho!"

Outside in the parking lot, as they walked toward Tivo's vehicle, Paul was visibly shaking with drunken rage. As the bar door opened behind them, Osvaldo's voice came toward them, seemingly twisting through the dim neon Corona beer light reflected on the cars.

"Buey, castrado, ven aqui."

Paul turned to face the boy. Osvaldo was again on his toes, arms raised above his head as if holding banderillas He repeated his chorus of taunts.

"I am Zorro. Ask her, Cachudo. She is so good to me."

As Osvaldo pirouetted closer, Paul felt Tivo grab his wrist and put something in his hand. Tivo whispered to Paul,

"Toma esto. Le mata. Ahora. Kill him, my friend."

Paul looked down at his hand and saw a knife, the Corona sign's neon lights glinting off its blade. As the boy danced by them, Paul grabbed Osvaldo's hair, lifted his chin and cut his throat.

As Osvaldo fell to the ground a dark face, invisible to Paul and Tivo, moved away from one of the windows beside the door of the bar.

A contractor bag which they found stored in Tivo's trunk served as a shroud for Osvaldo's body. Tivo and Paul folded the body into it and placed it back in the trunk. They drove to the public launch ramp on Three Mile Harbor Road and there Paul and Tivo waded out into the water and sank the bag into the outgoing tide of the bay.

4

MARITZA WAS NOW in her seventh month. She had convinced herself that Osvaldo had left, disappearing from her life because he could not stay and be father to the baby. Also, she was sure that he would not, could not, challenge Paul for the right to be with her. She had no notion of foul play, of Paul's involvement with the youth's absence, but she did wonder why Paul seemed less withdrawn and sometimes even solicitous.

It had been Primitivo Vega who had sat with Paul the night after the murder and planted the seed.

"Paul, amigo, only half the work is done."

Twisting the cap off another beer, Paul, his face void of emotion, stared at his friend.

"The other half remains. La Puta, the whore is still alive and happy. And there will be another Osvaldo, my friend. Another prancing Zorro who will call you names to your face. And the next one might be dangerous and not just a boy."

But Paul was still numb from the knowledge that he had committed murder. He had never been a violent man and would not have thought himself capable of such an act. However, as they talked, as Tivo persuaded, Paul began to envision not only another confrontation, another Zorro, but also began to see life with a child that was not his, a child that always reminded him of his wife's infidelity and his own disgrace. Tivo was right. Maritza was an issue for him. Divorce her? Leave and start a new life elsewhere? But why leave when his life was his own? She, the whore, had ruined it. Or so Paul began to believe.

As he left work a week later, Paul saw Tivo's brown Honda waiting for him. Tivo patted the passenger seat and pushed open the door to let Paul sit down. Vega pushed a small pizza box toward Paul and pointed to the cold beers on the floor.

"I've found the men for the job. Salvadorian brothers from Patchogue. You were right, brother, no Ecuadorian would do this. Except, except me and only for you my brother."

Paul stared at Tivo silently. He could not quite believe what he'd just heard. A few days ago it was just a thought, a discussion between friends of a problem, one which they, rather he, Paul, had to face. Paul had actually dismissed the thought. And now this?

"They don't want much money. Just half a coyote fee for a relative who is coming. For them it is an act of honor for a brother who has been greatly wronged."

Paul raised a cautionary hand trying to silence Vega and then he spoke. "But Tivo, I don't" he paused, "I don't know if…."

"Today you don't know. But look at her again. Watch her talk to the other girls at the IGA. Watch them all touch that whore belly and laugh. I have seen them and they are laughing at you."

And so Paul went and watched and saw what Tivo had described, and it convinced him.

<<<>>>

Like most Cuencanos, most Ecuadorians for that matter, Primitivo Vega was a compact descendant of Incan stock. That made him five foot five, 110 pounds, black-eyed and with wonderfully thick black glossy hair. His nose and cheekbone were made somewhat less prominent than some because of several generations of DNA dilution with Mestizo or other indigenous genomes. But unlike many East End Hispanics he was legal, his parents having emigrated from Cuenca at a time when they could establish green card status and then citizenship. Tivo could have stayed in school and earned a college scholarship based on his grades and his gifted "fútbol" skills. But by the age of sixteen he was working two jobs and playing with the wrong men and girls. He became a fringe player in the community, a procurer, a Yosserian among his army of Ecuadorian workers. If you needed something for work, for home or for your vehicle, Tivo would, for a vigorish, make it appear. From whence it came no one asked. It was his procuring talent that stretched his horizon beyond Suffolk and into Nassau County and eventually into the world controlled by the Guerra brothers.

Molded by years of civil conflict in Salvador, Terzio and Segundo Guerra were hardened mercenaries. They were considered dangerous, unreliable and, depending upon whom you asked, called either scum or caca de caballo, horse shit, and they were as ugly as their reputations. They were both thick set in the upper body and perhaps a bit bandy-legged. Their faces scarred, mustachioed, and pock-marked, they looked the role of villains. Vulgar, almost pornographic tattoos graced (a poor word) their chests and upper shoulders and arms. Segundo's was such that raising his arm away from his body would spread female legs and reveal grossly distorted female pudenda in his axilla. They were simply very, very ugly men in every sense of the word.

The Guerras had a finger in everything illegal which was profitable. They had a Salvadoran/Panamanian fiefdom of several thousand with whom they dealt, and they managed to stay out of jail and thereby avoid deportation. Their files in the Patchogue Police barracks were thick with information about suspected illegal activities and copies of "suspect" interviews for various and sundry crimes. Never was there hard evidence that would permit their arrest and prosecution, but they were often among the "usual suspects" in many investigations. They managed a layer of protection which, like the Teflon-don of NYC fame, kept them just slipping out of prosecutor's fingers.

Tivo's contacts in Nassau had told him about the Guerras, and it was clear that they had arranged "disappearances" and that nothing was beyond their capability if the remuneration, was appropriate. So, when Tivo sat with them that Saturday evening sharing arroz con pollo and lap candy, they were very sympathetic to Paul's plight and offered their services as "men of honor".

5

As the *Ruby-Belle* drifted east over the inner rip close to the lighthouse near Shagwong point on a brisk outgoing tide, Dr. Jack Martin retrieved his weighted squid fly until the 650 grain tip of his fly line was near the tip of his rod and then he again let out the fifty feet of running line. It was cheating twice over, as it rested his casting arm and always kept the exotic fly at least six or seven feet down in the water column. His son-in-law, Arden, was energetically working a diamond jig on or just above the bottom in the twenty-five feet of water beneath the boat. It was their first drift that morning and both men were not as yet "in the game" because both had missed strikes.

It was a crisp October morning. The thermometer at the house had read 50 degrees Fahrenheit but the sun and blue sky suggested it would warm rapidly. On board the *Ruby-Belle* they had to sponge condensation from the console and cushions. With a dry place to sit they had cast off lines and headed out of Lake Montauk.

Midway through his next retrieve Jack's line stopped suddenly, and he pulled back briskly on the line, setting the hook into a fish.

"How about a ten-dollar bet on the first fish Arden? Up for that? You're jigging the bottom and should be in the zone all the time."

The young man turned toward Jack and was about to up the ante when he saw the bend in Jack's rod and the grin on his face.

"Why do they eat that damn fly anyway? The jig is more appetizing and I should be outfishing you."

"It's finesse and talent, my boy. Stick with me and you'll learn."

Arden racked his rod and reached for the large net stowed in the rocket launcher above the center console.

"This is a good fish Arden, he doesn't want to come up,"

The fish took Jack once around the boat and then finally, at the transom, he brought the bass to the surface and into the net. Jack slipped the barbless hook from its jaw and then picked up the bass with the BogaGrip.

"Almost thirteen inches! Yummy good eating so into the well."

He watched the fish resting quietly in the live well and fit the fly into one of the guides on his rod.

"OK, Arden, I'll run us up to the top again and the next drift will be all yours. No fly in the water to lure the fish away from your jig."

Jack took the *Belle* above the rip and kept her on course so they drifted over the productive structure, a reef-like elevation on the sea floor where fish would linger. A minute or so later Jack heard Arden grunt and set vigorously on the jig. The rod bent dangerously as line peeled slowly and steadily from the reel.

"Bottom?" queried Jack.

Arden tightened the drag and whatever was on the jig slowly began to move with the boat.

"I don't know, Dad. If this is a bass it must be a cow."

As they moved across the rip and the boat picked up speed, the line once again began to move off of Arden's reel.

"They've had a couple of sixty pounders but they were caught outside, not in here."

Once past the rip and into quieter and shallower water Jack stemmed the boat against the tide as Arden struggled to recover line.

"No head shake or anything. It's almost dead weight!"

They never would have guessed how prescient his words were but ten minutes later as the breeze pushed them toward the quiet water nearer shore an image began to form in the water next to the boat.

"Oh my God, Dad, Get over here! It's a body. A person!"

Jack took one look and went into action. He opened the forward hatch, dropped the anchor and fixed the line to the bow cleat. Then he went to the radio.

"Take my cell and call 911, Dad!"

"Let me call the marina first. They'll get the harbor police or Coast Guard out here."

Twenty minutes later the small pontoon Coast Guard vessel pulled alongside the *Ruby-Belle.*

"Dr. Martin? Mr. Alden?"

"Yup, right on both counts," Jack replied. "Do you have a good boat hook or gaff or do you need ours?"

One of the Guards was in a wetsuit and preparing to enter the water.

"Don't think you need to go in. We're only in eight feet and I think Arden can bring it up for you."

In five minutes the bloated and crab-nibbled body of a young male was on the Coast Guard boat and headed back to base in Lake Montauk.

Jack walked over to his son-in-law and put a calming hand on his shoulder.

"Tough. Doesn't happen often, I guess. Bad luck for you. For him! Whoever he is. We should have had a camera on board. You might have made the cover of Long Island Fisherman with that catch."

"Thanks Dad, after that harrowing experience, I need to catch a fish this morning to make the day right again."

Jack started the boat as Arden lifted and stowed the anchor and he prepared them for another drift.

6

TIVO HAD A plan to cover his part of the payment to the Guerras easily enough and even then some. For weeks he'd been watching the "Aero Banco", the cash express window in the Hispanic grocery in Montauk. Friday paychecks were collected and air expressed to Ecuador as cash on Saturday. The commission was minimal so business was brisk and it was even better every other Friday as many were paid on a bi-weekly schedule.

The Guerras had offered their 'services to Tivo for 10K. He agreed reasoning that Paul was good for 5K and he could cover the other half with an illicit bet at the Boleto.

And there was an added incentive for Tivo at the Boleto. Everyone who played the local lottery or numbers knew that occasionally the fix was on but, for the large part, the man who ran it played it straight. Also, no one had come forth to bankroll a competitive game. Old Francisco remained the only show in town.

One of the runners, a numbers bagman, had told Tivo to visit Francisco, to "stop in and say hello". Tivo left that visit smiling because he had been told to play a 2K wager the next week. Of course, a kickback would have to be made, but in Tivo's winning, the 5K for the Guerras was about to be raised plus an extra sum for his efforts. All he had to do was find the 2K.

Tivo checked the doors and windows of the store and of the health food shop adjoining it. Both were solidly built and alarmed so there could be no frontal assault. In the rear of the building were a dumpster, some trash cans, a 55-gallon drum and two doors. Both were certainly wired. About eight feet or so above the ground and mounted into a stainless plate with what looked like six large stainless bolts was the exhaust fan for the deli. Tivo knew that if he could remove the fan, he'd have easy access to the store and the cash.

On several occasions he'd visited the deli at lunch time. He chatted up one of the cooks who seemed to enjoy the attention. He took his half eaten grilled Cuban sandwich and followed her into the small kitchen.

"Hola, chica. So this is where you work? Do you do your best work here or elsewhere?"

He noticed that she blushed and smiled. He looked at the fan and saw it was not fixed on the inside.

"It must get hot in the kitchen. Do you get all hot working in here?"

She was young and attractive. Clearly worth pursuing when all his work was done.

"Well, chica, I have to go." He held up the remains

of his sandwich as he left the kitchen. "Is all your work this tasty? I shall have to try more of it."

As he left the kitchen he noted the simple hasp lock on the drawer under the "bank" window. It could all be done quickly and easily. He only had to wait two days.

7

ABOUT FIFTY FEET north of the railroad crossing on the west side of Abraham's Landing Path was a house that had recently been sold and left unoccupied. More a teardown than a fixer-upper, the original owners had finally realized that not many people wanted to be within spitting distance of the trains as they passed just south of the house. They had finally lowered their absurd asking price enough that someone was willing to make an offer and it sold. The two structures behind the house, a large shed and a larger garage, had both been rented by a young landscape gardener. He had more than once made a fair offer for the property but the owner had refused and then not renewed the man's lease. Months later, either too embarrassed or proud to call him, they sold below his standing offer, leaving no one very happy. The house was now shuttered and boarded closed.

Tivo wandered around and found an old root cellar or coal chute entry shaft with steps leading into the basement. The small underground space was little more than a furnace room for the coal burner now converted to oil. He found stairs and came out into the kitchen. Enough light came through the boarded windows to let him explore the parlor and dining room and toilet on that floor. The abandoned old furniture would be adequate for living there while he and the Guerras planned their business. Tivo turned on the valve under the toilet and was pleased to hear the water closet fill. Back in the kitchen he walked up to the old gas stove, a 40s model on legs, found a box of matches and lit a burner. The electricity was off but all else was functional. As long as they were quiet and careful it was perfect. Outside again he walked back to the garage and popped the padlock from the hasp and opened one of the doors. The space was essentially empty.

Tivo knew that it would be months before any demolition or work permits could be filed and approved. All he and the Guerra brothers needed was a week or two and then they would be gone, their work completed.

8

IT WAS FIVE p.m. on Friday, the magic Friday, Payday Friday, and Tivo was anticipating being flush with cash before the evening was over. He went to his Honda, drove the few blocks to the IGA and went inside. He picked up a ready-made sandwich and a six pack and stood in the check-out line. He could have gone to the express line but chose the register run by Maritza. She smiled warmly as she scanned his purchases.

"No mas, señor?"

Tivo shook his head and put a twenty on the conveyor. She was pretty. And with her now bigger pechas, those momma titties, she would be fun for the boys. The Guerras would enjoy their job. Puta! Whore!

Tivo drove east to Montauk and parked in the space behind Johnny's Bait and Tackle shop, from where he could watch the deli. The last customer had left some time ago and the cook had finished her clean up and was walking out. Finally, when the owner and his wife had set the alarm and turned off the lights, they exited the building and doubly locked the front door. At ten o'clock, Tivo drove to the area behind the deli. He positioned the Honda so that it somewhat sheltered him from view of passers-by, as he would be working. Then he put pliers, wrench and screwdriver in a jacket pocket and walked to the back of the building. Emptying the contents of the 55-gallon drum into a smaller can and dumpster, he inverted the drum under the fan and vaulted up onto it. The drum gave forth a resonant bass "boing" as it received his weight.

He turned on his small LED light briefly to confirm what needed to be done and then went quickly and quietly to work.

Greased by the exhaust from the kitchen cooking, all of the bolts were uncorroded and easily removed. As he put the sixth in his pocket the fan settled in its sleeve. Tivo slid the fan slowly outward and onto his shoulder. Its thirty or forty pounds of weight added to his own exceeded the tolerance of the rusted base of the drum and his left leg broke through a thinned area, tearing his jeans and badly lacerating his leg from the ankle to the knee before he finally wound up kneeling with his good leg on the drum. The loss of footing and sudden shift of weight caused Tivo to fall to his left, toppling the drum, fan, and Tivo onto the ground with a considerable and reverberating cacophony of sound. He had to bend rusted metal from around the rent in the drum before he could painfully extract his leg. He found and directed the LED onto the leg and saw he was bleeding profusely. A car had stopped, its headlights aimed on Tivo. He waved to his audience and then limped to the tan Honda and drove away.

The car moved slowly to the area Tivo had vacated. The driver, a fisherman headed to the beach at Ditch Plains, realized immediately that he'd interrupted a robbery and reached for his cell phone. There was a bit of typical autumn ground fog settling in from the beach only a block away so it was difficult to see the plate on the car, but he could tell it was a NY plate. The car? An old Honda sedan. The man? Short and stocky and probably Hispanic.

So the police report had only a vague description of car and driver but the detectives had a DNA sample from the blood on the drum collected and stored.

Finally back at home, Tivo showered and wrapped his leg in a clean shirt, took two Tylenol with two beers, and tried to sleep. It had not been a good night and he would have to deal, to bargain with, the Guerras with limited funds. That was not a pleasant prospect. Tivo had not been completely honest with Paul. The Guerras did want ten thousand US dollars for the job. But he was sure that after the two had enjoyed Maritza's body before they killed her, they would be happy with just Paul's 5K. If not, well, they could be dealt with. Vigilantes, good Ecuadorian men, would be happy to treat them to an early exit from the US. The police in Patchogue would love to have the Guerra brothers booked as murder suspects. And there might just be a witness somewhere out there.

9

PAUL MET WITH Tivo and the Guerras only once and that was to hand them five thousand dollars. The brothers looked at Tivo who mollified them with a look and a gesture. Since their arrival the day after Tivo's botched burglary they'd stayed at the safe house and had nightly traveled the short distance to the IGA to watch Maritza close the store and then leave for home

Each day the brothers, especially Segundo, became more descriptive of what they would do to Maritza before they would "cut the whore baby out of the whore mother's body". Tivo did not enjoy these rantings and the latest, "a whore sandwich", with Maritza positioned between the two brothers was too vivid for him. But he did have to admit that they did have interesting imaginations. He left the men and went to his own home.

Tivo was awakened at five a.m. by a throbbing in his injured leg. This was the first time that Tylenol and a couple of beers hadn't let him sleep through the night.

The pain wasn't just in the area of the laceration but now up and into his groin. He turned on the light and looked at his leg.

The swelling had increased markedly in the last twelve hours and when he pressed a finger into the flesh of his thigh it left a deep impression. He knew that he would not get back to sleep so he made some coffee and turned on the TV.

He knew that in spite of his twice a day washing and care of the injury the wound was clearly infected. Tivo was sure that he could not safely go to a clinic for medical care so he instead went to talk to the chica at White's Pharmacy in Montauk and she picked out dressings and antibiotic cream for him. She also slipped a dose pack of a third-generation cephalosporin into his package. By the following Friday scabs had given way to purulent, painful, draining wounds and he noted tender red lines running from the knee up to his groin. He could smell a sickeningly sweet odor to the wound, and he felt this was ominous. He knew he must see a doctor but tomorrow was the day they had planned to avenge Paul Hermanos.

For the Guerras, life in the closed-up house had not been bad. For the three days they'd watched Maritza come and go from the IGA, life for them was better than it should have been. They had spent Friday night honing their skills with two Salvadorian whores they'd brought in by train for the occasion, and when Tivo came limping into the house at ten a.m. on Saturday morning wondering why the men had not met him at the IGA, the mess strewn on the floor and the four undulating bodies on the sofas explained everything.

Showered and dressed, the whores were sent off to the train and the three men went over their plans one more time. It was simple and easy, an uncomplicated strategy for uncomplicated men. Tivo would drive the Honda to the IGA at six. The Guerras would wait near Maritza's car until she'd locked the store and approached her vehicle. They would grab her, take her keys and with Segundo holding her on the floor in the rear of the car, brother Terzio would drive out of the lot and then follow Tivo out and onto the back roads of Amagansett to the isolated area they had designated for their crime. It would be that easy. The Guerras needed a nap so Tivo went back home for a few hours.

He returned at six and then the three of them drove the few blocks to the IGA where Tivo parked in the NW corner of the lot. Segundo opened the door and stepped out onto the blacktop.

"Where are you going?" queried Tivo. "It's too early."

"Vega, you smell and besides, I'm hungry. I'll be back." Segundo strode toward the IGA and disappeared around the corner of the building.

"Your brother is crazy, Terzio. Someone will see him. He's a stranger here and perhaps someone will remember."

The older man looked at Tivo and then reached for the door.

"He's right, Tivo, you smell. And I also am hungry. We had a busy night and have to prepare for another." He followed his brother's path to the supermarket and found Segundo in the rear of the store by the rotisserie in the deli section. Segundo was waiting for a chicken to be quartered. He slipped the meat into a foil lined insulating bag. He turned toward his brother.

"Cervezas, por favor, mi hermano. Dos Equis."

As Terzio left to find the beer his brother chatted up the girl at the counter and then grabbing a handful of paper napkins he walked toward the front of the store. He found Terzio staring at Maritza. Segundo nodded toward her register, muttered "Mira, la puta," and then walked up to the conveyor at her station.

She smiled innocently at them not knowing why they had laughed when she had greeted them. They paid without speaking and then walked out of the store. A voice called to Maritza from the next register,

"Ritza, dos hombres feos!"

Yes, she thought, *two ugly men.*

Back in the Honda the brothers ate voraciously and sloppily, bits of skin and bone falling in the car or landing just outside on the pavement.

"You make my car a mess, amigos."

"Vega, at least the chicken smells better than you do. Come, eat some, you will need your strength."

Tivo declined, too anxious to be hungry.

Segundo belched loudly and looked at his watch. "Es la hora. Vamonos."

The brothers wiped their hands on the paper napkins and on the car seat and then brushed detritus from their jackets as they walked toward Maritza's car. Stopping a few yards away they leaned against a convenient laundry truck and sucked their teeth. Segundo elbowed his brother.

"First in the ass, brother. As a lesson to the whore. And then in the front. If we are lucky, we can show her the whore baby before she dies. But I will have to be fast with the knife."

It had taken a few minutes to get the last customer out of the store, and she'd had to say "no" to an even later arrival, but she had finally locked the office and set the alarm and now she had forty seconds to leave the store and lock the front doors.

Terzio looked toward the glass front of the store. "Light just out in the store. She is coming."

Moments later she was walking toward her car.

They stepped out of Maritza's line of sight and waited.

10

THE GAME SHOULD have been a lopsided victory for the Bridge Hampton Killer Bees but East Hampton had decided otherwise and had come to play hard. The Bees had scored on their first possession but then so did East Hampton leading many in the stands to believe that the highly rated Bees defense had missed the bus. Dusk was falling as the field clock ran down to zero with the score at 45-38 in favor of Bridge Hampton. It had been the kind of exciting offensive battle that even at the end of the third quarter it was evident that whoever was in the lead in the closing seconds would be the eventual winner.

Parents and coaches searched memory for a higher scoring and greater total yardage game and the sports pages in the next day's papers would confirm that the game set new records in many categories. Everyone, win or lose, left the field exhilarated. Two couples, seniors from East Hampton High, piled into the restored '57 Chevy belonging to one of the boys and left the parking area in a loose caravan of cars. Driving north they skirted town and headed for a new barbecue restaurant, "Ribs and Chix", that had opened during the summer and had at once become an immediate success as a hang-out for East End teens and not just a few of their parents.

The owners, Jasmin and Ty Green, had been trained by Ty's parents who ran a very successful southern style pulled pork palace just east of the Nassau/Queens border. Timing was perfect for the young restaurateurs to move east and set up their own eatery.

They sold no alcohol and vigorously discouraged brown bagging. Both teens and parents respected the house rules. Tonight over one hundred parents, students and friends had arrived for dinner and had quickly filled the inner spaces and spilled out onto picnic tables and tailgates to celebrate competition, friendship and a soft fall evening.

As they had for the last year Fred Allison and Jim McAfee were double dating the Stephenson twins, Julie and Caitlin. The two couples were inseparable and fast friends. The girls had early morning church choir rehearsal the next day, so the foursome helped pick up trash outside the restaurant and then after saying goodbye to the Greens they walked over to Fred's wonderful blue and ivory convertible.

With no booze on board and because he drove his car proudly and carefully, Fred traveled slowly across back roads toward Amagansett until they turned right and headed south toward town. Only then did Fred turn down the radio and ease the speedometer past forty. It was a straight shot home from where they were and they were early enough to enjoy a few minutes alone before the girls had to be home. A moment later, Caitlin, seated next to Fred and under his right arm bolted upright and screamed.

<<<>>>

When Maritza saw the knives in the hands of the two men approaching her, she assumed a robbery and offered her purse. Terzio took and opened it and found her car keys. He opened her car and they pushed her onto the floor in front of the rear seat where Segundo held her down with his feet until they were out of the parking area. Tivo Vega led the way in his own car as the getaway.

Patience was never one of Segundo's virtues so as soon as he had pulled her up onto the seat next to him, he reached for the buttons on her coat. Unbuttoning it he tore open her blouse, ripped apart her bra and began to fondle her breasts. But his big mistake came not from his hands but from his mouth. He leaned toward Maritza and hissed into her ear.

"Whore, we are going to take your whore baby out of your belly and feed it to the rats. But first we will let you play whore for us, all of us. For free you will fuck us. Just like you did Omaya. Poor little Osvaldo. We killed him and fed him to the sharks."

Maritza paled and grew cold. She felt her stomach knot and begin to turn itself inside out propelling its contents upward and outward as a projectile onto and into Segundo's face and chest.

"Bitch! Filthy bitch! Is this how you treat your lovers?" Wiping vomit from his face he reached into his pocket, pulled out his switchblade and held it in front of her.

Again, a bolus of bile and tortilla hit him as he lunged at her, stopping him, even making him move away from her. With great difficulty Maritza pulled her feet up and pushed them against Segundo, moving him even further from her and placing herself against the rear door. Terzio had slowed almost to a stop and was turning to view the combat in the rear seat. Maritza took the opportunity to feel for the door handle, find it and pull it up opening the rear door. She kicked again violently and tumbled out onto the road. Desperately she righted herself and ran stumbling away from the car and back toward town. Terzio had finally pulled off the road and they were now both out of the car and chasing her, Segundo cursing like a madman.

Tivo glanced in his rearview mirror and seeing no following car did a quick U-turn back to the south along the road. A few moments later he saw them highlighted in his high beams and watched as Terzio grabbed Maritza and threw her down onto the gravel shoulder. He pulled off the road near them and limped over to the melee now moved to the mown grass strip bordering the county road.

Segundo had his knife busy cutting away the remainder of Maritza's clothing from her body, wildly throwing the rag pieces aside. In moments she was naked and with Terzio's help he had turned her over onto her hands, knees and belly. He tore open his trousers and mounting her from behind he screamed at her.

"Is this how you did it for Osvaldo, whore? Did you let him do this to you?"

She couldn't scream. She couldn't even cry out. She did try to die but did not know how. She prayed for the help to die but the help did not come.

Segundo convulsed and turned toward Tivo.

"Your turn, amigo, and hurry while she is still fresh and alive."

Tivo turned away and shook his head. Segundo looked at Terzio.

"Brother, come. One more before we turn her over."

They switched places and while Terzio sodomized the woman Segundo shoved the end of his still erect penis at her face.

"Look, whore. You made him happy and he wants more. You are a good whore, puta."

Tivo limped away, unable to watch as the brothers rolled Maritza onto her back.

As Segundo entered her, he looked up and in an instant had lost his erection. Two headlights were coming at them from the north and were adding their brilliance to that from the Honda's headlights. He froze, illuminated full face and leaning over Maritza, he rapidly reached again for his knife and brought it up into the light.

"We have to go, whore, but first we take out the whore baby."

He began a cut at her right hip bone and carried it up and under her ribs and then across and down toward her left hip bone. But before he could complete the cut, Terzio had lifted him by the collar and was dragging him toward Tivo's Honda. As he struggled to lift and close his trousers Segundo thought he heard a scream and turned toward Maritza. He freed himself from his brother's grasp, spit in the direction of the woman lying on the road and tossed his knife into the field next to the road. The approaching car screeched to a stop as the men sped away.

<<<>>>

Caitllin Stephenson was fearless. She was out of the car and on the road beside the woman before Fred had turned off the ignition. She immediately recognized Maritza from the IGA.

"Call 911, Fred. Hurry and then bring me the blanket from the back of the car."

In a moment she had covered the unconscious woman and then the horror of what she was witnessing hit her and she collapsed sobbing.

The ambulance arrived in less than five minutes and was immediately followed by two East Hampton Police vehicles. Moments later Maritza was speeding toward South Hampton Hospital with an IV pouring precious warmed fluids into her body and a mask delivering equally important oxygen to her lungs and to her baby. The police cordoned the area, and while one group searched the ground carefully, Detective Captain McKeon stood next to his squad car in which the four teens were seated. Parents, notified by the police, began to arrive a few minutes later. They listened in quiet disbelief as Fred and Caitlan repeated once again what they had seen from the car as they approached.

There had been three men involved in the assault. Of that there was no question. Two were fairly well seen in the headlights and identified as short and dark, probably Hispanic. One seemed to be pulling the other who was trying to pull up his pants. The third, the one ahead of the others and headed toward the car, had a pronounced limp. They'd only seen him take a few labored steps as he struggled to enter and start the car but he was almost dragging the leg. His left leg, they agreed. Fred demonstrated the circumducting gait of a stiff or locked prosthetic leg. Could they identify them? Possibly the two best seen. But not for sure. Once again Caitlin emphasized how "ugly" they were. Not because of what they had done but because that was her first reaction to seeing their faces. Did they have weapons? Other than what they thought was a knife? No! Had the youths been drinking? An emphatic no and a choral "test us" was the answer.

Jim and Julie could only attest to the one man lurching along and the other two running more normally. From the vantage of the rear seat they could not be sure of more than that.

A few minutes later another detective team arrived, set up bright lights around the crime scene and began a second search of the area. They took fingerprints from Maritza's vehicle and DNA samples from the torn garments found where the woman had been brutalized. Slowly the footprint of the crime took shape. Using the teen's information, the detectives could see where Maritza had lain, the drag scuffs where Terzio had pulled his brother from her body and the strange heel prints where Segundo had dug in, struggling to get back into his trousers as they dashed to escape. Even the toe drags of Vega's strange gate shown clearly in the bright halogens. In the brush about twenty feet from the road they found the blood-stained knife.

McKeon stood, note pad in hand, and for a third and final time he went over what the young people had told him. They had no additions for him and he did not want them to begin to fabricate. They would have time to think about what they saw, clarify it in their minds and then, once again, go over it with him the next day. He reminded the four and their parents that they were the only witnesses to what might yet be a murder and that the testimony and recounting of the event might be required repeatedly. He also suggested that it would be prudent to have parents drive everyone home.

Before heading home himself, McKeon made sure that the crime scene was secured and the road blocked and fully cordoned at either access. A squad car and two officers were left to "coop", assuring no one would disrupt anything. In the light of day they would make a third sweep of the area, confirming the previous evening's findings and hoping to find another piece of evidence.

11

DR. JACKSON, CALL from EMS for you. Line one on your radio."

Charlene Jackson was the newest member of the SHH Emergency room team. She was handpicked by her boss because of her excellent credentials, her take charge attitude and her history of exceptional athleticism both on the basketball court and the Judo mat. Standing six-foot two, she fit her black skin like a glove and was able to take command in any emergency situation with grace and efficiency.

Charlene had heard the unit leave and wondered what they would bring back to her ER. It was too late for them to ask if she wanted to share a pizza so a call ahead meant something of significance. She sat at her desk, turned on the dispatch radio and crossed her fingers.

"Jackson. Go ahead, EMS."

"Hope you're sitting down, Doc. Mid-thirties Hispanic female, partially disemboweled, raped and probably sodomized. Also, I'm afraid she looks about seven months pregnant. Second liter of Ringer's running in and vitals are stable, if a bit shaky. No active bleeding at this time. ETA less than ten minutes."

When he heard nothing, the EMS tech was back on the air. "Jackson, you there?"

"Gotcha EMS. We'll be ready."

Charlene left her office and grabbed two nurses as she headed for the isolation and intervention suite. The room was equipped to start an operation and, if need be, even open a chest and clamp one of the intra thoracic great vessels in a temporizing and life saving measure.

Briefly she explained what was coming and what she wanted and in the next minute gave the registrar a list of chores: no patient would be seen in the next hour unless it was another crash; get a surgeon and an obstetrician in the ER immediately; notify the OR to get ready for a lap and a C-section. Also tell them to send Anesthesiology down to the ER stat, double stat. And, oh yes, notify Peds that a preemie might be on the way and then call the blood bank. Have their tech ready to work and have him get two units of O Negative ready.

Charlene opened a central venous pressure, subclavian access set and put it next to an open, sterile gown and gloves. She made sure the warmer had several liters of IV saline and had the nurses get absorbent pads for the floor which she expected to get flooded with irrigation fluids.

Two minutes before the estimated time of arrival

and they were ready, rechecked, locked and loaded. They sat down and waited. Finally, a short single toot of the siren was heard as the EMS team turned onto the road leading to the hospital. "One if by land": the patient was still viable and stable. "Two if by sea" meant sinking ship. They had all heard the one "boip" and knew they would be very busy.

"Good! We have a shot," was all Charlene needed to say as she and the two other women saw the flashing lights stop at the entry to the ER. She was putting on gown and gloves as the gurney came into the room. Maritza was carefully transferred to the operating table. Charlene removed the sterile cover from her patient and gasped.

"Oh, my God! Who the fuck…sorry, let's get to work. Warm saline packs in axillae and groins. Hang warm Ringer's solution in the peripheral line and let's get her central line in."

Someone quickly slipped a rolled-up sheet between Maritza's shoulder blades as Charlene painted the woman's neck and shoulder and upper chest with Betadine. She then dropped a fenestrated drape over the area and quickly felt for bony landmarks: sternal notch and the angle of the mid-clavicle. Without taking her eyes off of her small field or moving her left hand, Charlene picked up the syringe with its long needle. Carefully sliding the needle under her thumb and then under the clavicle toward the sternal notch she kept suction on the syringe. She began her mantra, "No lung, no artery, just…VEIN."

At once the syringe filled with dark venous blood.

"Gotcha! Damn, Jackson, you are good!"

Holding the needle motionless with her left hand she removed the attached syringe and slipped a flexible wire into and through the needle positioning it in the woman's subclavian vein. She withdrew the needle and after another brief maneuver she slipped a three lumen over the wire and past the vein into the vena cava just above the heart. Now they could administer huge volumes if it became necessary. But first Charlene withdrew thirty cc. of blood and put it into smaller tubes for the lab and the blood bank. As she watched the specimens head out of the room, she sutured the catheter in place and applied a sterile dressing. Finally, she attached a venous pressure monitor and began an additional infusion of warm fluid.

Charlene looked up and saw her surgeon walk into the room. She just shook her head and gave him a half smile with her eyes, wrinkling them just a bit.

"OK ladies, rape smears and a Foley." She took off her gown and gloves and walked toward Dr. Jack Acquavella.

As did most of the hospital staff, Jack Acquavella lived only ten minutes from either his office or the hospital and its O.R. When weather and spare time permitted, he could and often did walk to work. Well trained and well respected in the community he had none of the elitism or airs that his Milanese patrician ancestry might have left in his genome. Married and with two boys in lower school he was a consummate husband, father and staff member.

He leaned against the soft blue sterility of the tile wall of the room as Charlene finished her taping. If he was worried about what he'd been told it did not show. His maroon and white pin-striped button-down collar shirt was open at the neck and tie-less. He was a tall 6'3" and carried himself well. His chinos were neat and without designer logo. Bare feet fit comfortably into what must have been his after-work loafers. The ability to dress as he was attired at that moment was one of the main reasons he was in Suffolk county and not back in Manhattan. There was a time and a place for a suit and tie and Jack felt it was not in the ER after hours.

"Jack, it isn't pretty," Charlene said. "But she's stable and we can move her as soon as you say go."

As she spoke, the anesthesiologist walked into the busy room and Jack spoke to him from the board of monitors, watching Maritza's vital signs.

"She's a bit shocky but looks stable. Young, thank God, but she's lost a good portion of her blood volume. I think you'd better tube her before we go any further. Just in case she crumps. Dr. Jackson has not as yet dignified us with a look at the wound. Probably lucky!"

In moments Maritza was intubated and on a ventilator, thus stabilizing at least one more system. Charlene regloved and was about to uncover the woman's abdomen when the obstetrician arrived with fetal monitor and Doppler in hand. Grady Liebovitz was the kind of doc every patient fell in love with. Always smiling and showing perfect teeth, curly rust colored hair always slightly tousled, alligator belt just a bit low under a minimal middle-age pot, he had a voice that should be in the movies. And he was good! "Give her a dose of Betamethasone as I expect we'll be sectioning her," he said. "If she is only seven months, I'd prefer a second dose in twelve to twenty-four, but we have what we have."

"Dr. Jackson." It was the registrar on overhead. "Police have a tentative ID and I ran our computer. Nothing in it. Name is Maritza Hermanos, a thirty-six-year-old Ecuadorian who works at the IGA. Probably illegal. That's it."

They watched as the steroid was hung and run into the IV The drug would stimulate maturation of a fetal lung and worked best over a day or two. But in this emergent situation Grady hoped that having the strong medication cross the placental barrier into the fetal bloodstream would at least mean the newborn would have it on board. Everyone in the room knew that the best place for a seven-month fetus was in the uterus until it was a month older. An irritable uterus, premature labor, could be dealt with. Contractions could be stopped with a tocolytic agent or good old ethanol if that were needed. But any hint of fetal distress or compromised placental blood flow or other maternal health issue should override all consideration. A baby in the ICU, even a small baby, was safer than one in a shaky environment.

As Charlene removed the sterile drape from Maritza's chest and abdomen, what struck them, other than the horror of the fact revealed, was the bizarre image created by the young woman's breasts and nipples and the inverted "U" incision. Looking at them was in effect an unhappy face, a very unhappy face. Quickly Charlene poured more Betadine over the lower abdomen and groin and Dr. Leibovitz gloved and stepped to the table. While Charlene shot a generous amount of sterile gel onto the abdominal skin above the pelvic bone, Grady began to move his Doppler probe, searching for the placenta and the fetus.

"Reasonable placental flow. There, look at the color display. Constricted but OK. Amazing. And let me just, there, there is the fetal heart and notice 'he' is moving. But I'll bet he's still chilly. Let's get him upstairs. Jack I'll be ready as soon as you let me in the field."

"No you don't, Grady," Jack put an arm over the obstetrician's shoulder. "You start this one with me, buddy. You are needed." And the two men started for the door. Jack stopped,

"Here's the blood. Take time to warm it and then push one and start the second. Charlene can you join us? We'd be glad to have the hands."

Grady Leibovitz turned back toward Charlene and added, 'Jackson, he just likes a young body next to him in the OR and mine won't do."

Charlene laughed then said, "If it's clear here I'll stay with you. I'll escort her with Anesthesia and then stay if I can." She turned to the nurses behind her and added, "I want to be ready to roll in three minutes. Check on the OR and the elevator."

In less than two minutes they were on the elevator on the way to the OR.

12

PREPPED AND THEN draped in an operative field that went from her neck to her thighs, Maritza Hermanos and her unborn son were given into the hands of the team now assembled in the operating room. The head nurse had to rally her staff's courage when they first saw the wound and pregnant belly but they were all now ready to do what they were well trained to do, save lives.

Under the drapes a fetal monitor positioned less than ideally on Maritza's loins kept them apprised of the intrauterine inhabitant. They were concerned lest an already stressed fetus be endangered by the addition of anesthetic agents and sedatives into his system, so the anesthesiologist used as little as possible to keep his patient just asleep, amnesic and not moving.

With a full staff that now included Charlene Jackson, Jack Acquavella began exploration of the wound and abdomen. Beginning at the right iliac crest the abdominal wall, all layers of its musculature, had been divided into the peritoneal cavity. This continued to be the case upward and then medially toward the base of the sternum but then the wound became more and more superficial until only skin and underlying fatty tissue were divided at the left iliac crest.

Although the expanded uterus had pushed most of the abdominal contents upward, compressing them above it, portions of her large and small bowel were still in the depths of the abdomen. They all knew that a knife blade moving in the abdomen could nick or puncture almost any organ and that the entire abdominal contents would have to be visually and manually examined. But in spite of the fact that Maritza was partially eviscerated at the crime scene, they saw no intestinal contents, no food or feces or bile, free in the abdomen. This was a favorable finding of miracle magnitude. Terzio's horse collaring of his brother mid-assault with his knife had probably saved Maritza's life, but only time would tell.

Jack Aquavella spoke first. "I've got to have more room to see everything and we need to look at everything. Absolutely everything."

He deepened the incision across the midline and down the left side until he could lift a flap. completely exposing the contents of her abdomen. He then took cultures of the fluids in the abdomen and especially in the deepest pelvis. Then he and Grady examined every inch of stomach, liver and intestines. Except for a partial laceration of the cecum next to the appendix everything else was uninjured. The small defect was repaired. Jack looked from Grady to Charlene and shook his head.

"I know the Turks did this in their, hah, ethnic cleansings in the early nineteen hundreds. They even cut open a uterus and took out the fetus while the dying mother watched. The coco lords have even done it recently in their battles of revenge. But here? Now? I never could have imagined such brutality." He paused and turned to the next pressing issue.

"OK, team, what about Junior?"

Charlene spoke up at once.

"I vote out. Get him out alive."

Grady Leibovitz, as the man of the hour, studied the fetal monitor and then wet his hands and slid them down the sides and then around the uterus that was filling most of the abdomen. He paused. Turning his body slightly he lifted and peeked into the depths of the wound.

"Direct one of those overhead lights down into the pelvis."

One hand came out with a firm, lemon sized blood clot. Then he felt carefully again. Resting his hands on the drapes he was quiet for a minute.

"Firstly, this is not a clean wound. It was made on a roadside assault by filthy people. Sorry. No matter what we do preventively and prophylactically she may yet pus it out. That means a mess and a huge risk for Junior. Add to that, she is not going to be a good candidate for a vag delivery any time soon. Secondly, my Doppler suggests that he is thirty-four weeks or close to it. No sweat there. Lastly if for some reason other than infection she crumps, he's a goner."

He put his hands back down along the uterus and came out with a fresh blood clot. He felt again and then reached for and carefully positioned a retractor.

"She's got a small hematoma in the uterine wall and some active bleeding. It must have been lacerated with the very first movement of the knife. That clinches it, team. I agree with Dr Charlene. Out he comes. Do we have more blood in the room?"

There were two more units of red blood cells in the warmer and Grady asked that one be administered while he readied for the C-section.

"When did you last see a section, Dr. Jackson?"

Charlene couldn't remember exactly but it had to have been as a third-year student and that was now—how many?—seven or eight years ago.

"It's been a while, Grady."

"Then you can assist me. Charlene please change places with me."

Moving to the right side of the table he placed a retractor under the lower extension of the abdominal wall flap and gave it to Jack.

"You recall that we like to make an incision as low as possible across the uterus. That makes for stronger healing and less bleeding. Once I make the incision, I want you to slip your right hand up and into the uterus and boost the baby toward the opening. Don't be surprised at how much pulling we might have to do to get Junior out. He'll still be a heck of a lot prettier than if he came through the birth canal."

"Evening. I see I'm not late." The voice came from the neonatal intensivist, who entered the O.R. "I'm ready to receive."

"Great, he still looks good on monitor so I'm starting."

A few moments later Grady passed a mewling, kicking baby off the field and began delivering the placenta.

"Frank, please push the pitocin," he said to the anesthesiologist. "There, prep this for freezing." He passed the placenta to the nurse at the foot of the table. "Stem cells. Everything today is stem cells. I hope the expense of what we're doing will pay off, at least once in a while."

They all watched the uterus respond to the pitocin and Grady's gentle massage and when it had shrunk to his satisfaction and irrigation showed no bleeding, he looked at Charlene.

"Jackson, follow my sutures for me. We're ready to start to put her back together again." In a few minutes the hysterotomy had been securely closed. "Through at this end. Shall we rinse her some more before we close the abdomen Jack? Dr. Jackson thanks. You are now free to move about the country. Doc, how's he doing?"

Jack rinsed Maritza's abdomen with an additional two liters of warm saline, removing any remaining blood clots and any potential contaminants. The two men reconstructed her multiple muscle layers, restoring the integrity of her abdominal wall. The skin and underlying fatty tissues were lavaged once again with saline and a dilute antibiotic and then only partially closed as a precaution against infection. Her closure could be completed with steri-strips thirty-six hours later if the wound remained clean.

They now methodically prepared to move Maritza to the ICU across the hall and Junior to the Pediatric ICU.

<<<>>>

Back at the safe house Tivo had a difficult time keeping Segundo from wrecking the place and possibly even trying to kill his brother. He had gone ballistic, berserk. He stormed toward Terzio, his arms flailing wildly.

"Fuck you Brother. One more second and that whore baby would have been on the road and under my feet."

Terzio stood his ground and tried to assuage him. "One more second and the people in the car would have seen all of us. Then what Brother? Then what?"

"I would have killed them too." Snarling and face-to-face with his brother he drew back an arm as if to strike out. Tivo winced with pain as he threw himself between them.

"We all just better hope she dies or we are all in trouble, amigos. Enough of this madness."

Tivo went to the kitchen and took the now cooled pot of boiled water into the bathroom. He unwrapped and prepared to bathe and redress his leg. There was much more pus than a day ago and bits of necrotic flesh fell off as he'd unwrapped and then washed it. He generously spread the last of the antibiotic cream over the wound and rewrapped it in sterile gauze and then put on his jeans. He'd had to slit the seam to the knee so they would fit over the dressing and swelling.

Segundo came into the kitchen and glared at Tivo. He stood nose to nose with him and hissed, "Vega, you are beginning to stink. In fact, you stink so much that I may have to get rid of you very soon."

By the sound of his voice Tivo realized that the man was serious so he went out to his car and drove home.

13

IT WAS SUNDAY morning and Detective McKeon sat in his office waiting for the phone to ring. He'd had breakfast with his family and ordinarily at this hour he would have been sitting in church with them. But the morning was anything but ordinary and as he left for his office, he'd reminded his family to pray for Maritza and her baby. Not many people on the East End had as yet learned of the horror of the evening before but the McKeon family knew.

Dressed in his working clothes, a shapeless gabardine suit with signs of early shine, Thomas Finnerty McKeon looked like a gumshoe. A tormented few hours in bed had left him edgy and as a result there were two tiny pieces of toilet tissue stuck onto razor nicks on his face. His wife had confiscated yesterday's shirt so the one he wore was starched and neat. He'd have worn it and a good suit to church had this morning not been extraordinary. Stocking feet, freed from his shoes, were up on his desk. He looked at the clean and empty ashtray and reflexively his right hand went to his empty shirt pocket. Even after two years the brain remembers moves that once meant comfort and relief of the addictive craving. He laughed and shook his head incredulous that his body reflex still responded. He took his cell out and made sure it was on and put it on the desk and then walked to the half pot of fresh coffee and filled an almost clean mug. He looked at his injuries in a wall mirror. They were no longer bleeding but it wasn't yet time to moisten the papers and have them come off. *So that's the map of Ireland I'm looking at,* he thought. *I guess it ought to be. My parents sure looked like the part.*

Back again in his chair he considered the next few days. He knew that the Suffolk and State Police would step in and participate in his investigation only if a murder had occurred or if he requested their assist. So far he only needed to bring them both up to speed. As of an hour ago both victims were alive so he was still running the show. Of course, both offices would offer manpower and laboratory assist if he wanted it, but they'd respect his autonomy until they were forced by events to step in. He hoped and prayed for the sake of the woman and her infant that would not happen. He glanced at his watch and realized that at this moment Father Colgin would be offering communion to the penitent of the parish. Finally, his phone rang.

<<<>>>

During the first dozen or so hours in the ICU, Maritza's IV fluid demands were huge. To keep her central venous pressure at an appropriate level the staff had to continually administer large volumes every hour. She poured fluid, her own plasma, into the spaces between the cells of her entire body. It was her body's reaction to the massive trauma it had sustained by both the brutal assault and then the extensive operative procedure. This fluid, not in either the cells or the blood vessels, was essentially in a "third space" and functionally lost to her. It could neither help in keeping her blood pressure in a normal range nor, as a consequence, could it speed blood and oxygen to vital organs. So the staff had to continue to infuse fluids to keep her blood volume replete as it leaked out from injured and stressed capillaries. But in about twenty-four hours her body would begin its slow self-reparative activities and her fluid demands would decrease. At least that was the hope of the entire staff.

The South Hampton Hospital Administrator had requested around the clock security for the ICU and the police had stationed an officer there immediately. No one knew or could anticipate what the mad men who had committed this crime might next do so they protected Maritza as best they could. The police were also anxious to be present when Maritza was removed from the ventilator and they could interview her. No one, not even the police, would even think about any other outcome for the woman. Everyone involved in her care to this point only wanted to see her awake and able to describe or name her assailants so they could begin the search that would lead to their apprehension.

The county and state DNA files would be run against the materials collected at the crime scene and from the rape smears but that would only offer slim hope for a match. Unless the teens could positively pick a face out of the mug books Maritza would have to give the authorities the information they needed.

<<<>>>

The three men sat at one of the corner tables in the bar, empty shot glasses and beer bottles adorning much of the surface. The large screen TV. would ordinarily have a soccer game projected on it. Sometimes a split screen would show two matches, especially if a Central American team was playing. But today nobody was watching soccer. Earlier in afternoon rumors began to spread over the East End about a brutal attempted murder of a woman identified as Maritza Hermanos. On the plasma screen was an interview with a surgeon and an ER physician, the people who had hopefully saved her life and that of her baby. When the interviewer expressed disbelief that the two had survived, the surgeon reiterated that both were stable and although they were still listed as critical, he was hopeful. As the camera zoomed in on the two physicians, the reporter described them as "heroes" and thanked them effusively for their service to Maritza and the community.

Segundo stood, walked up to the screen, and stared at the faces and names. Returning to the table he looked at the other two and spoke softly.

"If the whore lives, they will die. They will both die. I will kill them, I promise you. And if the whore lives, I will kill her too. This also I promise you."

The TV. switched to a probing interview with the very capable and cautious chief of police.

"Sir, we know there were witnesses to the crime. Can they identify the attackers?"

"As yet they have not."

"What do we know about the men? I have heard there were three."

"That is correct."

"I have also heard that they were probably Hispanic. That would make this a crime on their own people. Isn't that correct?"

"Yes."

"And I have heard that one of the men was injured. He had a pronounced limp."

"That is the same information we have."

"Can you identify the witnesses?"

"It would not be proper or safe to do so. No, I cannot."

"Chief, I have names. Could you confirm if they are correct?"

The look on the face of the commanding officer clearly was one that meant only one thing to the interviewer, that those names had damn well not be aired now or ever unless it was by the police. He raised a warning finger and then turned away from the cameras.

Segundo stared at Tivo and growled at him, "You, cojo, invalido, you and your leg may get us caught.

No more in public for you. Better in fact that I feed you to the crabs or the rats."

He finished a shot, put some money on the table, and headed for the door. His brother and Tivo followed slowly. Tivo did his best not to limp, to walk normally, and he kept one eye always on Segundo.

For the next three days Segundo would watch the comings and goings from the South Hampton Hospital. He followed Charlene Jackson to her apartment and then he identified Jack Acquavella's car and followed the route he took to and from the hospital. What he was thinking no sane person could imagine. But he watched, memorized, and planned.

14

Basketball in her lap, Charlene Jackson sat uncomfortably and as she ate her breakfast, she thought about the savaged woman now in her third day in the ICU. The attack on Maritza presented her with her first challenge to the Hippocratic oath she had sworn as she received her MD. If she was ever faced with the challenge of treating one of those bastards, she was not sure what she would do. She slammed the ball into the floor so hard that it bounced up and hit the ceiling, resonantly snapping her back into reality and scattering The King and I.

"Technical foul, Jackson! Sorry boys. Come on and have some of Mom's breakfast."

Her two Siamese came slowly toward her, crossed blue eyes querulous after their rude awakening.

"Well, it looks like both Mom and Junior will make it OK. But questions, Charlene, and answers. Like where is Poppi? Who were the attackers? Why? That's the big one, isn't it? Why? And, yes, are they gone, scared off by their failure or are they still around?"

She looked at the clock, cuffed her cats, and prepped for work.

Segundo Guerra watched as Dr. Jackson left her apartment. A light jacket over her clean scrubs and her stethoscope draped around her neck, she began her easy ten-minute jog to the hospital. He looked at his watch. Six a.m., she was punctual.

He stepped across the street and went to her door. Conveniently her apartment was on the ground floor. He slid a piece of flexible plastic between the door and the jam and since the dead bolt had not been thrown, he was inside in a second.

A pair of Siamese cats stared tangentially at him and for a moment he thought about killing them. Curious, he went through several drawers and then the fridge. Pulling a drumstick from a roasted chicken, he closed the door and looked around while finishing his snack. He tossed the bone toward the cats and started for the exit. As he left the apartment the loose braided rag rug Charlene used as an inside door mat slid under his feet so that its edge became caught in the door as he closed it.

<<<>>>

Before going to her office Charlene walked up and into the ICU to check on Maritza. Her boss was already at the computer. He always seemed to get to work before she did. And she was always an hour or so early. She stood hands on hips looking at him until he turned around.

"With a babe wife like yours, Doc, why are you always here so early?"

Matt Colicchio rotated his chair so he faced Charlene. Bright eyed, a neat full beard and head turning handsome he was what Charlene considered arm candy for any woman. Turning around again to the computer he scrolled back so Charlene could see all of Maritza's data.

"She's fine. We'll extubate her in an hour or so but she needs to burn off a bit more sedation before we do. Let me know if you hear anything from the Police. I'll be up here most of the day."

Charlene walked over to the nurses' station where morning report was underway and sat down next to the significantly pregnant charge nurse Evangeline Yancy-Colicchio, Matt's wife.

"Boss says she's about ready to wake up, Yancy."

"We've just been talking about her. She's going to have quite a belly ache still but physiologically…" She trailed off and turned more toward Charlene.

"Her head, Charlene, that's what I'm worried about. Her poor psyche must be as bruised as her belly. Probably worse."

"Agreed. This is going to take a lot of woman to woman work by all of us. I'll get Psych to give us some help and guide lines, and meds if we need them. Carry on ladies, and thanks."

Charlene walked over to bed three and picked up Maritza's hand. The woman tried to withdraw so she released and patted. When she then touched her cheek Maritza opened her eyes, furrowed her brow and quickly squinted against the bright lights. Charlene bent and spoke briefly to her, hoping that some of her message would get through the mental haze of a third day of sedation in the eternally bright ICU.

She poured herself a cup of fresh coffee, chatted with Matt, about her conversation with his wife and then left the ICU. It was finally a civilized eight a.m. and she was ready to start her day, but back in her office in the ER she saw a message for her to call Detective McKeon, and a second message from the DNA lab down county.

The fact that the detective was on his cell so early in the day surprised her. She'd always visualized a peaceful life for the East End police forces with regulated eight-hour shifts, lots of down time and little excitement. But the last four days had been anything but that for everyone involved with Maritza.

McKeon told her about Tivo Vega's visit to the pharmacy and asked her to put hospital Security on alert for his possible visit to the ER. He doubted he'd show but had to be considered armed and dangerous.

The lab only confirmed what she already knew from their own efforts, that there had been two men involved in the rape. Once again, the usually placid Jackson seethed with rage.

The morning was hum-drum: a dog bit its owner, a hammer crushed finger, a fender-bender, colds, two tummy aches and a dementia. At two p.m. Charlene saw an empty waiting room and walked up to the ICU where she found Maritza, now extubated and breathing on her own, lying in bed and sobbing quietly. She would respond to no one and acted as if she heard nothing spoken to her. Charlene pulled a chair next to the bed and drew a curtain partially reducing the glare of the lights. She hoped to set a mood conducive to talking or at least listening. As an icebreaker, and before sitting, she decided in favor of a little "hands on" doctoring so she gently reached for the white sheet covering Maritza.

"Let's see how you're healing, Mommy. I'll be gentle but I'm afraid my hands are a bit chilly."

She slowly drew down the sheet and as she did, she placed a clean towel over Maritza's engorged breasts.

"We need to get your baby in here so he can start nursing. He should be up to it today or tomorrow. Hey, this looks fine. You're healing nicely. No problems here, lady."

She replaced the sheet and sat down. She lingered at the bedside, waiting for the conversation to continue, but once she had counted to sixty Charlene began to talk again. After ten minutes of generalities and pep talk, she bent close to the woman's head and whispered,

"It's fine just to listen. You don't need to talk now. I'll be back later and maybe then we can chat."

Back in her office again, Charlene called a psychiatrist who she felt would be glad to help them on a pro bono basis. When she'd related the story of the last four days there was silence on the other end.

"Are you with me Doc?"

"Yes" and another pause. "Look, we have no way to tell how this woman will respond, how quickly she'll recover…if at all…and how she might be permanently stigmatized. A lot will depend on the circumstances of how and why this happened, facts you don't yet have, and how good her support group will be. Does she have any family?"

"As far as I know she only has a no-show husband."

"She'll need a lot more than that. While she is with us we can do a lot but when she's ready to leave…I can't say. Should we meet her together tomorrow?"

<<<>>>

When Tivo didn't make a morning appearance for breakfast the Guerras were just as happy. He came in the night before and they'd forced him to sleep upstairs behind the closed door of a room with the windows opened. In the early afternoon Terzio went up to check on Tivo and found him incoherent, partially obtunded. The stench in the room was overwhelming so he closed the door and went back down stairs.

The brothers sat quietly. Segundo had stopped ranting and seemed distant and when Terzio tried to talk about their upstairs problem, his brother only shrugged.

"Leave him here brother, he will be dead soon enough."

Terzio knew that they themselves had to leave, to find a way to disappear. But he knew that his brother would not go until he'd avenged his failure and completed what was now a mission for him. No talking would change that. Terzio thought about just getting up and leaving his brother to his own fate but he couldn't do it. He was blood and you didn't do that to blood.

Segundo stood and walked toward the kitchen and the way out.

"I'm going for a ride in Vega's car. I won't be long."

He drove the old Honda east on Route 27 and then onto the Old Montauk Highway and finally pulled into a burger joint from where he could watch Jack Acquavella's office. He bought a cheeseburger and fries and sat in the car eating and waiting. At five-thirty the surgeon came out of his office and went to his vehicle and headed toward Quogue. Segundo threw the remaining food out of the car and drove after him, pulling in behind him and tailing him closely. As they came to one of the bridges over an inlet from the bay, Segundo overtook Jack and forced him into the wooden posts and guard rail. When Jack stayed on the road, he hit him a second time trying to force the car through the barrier and into the water. Jack's car stalled but the railing held.

Now in front of Jack, Segundo did a U-turn and tried for a third time to push Acquavella into the water but in his haste only hit the rear end a glancing blow. Segundo then sped back east, angered by yet another failure.

Jack was shaken but not hurt and he had managed to see the license plate and jot down most of the information. And he certainly had an up-close and personal look at the driver. His call to 911 brought two familiar faces from the precinct. Jack's car was still drivable, so they moved off the bridge and pulled off the road into a safer area and Jack began his story. One of the officers immediately called in the information on the Honda, hoping that someone might yet see it on the road. They had just about finished the writing of their report and were about to send Jack on his way home when the radio in the squad car came to life. The announcement stunned the officers. The locked and dented Honda had just been found in the handicap parking area next to the entrance of the hospital. The man behind the wheel seemed unresponsive and a stench was coming from the car.

When minutes later they arrived at the hospital, they found Detective McKeon and Charlene Jackson had jimmied the door and Tivo Vega was being placed on a gurney. Despite the efforts of the ER team, within the hour Tivo had succumbed to cardiac arrest due to irreversible septic shock.

As McKeon walked Jack back to his car, he took out photos of the Guerras. Jack pointed to Segundo.

"That one. No doubt about it. Ugly fucking bastard! Sorry."

"No apology needed for an appropriate description. I don't think you need to worry but we'll have a watch on you and your family until we find them."

<<<>>>

When Charlene arrived home that evening, she had to push against the door wedged shut against the floor mat before she could enter her apartment. Even a quick glance showed her that she'd had a visitor so she stepped back outside and called the police.

Five minutes later and with an armed escort she reentered her apartment. Within the hour finger prints had been recovered and not long afterward they would be matched with prints found in Maritza's car.

15

ALTHOUGH ORIGINALLY SHE had said no to police protection for herself, after her break-in and what had happened to Jack Acquavella, Charlene was not unhappy when at six a.m. the next morning she stepped out the door and saw a police cruiser parked at curbside. Inside the car, chin on chest, was Officer Franklin Pierce. Through the window she saw he was tall, black and beautiful, definitely a stud muffin.

"Where have you been all my life?" she said as she tapped the window.

The window opened and then the door as he unwound himself from behind the wheel. "Sorry Doc, it was a long night."

Charlene turned his name tag so she could read it and then let him have both barrels of intimidation.

"I could have shortened it for you if I had known you were here, Officer Pierce. But thanks anyway. I can make it safely on my own from here. You got the duty again tonight?"

"Yes, sir, ma'am. As low man at the barracks I pull the all-nighters."

"Well at least I can feed you this evening. Date?"

He nodded a still sleepy "yes."

Just a few months ago Charlene would not have had many free evenings but the addition of a new ER physician as coverage every other night had greatly improved her lifestyle. Now she had time to read, get some extra sleep and it had meant a few extra hours with the basketball, often one-on-one with Matt.

The ER was its usual early morning quiet self so it was easy for Charlene to leave for her session in the ICU. She met the psychiatrist outside and they walked into the family room together. Jason Springler, MD was not the person you'd pick out of a lineup as "the shrink". He looked more like a surfer dude, tall and muscular, tanned and a bleached blond rinse on his naturally curly hair. Jackson chuckled quietly as she visualized him on his board at Ditch or Long Bar, but he had a rep for excellence in crisis intervention and was occasionally called on by the police to lend a hand and mind in such settings.

"Charlene, as I told you, we can't predict but we can help and adjust that help as we see fit. Until we see her and evaluate her over the next few days…" he tailed off and gave a hands apart "who knows" gesture. "But someone needs to be with her all the time, especially if the police interview her today. I can help with that this morning but not later." He rose and offered Charlene a hand. "Let's see where we are, rather where she is, this morning."

As they approached the ICU, they saw Yancy standing with her hands on an isolette; a little black-haired head just visible at the end nearest Maritza. Springler put a restraining hand on Charlene's shoulder. They watched as Maritza looked silently at Yancy, then, propping herself on an elbow, she reached out and drew the isolette toward her.

"Is it mine?" she asked hesitantly.

"Yes. He's your son and he is fine. A bit small right now but he will grow. He doesn't have a name yet. In fact, your husband has not come into the hospital yet. We have not been able to find him." Mid conversation, Yancy had switched to Spanish hoping to relax and draw Maritza out from her funk. "We have been feeding him." She indicated the small tube in his nose. "But he is ready to nurse. You seem to have plenty of milk."

Maritza could feel the bra constraining her engorged breasts and nodded affirmatively.

"Do you want to try?"

Fresh tears began to form and run down Maritza's cheeks. She started to turn away from the infant but gritting her teeth she elbowed her way into a sitting position against the head of the bed and her pillows and spoke softly to Yancy.

"Tratemos, let's try." She reached out for her baby.

Charlene observed that Maritza's nipples did express milk easily. They positioned the baby appropriately until his fine plastic naso-gastric tube didn't interfere with his suckling. Soon, exhausted from his efforts, the little boy fell asleep but a few moments later he was awake again and rooting and then feeding.

They had watched for almost twenty minutes before Yancy saw them. Charlene pointed to Springler and then Maritza. Yancy shook a definite "NO" and mouthed "later". As they walked out of the ICU, Springler went over a list of signs and symptoms, a depression dictionary, and suggested Charlene set up the police interview for one p.m. tomorrow, his next free chunk of time.

"What we saw was good. Just make sure the nurses give her quality time. Also make sure she eats. Stoke the furnace."

When Charlene returned for a visit late in the afternoon, both mother and infant were asleep so she went back to her office. Hunkered down at her desk she watched her boss and his wife leave for home. Nurse Yancy was due in what? Two or three months? Almost shotgun numbers she thought as she remembered the spring wedding. Quick work there, Colicchio, but fun work!

Up to this point in her life Charlene had not felt the pull of maternal instincts. It had always been college, med school and then work. But watching Evangeline blossom in her third trimester and then seeing Maritza apparently pulled from the possibility of a profound depression by her baby, Charlene began to feel something tweak inside her. The boys, The King and I, were simply not family enough. But how did an ER physician meet Mr. Right? She looked at herself in her introspective cerebral mirror, before her stood a black goddess. She laughed at the thought but there it stood, six two and a half inches of beautiful, intelligent, sexy-bodied African-American womanhood. Sure, she was intimidating, but there must be a brother out there, a brother to satisfy her, who loved being intimidated. But where to look when you worked so many days and nights? Options were sorely limited, damn it!

Before she went home that evening Charlene stopped once again to see Maritza. She stood next to the isolette and spoke quietly to the sleeping infant.

"Well young man, you didn't expect to arrive until next month, did you. But it is warmer now and better weather to begin life. You and your mother will have some nice long walks before it starts to get cold."

She noticed that Maritza had awakened and was looking at her so she put her hand on top of her still swollen hand and sat down.

"Every woman here fears having to endure your horrible experience and every one of us will help you. Just talk to us when you are ready to talk." She touched Maritza's cheek and then reached for a tissue to wipe the tears that had again started.

"Tomorrow then."

Back at home she fed the boys and unpacked the groceries and prepped for her guest to arrive. She made a roast chicken, Mama's style, and fixings Mama's Style, and then some Dulce de Leche. Dinner involved small talk mostly, identifying who each person was and, superficially, how they got to where they were that night. At ten she walked Franklin Pierce out to his patrol car. The cats, unused to company or fancy table scraps, stayed in their cat tower and stared at the intruder until he had departed.

At six the next morning Charlene jumped twice on the bumper of the police car and waved a goodbye to Officer Pierce.

"Definite prospect there, Dr. Jackson, definite possibilities. Momma would just love him."

Two blocks down the road she thought she saw someone cross the road quickly to fall in behind her. She nudged the stethoscope hanging around her neck to unbalance it but it refused to slide. She nudged again and it slid from her neck onto the pavement, her left hand purposely grabbing at air. Almost without breaking stride she stooped to pick it up and glanced behind her at the hatchet-faced, ugly fireplug following her.

"Uh oh, Dr. Jackson, we have company. Do we call 911? No, we do not. This is what we have trained for. But do we want to risk getting hurt? Fucking-A we do! Bring him on, the poor bastard!"

Scope back around her neck, Charlene fine-tuned her senses to any sound behind her. It was like an exercise with the judo instructor when in his attack from behind all she would hear was his breath-in or the movement of coarse material rubbing against coarse material as he raised an arm.

She heard footsteps quicken but not yet closer. The short man would have to hurry, run in fact to accelerate against her long stride. She slowed she hoped imperceptibly and then counted to five, her estimate of the time it would take him to close on her. She turned and dropped into attack position. Fifteen feet away Segundo faltered momentarily but then raised his right arm, the one with the knife in it, and ran toward Charlene.

Bracing herself, her left leg slightly in front of her, she locked her thumbs, formed a strong cup of her two hands, and brought it quickly upward onto his wrist behind the knife. Continuing the fast upward motion, she clamped her hands vise-like on his wrist and forearm, pivoting inward and around, ever lifting and rapidly dislocating Segundo's shoulder. Maintaining her tight grasp on his now backward facing arm she shoved him face first onto the pavement. She was amazed at the "thonk" his head made as it hit the ground with no mat under it. The knife landed harmlessly twenty feet away, rattling to a stop in the street. Before releasing his arm to let it fall flail at his side, Charlene managed a vigorous kick to his crotch. She brought her foot back for a second kick, hesitated and just sat down as hard as she could on his back and took out her cell phone.

When the precinct answered she asked them to please radio Office Pierce and send him around the corner.

"My judo instructor would be proud of me!" she said to no one in particular as she awaited Pierce's arrival. The cruiser pulled up less than one minute later and Pierce jumped out. She glanced at her watch and then at the man who stood above her, a look of disbelief on his handsome face.

"My White Knight will need a better response time. Book him, he tried to kill me. Oh, when do you get a night off Pierce? Laaatah, bruddah."

Charlene gave her victory saunter her best imitation of a pimp-roll as she walked the last few blocks to work. She glanced at her watch again, "Damn, I'm gonna be late."

16

ON ARRIVING AT the ER Charlene said nothing about her morning adventures, but seeing no one in the waiting room she went directly to the ICU. She found Maritza pushing food around on her tray but not really eating. Until after today's police interview, she felt that Maritza did not need to know either about Tivo Vega's demise or her own take down of Segundo Guerra. There was no need to stir an already roiled pot.

She pulled a chair toward the bed, reversed it and sat down, her long arms resting on the chair back.

"Not hungry?" She saw a slight shake of Maritza's head.

"Walk yet this morning?"

Another no.

Charlene looked at the isolette with the blue blanket swaddling the baby.

"Feed him yet? Mommie, you both need to eat. Maritza, I was in the ER when they brought you in. A lot of people did a real good job getting you to where you are today, but now we need your help if we're to make progress and get you both out of here. Every day…" She paused and switched tracks.

"Everyone wants to find the men who did this to you, so this afternoon I'll be back with the police and another friend of mine. With your help we'll find and punish the three of your attackers."

Maritza had turned from Charlene and was sobbing.

"Crying helps but so does talking. Not all at once, just a bit at a time. So, we'll start after lunch." She stood and called to the Nursing Station, "Yancy, can you get this tray warmed up?"

When she sat down at her desk, Charlene found a message from McKeon. He wanted to talk to her about her morning escapade, so she called his office and the conversation began predictably with a lecture which Charlene interrupted after just a few sentences from the detective.

"Sir, you're right I am more valuable alive. But you have to understand that with my training I'm more dangerous than that dope was with his knife. Besides, if I'd hollered for help he wouldn't have a dislocated shoulder, a headache and sore nuts. Sorry Detective but sometimes a girl's gotta do what she's gotta do. Now about this afternoon."

She heard McKeon laughing and then cough as if some coffee went down the "wrong neck".

"Truce, Dr. Jackson." And they discussed plans for the afternoon interview.

Later that morning Charlene was surprised to see two South Hampton police arrive with a shackled and orange clad Segundo Guerra brought into her ER for an attempted reduction of his shoulder injury. She stood and returned his glare and dropped into attack position and growled at him.

"Hippocratic Oath aside guys, couldn't you have taken him somewhere else, like to Kavorkian? I'm not sure I have enough Valium in the entire hospital for that bastard. But then euthanasia is much too good for him. Follow me." She feigned a pass at Guerra and growled again and then led the trio into one of the exam rooms. An hour later he was led groggily back to the squad car, his right arm Ace bandaged to his chest and the jumpsuit arm pinned up.

<<<>>>

After feeding her baby and eating most of her lunch Maritza had fallen asleep. When she woke, Dr. Jackson and two men were sitting near her bed. One was in a police uniform. The other man, much younger and in a white coat, sat nearby.

Charlene stood. "This is a much prettier picture than when we talked this morning. Isn't it Maritza?"

Almost with a smile she nodded yes. Charlene then introduced the others and explained the presence of the officer and his desire to talk to her.

"Or we can just listen if you want to talk. We all know some of what happened to you but we need to know more, Maritza."

Slowly she began, starting with the kidnapping outside the IGA and then the drive away from town.

Charlene asked the questions as they were needed. Her first interruption was to ask for names.

"Did they call each other by name?"

"Yes. The man in the back with me called the driver Terzio. The man in the other car was Vega. The one in the back kept asking 'can you see Vega?'"

"What did the driver call the man who was with you? Do you recall?"

She shook her head. I think he called him brother."

One of the officers gave Charlene a prompt.

"Did he call him Segundo?"

"I don't know because he started to take off my clothes and told me that he had killed Osvaldo. Then he said he was going to kill me and Osvaldo's baby." She paused and then sobbing tried to continue. "Then I got sick all over us and I think I fell out of the car. But I don't remember anything else until I woke up here."

At this point and with a nod from Springler, Charlene stood and reached for the tissue box for Maritza.

"I think that you have done very well and we have more than enough for today. Thank you, Maritza."

Jackson and the men went to a conference room where a thermos and cookies were on a table. Detective McKeon looked at Charlene and initiated the conversation.

"Killed Osvaldo? And now they were going to kill his baby? Jackson do you know anything about this? We just got an I.D. on the body in the morgue. It's an 18-year old by the name of Osvaldo Omaya. We'll know more when we get a look in his room at the boarding house where he lived. His baby?"

He poured himself a cup of coffee and stood. As he sipped he walked and kept pointing his free index finger in a true meaning of life gesture.

"Maritza is how old? Thirty-six? And her husband Paul Hermanos is forty-four according to DMV. Doc, we need to dig deeper into the motives here. This crime was committed for a reason we have yet to decipher. You can help by gaining Maritza's complete trust. Maybe then she will reveal some intimate details to you, woman to woman. In the meantime, we also need to find out more about Osvaldo Omaya. And we need DNA results on him and Segundo Guerra. And we need to find big brother Terzio. Patchogue is faxing us all the info they have on those two so we can add it to the picture we already have. If he shows in Nassau, they nab him. But if he goes underground it may take time." He returned to his seat at the table and held his cup in both hands, rotating it slowly. "And then there is Paul Hermanos. Where the hell is Poppi? If he is THE Poppi! And then there is Tivo Vega. Who was he and how did he fit in? Again, thanks, Doc. You know how to reach us and we'll let you know anything and everything. And do me a favor, if you will and let us take down Terzio."

He left. Charlene and Springler sat alone in the room each with a half-eaten cookie in hand.

"Jackson if it weren't for the aggression and the deaths this looks like it is going to have the makings of a TV soap." Springler pointed toward Maritza's bed. "Big doings there." He stood and paced the room. "Hypothesis! Maritza told us why she was attacked."

Charlene followed him with her eyes and then turned in her chair.

"She told us the baby wasn't her husband's. Or at least that's what the 'brother' said. And if not fact, why would she even offer it to us? And without a denial. Go slowly but find out what you can. It's amazing but she does not seem to need me or my medicines at this point. We'll talk tomorrow. OK?"

They walked down and into the ER and then Springler left for his office. There were no waiting patients and the evening Doc was due in ten minutes so Charlene left for home.

She reworked the "Springler Hypothesis", adding her own caps and quotes. Even if he were correct, who would commit such a heinous act? Only madmen. And Segundo had been crazy enough to attack both her and Acquavella, the dumb bastard!

"Menu time, Dr. Jackson. What do we feed the man tonight?"

The small grocery store she entered actually centered more on the butcher counter and case in the back. The front half of groceries was more an accommodation to the butcher's clients than an effort to compete with IGA and the others. His meat was the best around. It was pricey, but what wasn't today? Aged, tender and well-trimmed beef had kept regulars and special occasion diners returning. Recently he had brought in organic bison and beef raised on the North Fork. Grass fed, hormone free meat was a novelty a few years ago but this summer he could not keep up with the demands of the health diet driven summer residents. And now the regulars, the full timers were continuing to buy. Charlene had treated herself on only one occasion and tonight was certainly an occasion.

She bought two inches and a half thick, boneless NY bison strips and watched hungrily as the butcher liberally seasoned them with "the rub" and then wrapped them in dark red butcher's paper. Sticker shock. But she thought Pierce might be worth it. Time would tell.

<<<>>>

Maritza awoke the next morning and looked over at her roommate. Baby Boy Hermanos was still written on the card taped to his isolette. Twice during the night he had fussed and she had brought him to her breast. In the dark she had not seen the little smile as he recognized her warmth and her smell. Sometime late last evening one of the Hispanic nurses, or perhaps she'd been an aide, Maritza didn't know the distinction, came in and sat with her. They spoke for almost an hour. Sadly and tearfully Maritza related the tragedies of her first life, the loss of Mundin and then Jose. The guest had heard rumors about the baby, staff do gossip, and everyone knew that as yet Paul Hermanos was a no show, but she avoided this topic in their conversation. She rose from her chair and moved to the edge of the bed.

"He is strong now; see how well he feeds? He is strong like Jose was strong, Madrecita." She stroked his soft black hair. "You look like a Jose. Creo que sí, Jose." She then embraced Maritza and said good night.

Maritza used the braided gauze rope attached to the foot of her bed to pull herself up, a movement still too painful without the assist, and swung her feet over the side of the bed and slowly stood. She picked up her baby and gazed at his wrinkled and worried brow. Then she brought him tight to her.

"Sí, tú eres Jose, Joselito."

She moved his rooting mouth to her breast, sat down, and began to cry. She cried until there were no more tears in her. In the morning she had the staff edit the name tag.

<<<>>>

During her early morning visit with Maritza, Charlene tried to open a conversation about Joselito's exact parentage, but Maritza was not ready to discuss the issue. Charlene persevered with a second question.

"Didn't you tell the police that Segundo said he was going to kill Osvaldo's baby?"

Maritza nodded yes.

"Does that mean you know something that I don't?"

She shrugged and turned from Charlene.

"OK, not ready yet. I can see that."

She plopped down on the edge of the bed but did not continue the questions.

"Today we are going to move you out of the ICU. There's a nice quiet room ready for you. Don't worry about being safe or alone. The police guard is still nearby and you'll get as much attention as you did here, probably more because it is easier to visit. But you still need to tell me more." Charlene paused briefly and then pushed one more time. "Have you heard anything from your husband?" She knew what the answer would be but asked anyway. Rising from the bed she waved a goodbye, "I'll see you later in your new room."

Charlene knew that paternity could be determined if Paul Hermanos finally appeared and agreed to DNA testing. IF! But where the hell was he? Why was he a no show if he wasn't complicitous at least tangentially? She needed to talk to McKeon.

<<<>>>

Long ago, when he was a member of the Salvadorian terrorist underground, the Salve trucha, Terzio had learned how to become scarce. When he saw his brother's face on the front pages of the newspapers, he became a virtual hermit. Living in the safe house by day, only late at night would he venture out to seek an out of the way fast food shop. As he made plans to escape the area, he followed progress of the search for him in discarded newsprint he collected at night. Jail was not an option. He knew that Segundo would not live long when finally incarcerated. Fellow inmates did not like those who had abused women or children, and that put his brother in the hot seat.

He knew he'd have to ration his money and lay low until the authorities thought he was no longer in the area. Terzio figured he was better off in the safe house than in Patchogue where hundreds would be happy to finger him. His one aggressive move was achieved late one night when he switched license plates with an old seemingly abandoned vehicle, hopefully creating another layer of cover for himself.

<<<>>>

Maritza's move out of the ICU took but a few minutes as she had little packing to do. Before she left, the staff brought in a small cake purchased at a local bakery and tried to make the event somewhat cheerful for her. Everyone promised daily visits and help with Joselito.

Her new room overlooked gardens and had a visitor's sitting room across the hall. Jose and all his baby supplies, as well as her own nursing material, were now to become part of her daily routine. She was going to begin to become mother-in-charge. Although the thought frightened her, Maritza knew that both she and her baby would soon be able to leave the hospital. Her concerns were for their safety and her inability to be self-sufficient. She wondered why Paul had not come to see her and his absence made her even more anxious. Soon she was certain that he too was dead.

But she would not be either alone or uncared for. The hospital's social service network already had her and Jose registered for Medicaid and they were exploring a home health aide for her until her life stabilized somewhat.

The girls and her boss from the IGA had made brief visits to the ICU but now that she was in her own room, they made much more frequent trips to the hospital. Her boss told her that her job was available to her when she could finally return to work and all the other women offered to help with day care for Jose. When Clea Schwartz, the social worker, came for another visit, Maritza asked her if she could return to Cuenca where her mother could help her with Jose and she could start a new life. Of course, Maritza knew that she could not leave until after the trials of both Guerras, she was sure of that, but then she had an idea. Clea sat with Maritza and was busy filling out yet another document when Maritza tapped her on the shoulder.

"If I can't go home perhaps my mother could come here. She would need a visitor's visa. I'm sure you have a paper for that as well. She could help me with the baby and you would not need to find someone I did not know. And then we could go back to Ecuador together." She'd played all her trump cards at once, and Clea stared at her, wondering where she had learned to manipulate the system.

It sounded an absurd idea given the political environment surrounding illegals, but with the notoriety of this case who knew what might happen with the right people pulling strings? Clea's neighbor was a NY state assemblyman, and the next evening she paid him a visit. A savvy and well-connected politico, he called the office of the junior senator from NY, and her offices obtained clearance to make a few calls. Soon it was done.

<<<>>>

They had gone to dinner at Nick and Tony's and then walked the streets and lanes of East Hampton. Charlene had slowly drawn Pierce out of his shell and was delighted to find an amusing and well-educated man hiding inside. Walking south on Main she had looped her arm through his and then directed the scattered conversation into a purposeful discussion.

"So, let's just look at this again, Pierce. I'm what, six months older than you? That bother you? I might say I've had an excuse for not getting married the last eight or nine years. But how about you, Pierce? What's your excuse?"

She could feel him laughing as she leaned against him waiting for his reply.

"Is this a proposal, Doc? Aren't you rushing things just a bit? Actually, I've had to spend most of my free time working to help Mom and the other kids. We, mostly she, put four of us through college. Only community college for two, but college. I had to help pay for them and be big brother. We lost Dad early on. He just up and gone. Didn't hurt and probably helped. Then there was the Academy and here I am. Just took me a while to get here."

They stopped in front of one of the women's boutiques and she saw their reflection in the window.

"Pierce, look at that couple. They are awesome together. Jesus, look at those dresses! What kind of buttless, skinny thing would wear that? Have you seen Serena's line of clothes in her TV ads? Now there are some dresses for me. Pierce, are you ever going to kiss me?"

A tired but happy Dr. Jackson walked to the ER that next day. She visited Maritza briefly and encountered continued resistance to any discussion of Osvaldo, so she went to her office and called Detective McKeon.

With no help as yet from Maritza, they only had pieces of a puzzle which they could move around until some might fit together. DNA from the presumed Omaya corpse could be matched with Maritza and Joselito. That was easy to do, and a match might give them the leverage they needed to get her to talk about it. They agreed that they needed more pieces to have something to work with before finally fitting together the puzzle, no matter how much like an Escher puzzle it became.

But again, the big question was always of Paul Hermanos and Terzio. Where were they?

Maritza spent most of the day walking and trying to become more flexible. Her incision was painful but no longer required analgesia except at night. She fed and changed Jose as needed and began to anticipate her mother's arrival. Mrs. Schwartz had brought that wonderful piece of news to her only a few hours ago. The arrangements and her eventual travel would take at least a week to complete, but it was going to happen.

As the food service picked up her empty dinner tray, Maritza turned and saw her husband standing in the doorway. He looked haggard and in need of a shave and shower but he managed a smile and a gesture of hello. He looked at the bassinette next to her chair and again gestured.

"Nuestro?"

"Es mi niño. Pero nuestro, quien sabe?"

"When can you come home, Maritza?

"Do I have a home, Paul? My mother is coming next week and then I will leave the hospital. Niño is still small."

When Paul had walked into the hospital and identified himself and asked for the location of Maritza's room, the receptionist had quietly notified security and the charge nurse on the floor. Security then called the South Hampton police. Shortly after Paul had pulled up a chair to sit next to his wife, an officer walked into their room.

"Mr. Hermanos, when you have finished talking to your wife, we need to talk to you."

Paul nodded, rose and said goodbye to Maritza. Together Paul and the officer walked out of the hospital and up to the waiting patrol car.

"You can ride to the barracks with us. We'll bring you back to your car after you answer some questions."

Although McKeon suspected Paul might have had some hand in the attack on Maritza, they needed some reason, some tangible evidence, before they could hold him. There were enough questions that needed answers, and McKeon hoped that just watching Paul outside of jail might be of help finding those answers.

It was a gamble but one McKeon hoped that would pay off handsomely.

The two men sat alone in McKeon's office. Paul seemed calm, considering where he was.

"Where have you been this last week?" McKeon asked.

"Mostly drinking and sleeping with friends."

"Do you know that Tivo Vega is dead and Segundo Guerra is in custody?"

Paul nodded an affirmative. "From TV."

"The Guerras told Maritza that they had killed Osvaldo Omaya and that they were going to kill her and Osvaldo's baby. Is that your baby or Osvaldo's?"

"I don't know."

"Then we will do a test to see. You will agree to that?"

He agreed, hoping for the chance that…well, just hoping.

"Fine. I'll arrange it for tomorrow morning when you are visiting your wife. Where can we find you?"

"I will be at home now." He gave the address and phone number.

"Have you seen Terzio Guerra?"

"No."

"Have you any idea where we might find him?"

"No."

"Mr. Hermanos, we still have a lot of unanswered questions and we might need your help, so please stay where we can reach you. We will see you in your wife's room at eleven a.m. Agreed?"

Paul nodded yes.

"Officer Hannon will take you back to your car. Thank you, that will do for now."

Paul rode in silence back to his car and then home. If in fact Segundo had told Maritza that he had killed Osvaldo, and Tivo, the only witness, was dead, could he survive this? Could he escape detection? Surely he didn't deserve it but someone needed to provide for the baby. Could it ever be their baby and part of a family?

After he had showered and changed, Paul drove to Montauk and, not knowing that it was where Tivo had been hurt, he parked by the Ecuadorian deli. For Paul it was a refueling spot after a walk along the bluffs that ran east toward Ditch Plains. He walked to the dead end on Surfside Street and cut along the path lined with rosa rugosa that were heavily bent by hips the size of quarters, and emerged out upon the bluffs. The near flood tide nearly reached the base some forty feet below. Due to the relentless erosion, the first house to the west of that point had finally been moved back from the edge and was rehabbed and again occupied. In the cloud-filled sky, the ocean seemed gray, a lifeless mass. Without sunlight sparkling on the wet rocks, the sea and the spectral spray, usually vibrantly alive, now looked dead.

"Mi vida," he spoke softly, "oscura y sin salida."

He took a step toward the edge and then turned and walked back to his car and his "dark and dead-end life."

<<<>>>

The next morning Paul arrived in Maritza's room and found McKeon waiting for him. After a few minutes with his wife and baby he followed the detective to the phlebotomy lab. Holding a taped piece of gauze over the puncture site in his forearm, Paul walked with McKeon to the empty coffee shop where the two men sat. Paul rose and went to add sugar and milk to his cup and then returned to the table. Unlike his demeanor during the interview yesterday, this morning Paul seemed relaxed. The detective sensed vulnerability in him and an opportunity.

"Mr. Hermanos, why did Segundo Guerra say that they were going to kill Maritza and Osvaldo's baby?"

Paul took a sip of coffee and looked at McKeon.

"Why did he say Osvaldo's baby?" McKeon prodded.

"Because I probably can't have babies."

"You seem a healthy man so why is that?"

Paul explained the couple's infertility issues and his own subsequent testing. The admission seemed to shake him and he nervously played with his cup. McKeon waited, looking directly at Paul.

"After that news you know how men get. I just couldn't do it. We would try but it was no good. So we...I guess I stopped trying. And then Maritza was pregnant."

Again he stopped and shook his head and started to say something but remained silent. Looking at McKeon he shrugged. Tears formed in his eyes.

"Not easy for anyone, Paul, but what happened?"

"I was angry. I stayed away. I didn't go home much because I was drunk. And I even talked about her at the bar."

"What bar?"

"Quito-Quito"

"I know the place. Alone?"

"Yes, usually."

McKeon motioned for him to continue.

"And sometimes with Tivo."

"You were friends?"

"For a long time, many years."

"And with the Guerras? Did you drink with them?"

"No. I don't know them."

McKeon now pushed his advantage aggressively.

"Paul, why did you disappear? Were you involved with what happened?"

Paul sobbed and covered his face with his hands. "I was ashamed. I felt somehow to blame."

"Are you?"

"I don't know. I just don't know."

McKeon felt it was time to end the questioning so he put a hand on Paul's shoulder. "Go see your wife."

McKeon drove back to the barracks certain that Paul Hermanos was in some way more involved than he admitted. As yet they had gotten nothing from Segundo Guerra. He remained hostile and silent except for denying that he was involved in the attack on Maritza.

When he had all the DNA information in hand, he could again confront Paul, but until then they'd keep a close tail on the man lest he try to bolt. McKeon would talk to Jackson again, and armed with his information from this morning she might just get Maritza to tell her the truth. They might get some of their puzzle pieces to align, even to fit together.

His team talked to the Quito-Quito regulars and the only fact they corroborated was that Paul had defamed his wife during several besotted evenings. No one would give further insight nor would they indict either Paul or Tivo Vega. No one seemed to know about Osvaldo Omaya. Which McKeon knew meant they were being closed mouthed about the truth. Today, however, that would change.

McKeon had taken coffee and a sandwich into his office and had closed the door behind him. He needed a quiet hour or two in which he could rethink what he had written earlier that day. It was a "Where are we?-Where do we need to be?-How do we get there?" didactic, three columned working plan. He wanted to concentrate on the third part, the "How".

Seeds from the ripe tomatoes in the sandwich fell onto the paper with his first bite, but before he could wipe them up with a napkin his intercom buzzed.

The street and traffic noise he heard meant public phone. The heavy accent was clearly Hispanic.

"Omaya, the boy, he was at the bar. Quito bar. Hermanos was drunk and they called him Pistola Muerta. You understand?"

"Yes, dead gun. Because of no babies?"

"Sí, no babies. But Omaya was also drunk and told him. Told Hermanos that he had fucked his wife. Vega was there and took Hermanos outside fast and the boy followed them, Vega and Hermanos."

"Did you see what happened?

"Maybe yes, maybe no."

The line then went dead.

McKeon reached for a pen. He went to the "Where are we" and added a very significant piece. It was as yet hearsay but probably the truth. It made sense. Perhaps tomorrow Osvaldo's mother would have more information for them. With his next bite mayo oozed out and fell next to the tomato seeds.

17

Sixteen-year old Celeste Omaya's prayers had finally been answered. Her parents had sent the money needed for her to travel by coyote from Cuenca to the US. She was at last, after a seemingly endless five years, going to join her family in New York. So, she kissed her grandmother goodbye and joined a group leaving for the coast, the Coyotes and a perilous journey north.

Her trip might have been uneventful but for a meeting of the heart somewhere in Mexico. A handsome young man from Guayaquil, who was twice her age, began to be attentive and protective of her. He shared food and water and occasional treats that she never could have afforded and, slowly, inexorably he taught her about love. It was difficult to find moments alone together but they found a few. They apparently found just enough for Celeste to become pregnant.

On the first morning after crossing into Texas, a helicopter suddenly appeared above their group of travelers. Paul Hermanos gave Celeste his food and water, moved her into the protection of a clump of sage and gave her a hurried kiss and a warning.

"Don't move until night. If I don't get back to you the town is just a few hours directly in front of us. Remember to find the bus station and the coyotes will be there. But I will find you."

He didn't come back but she did find the town and the next contact. The six who had not been arrested were piled into a van and thirty-six hours later she reached Peekskill, NY, and her family. Seven months later the son of Paul Hermanos was born.

<<<>>>

An important corner of the puzzle was uncovered when the police searched Osvaldo's apartment. As they began a second day of sifting through the remaining boxes and drawers, the detritus of a tragic life, the post was dropped in their laps. A brightly colored envelope, clearly a message of celebration, had a return name and address. It was a birthday card from Celeste Omaya and had been mailed in Peekskill only a few hours away on the mainland.

The next day the Westchester police had found her where she worked as a live-in nanny for a family in Chappaqua. The sad news of Osvaldo's demise rallied the family around Celeste. As she left to go home, they assured her that she was loved and needed and that they would help her in any fashion.

At seven a.m. the next morning the Peekskill police met her and drove Celeste to the South Hampton Barracks and a sad meeting with Detective McKeon. In her mind her son had always been everything a mother could wish. He'd been a good student, a superb futbol player and he was growing into a kind young man. What happened last year still confounded her.

At a soccer game between a local sports club and one from Suffolk county, Osvaldo had met several young men, all Ecuadorians and all working for the same landscape firm which sponsored the Long Island team. Lured by the offer of a job and most certainly by the many chicas at the game, Osvaldo told Celeste he was moving.

Devastated she tried to remind him of his college plans, her plans for his education. They were temporarily on hold, he told her. He wanted a job and to earn his own way. She could not dissuade him and a week later he was gone. They spoke regularly and he seemed happy for he always talked about his work, the soccer games and his growing bank account. Celeste finally felt that his decision might not have been such a bad one and was again proud of her son.

This was the story that she would tell McKeon. This was the story that repeated itself in her mind during the four-hour ride to his office. How did this happen and why? She had as yet no answer.

McKeon looked consolingly at Celeste Omaya. She looked much older than thirty-four and today she looked exhausted. But her grief did not completely hide the features that said "I was once a beauty, and if it were not for this…" Diminutive, like a frightened, dark eyed little bird, she held her arms around herself as if trying to keep warm. Only a day ago she was a cheerful Nana for two lovely children she treated as her own; with Osvaldo gone her world had constricted. She was devastated.

Detective McKeon's chair squeaked quietly as he leaned back, rocking gently. He straightened and leaned toward Celeste.

"Paul Hermanos was Osvaldo's father? Is that what you just told me Celeste?"

"Yes, Officer."

"I can tell you that we think we know who killed your son. But there is something else. The people who attacked Maritza Hermanos told her that they knew that Osvaldo was the father of her baby."

She started to speak but paused, shaking her head slowly in disbelief.

"That means…" She took a tissue from her purse. "That means that baby is my grandson. Does it not?"

"Perhaps, Celeste. When we have done the DNA studies, we will see what comes of that information. No matter what there is still the case of Paul Hermanos."

She looked at McKeon and she stiffened noticeably.

"I don't think I want to see Paul."

"You may not have to. But we can wait until we know more. Would you like to visit Osvaldo's room and take anything with you?"

"No. If I do have a grandson, his child, that will be all I could want from my son. Other than my memories of him. I will wait until I am able to see the baby. Now, if you can just take me home."

An even older and wearier woman walked slowly out of McKeon's office, prepared for a long ride home.

McKeon sat back again, rocking and digesting. He decided he had to talk to Jackson and then to Maritza before any DNA testing was done, so he headed out to his vehicle.

<<<>>>

The two women were seated in the nurses' station across the hall from Maritza's room. Clea Schwartz, the social worker, was speaking with the hospital switch board. Soon a communal phone began to ring in the house where Delia Ponson, Maritza's mother, lived and Clea passed the phone to Maritza. It was almost seven a.m. in Cuenca and everyone would be at home preparing children for school and men for work. When a very young voice answered, Maritza identified herself and asked to speak to her mother.

"Es para Tia Delia. Tia Delia, Tia Delia, Venga aqui!" The excited little voice faded as its owner ran to find his aunt. Moments later a familiar voice answered and Maritza was speaking to her mother. Clea had prepped the conversation between the women so that daughter would give only some information and that mother would understand that she was coming to NY for a visit and then eventually she could take Maritza and her baby back home. But she was to make no mention of the attack.

"Nona, Maritza? I am a grandmother?"

"Sí, Mama, un hombre pequeño."

"You are well, my child?"

"I am OK now but I had some problems. When you come you will learn all."

The details of Delia's trip were arranged through consul and embassy contacts, and an almost VIP service assured a no "snafu' journey for her. At JFK her non-stop flight from Quito would have an escort waiting at Immigration, and then Maritza and Clea would meet Delia in a hospital van.

<<<>>>

Charlene was suturing a laceration over the bulging left bicep of a local construction worker. He'd been lucky that the piece of blade from his tiger saw hadn't hit his neck or face.

"Make it a plastic closure, Doc. I still got a few centerfold years left. You know how vain men can be when they got looks."

He kept her laughing throughout the twenty-minute procedure, and for the last ten McKeon leaned against the door to the room, enjoying the show and banter. Charlene added steri-strips over the sutures as a "just in case" because she knew he'd be back on the job within the hour.

"Have you had a recent tetanus shot?"

"Half an hour ago, Doc. Stitches out when?"

She was about to say ten days but seeing the biceps and pecs she told him two weeks. She took off her gloves and tossed them onto the tray with the disposables. As she washed up, she looked at McKeon.

"You, Detective, know something that I don't. That obvious cat ate the canary look is staring at me. Come on into the office."

Closing the door behind him he sat down on the chair Charlene pushed at him. When he'd finished telling her about Celeste Omaya, Charlene buried her face in her hands. She peeked at him from between her fingers.

"Detective, his own son cuckolded him? That's what you expect from the DNA results isn't it? Wow. Double wow."

"Looks that way, if Guerra was telling the truth."

"Paul know?"

"No. It isn't the time to tell him. I still suspect he's more involved than we know or he'll admit. But I'm going to talk to Maritza."

"I'll stop up there later. I'm overdue for today's visit. Wow! See me before you leave?"

She watched him leave the ER and then turned to see what was waiting for her.

McKeon found Maritza on her way to the Day Room, singing to her baby. They sat together in the warmth of the solarium-like space filled with flowering plants.

"Flowers like in Cuenca, Maritza?"

"Yes, tropical flowers, señor."

"Paul told me that the baby might not be his. Do you think you can tell me why he said that?"

Slowly she related the story of the clinic visit and the discovery of Paul's sterility.

"Do you know why, what happened to him?"

"Yes. When he came to the States with the Coyotes there were many sick children. Children with paperas." She puffed up her cheeks and looked for the English word.

"You mean mumps, rubella virus."

"Sí, yes, mumps. Paul got mumps when he was twenty-eight and it also went to his cajones. Testes?"

"Yes, I understand."

"But we tried many times for a baby."

"And then you were pregnant."

Maritza turned away and began to cry. He asked only one more question.

"Osvaldo?"

Without facing him she nodded yes. McKeon rose and gave the distraught woman a hug and left her to her misery.

<<<>>>

The front page of the day-old tabloid caught his eye. Again! It had been a portrait-free week but here he was again on the front page. Terzio glanced at his reflection in the mirrored window.

An almost two weeks growth of beard helped. So did the longer hair pulled into a pony tail. But he still looked too much like the picture to be out and about, at least in daylight. One night he had driven into Nassau to use an ATM and was delighted to find that it had not yet been frozen. He maxed out and hoped it might lead authorities astray. The next night he did the same thing in another town. The two grand in his pockets could tide him over for a good length of time, but eventually... Yes, eventually something would have to change. He wondered if the Coyotes worked backwards, getting you out of the US instead of in. He'd have to trust someone in Patchogue to get him the information and the money. It was madness, but that just might be what it would take to escape.

<<<>>>

Charlene heard Maritza talking to someone so she peeked into her room and saw her lying in bed with her baby held above her. Maritza chatted to Baby Jose, who seemed to be enjoying his high perch. Charlene knocked, walked over to the bed, and reached out for the infant. Holding the little creature on one hip she bounced him lightly.

"What were you telling him?"

"Just that I wasn't sure what I should call him, Jose or…"

"Or Osvaldo? Maritza, that's your decision. Who he will be won't be determined by his name. You will make him into either an Osvaldo or a Jose when you decide which you would rather have him be."

"You spoke to Detective McKeon."

"Yes."

"About Osvaldo?"

"Yes. But again, I tell you to make your son the man you would have him be. He should have that name. Do you understand what I am telling you?"

"Yes, Doctor. And for that reason he should be Jose."

Charlene held Jose up in the air above her head.

"Your mother arrives tomorrow doesn't she? She doesn't need to know everything. Parts are best forgotten Maritza. At least for tomorrow. Those are hungry sounds, Jose. You need Mommie and I have a date."

Charlene walked home wondering which of her vast wardrobe of six outfits Pierce would like to see tonight.

<<<>>>

Delia's arrival and disembarkation went without hitch. After a reunion and introductions and Maritza's assuring her mother that Clea spoke perfect Spanish, the three women walked out of the LAN terminal. Five minutes later they began the circuitous route out of JFK and onto the Belt.

Very quickly Delia put a halt to the impersonal chitchat.

"Where is the baby? What is his name?"

"Mama he is still in the hospital. He was small but he is fine."

"His name!" she persisted.

"I am not sure."

"And why is that, my child?"

"Mama, I call him Jose. Joselito. But..."

Maritza began the long story of her marriage to Paul Hermanos and his sterility. Finally, tangentially she spoke of her indiscretion, her affair with Osvaldo. Her mother clucked warningly but told her to continue. Maritza told of the attack and her stay in the hospital.

When she spoke, the anger in Delia's voice was easy to hear.

"Who were these men? Surely not Ecuadorians!"

"Mama, one was but two were banditos from Salvador. Tivo Vega was a Cuencano. His voice, Mama."

Maritza felt her mother suddenly stiffen beside her and her hand close firmly on her daughter's arm.

"You said Tivo Vega, Primitivo Vega. Are you certain of the name?"

Maritza nodded affirmatively.

Delia released her daughter, opened her purse, and took out a rosary. She began a tearful prayer. After a few minutes she stopped crying and sat up stiff and upright and looked at her daughter.

"My child you are not alone in your mistakes!" and she began a story that shocked the two listeners.

<<<>>>

Detective McKeon sat at his desk and looked at the papers in front of him. Just a few days ago he was not sure who had fathered Maritza's baby. Then the East Hampton clinic had faxed him the results of Paul's semen analysis and it appeared he was in fact a Pistola Muerta. Then there was the anonymous phone call. He wondered what law enforcement would have done with these facts fifty years ago. He knew all they would have had were ABO blood types and a best guess. But in front of him was the gospel according to Watson and Crick.

The lab at Stoney Brook had received the buccal smear from Joselito, blood from Paul and Maritza, and samples from the corpse of Osvaldo. And now McKeon knew. What was that song from the 50s he'd heard as a youth? "I'm my own grandpa?" Well Paul Hermanos came damn close.

Young Osvaldo Omaya had died not knowing that he'd impregnated his father's wife. He'd died not knowing his father had wielded the knife that took his life. He'd died not knowing his father.

<<<>>>

Delia Ponson grew up in a prosperous and privileged Cuencano family. Her father was a politician and public figure who lived on his inheritance, his salary, and graft. Delia was an attractive and precocious child and by the age of twelve she looked like a young woman. She was invited into a circle of older young people from families of means and felt pressured to be accepted by her friends. To call her promiscuous wouldn't be fair. She experimented as did many of the older girls but she knew nothing of contraceptives, so during a coupling with one of her three or four beaus, a precocious egg met an almost as young sperm and they set up housekeeping.

To avoid scandal and because she did not know whom to indict, the family ferreted Delia away to a small village until the birth of her son. A family greatly in debt to Delia's father was persuaded to adopt the little boy and in exchange their debts, financial and politic, were discharged.

Primitivo Vega was raised as their own child and he never knew his birth mother. Delia was later betrothed to another of her father's friends and Maritza was the only product of that short and unhappy union.

Until this day Delia had never spoken of her first child and now, unfortunately, Maritza's half-brother was not only dead but had been accused of killing the father of Maritza's child.

The remainder of the ride to the Hospital was in almost morbid silence.

<<<>>>

McKeon collected the papers from his desk, put them into his case file, went to his car and drove east. Nodding to the plain clothes officer who was watching Paul's house, he pulled into the driveway and went to the front door. After his second ring and a loud rap Paul opened the door. He was unkempt and the inside of the house smelled like a frat house on Sunday morning. He motioned McKeon in and brushed detritus from a chair.

"You haven't gone back to work."

"Maybe next week. I do need the money."

"Mr. Hermanos, do you remember Celeste Omaya?"

For a brief moment he looked up at McKeon but he remained silent.

"Do you remember her?"

A shrug and then a nod and finally, "Yes."

"I know that was eighteen years ago. She had a baby, a boy. Your boy. She named him Osvaldo. That boy, your son, died last month."

"Vega," was all he could say through his sobbing.

McKeon rose and left, glad to be in fresh air. His intuition still told him that closure in this case eluded him and that Hermanos was not, had not been, an innocent bystander in the events. He was guilty, McKeon was sure. But guilty of what?

18

Disquieted by the visit McKeon sat in his car. It was true, they could easily keep tabs on Hermanos. He had stuck around so far and McKeon was confident that he would not try to scram. God, do we still use that word, he wondered.

The search for Terzio Guerra was at a standstill even though every barracks, all newspapers and TV stations, and most emporia had his picture. Whenever he asked for a refresher his face would appear in all the media. McKeon was convinced that Terzio would show. Sooner or later he would foolishly feel confident enough to step out into the daylight. When or where or how disguised he wasn't sure. But he would show. They always did.

Once again, he needed to enlist Charlene and as it was still early enough, he went to the hospital and walked into her office.

"Well, good afternoon Detective McKeon." She gazed at him over the pages of *Women's Wear Daily* and smiled. "Not mine. I found it in the waiting room. But a gal's gotta keep abreast of things. Chair?"

McKeon sat and relaxed. *Something about this woman puts you at ease,* he thought.

"Think we still need to keep a watch on you, Charlene?"

She closed the glitzy mag and sat up quickly.

"Aha! So that's it. I'm taking up too much of Pierce's time, am I? Sorry about that, but…"

He cut her off with a wave which meant stop.

"What? You and Pierce? I must be blind or just getting old. He's a great officer, Charlene, and a good man too. No, young woman, it's nothing like that."

He then explained that tomorrow she might expect a visitor and exactly what McKean would want her to do. He left smiling at his own marked presbyopia.

Back again in his office, McKeon found a note on his desk. As he read it, it became clear that he was going to be late for dinner and that his wife needed to know. He put his cell down and called in the night sergeant who had left him the note.

"I put the two new pins in the map. Both are ATMs. Keep the accounts open or close them?"

The map was dedicated to Terzio Guerra but it hadn't had a single addition since that Saturday past and now both yesterday and the day before he had surfaced in Nassau. McKeon tapped the two sites.

"He's not there. These are too close together; it would be too much exposure. It's smoke, smoke and clouds. He's here, right here damn him, but where?"

McKeon waved good night to the desk and went to his vehicle.

He's a pro, that's for sure. So it won't be easy. You expect an amateur to run but this man is here, hunkered down. Thinking that, McKeon considered retracing and squeezing Segundo. Perhaps even water boarding him. His soliloquy complete, he drove slowly home to dinner.

<<<>>>

Delia had not yet met her grandson. They had arrived on the East End too late in the day and she had been driven directly to the Lopes's home where she would be rooming. For years Candy Lopes had worked at the IGA with Maritza and they had become best of friends. When she learned of Delia's visit, she offered a room.

They had planned for Delia to arrive at the hospital about mid-day next, a time when Joselito was usually at his best. Bathed, fed and rested he would be alert and entertaining.

Charlene had stopped in early to see Maritza and found her singing to Joselito who lay drowsily in the midst of a diaper change.

"Hola Mama. Buenos dias, hombre pequeño." She roughed the baby's black hair and watched his mother at work.

"It seems so long ago, Doctor, so long ago that Mundin..." Maritza shook her head sharply, repressing tears. "No mas, no more crying, Doctor."

"Big day today for both of you. Are you nervous?"

"A little."

"I'll come up around lunch time. By then Nona Delia will be busy with her grandson."

As she left the room Charlene knew that her next visit would disrupt what would be a very happy family scene.

At two p.m. Charlene was able to leave the ER and return to Maritza's room where she found grandmother playing with Joselito. She greeted Nona and then plunked down on a chair in rather non-doctorly fashion. She changed her position as if uncomfortable, attracting Delia's attention. When Delia saw the furrowed brow and disquietude of her daughter's physician, she turned toward her.

"Is there a problem, Doctor?"

"Not really. Not in my mind. But, ladies, there is another grandmother, Celeste Omaya. She is Ovsaldo's mother. She knows about the baby and wants to visit him. She wants to meet all of you."

Maritza was immediately agitated and looked angrily at Charlene. She started to speak but was preempted by her mother.

"That's fine, Dr. Jackson. More grandparents are better for any child and we will welcome her as part of the family."

"I agree with you Delia. Jose can only benefit. Celeste will come here tomorrow afternoon to meet you. But there is more."

Maritza had begun to pace nervously. Charlene rose and guided her toward the bed.

"Sit here, and Delia, here also. She patted the bed so Delia would be sitting next to her daughter and might help her in the next few moments.

"Maritza, Paul was Osvaldo's father."

Maritza's head and shoulders convulsed. "No!" she wailed. "How? No, it cannot be! It just cannot be!" and she fell sobbing into her mother's arms.

Charlene waited until their eyes had met once again and then continued the story of Paul Hermanos and the sixteen-year old Celeste. When Maritza was again able to speak, she held out a hand to Charlene.

"She must come. Jose is as much a part of her. But how will I do this? I will need help, much help."

A few minutes later Charlene was in her office finalizing the next day's plans with Celeste.

<<<>>>

The driver was a pleasant young man. He worked for a funeral parlor on an as-needed basis and drove for the "Ecua-go" service to fill his days and his wallet. He was legal as were his parents. Just seeing him and listening to him chat to her during the long ride from Peekskill made Celeste sad for she thought almost continually about what might have been. What should have been.

When they finally stopped at the entry doors he turned and said, "I'll tell reception that you are here. I'm sure they will have someone waiting for you."

He was back in a moment and opened her door. "Come with me. I'll be waiting for you and when you are ready to leave, security will call me."

A woman met them as they entered, introduced herself and, taking the obviously nervous Celeste by the hand, led her to the ER. She knocked and then opened Charlene's door.

"Dr. Jackson, this is Celeste Omaya."

Celeste could not help but laugh when the doctor stood, towering above her and offered her hand. All anxiety seemed to leave her. She gazed around the office until she fixed on the picture of the young Charlene. Celeste walked closer to the frame and then turned back to face the very tall black doctor.

"Dios mio, now I understand; You are a basketball champion Brava!"

Together they walked to the day room where Delia, Maritza, and Joselito waited. Charlene made the introductions as casual as she knew how.

"Nona Celeste Omaya, this is Nona Delia Ponson." She paused while the two women embraced. "And this is Maritza, and here is your grandson. Ladies, I will be at the nurse's station or in my office."

Delia lifted Joselito from his mother's arms and carried him to Celeste.

"What is his name?" Celeste asked, taking the baby in her arms.

"Jose. It was so…. Jose."

Celeste held him up above her and watched him smile and then she spoke to Maritza.

"My child, you and he are gifts to me from God. He is like a little God to me, un Diosito and that is how I will call him."

Three hours later Celeste was back in the car headed home. Phone numbers had been exchanged and plans had been made for a longer visit the next weekend when Celeste was free to travel. By the end of her visit, it was clear that Jose would have all the love a child could want and that his mother would have enough help until her life was once again stable.

Since Delia had arrived Paul had once again been a no show and if he was planning to be a part of this family, he certainly wasn't showing it. It vexed the two women as they knew that at some point he would have to be dealt with. All the doctors involved with Maritza and Jose had hinted at her approaching discharge, and she and Delia had discussed it more than once. The dim aura of Terzio Guerra skulking about made them nervous and both had become increasingly suspect of Paul. They had both concluded that it would not be wise to move back into Paul's house.

Delia had enjoyed staying with Candy and Matteo Lopes and had been using their kitchen liberally. Daily she arrived at the hospital with home cooked Ecuadorian food to the pleasure of her daughter and the nurses. A renter had recently vacated the apartment in the Lopes's house, and they insisted that Maritza use it when she was discharged. Delia would have time to ready the space and everyone was delighted with the prospect of having a baby in the home.

Delia and Candy had decorated a room for Maritza and Jose. The old crib had been cleaned and re-assembled and a visit to K-mart had provided the other essentials of new baby care. When they also received the "going home" supplies from the hospital, they were well stocked for a month.

Seventeen days after her very tumultuous admission Maritza and her baby left the hospital. No fanfare, no publicity, they just made a quiet escape to continue convalescence and for Maritza to re-learn being a mother.

Friends from the IGA had taken her car from the police pound, sanitized it, then detailed it with such care that she did not recognize it as her own. She was cautioned against driving for two more weeks but she could do most anything else. The police had a plain clothes presence at the Lopes home and planned to keep it in place until Terzio was apprehended.

Mother and Jose had doctor visits scheduled at one and two months, but she knew not to hesitate to call either Charlene or the Pediatrician if they were needed.

19

TERZIO WAS RESTLESS. Almost a month had passed and there was not much left of autumn and he knew he could not winter over in the unheated safe house. A few days ago he had called a friend in Patchogue, a member of his group of disreputable associates, and quickly learned that he couldn't safely go there. There may have been honor among thieves but the Guerras had dishonored themselves and were not welcome in the area. The words he'd used were succinct...you will not last a week. So Terzio needed to move. And he needed money. His last ATM visit had tapped out that source and he'd been reviewing his options, a robbery or a low visibility job.

To save money he drove less. He "borrowed" a bicycle and used it at night to get to his eateries. On his varied and circuitous journeys he'd noticed that one house had been dark at night, never a light for over a week. He watched and concluded the owners were away so he planned a break-in. Many homes in the area had lawn or window signs warning of home security systems but this one did not.

In case he needed his car, he parked it a short distance away on a parallel road and cut through yards to approach the house from the rear. He quickly found a kitchen window unlocked and slid it open. He felt a cramp in his abdomen begin before he stepped into the house so he stepped aside, lowered his trousers and defecated in the shrubbery.

Carefully he stepped into the kitchen. He felt hot and uncomfortable, nervous, so he fumbled for his jacket zipper. Taking off a glove he unzipped his jacket and put the glove in his pocket. He used his small flashlight only intermittently, mostly feeling his way into the adjacent dining room. Exactly forty seconds after he'd entered the house, the alarm went off.

He went out rapidly, not even pausing to close the window, and cut tangentially across the same yards to the next street and his car. The light rain had wet the leaves and he made no noise as he ran. A light went on in the house immediately next to the one he'd entered. He drove away without headlights in the direction he thought the police might be least likely to use.

The investigating officers saw and smelled a failed burglary and they did nothing but lock up and notify the alarm company. When the report came across his desk the next morning, McKeon called one of the team and asked if they had dusted for prints. Quickly they were back at the house and at work. The surfaces were all spotless, as if they all just been cleaned, so it was easy to find and digitally lift prints and get them back to the lab and the computer. That afternoon it became clear to everyone that Terzio Guerra was still on the East End and hiding somewhere nearby. But again, the question was "Where"?

<<<>>>

Terzio sat in his car with a large cup of coffee and thumbed through an East End Employment weekly tabloid. A half page ad for day laborers caught his eye and he tore it out and set it on top of another shard on the seat next to him. Nothing else in the flyer interested him so he returned to his two gleanings. On the larger one there was a map showing how to get to *The Milk Pail,* an apple farm south of East Hampton town, and a request for pickers. Pay was by the hour. It was certainly out of the way and would have little exposure so he decided it was worth a look.

He neatened his beard and hair into a Che Guevara look, put on clean clothes and took a ride. Riding east along back roads he drove by the aristocratic homes of the south shore headed toward East Hampton. He'd no idea that such homes existed as those he glimpsed behind hedges or through driveways. Homes of royalty he thought, of kings, princes, and presidents.

Then suddenly the estates ended and farmland began. He saw manicured orchards and hedgerows, glossy black cattle and bicolored sheep that all looked brushed or curried. Then he saw the understated sign, *The Milk Pail…pick your own apples…Weekends only.* He parked and got out of his car. He looked around and was pleased by the isolation of the place. It gave him a sense of security so he went forward to the farm stand and introduced himself as Manuel Faust. Because he seemed polite and presentable, he was hired as a picker and was to begin the next day.

He had spent part of his childhood on an uncle's farm in the Salvadoran mountains and seeing the fruit trees and the animals in the adjoining fields brought back fond memories of those summers. As youths he and his brother rode bareback through the plantations of fruit and nuts and of cacao trees growing in the floral shade of the madre de cacao. To be happy and to be paid at the same time made him wish his life had developed differently. But he was now who he was and that was unlikely to change.

Three days later, on Saturday morning, Jack Acquavella packed his family into the Volvo wagon for the trip to *The Milk Pail*. Since the kids had been big enough to carry a bucket it had become a pilgrimage everyone enjoyed. From their bounty, Felice, his wife would assemble and freeze pies and put up applesauce just as she'd learned to do in her mother's kitchen. All wearing their colorful rubber boots, the family of four walked through the dew dripping fields along well signed paths toward the orchards. They always picked at least four varieties of apples, a peck each of Galas, Mutsu, Macoun, and Staymans, a perfect blend for pie but also for eating.

A tractor came toward and slowly overtook them as they stood aside. There were three men sitting on the flatbed it pulled. Just ahead of them it turned right onto one of the lanes into the orchards.

Jack paused, his eyes following the tractor. For some reason he was suddenly greatly disturbed. Then one of the men turned for a moment and glanced back toward Jack and his family.

Jack kept shepherding his family forward until the tractor was out of sight and then caught Felice by the arm and spoke softly to her.

"Honey, the third man on that tractor was Terzio Guerra."

She looked at him in disbelief but she knew Jack well enough to trust his astute clinical intuition and also his judgment. He was rarely wrong, damn him. She called to the boys who were now a few steps ahead of them.

"We've got to go back for a minute. Dad's beeper just went off and we forgot the cell phone in the car. Hurry up."

There were momentary "aw, Dad"s and a "but Mom, I didn't hear it" as they started back to the stand and its office. Jack re-introduced himself to the wife and proprietress and escorted her into her office.

"Look, I may be wrong but I don't think so. I believe one of your workers on that tractor, the one with the beard, is wanted by the police."

He hadn't needed to go beyond the name. She'd already picked up the phone and called the East Hampton Barracks. She knew everyone in the unit and when the desk sergeant heard her voice, he was polite and attentive.

Ten minutes later a squad car pulled silently into the *Milk Pail* parking area and three officers emerged.

Jack penciled in a beard on one of the photos they had brought and all were satisfied that Jack had been correct. Fortuitous luck? They didn't care. All that mattered was that for the first time in months they might be, close to Terzio Guerra. Until he had contacted McKeon in South Hampton, the captain had told his team to sit tight.

They walked to where the workers vehicles were located, put a wheel lock on Terzio's car, and went back into the office. Just in case a *CLOSED* sign was put up on the entry to the farm and people who stopped were invited back "after lunch" for a free bag of apples.

Something had also clicked with Terzio. The man in the field with his family, did he look like the surgeon he'd seen on TV.? Could it be? He certainly had watched as the tractor went by.

Excusing himself and promising to catch up he'd hopped off the tractor and cautiously made his way back toward his car. He crept behind a hedgerow fence that ran toward the road and the fruit stand. He saw the group around his car so he quickly worked his way back into the depths of the orchard and out of the south-east corner and into a pasture. He put his hands into his pockets and leaned against the split rail fence for a minute, planning his next move when it nuzzled his jacket. The bay mare had smelled the lunch apples in his pocket and wanted them. He fed her one and patted her withers. By the looks of her she was a jumper. Her long, strong legs and muscular hindquarters were built for elevating and not for speed. While she looked for another treat, he held her mane and cautiously, using the lowest fence rail as a step-up, he swung onto her back.

This was new to her. Not the weight, but having no bridle, bit or saddle. It was in fact nice. Terzio skillfully guided her into a slow trot and then a canter, taking her away from the orchard and eastward across the south side of East Hampton. Without hesitation and to the pleasure of both horse and rider, she took a low fence. As they traveled across the edge of a golf course he stayed in the rough or the trees until he was on the beach. He continued east until he thought he was close to Amagansett and then cut north. He came out onto Route 27 near the firehouse and in moments he was on the back roads north of town. He was amazed that he'd seen only a dozen or so golfers and then no one until some of the Firehouse staff. But it was still early on a late fall Saturday morning and most of the East End was still abed or breakfasting.

About half a mile from the safe house he left the mare in a fenced pasture and walked back to his hideout with twenty dollars and an apple in his pockets.

<<<>>>

Between ten and eleven o'clock that morning a series of calls came to the desk at the East Hampton Barracks. They were all reporting a bearded man riding bareback on a lovely horse. Although the sergeant on duty had duly recorded the first call, he'd thought nothing of it, just a prank, a Lord Godiva, but the man was clothed. But after several more calls, the last from the Engine Company, he went into the boss's office with his list.

"Captain, look at these calls."

Captain Dean Sciavone had been waiting to hear from his team in the orchard. He quickly scanned the list and walked up to the laminated town map on his wall. He marked each call with a circle of erasable marker. From the westernmost he drew a short line to *The Milk Pail.* He picked up his dispatch radio and called his team at the farm stand. They were briefed and told to carefully check on the tractor and the pickers. They were to assume Guerra was armed.

In the orchard they found the tractor and confirmed that "Faust" had left and not returned. At the adjoining farm a quick head count confirmed one mare missing. The officers headed back to barracks and Jack took his family home, their picking rescheduled for tomorrow.

Detective McKeon had arrived in East Hampton, and the day room was now crowded. He stood in front of the map and addressed the group of twenty.

"The lathered mare was found here, north of the firehouse, so Guerra's on foot and probably not far away."

He drew a circle about a mile in diameter with the firehouse as the center and then made a pie-chart out of it with six equal wedges.

"We have a few more hours of light. Let's make the most of them. He's most likely on the north side. Too many people south of 27. So, let's search these three sections carefully this afternoon. I'd just do a few random questionings to the south. OK with you Dean?"

Sciavone nodded assent and began to divide and assign the men.

"Everyone back by five please so we can plan tomorrow."

<<<>>>

Terzio heard the car pull up and then he heard the officers talking. He slipped quietly into the kitchen and then part way down the stairs to the cellar. If they started in, he wanted to be able to shoot and not be seen.

They came onto the porch and tried all the windows and doors and a flashlight shown briefly through the boarded windows. They left the porch and he heard them circle the house and then head to the outbuildings. Soon he heard the car pull away. Somehow, perhaps in the near dusk of the late afternoon, they had not seen the root cellar entry. Terzio shoved his revolver into his waist band and sat down.

"Too close. They'll probably check everything again in the morning." He lay down on the old sofa and tried to sleep.

Terzio didn't know it but as he rested, the media of the East End were preparing to display his "new face" to the world. Also, they would broadcast that he was in Amagansett and considered armed and dangerous.

During the night something transformed Terzio. The DNA that drove his brother, and which he shared, came out from where ever it was hiding and took over his mind. He sat up and spoke to his brother.

"Segundo, if I am going to die it should not be with our work unfinished."

In the pre-dawn he left the house and carefully zig-zagged his way to the trees and shrubbery behind the IGA. "Time enough has passed and the whore is probably back at work. That is my only hope."

He sat and waited.

By eight o'clock all the staff was in the store and the first customers had begun to arrive. Terzio went to the front of the store and stood peering between the large, bright sale signs which covered most of the glass. Slowly he moved along the windows and stared at each of the cashiers. As she turned to talk to her neighbor Candy Lopes saw Terzio looking at her and she calmly reached under her register and pushed the alert button. The 'robbery' signal went off simultaneously in the office and in the police station.

Candy walked slowly toward the rear of the store and stopped her boss as he came out of his office, a fully licensed 9mm Glock in his hand.

"He's out front. Guerra's out front."

He pushed her into his office.

"Stay here and call the police."

Lloyd Carver, ex-NY cop and now IGA franchise owner, went out the back door and calmly walked along the east side of the store toward the front. He heard a faint siren in the distance begin to grow louder.

But so did Terzio, who paused and turned toward the street just as Carver stepped into view.

"Guerra, on the ground."

Terzio turned slowly to his left to face Carver. He smiled and pushed back his jacket and drew out his revolver.

"Please don't," Carver called, and then squeezed off two shots both hitting Terzio in the chest. Moments later a patrol car screeched to a stop in front of the IGA.

The scene was cordoned and after the police photographer had completed his documentation, the corpse was taken to the morgue.

DNA reports would show that Terzio was the second rapist and that would begin to have some officials looking toward closure. But Detective McKeon was still unhappy. He was convinced a big piece was still missing from his puzzle, the large Paul Hermanos piece that fit right in the middle.

<<<>>>

McKeon sat with a shackled Segundo Guerra in the interrogation room. He hoped that he now might get him to talk and give him the information he needed to close this case. When Segundo was told of his brother's death he laughed and snarled, "Never. You won't get him. Never."

Shown the pictures taken outside the IGA Segundo just shrugged.

"Maybe he's luckier than me."

As McKeon rose and walked around the small room Segundo's eyes followed him.

"Guerra, I need to know more about Paul Hermanos."

"His wife is a whore. What else do you need to know?"

"Who killed Osvaldo Omaya?"

"How the fuck would I know?"

"You told Maritza that Tivo Vega killed him."

"So there, my friend, you have your answer."

"Someone told me something different. I believe Paul Hermanos killed Osvaldo."

Segundo was silent.

"Guerra, you're going to be tried for rape and attempted murder and you'll probably go to jail for the rest of your life. You'll sit in jail and know that Hermanos is walking around Amagansett, free as a bird. Because, Guerra, I have nothing against him and no one else alive who might know the truth except you."

"And you're that someone else, don't forget you're that someone else!" He spit out the words venomously.

McKeon walked out of the room, nodding to the officers waiting outside and Guerra was taken back to his isolated lock up.

Pushing papers angrily around his desk McKeon's frustration with Segundo kept him from thinking clearly.

"Your 'someone else', Segundo, has not been forthcoming. If you don't hear from him what do you do? You will have to play Hermanos. But how, just how?"

20

THE POLICE WATCHING Paul Hermanos knew that he had returned to work and that he had not re-visited Maritza. He'd seemingly detached himself from her and Joselito.

During one of her visits to Amagansett, Celeste Omaya had once again, at his request, met with McKeon. He had become convinced that he could extract a confession from Hermanos if Celeste were to become the catalyst. She had agreed and McKeon set his plan in action.

Paul arrived at the barracks punctually and was escorted to McKeon's office. The Detective greeted him cordially and motioned to a chair in front of his desk.

"Mr. Hermanos, I wondered why you haven't visited your wife since she left the hospital."

Paul began as if to speak but only gave a gesture, a stuttered physical, non-verbal "I don't know why."

As McKeon studied Paul, he let some trace of doubt, perhaps his miscalculations, of Paul's guilt enter his thoughts. Hermanos had cleaned up well. His clothes were neat and clean, his hair trimmed and he was freshly shaved and showered. Maybe, just maybe, McKeon had been wrong and it had been Vega.

"Mr. Hermanos, Tivo Vega was Maritza's half-brother." When Paul said nothing, he continued. "Delia Ponson was his mother. She made a mistake when she was only a child. But the blood tests prove it was true. If I am to believe the facts I have, then Tivo Vega killed your son and had a hand in almost killing Maritza and her baby. Is that what I am to believe?"

McKeon watched Paul beginning to become fragmented, very disturbed and trembling, so he bent toward his intercom and spoke softly. Moments later Celeste Omaya was escorted into the room. McKeon rose and motioned to the chair next to Paul but said nothing.

She sat quietly for several seconds and then turned to face Hermanos. She addressed him with the Spanish Pah-ool pronunciation of his name.

"Paul." She paused as she had been coached to do and then continued. "Tell me what happened to our son. Tell me what happened to the father of my grandchild."

They watched him register shock and turn pale. Paul felt his stomach begin to convulse violently. Retching he put a hand over his mouth and looked at McKeon who pointed to a door. They could hear him vomiting and then the toilet flushing.

Paul was drenched with sweat and was vomiting again. As he wiped his face he saw the partly opened window next to the commode. As he again flushed the toilet he opened it further and dropped out of it onto the ground at the edge of the parking lot. He raced to his car and drove out onto old Route. 27, headed east.

A minute later McKeon rose and walked to the toilet. He knocked and then opened the door to the empty room. He was annoyed with himself but at the same time felt smugly vindicated. He alerted the East End barracks and initiated a search for Paul.

<<<>>>

Paul had always felt that he would eventually be found out and held as a murderer. But he had used the cover of Tivo's supposed guilt to let him suppress, almost deny, his reality. Until the confrontation with Celeste he had succeeded. But it was different now and he did not know what to do, what he would let himself do.

For almost an hour he drove eastward on back roads, finally turning north and then, when he reached the water, again east along the water in Montauk's north shore. The road abruptly ended at the charter boat piers in front of Goswell's dock and restaurant. He parked and sat. It was early afternoon. He got out and walked into a nearby liquor store and bought a quart of rum. Drinking from the brown-bagged bottle he wandered the docks. Soon he heard a group of men speaking Spanish, Ecuadorian Spanish, and he followed them toward the *Lazy Bones*. The boat was being fitted for an afternoon party charter of porgy fishing, and the group was waiting to board.

One of the men turned toward Paul and raised his own brown bag in a friendly salute,

"Salud, pescador!"

"Salud," Paul returned and drank heavily from his bottle.

"Venga, amigo. Join us today. The fishing has been excellent."

Paul had the tariff needed to board and he stepped unsteadily onto the boat. As the *Bones* moved slowly out of Lake Montauk and turned east toward Montauk Point the crew passed out tackle and the fisherman began rigging the rods.

"Cuanto plomo? How much lead?" someone asked.

"Six ounces" was the mate's reply.

Paul saw people rummage through the boxes of lead sinkers, each taking a few six-ounce sinkers and then move toward the railing, waiting for the first stop and drop.

The *Bones* passed the lighthouse and began to slow about a mile off Caswell's. While the crew passed out bait pails, Paul stood next to the boxes of lead. Slowly he filled his pants pockets and then his jacket with sinkers. Then he picked up a dozen or more egg-shaped leads and painfully swallowed them, washing them down with the rum.

The load claxon startled him. He watched as everyone picked up pieces of clam and baited the three hooks attached to each line. At the second horn they lowered their lines to the bottom.

Paul picked up his rod and walked to an open space on the stern. Everyone was engrossed in the fishing so they did not notice him step up onto the gunwale. Paul set down his rod and stepped off into the water. The men who had been on either side of him seemed to freeze in disbelief, staring at Paul's slowly sinking image. Finally, they shouted in unison,

"Man overboard!"

Paul did not resurface, and in the swift tidal current the efforts of the crew to snag him with rods and hooks was futile. The Captain radioed the police and Coast Guard. Because the other fishermen could identify Paul as Ecuadorian and the alert for Paul was fresh in their minds a search of the dock area was begun. Paul's car was found about two hours later.

Four days later during strong sustained southeastern winds, Paul's body washed ashore in Hither Hills.

Tempered Steel

The Folly of Revenge

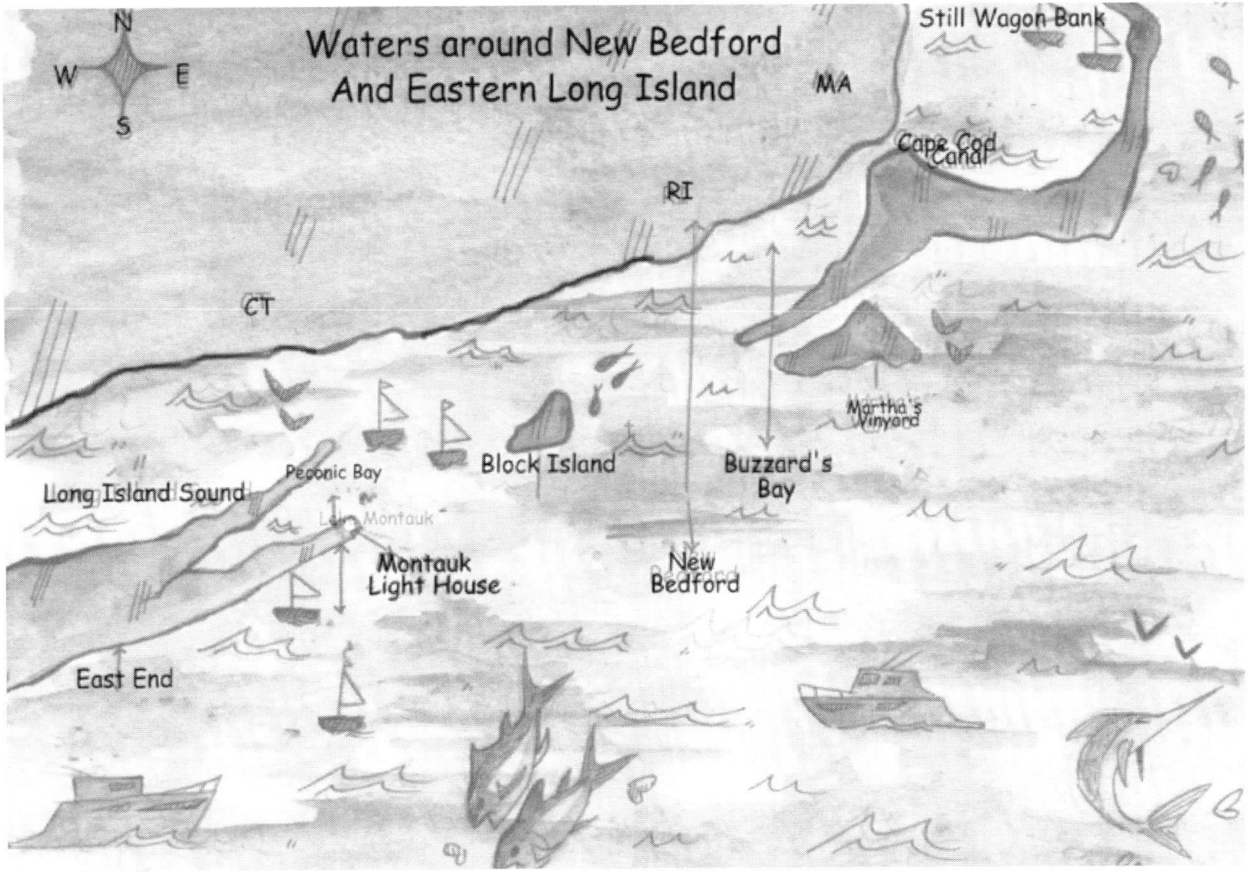
Waters around New Bedford
And Eastern Long Island
N
W
E
S
MA
Still Wagon Bank
Cape Cod Canal
RI
CT
Martha's Vinyard
Block Island
Buzzard's Bay
Peconic Bay
Long Island Sound
Montauk
Montauk Light House
New Bedford
East End

1

Day 1: Wednesday, July 23

STORZ'S BODY WAS found at six-thirty a.m. on a quiet, mid-summer morning by the owners of the boat moored next to his. They had not yet stepped onto their own vessel and so had managed to collapse onto a nearby storage box, take out a cell phone, and dial 911.

Stortz lay in a pool of blood on the stern decking of his 26' Whaler. Splatters of blood covered most of the area and the gunwales, strongly suggesting an upright, violent struggle had taken place before he'd fallen to the deck. The Montauk Police had cordoned off the portion of the anchorage, the right angle of decking, perpendicular to and leading from the main walkway out from the East Lake Marina. Their photographer had just begun his work when Chief Detective Thomas Finnerty McKeon of the South Hampton Barracks arrived with his coroner, Eric Hampson.

McKeon twice walked the length of the mooring, nodding to the other officers as he passed them. He wondered if what he was seeing was, in fact, possible and if he was not still asleep and this was one of his recurring nightmares. After finally greeting his friends from the Montauk Barrack he looked at Hampson, who simply shrugged. At this point there was not much to say. They put on paper booties and vinyl gloves and moved to step down into the boat. McKeon, now acutely aware that this was not a dream, paused, staying Hampson's next step.

"Christ, Eric, how?... I just hope this isn't a replay of last month!" He steadied himself as he stepped over the gunwale into Storz's boat, then he offered Hampson a stabilizing hand. The two men squatted on either side of the body which lay face up in a darkening pool of freshly clotted blood. Hampson looked across at his boss.

"Tom, this looks like his total blood volume on the deck. Look at his neck." Hampson pointed to the two perfectly round half-inch holes on either side of Storz's neck. "They're just behind the trachea and must have tracked through all the great vessels, both carotid arteries and probably the Jugular veins. Look at the gunwales and the mooring lines. And the center console. The entire stern has blood on it."

"So he must have been standing when he was shot?" McKeon queried.

Hampson looked at McKeon, stared at him and shaking his head in disbelief. His silence did manage to get McKeon to rephrase his question.

"OK, just hoping…until he was gaffed?"

"Yes, I'm afraid so. This is not a bullet wound in any way, shape, or form."

Standing, Hampson pointed to the deck of the boat. "Bloody footprints, and some skid marks. Again, all the signs of a brutal struggle before he fell and finally bled out. And Storz is what? Six-foot two?" He looked carefully at the corpse. "And two hundred plus? And very fit."

McKeon rose and walked two steps to the stern which was moored to the dock. He looked upward. "But no bloody footprints on the dock. So where did he go, and how, without a trace? Again? Eric, do you believe in agains?"

Looking around him McKeon noticed that the mooring next to Storz's port side was occupied and the boat had a few drops of blood on her hull. The slip to the starboard was vacant.

"Either he sat on the pier and took off bloody shoes and clothes so he wouldn't leave a trail or he hopped into his boat and left. How long ago? It's now nine a.m."

Hampson reached for the instrument bag he'd left on the pier, took out a digital thermometer, and put it into one of Storz's ears.

"Ninety degrees Fahrenheit, and the air temp this morning was sixty-eight, so he cooled slowly." He lifted one of the body's arms. "Rigor mortis is almost complete. So I'd estimate he died between eleven p.m. and two a.m."

Other than the neck wounds McKeon saw little of note: tattoos on both forearms and the left lower leg, a T-shirt that read "Get Bit in Montauk", and old, stained khaki cargo pants. Storz was wearing no socks and only one low-cut sneaker. They found the other under the transom, apparently kicked off in the struggle. McKeon would wait until photos were completed before they emptied the pant pockets. Looking further he found two beer bottles under the port gunwale close to the bow. Both would be bagged for prints and DNA, as would the roach he found nearby.

It began to look like an affable conversation in the bow had turned ugly and then moved to the stern as if someone was trying to leave the boat and get to the dock. McKeon searched for a gaff but none was evident anywhere on the boat. He then motioned to his team and the photographer and told them to get busy.

He went to the center console, opened the cabinet below the controls, and carefully bagged a phone, a pack of cigarettes, a set of keys, and a half empty box of condoms. That was it. No cards or papers, no phone book, no flashlight. Glancing at the windshield he saw it held only the appropriate stickers, certificates, and a few tuna lures on an attached piece of Styro. Four trolling rods stood in the rocket launcher above, the reels clean and full of heavy monofilament, Spro snaps attached lines to the reels. The bait wells were empty and clean as were the holds. All would be checked again and dusted for prints, but McKeon guessed they'd find nothing.

"Eric, let's let the team do their work. Up and out. Gentlemen, when you're finished please empty his pockets and call me for the contents. We won't be far."

They both stepped up and out of the boat and after taking off booties and gloves and putting them into a garbage bag held by one of the officers, they stepped over the yellow barrier tape and onto the main dock.

Looking toward the marina, McKeon saw about twenty people gathered around a restraining policeman. Motioning to Hampson, McKeon sat down on one of the large, locked storage boxes most boat owners had on the pier.

"Again, Eric. I know, I already said that. First in Amagansett and now here, both on their boats and both gaffed through the neck." He reached for his breast pocket and laughed. "Ten damn years and I still reach for the cigarettes!"

As they passed by with the body bag, one of the officers handed McKeon a ziplock which held the contents of Storz's pockets.

"Did you get his address from his license?"

One of the men nodded.

"Good, give us half an hour here and then we'll check out his bungalow." McKeon put on fresh gloves.

In the wallet were his driver's license, a Mastercard, an outdated Aetna card, and eighty-five dollars. A folded piece of paper, an old restaurant receipt, had five last names and telephone numbers written on it.

McKeon stood. "Eric, it's early. Do you have time to follow me to his bungalow for a quick once around before the boys comb through it?" Hampson nodded an affirmative so they moved slowly toward the crowd on shore.

"Let me talk if need be. Less will be more for now."

The marina manager waved to McKeon, and the detective motioned him forward but raised a cautionary finger which promised "more later. Just a briefing for now."

McKeon began. "When things are cleaned up a bit these folks can get to their boats. I'd like to speak to whoever first found the body. Is he here?"

Frederick "Shag" Stickles, who'd owned and managed East Lake for twenty years, was in his fifties, still trim and tan with graying temples, and dressed in his manager's uniform: a clean tee, pressed khaki shorts and sockless in Docksiders. He knew McKeon from church. Turning back toward the gathering he pointed to a man standing with his arm around a woman's shoulders.

"They are the Raysers," he said to McKeon, "and they had the misfortune." Shag motioned to the couple, "Harry, Fran, please come here."

They made intros, shook hands and followed McKeon as he moved a few steps away from the others.

"Tell me about it, please."

Harry cleared his throat and began. "Sir, we are moored next to Storz and we were heading to our boat for a morning striper outing. It wasn't until I'd almost stepped down onto my boat that I saw. Fran almost fainted and I had to help her find a place to sit down. Then I dialed 911."

"Did you see anyone else around here?"

"Just one boat, the 'Numbskull'. They were starting to leave. From much further out in the mooring."

"No boat next to Storz? No footprints?"

"That slip has been empty all season. Don't know why as it's a choice spot."

McKeon handed Harry his card. "Did you know Stortz well?

"He was kind of quiet; we usually just exchanged a nod or a wave. We never had a chat or beer or anything. So, no, we didn't know him well."

"How do I reach you?" After he'd entered their number in his cell, he thanked the couple and told them to call him if they thought of anything at all. Then he turned back to Stickles.

"I need a minute alone with you, Fred, in your office."

That office sat to the side of the marina's supply shop, a tackle, bait, grocery, and repair supply store wrapped into one. Before they sat down McKeon introduced Hampson. Stickles put his palms down on his desk and took a deep breath.

"This makes two, doesn't it, Tom?"

McKeon nodded. "I almost hoped you wouldn't remember. Do me a favor. Quietly find out from people who might have known Storz anything you can. His fishing friends, drinking friends, girlfriends…anything from anyone. And try to keep note of whom you talked to so you or I can follow up IF you hear anything. Oh, yes, did Storz keep a gaff on his boat?"

"Yes. He had to because he needed it if he hooked a big tuna."

McKeon tapped his note pad, pausing before he asked his next question.

"Shag, when you left for home last night was the restaurant still open?"

"Yes, a couple of tables. That was nine-ish."

"I would like to chat with the staff. When will they be in, and is it the same crew?"

"Yes, same two waitresses, the bartender, the cook and his helper. If you come any time after three, they'll all be here."

McKeon rose and extended his hand to Stickles, "Let the folks go to their boats but keep the path to Storz's shut for now. And please don't talk to the papers or news people. Thanks, Fred. Eric, let's head to Ditch Plains."

2

Sean Storz had motored into Montauk seven years ago, towing his Whaler behind a twenty-year old Ford pickup. He'd bunked initially at the Crow's Nest until he'd found a small rental in Ditch Plains which he'd paid for monthly in cash. He'd never missed a payment. All his transactions around the East End were in cash except for a few on the Mastercard which had a direct bank payment from a Citibank account opened initially in New Bedford, Mass. That account had a five-figure balance at all times.

He had recently turned forty-three years old and had no family of record or with whom he corresponded by either phone or mail. He had no computer. Only what I've mentioned, along with several ounces of weed McKeon found during a quick but thorough look through Storz's cottage. They chatted with his landlord who lived next door and who had come out when the police vehicles arrived.

Sure, there was grass and Storz was not beyond sharing with him or with friends. Who were those friends? McKeon came away with a list of six names. The others were unknown to the landlord.

Hampson had to get back to the hospital to do the post on Storz. As they had no evidence of a family of record, and it was a homicide, permission for the post was unnecessary. He was anxious to get to work.

McKeon heard his stomach growl and looked at his watch which told him it was two hours past lunch time. He was at that point in a man's life when a relatively sedentary job put great stress on an almost fifty-year old's waist line and he was ever mindful of his wife's thoughtful, calorie-conscious care when feeding her family. He looked at the lines at the food trucks in the Ditch parking lot and decided to head into town. Montauk, he knew, would already be abuzz about the murder and he decided the best place to hear some of that buzz would be at the Shagwong.

A parking place opened up directly across from the restaurant/bar that was probably most famous for a somewhat fuzzy photo taken at the Andy Warhol Cottages of a purportedly topless Jackie-O. It was hung on the wall amongst mostly grip-and-grin shots of large striped bass. As he backed into the space, he saw several men walk into the Shag, all of whom seemed dressed as archetypical fishermen. Or so it registered in McKeon's mind. It took almost a minute before a break in traffic allowed him to cross. So much for pedestrian rights of way when town was busy. He entered the Shag and at once confirmed he was right on in his supposition, for in the dimly lit rear of the room, at the end of the bar, about a dozen people, all but one of whom were men, were in an animated discussion. There were three empty stools mid-bar so he sat down, picked up a menu, and ordered a glass of Sam Adams from the young, black-haired, blue-eyed girl bartender. He spent longer than needed looking at the menu but he was listening to what he could hear of the conversation down the line. Pushing his empty glass forward he nodded to the young woman. When she delivered the refill, he ordered a tuna burger, rare, with coleslaw and no fries.

When she delivered the burger, he asked her if she had known Storz. She hesitated but then spoke.

"Sean? Sure'n I knew the man. He was a good tipper and will be missed."

She was one of the dozens of Irish summer help that flocked annually to Montauk and her brogue was as thick as her lustrous black hair. She started to move away but McKeon called her back and showed her his card. She balked and slowly edged along the bar.

"What is it, sir? Me? I have my papers!"

"No, miss, no, it's not you at all. I'm interested in Storz…in charge of the investigation. From the conversation over there everyone in here knows what happened."

"That he's dead, sir? Yes, that's the word, it is, sir, but…"

Raising his hand, McKeon tried to calm her.

"Are any of those men people who you'd call his friends?" He took out the list of names he'd been given by the landlord and pushed it toward her. "Are any of these names in that group there? These are supposed to be friends of his."

She looked at the list and then at McKeon. She started to speak and then stopped.

"I'm not sure, sir. I'm afraid…" And she turned away from him.

"Sorry young lady, I understand. No more talk."

Pocketing the paper, he took a bite of his meal. The thick rosy tuna tasted more like veal than fish and it was superb. Halfway through his lunch he thought he'd take a chance and try his luck. He also was Irish, was he not? He took out the list, looked at it, and then called out the second name, "Wakeland?", but he got no response. A minute later he tried number four. Quietly he called out, "Van Winkle?", and a face looked up at him.

McKeon then spoke directly to the face, "Tommy, can I see you a moment?"

Hesitantly Van Winkle left the group, moved along the bar, and sat next to McKeon.

"I saw you show your ID to Bridgit."

McKeon smiled, "Very observant of you. I doubted anyone had. Yes, Chief Detective McKeon, South Hampton Barracks. I'm here for the obvious reason and Storz's landlord told me you were one of his friends."

"I heard you call Fred's name also. We both were friends of Sean's. Not many of us though. What can I do for you, Detective?"

"Tommy, if you both heard and saw me, I think you can guess."

"Do I know any reason why someone would want to kill Sean? No, Officer, I do not."

"He wasn't selling any of the weed we found in his bungalow? Or anything else?"

Tommy laughed. "No, Sean only shared that with four or five of us. It never left his house, as far as I know. As for hard drugs, you can't do that and fish solo for tuna and survive on this ocean. Not when a good fish can pay half a year's bills. No, no hard drugs at all." He paused and then continued, "Fred's out fishing. Who else is on your list?"

"Michaels."

"He's not here either. He crews with Fred on the *Suzie-Q*."

McKeon gave Tommy his card and asked that he keep his eyes and ears open for anything that might help. He patted Tommy's shoulder and waved to Bridgit for his check.

As he was leaving, Van Winkle followed him. "Sean's the second one to get murdered?" McKeon nodded an affirmative.

"Who's next, Officer?"

"That, young man, is something that it is my job to prevent." He started toward the door but paused, "One last thing, Tommy. Did Sean keep a gaff on his boat?"

"Yes, always, and it was as neat and clean as his tackle."

And with that McKeon left the Shagwong. But not before he glanced at the photos on the wall. He looked at his watch. It was already three-thirty so he headed back to East Lake to talk to the kitchen crew. He wondered where the day had gone. He stopped in at the office and, with Stickles in lock step, he headed to the waterside restaurant.

One middle-aged woman sat at the bar chatting up the handsome bartender. Shag tapped her shoulder.

"Susie, have to ask you to move for a few. Business with my staff."

Not happily, she picked up her martini glass and prowled out onto the moorings, searching for another young man.

Stickles spoke to the bartender, "Get everyone here for me, please. Just tell them to drop what they're doing."

The chef, his helper/washer, the two wait girls, and the bartender sat at a far table and Shag introduced McKeon. Perching cautiously on the railing next to the table he took out his note pad and a pen.

"You all know of this morning's events, but I'm interested in last evening. When did you finally shut down?"

The chef, a slender and handsome red-headed youngster probably in his twenties, dressed in a surprisingly clean and starched jacket, stood up. "I plated my last dinners, two of them, at nine-thirty."

"Who got those meals?"

The younger of the two wait girls raised a hand, "I served them to the Sizemores."

"Familiar people?"

"Yes, regulars."

"Who else was still eating?"

"Only three other people still here, the Chopins and Arnie Lenz. Again, Detective, they are regulars."

"OK, good. But at any time last evening was a total stranger here? Alone?"

A universal "no" was his answer.

"Let's stretch it a bit if we can. How about the night before? Any notable customer? A newcomer?"

Again a "no", so McKeon stood, put his unused pad in his jacket pocket, thanked them, and walked away with their boss.

"I'm not surprised, Shag. Whoever he is he certainly didn't want to be seen. Clearly a new face would stand out around here. Thanks, I appreciate the effort."

McKeon offered his hand and then moved toward the parking lot and his vehicle. As he walked down the ramp from the restaurant, he saw his reflection in the marina shop's large window. Not long ago, Gaby, his wife, had tossed out his summer work suit, commenting that the rayon or polyester shine hurt her eyes. He had to admit that the new dark blue poplin was handsome, flattering he supposed. He stood tall, stretching his six-foot frame, turned sideways, and saw he was not quite what you'd call svelte but OK for the end of the fifth decade of life. He ran a hand through his slightly curly black hair and winked at the image, "Handsome Irish devil, you are, McKeon." He whistled a tune that came to mind, one appropriate for the marina, probably an old sea shanty tune but he wasn't sure of its origin. He tried to sound like a penny whistle.

<<<>>>

Back at the Barracks, McKeon pulled the file on last month's Sayger murder, found a new manila folder, and went to his desk where he named and dated it. Then, almost growling, he turned his chair around to the antiquated computer he abhorred because of its slowness. It rested on the windowsill, which was its home. He booted it up. Pen and paper had been just as hard for him to give up as had been the cigarettes. Well, anyway almost as hard. But he was becoming more facile and fewer and fewer spell check words appeared on the screen. And he did print out everything he wrote so he still did have papers to shuffle and cut and paste (he still refused to learn how to do it on the computer) and edit his thoughts as the facts demanded. Before he began working, he turned back to his desk and the intercom. Moments later Audrey, his clerk, knocked and entered. Starched and smartly dressed and efficient was how he always viewed and described her and today was no exception. Her blouse was Mediterranean sea-green and her white, mid-calf skirt looked as if she'd not yet sat in it. Her shoes, stylish flats, matched her blouse perfectly. He wondered how she did this on a regular, daily basis.

"Boss."

"Audrey, please check the DMV and post office to see where Storz was licensed and lived before he came to Montauk. Thanks."

He turned back to the PC keyboard and began to type. An hour later he picked up the pages from the printer and sat again at his desk. He opened the Sayger file and read through it once again. As if he'd ever have to refresh his memory of the event. It was there, able to be called up, just as if it was the photographs in the file: the body in the stern of the 33-foot Contender lying in a pool of blood, the two wounds in the neck, and no gaff on the boat of a man who'd also been a solo fisherman.

He looked at the coroner's report which showed evidence of old IV drug use: some sclerosed and scarred arm veins, and a couple of healed liver abscesses. There was no evidence at all of recent drug use in the negative tox report, except for a trace of cannabis. But these days weed would be as common a finding as coffee…if there were a test for coffee blood levels.

Sayger, thirty-six at his demise, had also been a loner: divorced in his early twenties and with only a long-lost brother somewhere down south. But he'd never been a problem at his marina or in town. He'd arrived in Amagansett about eight years before, after having left Fair Haven, New Bedford, Mass, where he'd been a fisherman on a commercial boat.

McKeon, at this point, saw only one connect: the commonality of the gruesome murder of two fishermen. Oh, yes, and the gaff missing from each boat. With Sayger's murder only his own DNA had been found. There had been no beer bottles or roach to hopefully yield some information. He replaced the papers into the respective folders and walked into the day room where three patrolmen were busy at work. They were in the spiffy uniforms common to Suffolk County Police but not the jodhpurs of state or motorcycle officers. Their black regulation footwear was always shined and helped McKeon to remember to keep his own shoes buffed. He walked over to and sat on the desk of Officer Franklin Pierce.

"Pierce, do me a favor and stand up."

Obliging, the young man stood and looked at his boss. "Turn around, maybe, Boss?" he quipped.

"Don't be a wise ass, Pierce. How tall are you?"

"Six-two and a half in socks, Boss."

"OK, I'm five-eleven plus, so if I stand on two phone books…" He walked to a shelf, pulled out the books, put them on the floor, and stepped up onto them, "…I'd now be about six foot two. OK?"

"Looks about right."

The conversation had drawn the attention of the other two men and Audrey.

"Pierce, do you know what a gaff is?"

"Do you mean, like, if you slipped off of those books by accident and it made me laugh?"

"Will someone PLEASE help Pierce?"

"Pierce," came a reply, "like the hook on a fishing boat to gaff fish and haul them on board. What the heck were you talking about?"

Pierce probably blushed but it couldn't be detected under his ebony complexion. "Sorry, Boss, yes, a gaff-gaff. Yes, I know."

"Who has an umbrella handy?" One magically appeared and McKeon directed Audrey to give it to Pierce.

"Now, Pierce, hold it by the point, the tip, and not by the handle, and see if you are tall enough to poke the handle through my neck while I try to stop you."

"Boss?"

"Just try!"

As the tall officer approached McKeon, his boss tried to fend him off and keep his balance on the phone books. By holding the umbrella only at shoulder height, Pierce was able to deflect his boss's arms and put the handle on McKeon's neck.

McKeon faced his audience and asked them all to stand. "Who's shortest?" he queried. The consensus was that it was Audrey. Playfully she held the umbrella like a sword and feinted once toward McKeon but when she saw his face, she quickly switched ends. Try as she might, even against McKeon's only half-hearted attempts to stop her, and even on tip-toe, she could not get the umbrella handle anywhere beyond his mid-chest.

"Thank you, lady and gentlemen. Given that both murder victims were over six feet tall and the wounds were in a level plane across the neck, not angled up or down, what can we hypothesize?"

"He, the murderer, was as tall as I am. Or close to it if not taller," Pierce volunteered.

"Precisely!" McKeon turned and went back to his office.

As he was getting ready to go home his intercom buzzed. It was Shag Stickles from the marina.

"Yes, Shag."

"Tom, I remember that the slip next to Storz's was rented about six months ago. A man came in and said he was a friend of Sean's and wanted to rent the slip next to him. It was OK by me so he gave me six month's rent and filled in the papers. When I tried to reach him for this month's rent the phone number was dead, not in use. And Tom, the funny thing is he never used the slip. Not once."

"Shag, do you remember him?"

"Vaguely. Big guy, tanned, and maybe fifty-ish. Looked like your everyday fisherman. It was quite a time ago, so…"

"I want those papers to see if we can get prints or DNA from them…other than yours and Betty's. I'll send someone over for them now." McKeon replaced the phone and walked into the day room.

"Gaff-man Pierce, I have a job for you!"

McKeon went back to his office and picked up his phone to call the Three Mile Marina in Amagansett. He asked to speak to the manager, Ferdie Lopez. Ferdie was a descendent of one of the earliest Portuguese families to settle on the East End, and his children were good friends with McKeon's.

"Ferdie, Tom McKeon."

"News travels fast. It's all over the place already."

"Right to the point then, I guess. Ferdie, who leased the slip next to Sayger's? The one that was empty?"

"Well, I can't say I know. Some time back, well before the murder, a man came in and rented it for half a year. He said he was a friend and wanted to surprise Sayger. Why do you ask?"

"Do you remember him?"

"Marina, my wife, rented it. Hang on." A moment later Ferdie was back on the phone.

"She says he was pleasant enough. He was a big guy, probably a fisherman, but he never docked his boat. That help?"

"Yes, it does. Ferdie, find those papers and put them in a safe place for me. Someone will come for them in the a.m. I'm looking for prints, Ferdie, and DNA if we get lucky."

McKeon leaned back in his chair, hands behind his head, and he began to massage his neck. It felt good so he closed his eyes,

"So, what, Detective, what if you do find the same prints on the two sets of papers, prints from the same no-show? And then find them on a beer bottle? What does that get you? Linkage, and prints to run to see if he's a known bad guy. Is that so bad?" he said to no one in particular, except it wasn't to no one as Audrey was standing in front of his desk.

"Time for me to slink home, Boss," and she left as quietly as she'd entered, the only sound was the sleeves of her blouse rubbing crisply on the bodice.

McKeon swiveled around to face the dreaded PC, typed for about ten minutes, and sent the entry to the printer which began to respond as he exited his office.

"We have not had a murder here since when? Seven years ago! Vega, Omaya and the Guerras! Someone should write a book about that summer. And now we have this mess that looks like a serial killer. Hah, and another book in the making! Making? This, Detective, had better well be solved."

Driving toward home he couldn't imagine what would make someone murder so brutally. The victims must have been held upright on the gaff while they sprayed blood until there was almost none left for the heart to pump. And then they fell to the deck. Had to be a damn strong person to hold up, and hold off those two men as they fought for their lives suspended on the end of a three-foot long gaff.

Thinking back to the Guerra brothers and those brutal events of seven years ago, he recalled that they were committed by outsiders, not real East Enders. Could that be a key to these murders as well? McKeon knew that it would take quite a bit of work and lots of luck to get the answer, always lots of luck.

3

McKeon parked partway into his driveway because his teenage son and daughter were having a two on two basketball game with the neighbor's kids under the hoop he'd hung above the garage doors. They all waved as he went onto the screened back veranda and then through the open door into the kitchen. The aromas greeting him assured him of another wonderful meal prepared by his wife Gabriella, the consummate wife, mother, and cook, in whatever order you chose to rank them. She had just closed the oven door where striper, in a sort of Italo-Provencal style, was baking. It was a fish a friend had taken from the beach Sunday night. Gaby gave him a peck and handed him a glass of well chilled Vermentino.

"Probably should be stronger, Tom, after what I've heard." She'd left no need for him to say any more. "These are the coolest days we've had all summer, so let's sit outside."

A stunning brunette, at five-foot nine, Gaby reflected the height of her Milanese ancestry and moved with their noble grace. She moved out to the veranda, sat on the edge of a chaise, and wrapped her long skirt over her elegant legs.

Taking off his jacket, tie and shoes, McKeon followed his wife out onto the veranda and sat facing her. Gaby called to the foursome in the driveway, "Dinner is in ten, so you two might want to quickly clean up." After two more changes of possession, the ball went into the rack in the garage, the four high-fived and two headed to their respective homes.

"Do they know, Gaby?"

"I don't think they have been on their phones or in front of the TV."

McKeon looked at his wife, sadly shaking his head and raising his eyebrows inquiringly.

"Yup, TV. Even a shot of you leaving East Lake. It's being hyped as the East End's first serial killer. As if it's kudos or a claim to fame for us. It's sickening."

"I didn't see a camera or even press. But all it takes is someone with a smart phone video who then offers it to the local station. How did I look in my new suit?"

"About five pounds overweight, dear."

He lowered the back of his chaise a notch and sighed. "Well there are some features of commonality in the two crimes that give the serial killer theory more than a little bit of credibility. But I need more wine." He pushed himself up, went back to the fridge, refilled his glass, and then collapsed into his chair at the head of the McKeon eat-in dinner table. Five minutes later their children were helping plate and serve dinner.

Halfway through dinner McKeon blasphemed, a definite no-no at Gaby's table. He reached for his wallet and took out the slip of paper that was in Storz's wallet and, getting up, muttered, "McKeon, those people named their boat *Numbskull* after you! Be right back and, sorry, dear."

He called the Barracks and gave the five numbers to the sergeant on night duty, "Get the phone company to validate them—names and numbers—and get back to me when you have the information."

After the call back from the Barracks, and when the kids had gone off to bed, McKeon helped his wife clean up after dinner. Apologizing again, he explained his transgression.

"I'd forgotten I had a slip from Storz's wallet with five phone numbers on it. That last call from the Sarge gave me names and addresses. Dare you to guess."

Hands on hips and apron his wife gave him "that look" and she said, "Of course one of them was Sayger's was it not?"

"Yes, and three others are on the East End and the fourth is on the Jersey shore, and that is like another Montauk. By chance I met one of the three today and now know of the other two. Somehow, I have to find the commonality amongst them and, perhaps, a common enemy. Tomorrow, my love. Now for that last drop of Vermentino, l'utima goccia, mia moglie. And I've not had a single Italian lesson!"

Gaby's apron landed on his head.

4

Day 2: Thursday, July 24th

EARLY THE NEXT morning McKeon hopped into the shower and exited almost as quickly. There was essentially no hot water. Telling Gaby, he put on his bathrobe and went down to push the start button on the coffee pot and then took a peek at the outside thermometer. It read sixty-two degrees. "Thank you to whoever set the temperature in July for this past week."

He went into the basement, pushed the restart button on the hot water heater, and returned to the kitchen where he put four eggs on to soft boil. He sliced the last two "everything" bagels Gaby had bought yesterday at Goldberg's and put them in the toaster. Soon the aroma of toasting seeds and garlic filled the room. He set the table for two, added butter and a small pitcher of two percent milk and finally a jar of homemade rose hip 'honey'. As the egg timer went off Gaby entered the kitchen.

"You didn't wake up once, dear, and I only had to roll you off your back twice. Murder cases must agree with you."

Not dignifying her with an answer he held her two eggs about three feet over her palms and said "Catch!" and as she shot her hands out, he gently put the eggs on her plate. Realizing she'd touched a tender subject inappropriately, she apologized. After breakfast McKeon showered and dressed, filled his carry cup with coffee, kissed Gaby, and went to his car. He knew that the names other than Van Winkle belonged to commercial guys who would probably already be on the water, but still he'd try to reach them.

Entering the day room, he tapped Pierce on the shoulder and pointed to his office. On his desk in front of his chair he found a large envelope from the East Lake Marina.

"Pierce, this goes to the lab for prints and DNA and then you go to the Three Mile Marina to pick up another envelope for the lab. And thank you."

McKeon took the slip from his wallet and set it next to the hand-written page left by the night sergeant, the names that matched the phone numbers. Lightly, with pencil, he drew a line through Sayger's name and then reached for his phone. Skipping Van Winkle the next name was Mike Michaels. On the third ring his call was answered.

"Mr. Michaels?"

"Yes, who is this?"

"I'm Detective McKeon, South Hampton Barracks." Choosing to remain vague he said, "No doubt you have heard about yesterday's events."

"You mean Sean? Yes, I have." The accent was New England, not Montauk.

"Can you come in for a chat this morning?"

"A chat about what?"

"Your phone number was one of five on a paper in Storz's wallet and I think it is in our mutual interest to have a conversation."

"I was about to go out fishing."

"Let me put it this way, Mr. Michaels, either you come here or I send a ride for you. It's your choice."

After a period of silence came the expected, "I'll be there in about half an hour, Detective."

As he waited for Michaels, McKeon made one of his signature graphic flow sheets. He wrote the four names plus Sayger on the horizontal X axis. Downward along the vertical Y axis were age, phone number, occupation, domicile, time on East End, origination, and, lastly, common link. It was complex but, for him, navigable and readily mutable. He hoped he would chart intersects from the two axes and come up with something… anything that would help. Unfortunately, besides the fact that both victims were avid fishermen, the only glaring and common link he had for Sayger and Storz was death. He turned to the computer and made several notes about the importance of finding a commonality to those still alive. He was saved from further typing by the intercom and a call from the coroner.

"Good morning, Eric I didn't expect to hear from you today. What do you have?"

"It's only the gross, Tom, but it is interesting. There were some scars in the liver and on two heart valves. They suggest liver abscess and endocarditis but, again, I'll need the micro to confirm. Also, a couple of old sclerosed arm veins. It all suggests past IV drug use. Perhaps, just perhaps, this might be the link with the two murders."

"Nothing new?"

"No, but we'll await the final toxicology reports. I'll bet they're negative except for a trace of cannabis again. Just like the prelims."

"Thanks, I think one of the names on that list just arrived."

McKeon opened the door to his office and Audrey waved to him. The man at her desk turned toward McKeon and held out his hand.

Mike Michaels was a big and burly man. In his late thirties, McKeon guessed. He had red curly hair and a neat flavor saver mid-lower lip. He was dressed in a clean T and jeans that looked almost as if they'd been ironed. Michaels noticed the detective's eyes on his jeans and laughed,

"Pants hangers, a trait instilled by my mother. Slide them in wet and let 'em dry. It makes them look pressed. Helps attract the ladies, Detective."

McKeon nodded. "Mr. Michaels, first of all thanks for coming. I don't like to force issues."

Michaels nodded affably. McKeon escorted Michaels into his office and offered him a chair. Passing him a sheet of paper McKeon asked him who on the list he knew.

"All of them." Michaels responded.

"How?"

"We are all fishermen."

"Is that the only connection? You're clearly not from Montauk. I'd bet either Maine or Massachusetts."

Michaels smiled, "I don't sound like a maniac, Detective. That's pure New Bedford you hear."

"As was Storz. And Sayger was from somewhere around there. And I'd guess Van Winkle from talking to him. So, Mike, how well did you know them?"

"We were friends, fishermen in and around New Bedford."

"Mike," McKeon paused, thinking how to couch the question, "did you have anything else in common? Did you ever have a drug habit? I need the truth."

Michaels held out his left arm and pointed to a trace scar line running up from the base of his thumb. "But I've been clean for six years. Oh, maybe I'd share a toke now and then with a friend, but nothing else."

"Autopsies suggest past IV drug use in Sayger and Storz. What do you know about that?"

"They had been clean at least as long as I have and they were clean until…" Michaels stopped, seemed to regroup, and began again. "You see, Detective, it essentially ruined our lives. The drugs. Sure, we were not the only ones, but…" He shifted uncomfortably in the chair, clearly trying to organize his thoughts. "You really can't be a fisherman on a trawler and feed a habit. Lots tried it and it destroyed them. Many died, OD, AIDS, you name it. Each of us on that list, in our own way, came to that realization. We might just have been fishermen, sir, but some of us have brains enough to know when..." he paused again and McKeon waited. "You get a rep and soon you can't get a job and, well, you know, you have to have money to feed a habit so it's a job or…" again, he paused. "We all knew that to start a new life; sometimes it takes a major change, and if you're a fisherman you have to be in a fishing town. Montauk fit the bill. It was a no-brainer to head down here. Took some time but, as best I can tell you, everyone on that list is or was doing OK."

Michaels wiped his face with his hands and looked at McKeon's coffee cup, "Sure would love a cup. Detective, I haven't ever told that story to anyone."

McKeon asked Audrey to bring him a cup, "Cream and sugar?"

"Both please," was the reply.

As Michaels collected himself McKeon completed making notes. Putting aside his pen, he folded his hands in front of him on his desk.

"Mike, I appreciate your candor but I must ask you a few more questions. Firstly, do you own your own boat?"

"No, not as yet, but I hope to soon. Why?"

"I'm not sure as yet. How about Wakeland or Van Winkle?"

"Only Tommy. Fred crews with me."

"Have you had any calls from anyone in the last months who is still in New Bedford?"

"Not as I recall. Reason?"

"Again, I'm not sure. I can't say why, but it might be important. Do you have any idea at all who, here on the East End, might have wanted to see your two friends murdered?"

"Detective, if we're fishing, we don't have much time to make enemies. At least not that kind!"

"What did that mean, at least not 'that kind'?"

"I guess we all step on toes, maybe talk to another guy's girlfriend. Maybe not be exact in locations about where and when we found fish. That's about the extent. Someone might get pissed but not for long."

"You're sure about no calls?"

"Yes, well, yesterday there was a call but no message…late afternoon. I was out fishing."

"That was my call," McKeon admitted. "Mike, I can't yet prove it but I think there is a link between the murders of your two friends and my guess is that it comes from your past, your lives in and around New Bedford. IF that is the case, the rest of you may well share that link. Again, that's a hypothesis, but right now it's the strongest, call it intuition if you wish, the best I can come up with. So, with that, I suggest you let me know of any calls or visits from people of that last life. Did Fred go out fishing today?"

"Yes, he did. They'll be short-handed today."

"Will you meet the boat when they dock and ask him to call me? My cell is on the card." He handed

Michaels two of his cards. "And Tommy was a no-answer this morning. Is he out?"

"Yes, I'm sure of it. Some bluefin were seen yesterday only twelve miles out and he hasn't filled his tag. One fish, a giant, is really big bucks."

"Where does he moor his boat?"

"Montauk Yacht Club. He must know someone there as it's far too pricey for most of us. But there aren't near as many boats there these last few years. More and more open slips."

McKeon perked up at the last statement, "Really? Open spots there?"

"Yes, seems to vary with the economy and price of fuel. But yes, everyone seems to have a few open spots."

"Mike, who runs the show there, manages slip rentals?"

"Well, when I called, I couldn't get past some b…, sorry, woman, who wouldn't say anything but 'stop in for any and all information', so I can't help you there."

"When do you think Tommy will get in?"

"Dunno, but I can give you his cell."

McKeon jotted down the number, rose, and walked around his desk. "Mike, you spoke under duress but I want you to know it was in confidence."

"Father Confessor, Detective McKeon?"

"Sort of that," he chuckled, "but also I hope you get the sense that I think you and your living friends ought to watch your respective and collective backs and ought to keep in touch. I have no basis for saying or doing more than that. When I do, you will know.

Again, thank you. This has been a most welcome discussion. Let me show you out."

He put a hand on Michaels's shoulder and they chatted amicably as they walked to the Barracks door. Going back into the day room he found Pierce making a fresh pot of coffee.

"When that's ready, please bring me a cup along with the print reports." McKeon closed his office door behind himself.

5

He awoke shortly after dawn when the sunlight, peeking through the incompletely closed dusty and faded draperies, glinted across his face. Rolling over, he cursed his situation and pulled a pillow over his head. He must have fallen back to sleep because the horn of the eight a.m. ferry roused him. He threw off the sheet which was his only cover and reached for his boxers. When they seemed too soiled to make a desirable undergarment, he tossed them onto the ever-growing laundry pile in the corner. Walking to a cabinet, he picked out fresh underwear and went to the bathroom. After a shower and a needed shave, he put on his skivvies and opened the drapes, letting the morning sunshine envelope the room. The bedroom was spacious, probably eighteen feet square, but clutter occupied most of the space. Besides the funky laundry pile, the room held a small desk, a bookcase, a couple of foot lockers, and a clothes cabinet built like a doorless armoire. And yes, there was some fishing gear mixed in here and there. Walking through an equally cluttered living room he reached the small, galley kitchen and rinsed the grummy mess from the bottom of the coffee pot. He refilled the machine and pushed start.

Had anyone knocked on his door, and if he dignified their presence by opening it, they would have been greeted by a six foot three, graying and frowning muscular man in boxers, and the intruder probably would have found some excuse for leaving immediately. Such was this man's morning appearance. It did not bode a warm welcome to anyone.

Kicking at the pile of mail lying to the side of the slot in the front door he nudged out a copy of *On the Water*, a fishing magazine dedicated to northeast fishing, primarily in the salt. The cover showed a man dressed for winter and holding up a large striped bass. "Catch More Winter Bass" was scripted in large print beneath the angler. After thumbing through the first pages he looked at the coffee maker and saw that enough of the elixir had percolated through to fill a cup so he did just that, unheeding the sizzle and burnt coffee smell of continued dripping while the pot was in his hand. Taking a careful sip, he walked back to the bedroom desk which sat under a large window. The wall behind the desk resembled the "wanted" posters of years past that hung in the post office. Five faces, all poorly photographed but recognizable, and two had a large red "X" drawn through them. The red magic marker lay on the desk beneath the photos. Also on the desk was a framed photo of a young man with a striking resemblance to the person now seated there.

The man opened the magazine to the lead article and, taking another sip of coffee, said, "Let's see what these dick-heads have to say about catching fish." After another sip he picked up a pen and started to read. "WRONG!" he said, crossing out a couple of paragraphs. "Wrong again, asshole," and he crossed out three more paragraphs. And so it went until he violently tore out the entire article with its lovely pictures, crumpled it angrily, set a match to it and tossed it to become ashes in a metal trash can beside the desk.

"You should all burn in hell, all of you. None of you knows anything about fishing, you damned bunch of druggies!"

He finished his cup of coffee but before refilling it he went to the bathroom where he fought the tops off of two orange CVS Rx vials and swallowed a pill from each of them.

<<<>>>

Pierce knocked and then went into his boss's office and handed him a folder.

"Print info, Boss."

"Sit down Pierce." McKeon pointed to the armchair next to the window. "What's going on with Dr. Charlene and your tadpole?"

"Well, she's six months and he looks fine on sono. You knew it was a boy?"

McKeon nodded. "Company for his sister. She's what, three now?"

"Yup. You know, Boss, without Charlene's mama and my mama able to help out, it would mean child care and that is not what we want. And now, with a third ER Intensivist at the hospital, Charlene has more free time. Her boss, Colicchio, is a gem. Is that the word? A great guy. He has two kids of his own so he understands. Anything else, Boss?"

"No, thank you. Please send my best to your ladies, all of them." As Pierce left the room McKeon picked up and opened the folder.

6

McKeon took out the report on the prints lifted from the two rental slip applications. There was one set common to both with enough good prints to be evidentiary in any court. He pressed his intercom.

"Audrey, see if the prints from the beer bottles on Storz's boat are available and also if any prelim on DNA from the same, and the cigarette butt."

He went back to the Sayger file and, just as he'd recalled, only Sayger's prints were found on the boat. Those beer bottles suddenly became more important. He turned to face his nemesis, Mr. Crummy Computer and entered the print information. As he walked toward the printer Audrey knocked and entered, handing him two faxed pages.

"Fresh coffee? Chief, you have missed lunch, but there are a couple of slices of pizza in the day room and I can warm them for you."

"Both sound wonderful. Thanks."

He scanned the faxed pages: no prints on one bottle and just Storz's on the other. There were two distinct DNA patterns, one from each bottle and both on the roach.

"So, he wore gloves but he swapped spit for the lab. Here we go!"

McKeon made the assumption that the prints on the forms belonged to the man with what he called "alien DNA". He called Pierce back into his office and told him to have the lab scour the lease forms for DNA.

"Have them check all the prints common to both forms and any stains on them. Thanks, Pierce."

Audrey came in with his lunch, and as he ate he mused about how hard it had become not to leave a trail. DNA, prints, cell phones, computers, game boards—all had dangling participles which the astute investigator could legally or illegally grab hold of and pull on, bringing down a lot of incriminating detritus. Yes, add to that the fact that your laundry and trash and toothbrush and comb and what was once thought of as waste were all becoming invaluable.

He wondered about the cell phones of the victims. They'd not found one belonging to Storz and somehow checking Sayger's seemed somehow to have fallen through the cracks or it had not been shown to him. He called Pierce again and handed him the Sayger file.

"Get cell and hard line records for April through June. Same for Storz, but through today."

It was already four-thirty but he buzzed Audrey and asked her to get the Montauk Yacht Club on the phone. When his phone lit, he picked up. At the third ring a voice said, "Club desk, can I help you?"

McKeon identified himself and asked for the club's manager.

"He usually doesn't take calls. Can I take a message?"

"No, you cannot. I am sure he'll answer a call from the police, so kindly connect me now." His voice was firm but not overly so and it prompted a polite "Please hold." A moment later the line was answered.

"Dempsey here. To whom am I speaking?"

McKeon again identified himself and added, "Mr. Dempsey you are well shielded from calls, but I had to persist."

"Call me Chris, Detective. How can I help you?"

"I believe Tommy Van Winkle rents a slip from you."

"Yes, indeed he does. He's a good man and a very good angler. He just came in with a very nice bluefin that will keep him in top financial shape for a while."

"That's nice but I need to know if the slips on either side of him are rented and, more importantly, if they are being used."

"Just a minute and I'll give you that information."

He heard Dempsey push back a chair and the sound of something heavy hitting wood.

"I'm back. I needed to get the ledger with up-to-date info. I believe I know the answer but wanted to check. Slips on both sides are rented and actually used by long-standing members."

"Is there an open slip nearby?"

"Not really, but the slip directly across the dock from Tommy has been rented. But the guy has never moored a boat. A bit unusual here."

"What do you remember about him? Looks, height, talk like a local—anything at all? And is Tommy still at the marina?"

"Yes, he's icing his fish and waiting for the Japanese buyer. Why?"

"Could you please ask him to pop in to see you while we are talking? About the other slip's renter?"

"Detective, that was a while ago and I see so many faces from so many places that the newcomers are a blur. Ask me about any long-term client and I can tell you how many false teeth they have. Sorry about that."

"Do you have the documents he filled in? The originals?"

"Yes. Sure. You want to see them obviously."

"Yes, I do, and I can…"

"Hold on a second. Be right back." McKeon could hear the loud speaker in the background,

"Tommy V, this is Chris. Please come to my office on the double."

A pause, and then: "Again, you were saying, Detective?"

"I will send someone to pick them up. Now, if it's OK with you."

"I'll be here until seven and then my assistant until nine. Hang on, here comes Tommy."

"Yallow, Tommy here." The accent was more noticeable now than in the Shag, probably because McKeon was looking for it.

"Tom, Detective McKeon. We met briefly yesterday."

"Yes, I recall, sir, what's up?"

"Well, I've learned a lot since then. I had a long talk with Mike Michaels in my office today and think we really need to chat."

"You talked to Mike? I thought he was fishing!"

"I caught him before he went out. I believe it's in your best interest that I meet with you. Preferably this afternoon if you can. Is your fish safe?"

"Yes, iced and safe and the buyer can't meet me until nine tonight. So, I have time. How about we meet half way? Say, Citarella in Bridge Hampton. That way I can get a bite to eat."

"Fine. How about in thirty minutes? No, make it forty so you won't have to speed and get stopped. Thanks. Hand me back to Chris."

Chris Dempsey fit the mold of marina boss. He was decisive yet friendly but was obviously perturbed by what he had heard and spoke carefully, "This is about Sean Storz and Sayger, isn't it?"

"Chris, for now, you can do us both a favor and keep this conversation to yourself. It did not happen. Yes, it is about those murders and my hunch is that we may have more problems unless we can prevent them. Thanks for the help and expect one of my men there within the hour."

He hung up. "Pierce, come in here, please "Please tell one of the evening guys I need him."

McKeon speed dialed Gaby and asked if they could dine a bit after the kids, say seven-thirty, and he asked her if she wanted anything from Citarella. He had to grab for a pen and paper for her requests and the young patrolman watched and listened as McKeon repeated the list. The patrolman rolled his eyes and whistled.

"That grocery list is my entire week's paycheck, Boss."

McKeon grimaced. "I know."

"So, what can I do for you?" the young patrolman asked.

"I need you to go to the Montauk Yacht Club to pick up some documents."

When the newest recruit was on his way to Montauk to perform his duties, McKeon headed for Bridge Hampton to meet Tommy Van Winkle and do some grocery shopping.

7

IT WAS A commercial tag day, a day when you could fish for profit, keeping a specified number of fish for sale. He had come back with his legal limit of striped bass and a couple of small "football" tuna for the table. It had been a very quiet day on the water with no other commercial boats in sight or on his radar so he'd crept close to the edge of Stillwagon Bank and trolled, sometimes quite illegally, just inside the protected area. But always he kept an eye on the radar and an ear to the sky in case a Coast Guard bird chose to patrol the bank.

In just two hours he had his four fish, all pushing forty-two inches, and he was tempted to hide a couple more but he feared any unwanted notoriety at this time. He had bigger fish to catch. One would be easy but the other two might be a challenge. But he'd beaten the odds most of his life and this time he was determined to win. He swung his boat to the west and leisurely headed home. It was time to make plans for number three.

<<<>>>

Tommy V, as he called himself, was sitting on the tailgate of his truck at the far western end of the always crowded, very narrow Citarella parking lot. As he saw McKeon turn into the area, he hopped down and motioned toward the far side of his truck, waving to the detective as he pulled into the space. Tommy met him by his door and handed him a cup of coffee. Van Winkle was in his fishing garb: a hoodie, cut-offs, and mid-calf boots.

"I had a sammidge, Detective. Do you want one?"

McKeon shook his head and pointed to the tailgate. "Will it hold both of us?"

"Sure, here," and he tossed over a cushion which McKeon adjusted and sat on. He patted the space next to him but Tommy said, "Chief, I listen better on my feet, so give me both barrels."

McKeon began with the facts he had and then went into his theory, which was well founded, but still a theory.

"Let me see if I have this straight," Tommy said. "Those two men were killed by the same person; someone you believe is part of our past and has some very significant grudge. And you think that because my boat abuts a vacant slip, I might be a target?"

"Yes. The past two slips, both of them, were vacant but paid for long-term. Both times by a no show. If his prints are on the rental forms here, then I'll be almost certain. So, Tommy, any contact at all that is unexpected you have to let me know. If you'd permit me, I'd set up a tap and trace on your line to cover you and see any missed calls. Your choice there."

"No problem for me with that, but what if I do get that call, then what?"

"Then the police will be listening, and when and if needed, will set up a way to intercept him and protect you. We will be your first line of defense. Second you must make sure there is no gaff on your boat, and we will need to arm you in some way. But let's get things set up with the tap. And, Tommy, I don't think he'd risk another attack after only a couple of days. Everyone is on high alert."

"Not unless he's crazy, Chief. What if he's certifiably crazy?"

They shook hands and McKeon took out his shopping list and started for the store. "Just watch your back. Any strange faces show up just call my cell. Bye."

McKeon took one of the carts from outside the shop and moved toward the entry. He'd been in the original East Hampton store years ago but had never been in this closer to home branch, some distance west on Route 27. He decided to cruise aisles from right to left as an organized shopper might. He passed through the veggies without seeing the haricots and mesclun that were on the list. Now cheese was on his left and the butcher cases on his right. A rabbit was item number three on the list and one was staring at him from behind the glass of the butcher's case, dull eyed and curled into a ball as if trying to keep warm. While it was being weighed, cut into pieces, and wrapped, he crossed to the vast cheese display where he was greeted by a pleasant young woman.

"Sir, can I help you?"

He read his list. "I need Parmigiano and Cacciacavallo."

"Both are just behind you. Pick a piece of Parmigiano with the least rind. It's a better value."

He showed her a piece and got a thumb up, then she pointed to the second pile. And again, she approved of his selection. "Anything else?"

"I remember that once Gaby, that's my wife, brought home what I thought was mozzarella but it was creamy inside, and delicious."

She picked up a plastic tub that held a baseball sized white cheese.

"Burrata, it just came in today and is divine!"

He nodded thanks, put the three cheeses in his cart, picked up his rabbit, and headed back to the veggies. About fifteen minutes later at the checkout he chose very wise words, "Please don't tell me the price, just show me where to sign!"

He picked up the two fancy shopping bags and headed to his car and home, nibbling one of the crusty baguettes along the way.

Dessert that night was a Lucullan feast of ripe Comice pears, the burrata cheese and a moscato from the island of Pantelleria, and it almost made him forget that the morning would bring another work day. But his reverie was interrupted by his cell phone. Michaels had met Fred Wakeland, filled him in, and Fred was dutifully calling. Twenty minutes later McKeon shared the last of the half bottle of moscato with Gaby and then they headed to their bedroom.

Gaby spoke to her husband from the shower. "That must have been the number five you were waiting to hear from. From what you say, and I infer from what I hear in your conversations, they must all be pretty good men."

"Yes, I believe they are and it's nice to see men who have cleaned up and can re-establish a life and make a living. It's a tragedy two are gone and, Gaby, we'll do our best to protect the others. Dry your back, lady?"

"I'll manage just fine, thank you, but a foot massage would be nice."

"Damned fetishes you women have. But it explains all the shoes. See you in bed!"

8

Day 3: Friday, July 25

IT HAD NOT been as restful a night for him as he had hoped, but McKeon was not surprised. Twice he'd awakened and lay reviewing the past day and planning for what might happen this day if Tommy received "the call". How would he do what needed to be done on such short notice? But in spite of himself, McKeon did manage somewhere between six and seven hours of reasonable sleep, enough for any middle-aged detective. He showered, dressed, and felt quite refreshed as he went down to the kitchen to make blueberry pancakes for the family. He'd heard the kids moving around in their rooms so he'd told them to plan to join their parents for a special breakfast. McKeon ate standing up by the griddle while turning out a total of some twenty-four large pancakes before everyone was satisfied. After he received a round of "great job Dad!" from everyone, he kissed Gaby and took his travel cup to his car.

McKeon's morning was dedicated to fulfilling the demands of his computer and then printing his entry and working on his graphic flow sheet. His "where are we and what do we need to get and how do we get there" puzzle had a simple answer: we wait until we know more.

He'd received clearance for the tap on Van Winkle's phone and considered doing the same for the other two men. But because he was the most vulnerable, McKeon was certain that Tommy would be the next person assaulted.

At noon Audrey buzzed that his lab was on the phone. They had carefully screened the two rental forms and found only one print that had DNA matching both a bottle and the roach. McKeon knew he had his man, but who he was and where he was still eluded him. Yes, probably in New Bedford, but in a big and busy seaport. The fingerprint search had turned up nothing and that meant he had no police record and whatever marine licenses he had pre-dated the mandatory fingerprinting. McKeon expected results on the third set of forms later in the day and was sure they'd show the same prints.

He walked into the day room and found everyone busy with paperwork. Except for Wednesday's disaster it had been a quiet week for the Barracks with only a couple of fender benders and one late night slugfest between two drunken friends. But it was Friday and Route 27 heading east was already bumper to bumper and would remain that way. Police cruisers could make time if needed by using back roads or commanding right of way on 27. Evening was just a few hours away and the watering holes would be overflowing and creating untold numbers of potential DWIs. He stopped at Pierce's desk and the big man paused and smiled at McKeon,

"Thanks for the evening off, Boss. The dinner and movie were great."

"Boss" gave him a pat on the shoulder and went outside for some still cool July air.

McKeon walked around South Hampton looking for a quiet place to eat lunch. The only reasonably short wait line was at the Jamaican food truck parked on a side street next to one of the town parks. He bought a curried goat wrap and a ginger beer and walked, still unrecognized, into the park. He picked a peripheral bench under a tree he could not identify other than being a conifer, and in front of a glossy-leafed, also unidentifiable, shrub. When only part way through his lunch he became aware of a constant, cat-like, scolding sound to which he'd been paying little attention. But when the vocal gray catbird landed on the bench railing and, spreading its wings, began to aggressively hop toward him, McKeon moved to the next bench and found solace. But not for long because a few minutes later his cell rang. It was the mother ship so he answered and learned that a call had come in from Amagansett Barracks about flyers that were being distributed both there and in Montauk. Someone was trying to organize an anti-Muslim rally for Saturday evening. He asked if any protesters had been seen in town and was told that they would check and get back to him. McKeon mused aloud, "I could maybe see that in Montauk, but in Amagansett?" As best he could recall there was not even a mosque nearby so why would this start now, on a summer weekend? He guessed that most people would be too busy standing in lunch and dinner lines or would be too happily oiled to give a damn.

He shook the piece of foil, giving what few crumbs remained to the lone pigeon watching him, then he walked to the recycle bins, foil in the trash and bottle in the glass only. Walking back to the Barracks he looked longingly at the window of The Fudge Store but he remembered both the Citarella goodies at home and the ongoing battle of the waistline and decided to forego the gratuitous calories.

Back at his desk he found a new fax. The same prints and DNA, a good sample, had been found on the Montauk Yacht Club papers and he knew he'd have to talk to Tommy V. again. McKeon had also decided it was time to talk to the chief in Montauk and discuss both protecting Van Winkle and a plan to apprehend the murderer if and when he decided to show. He was becoming more and more certain that at some point the man would show but was also certain that it would not be on a weekend when the marinas, especially the Yacht Club, would be busy all day and night, partying and fishing. The night time bluefish and tuna trips meant traffic all day and night. Lake Montauk would be a flotilla as it was every weekend, so there would be many eyes that would recognize a stranger. When he spoke with the Montauk Barracks, they'd agreed to meet on Monday morning and plan to do a walk through at the Yacht Club.

It was close enough to five and McKeon had spent the last hour with the Computer from Hell so he felt he'd earned an escape and even a swim. He walked into the day room and in his best camel voice said, ""What day is this? Does anyone know what day it is?" And, used to the routine, the crew responded, "It's Friday, start of a weekend, Boss!" He thanked them for the work during the past week and started toward home.

9

Day 4: Saturday July 26th

SATURDAY MORNING HE awoke and, after kicking a couple of beer bottles from his path, he set the coffee pot and went into the shower. When almost dry he reached for his medicines and took a pill from each orange plastic bottle. Walking into the bedroom he went to his clothes cabinet and reached for clean underwear but was greeted by an empty shelf. He slipped on jeans and a short-sleeved shirt, bagged his dirty clothes in a large mattress ticking laundry bag, and tossed it toward the front door where it slid to a stop atop the mail accumulating there. He filled a cup and took the two remaining pieces of pizza from the open box on the table and put them into the toaster oven. When he finally noticed a hint of burning crust in the air, he remembered the pizza, slid the two slices onto a relatively clean plate, and sucked his two fingers he'd burned in doing so. While his breakfast cooled to an edible temperature, he opened the draperies and windows and then, kicking laundry and mail out of his way, he strode to the front door and stepped out into the bright sunlight.

To his left, his truck stood outside the two-car garage whose doors stood open. Both sides of the garage were so filled with the detritus of his life that there was no space for the truck. One half held stacks of old lobster and crab pots, now useless live wells and many jerry cans. The other side was home for a fourteen-foot skiff, an array of old outboard motors on saw horses, and defunct fishing tackle.

Three sides of his property were lined by twelve-foot high, dense privet hedges isolating him almost completely from the world. The front was the exception as low shrubbery still let him see the street and passersby see him. But rarely did someone look into his yard. His home was in one of the more down and out areas of New Bedford. It was now a city where the failure of the fishing industry from the disappearance of cod and other bottom fish and the swordfish, which had been the basis of the economy, had driven people away to find a life elsewhere. Houses were left vacant and uncared for or were used as dormitories for the struggling newer immigrant population. Many waterfront buildings were lovely brick structures dating from the 19th century and were going the way of the nearby mill towns. The textile industry had vanished along with the fishing industry and those buildings not converted into seemingly glamorous yet empty rent stabilized housing were left to slowly decay. The wooden buildings and piers of the waterfront suffered all the more from neglect. But a few areas had survived and were used by the entrepreneurial types who could find fish and who plied the apparently resurgent scallop beds. These few could make enough money to buy food, keep a family and, all too often, buy drugs.

For some reason New Bedford was an easy access and entry port for the mercenary traffickers of weed and narcotics. Just as it had been during the days of Prohibition when, along with Gloucester, untold gallons of Canadian whiskey and, for years, West Indies rum reached docks and distribution. As in the last decades it had been drugs, marijuana, heroin, and cocaine by the hundreds of tons. Unfortunately, some of it leaked out into the arms and noses of the fishermen and their families. The results were devastating. Jobs, income, and lives were lost and families were destroyed. Those who could escape did so, and in so doing, the population of New Bedford dwindled even further.

This was the scene that greeted him later that day when, having shoved his laundry into two machines and given the Spanish girl who supervised them ten dollars to dry and fold, he parked his truck and walked down the dock to his boat.

<<<>>>

There were still some semi-private town beaches in the Hamptons, places where only residents with stickers on their vehicles and who were known to the local constabulary, could park and walk along narrow paths through grassy dunes to the beach. The public beaches were not fenced or really even separated from them and anyone was free to walk for miles along the oceanfront. But residents felt they could sort out the pale or freshly burned "intruders" from the healthily tanned locals, and they would look askance at these intruders when they tried to spread a beach towel or put up an umbrella on a "private" beach. Try to pull out a beer bottle from an Igloo and someone, usually in a uniform, or a lifeguard, would likely escort you off the beach.

From first light until the lifeguards set up their stands at around nine, the beaches were home to a few surf casters, joggers of all ages, playful dogs of every breed, and, of course, the rake tractors that manicured the sand every morning, burying the detritus or, if needed, carting it away.

McKeon had slept soundly until almost eight when Gaby sat down on the bed and awoke him with a kiss. "The kids were invited to go porgy fishing by Fred Janson and left about an hour ago. Get up and I'll fix your breakfast. Put on your bathing suit so we can hit the beach before the crowds."

After his morning ablutions he found his swim suit and was again glad he'd passed up the fudge. Looking at himself in the mirror he judged that Gaby was right and he had at least an additional five pounds to lose.

They'd packed a beach bag with essentials and McKeon had slipped his cell phone into his shirt pocket and then he and Gaby drove to the section of

South Hampton beach they preferred. It was an area in front of several miles of large private homes, well away from the condos and motels that bordered too much of the beachfront. At nine there were only a handful of people staking claims to an area of sand and most had not recognized the outgoing tide and had spread blankets well up on the beach and away from the water. The McKeons headed to the edge of the damp sand, spread a blanket and took off their cover-ups.

"They said it was to warm up today, Tom, into the low eighties," Gaby said. "First time all week! Also, they say that the onshore wind the last three days has warmed up the surf to almost seventy-five! I don't believe it but I'll let you know in a minute."

She rose, walked the twenty feet to the water, and let the next wave wash over her feet. The water was warm but the air temperature was still in the sixties and made the ocean seem warmer than it was.

"Come in, Old Man, even you can take this!" She waded out into the gentle surf.

After about fifteen minutes in the water they returned to their piece of the beach, toweled off, and shared a bottle of water. Gaby turned to her husband,

"If the kids bring home porgies, I want to fix them whole, the way my mother did. You'll have to scale them for me but then I'll fry them in olive oil with some garlic. She was always careful not to burn the garlic and she also added a bit of red pepper to the oil. I remember them being crusty brown and falling off the bones. We can pick up some corn on the way home, and I picked our first tomatoes yesterday while in the garden."

"What more could a man ask for, my dear? I know, come to think of it, a glass of Prosecco and then more of that vermentino. I think both are in the fridge."

McKeon's cell rang and he answered a call from the Barracks. "Boss, no protest tonight. County got wind of it and notified everyone that there were no permits. I thought you'd like to know."

He thanked the desk sergeant and then addressed Gaby's furrowed brow. "Some numb nuts have been denied permits to hold an anti-Muslim rally tonight. My guess is that no one would have shown up anyway."

A glance around showed that the number of beach goers had trebled. Car doors slammed in the lot and the first of the frisbees began to fly overhead both in and out of the water. The perennial overweight jocks were throwing a nerf football with increasing enthusiasm but increasing inaccuracy. When a group of twentyish girls began to set up next to the McKeons wearing what Gaby considered barely acceptable bathing suits, she got up and kicked her obviously mesmerized husband in the ribs, "Enough, Detective Lothario, you'd find nothing but trouble there. You are out of here!"

Obediently McKeon got up, carefully shook the sand from their blanket, and grudgingly put the gear in the bag. Looking at Gaby he said, "I wonder if they need sun tan lotion or would like the rest of our water?"

but his wife was already ten feet away and headed for the car. McKeon looked back at the group and shook his head.

They showered off briefly at the convenient building just at the edge of the parking lot, dried themselves, put on their shirts, and folded their towels onto the car seats to protect them at least a bit. The nearest farm stand, their favorite, was only a quarter mile out of the way. It stood on one of the few remaining open spaces close to town and the three acres were planted with the basic essentials: corn, tomatoes, herbs, and two rows of brilliantly colored zinnias. Most other items they sold came in from farms further out of town.

"Shall we plan for lunch as well?" he asked.

"Yes, certainly, and look, they still have bread and baguettes. You get a dozen ears of corn and I'll get the rest."

The corn, additional tomatoes, all the first heirloom varieties of the season, gorgeous heads of lettuces, half a dozen baby eggplant, and a bag of mixed herbs completed her shopping. They anted up and as they headed to their car, Tom handed his wife half an ear of corn. It was so sweet and juicy he wondered why you would want to cook it. Laughing and drooling corn juice, they stowed their treasure and headed for the shower and Saturday hair washing. Safely at home, when Gaby was stepping out of her bathing suit, she called to her husband,

"Oh, Officer, do you think you could give me a few minutes of your time?"

After finally showering they had a large salad, fresh corn, and the last of the burrata smeared on the still warm baguette. It was all washed down with the first half of the bottle of Prosecco. McKeon looked lovingly at his wife,

"You know, dear, the kids won't be home for a..." but a napkin in the face muffled the last words.

<<<>>>

His boat was in a row of a half-dozen Down Easters, the mainstay ships of New England ocean fishing. Broad of beam and with her enclosed cabin occupying most of the front half of the ship, she very much resembled a small ocean-going tug and she appeared sturdy and stable and was in far better condition than her neighbors. Her gunwales, which were almost waist high, added to her look of safety. When she was running, the whole boat seemed to tremble under the forceful vibration of the inboard diesel engine. She was equipped with outriggers for trolling, multiple rod holders and a 'tuna door' in her stern, a water tight door could swing inward about a foot above the water line so a big fish could be slid onto the deck and not have to be lifted over the side. State of the art radar, sonar and GPS graced most of the boats because to be safe and have a chance at a profitable trip you needed all of them.

He'd recently honed his radar skills so that he could now identify pelagic birds working over bait fish, the place where predators usually were to be found. It was this skill, knowing that the "fuzz" at the edge of his radar screen represented a flock of birds that gave him an advantage over many of the other boats. While everyone used to, and most still do, identify that 'fuzz' as weather or cloud or static of unknown cause, he'd learned to read it for what it was, a swirling mass of avian feeding frenzy. You'd find gulls and terns far from the safety of shore mixed with gannets, shearwaters and even some sub-arctic pelagic species which rarely ever went to shore. Under that cacophony, the water was usually churned to bloody foam by feeding predators, most usually tuna, his target species. Those tuna were once again of great value in a resurgent Japanese sushi market.

Now about twenty years old, she was still considered a relative youngster in the fleet. He had all his licenses and permits displayed but had kept her name and numeral registration in small letters on her hull. He could cover both easily with a piece of tarp that lay rolled up and secured above them. Pull two cords and he would become almost unidentifiable to strangers. He was sure of that. On his last striper trip to Stillwagon Bank he'd seen a number of swordfish basking on the surface as they loved to do, so today he was going to fish for them. He would rig his lures and baits much as one would for marlin if that species traveled this far north. He'd troll a spread of four rods, the two off the stern with teasers, attractive artificial lures meant to stimulate aggression, and the two on the outriggers would be baited with ballyhoo. Everything was meant to make a splash on or near the surface.

Stillwagon Bank was a marine preserve that lay where Massachusetts' Cape Cod Bay pours into the Atlantic, essentially between Provincetown on the Cape and Cape Ann to the north. The large expanse of water provided a haven for migratory species that could be hunted both commercially and for sport only to the north or south of the sanctuary. The Coast Guard kept a close watch on the region, which made risking fine or confiscation a good reason not to poach the waters. Nudging along the edge of the preserve could be productive, but most captains didn't ever want to get close enough to arouse suspicion and risk a boarding and check of their licenses or their catch. But a skilled loner, one who relied on his radar skills, could approach the Bank and come away rewarded.

From New Bedford it was easy to head northeast to the Cape Cod Canal, traverse it, and then continue through the Cape Cod Bay past Provincetown to Stillwagon. Once navigated, the journey plot was recorded in the ship's navigational system and upon exiting the canal it became an autopilot route that only relied on radar to alert the fisherman if another vessel was nearby. And so, an hour and a half out of his slip he was free to begin rigging for his troll along the western edge of the preserve which still lay about two hours away. He put a package of frozen ballyhoo into a bucket of seawater and took out a box of trolling lures, selected the four he wanted and reached into the cooler for a sandwich and a beer. An hour later he had rigged four ballyhoo and carried the bucket to the stern.

He put the first ballyhoo behind a black and silver skirt that looked like it belonged on a tiny, dashboard hula doll and ran it out about 150 feet behind the boat and clipped it to the starboard outrigger. The large marlin chugger, a plastic headed device about a foot long, he put out just as far on the port side. The two feather teasers were baited with ballyhoo in case of a short strike and placed just beyond the boats last wake, probably forty-five feet astern. A fifth rod was baited with the largest "hoo" in the package and it was kept in the bucket of water in case he quickly needed to get a bait in front of a recalcitrant fish. Everyone would say this is not how you fish for swords, but what did those a-holes know about fishing anyway! There were no boats showing on his radar so he took out a deck chair and sat down. He was still a good ten minutes or so from where he'd seen the first of the swords when he saw a disturbance behind the starboard bait. A bill flashed in the sunlight and the line popped out of the rigger clip. He picked up the rod and waited. Feeling nothing, he let out about five yards of line and began jerking the rod up and down, giving movement to the bait. The bill, black in the bright light, appeared again. He gave another yard or two and then began slowly reeling in the "hoo". When he finally felt resistance, he set the hook vigorously three times.

Upon being solidly hooked the fish raced across the surface and then sounded, headed for the ocean floor. He tightened the drag significantly and then carefully reeled the other rigger line toward the boat. Managing to keep tension on the fish struggling several hundred feet below the boat he was then able to wind in the two short lines and avoid any tangled tackle at the end of the fight. Reaching down to a hook under the stern he took out the gimbal belt and steadying himself he stepped into it one leg at a time and shimmied it up to his waist. With the rod now set in the cup of the belt he put his knees against the stern gunwale and began to pump the fish toward the surface. Although he knew there were usually no sharks this far north, he looked around repeatedly, just in case. Finally glancing at his watch, he saw an hour had now elapsed and both he and the fish were tiring. He'd only seen the head at 150 yards but he knew this fish would be at least a 300-pounder. But slowly the great creature came to the surface and soon it was unable to take line from the reel so he loosened the drag, preparing to let the fish move away from the boat rather than have the hook pull while he was landing it at the end of a long fight. When he finally saw the full length of the fish, he knew his estimate was far too low. Slowly he bent and opened the tuna door and backed up so he could reach his long-handled gaff stowed under the port gunwale. When the great fish lay on its side just off the stern, he put the rod in a holder next to the tuna door and reeled slowly with his left hand and when the massive head was even with the door, he struck with his right hand hooking the gaff above and behind the large eye. The fish thrashed wildly but he slid it into the boat. Picking up a hammer modified to have a long steel point on the end, he drove the point into the head between the eyes. The fish quivered once and was still. To get the fish to fit on the deck he had to curl it slightly and its size meant no chance of icing it so he covered it with towels which he'd keep wet with sea water allowing evaporation to keep it cool and fresh. Then he cut the gills to bleed the fish and, after putting the boat on auto pilot, headed home. A very happy fisherman, he slowly went about stowing tackle and hosing down the deck. Each rod had its lure removed and then was placed in the holder above the cabin, aptly named a rocket launcher. The fish was remoistened every twenty minutes or so and he throttled up to over twelve knots, burning more fuel than usual but getting home faster. He knew that he wouldn't have to work, fish for profit, for several weeks, this fish assured that, so he could plan his next trip to Long Island.

<<<>>>

At three-thirty, a horn sounded as a car pulled into the driveway delivering the McKeon teens and a bucket of eight cleaned and scaled porgies. They thanked Fred for the work involved but he said that the cleaning was a communal job effort and took almost no time. McKeon admitted it was early but offered him a cold beer. It was refused. Taking the bucket to the outside cleaning table alongside the garage, McKeon hosed off the fish and took the clean bucket and its inhabitants into Gaby's kitchen.

"Oh, my goodness," as she peeked into the bucket, "and sooo many. But I'll only cook half of them tonight and the others, Tom, I want you to fillet for me. That will be tomorrow's dinner. Please leave four here in the sink."

McKeon took his filleting knife from a drawer, picked out a small diamond sharpening stone and dutifully went back to the cleaning table. In half an hour he had eight lovely boneless and skinless fillets in a ziplock bag and ready for the fridge. The skeletal remains of the porgies he double-bagged and put in the fridge in the garage for later disposal. Returning to the kitchen he watched as Gaby was putting a sprig of rosemary and a slice of lemon into the cavity of the fourth porgy, placed it on a platter with the other three, covered them with waxed paper and put them into the fridge. Tom held up his fillets for admiring eyes and then put the baggie on top of the same platter.

Dinner was as good as promised and by eight-thirty the household was on shutdown and asleep. McKeon's silent cell sat charging in its usual spot on the nightstand next to the bed.

<<<>>>

Day 5: Sunday, July 27th

After a quiet Sunday breakfast and before heading to church, McKeon called the day room for a report from the desk sergeant.

"Boss, it was a quiet night. Someone set off some fireworks on the beach, two DWIs, both no issues, and a couple of noisy parties past deadline, but that's it. See you tomorrow, Sir."

After his homily, Father Keenan prayed for the soul of the murdered man and for peace and quiet on the

East End. As the parishioners left the church the priest took up his usual position at the front door where he greeted everyone. When he took McKeon's hand, he held it longer than usual and bent toward his ear,

"Do get the SOB, Thomas, before there's more agony."

Walking home the McKeon family discussed a Sunday outing, a routine event when work and weather permitted. Because of summer traffic on the roads a trip to the North Fork was voted down, but Sag Harbor was unanimously agreed upon as the destination.

"American Hotel or fish and chips?" he asked, full well knowing what the ladies would choose. They were, after all, over dressed for fish and chips. When he ID'd himself, the receptionist, daughter of a colleague, told him, "Just don't be late. One-thirty sharp, please."

They arrived into Sag early enough to permit a walk along the waterfront for half an hour and to try to calculate what it cost to maintain one of the large motor yachts moored there. The answer was always "much too much". Swinging back toward town they picked up their pace and arrived at their destination at one-thirty and were greeted cheerily by the young woman at the entry to the old hotel.

"Your table is outside on the veranda. Follow me. We have superb shellfish and both tuna and swordfish came in last night. You couldn't have picked a better day to come to eat!" When they were seated, she passed out menus, handed McKeon the wine list, and turning back toward her station added, "Enjoy everything!"

Gazing across at her husband, Gaby cautioned, "Just a glass dear. Is there a vernaccia on the list?"

As water and crusty rolls were set down McKeon ordered a half bottle of the white wine from the vineyards in San Gimignano, one of the Tuscan hill towns which they had visited last summer. The eclectic menu gave the adults a chance to be adventurous and the young people the opportunity for more conservative selections.

Gaby chose a scallop ceviche and then tuna tartar with a salad. McKeon had a dozen oysters which he shared with Gaby and Deirdre, and then grilled swordfish. Both youngsters had tuna burgers and fries, almost fish and chips but much more elegantly presented.

It was after three when the family began another short walk around town before heading to their car and home, all very content with their meal and the time together.

Dessert for their father was that his cell had not once called to him.

10

Day 6: Monday, July 28th

At work Monday morning there was little of a surprising nature, and a summer weekend had passed without a vehicular mortality, a bar room brawl, or a motorcycle ending up in the drink somewhere along the Old Montauk Highway. The only item on McKeon's agenda was to meet the Montauk Barracks chief at the Yacht Club at ten a.m. He signed off on some paperwork, looked at departmental email, responded where needed, and took out his diagrammatic flow sheet. The weekend had added nothing new but McKeon felt certain that someone existed who had rented three boat slips and had almost certainly murdered the two victims on their boats moored in the adjacent slips. But who that someone was still eluded McKeon. If only that someone had a police record, had screwed up once in his life, but he had not. McKeon hated to "use" Tommy V. but he was sure that Tommy was the next target and, therefore, essential to his capturing the murderer. What if he could hide an officer somewhere on Tommy's boat? That officer could hear anything unusual and know when to interdict. Or, what if he didn't even have Tommy on the boat and used someone as a decoy?

Well, in any event the options were limitless but the right one must be selected. When the next visit did occur, it would be late at night, and once the alleged perpetrator motored into Lake Montauk and tried anything, he would be trapped. There would be no escape. All of this would be part of the discussion later this morning with Chief Conklin.

Terrence Conklin was by ancestral rights an honorary Bonacker, named after the first settlers who plied Acabonic Harbor and farmed the community of Springs in the 17th century. His family had emigrated from Kent on the English coast in the mid-eighteenth century, and they were farmers, fishermen and a century later, constabulary. Few families merited being called Bonackers, and he was proud of the title. The local accent was nearly gone and few were still bay men who fished locally for a living in Gardner's Bay. Farm land was continually turned into valuable, almost priceless building sites as the once wealthy scions of the bay were no longer provided an adequate income from the land. Scallop rakes were traded for toolbelts to install lawn irrigation systems or ply another of the trade skills so in demand on the East End.

There were hold outs, and one of the most famous still existed: the fish farming and Rhodesian Ridgeback breeding farm tucked onto the north shore along the Napeague Stretch. Patrons could stop in and buy fresh fish, lobster salad, and goose eggs or have lunch at a shaded table amidst a menagerie of wandering domestic fowl. The dogs were exquisite, and a waiting list for a pup never got shorter. But few such remnants of a life from the past could be found without knowing where to look and how to listen. In one of those rare places where someone has been able to isolate himself and family from the inroads of modern life, if visitors were to close their eyes and listen carefully, they might just hear English spoken as it was by ancestors generations ago.

But the Conklins had left traditional old Springs life behind and had become East Enders. Terrence Conklin had become chief two years ago when his predecessor had won a modest lottery which, with his pension, would provide a comfortable retirement for himself and his wife. Terry was the natural replacement and no one in the Barracks groused at his appointment. He was taller and heavier than McKeon but no one would have doubted that their families both came from Anglo-Irish stock and that they might just share some genes as a result of some rural countryside hanky-panky in some past century.

At nine-thirty a.m., McKeon passed through the day room and made sure there was nothing of import, and then went to his car. Monday had begun warmer than any day of the previous week but it was still a typical end of July morning with the usual traffic of the "trade parade": worker and commercial vehicles headed east on Route 27 to job sites. By the time McKeon got on 27, the traffic had thinned out, and including a stop at a new Starbuck's, he pulled into the Yacht Club after only forty-five minutes travel time.

Conklin was in his cruiser talking on the phone but when he saw McKeon he exited and greeted his friend. They walked into the luxurious reception area, and because Conklin was in uniform no one interrupted their leisurely walk through the building, out into the marina area, and to Chris Dempsey's sanctorum. Ornate models of sailing ships and large oil seascapes adorned not only the main building but also Dempsey's office. McKeon assumed the few hotel/motel units were equally fancy. This was a first-class establishment built primarily for the privileged yachting set. McKeon had never been in the gift shop but he knew it was an extension of one of East Hampton's fancy boutiques

Dempsey was on the phone and nodded and held up one finger. After he quickly wrapped up the conversation, Dempsey stood and greeted the two officers and, looking at McKeon, asked, "Did you get prints off of the documents?"

"Yes, Chris, prints and DNA. That's the real reason we're here. The three of us need to look at Tommy's slip, the neighboring ones, and the suspect's empty one across the dock."

They followed Dempsey out into the marina area, walking past prime slips where they moored yachts up to 100 feet in length, boats that were in the seven to eight figure price range. They required permanent crews and burned in fuel in a year a dollar figure well above the average income of an upper middle-class Montauk resident. The further out the group went the more modest the boats became, the exception being the outermost moorings of the marina, those directly abutting Lake Montauk where the largest ships were tied up. They were much too large to navigate the inner marina.

They reached Tommy V's mooring where his spic and span 28" Parker was tied up, the immaculate boat reflecting the careful and thoughtful sailor owner. The boats on either side were of much greater significance. One was a classic twenty-year old Bertram with lots of teak, the other a somewhat larger sport fisher painted sea green to a foot above the waterline and then a sea-foam white above that. Across the stern her name was written in dark blue: *My New Wife*. McKeon looked at Dempsey who just smiled and gave an affirmative nod. Looking around to get his bearings, McKeon realized the dock they were on stretched north into the lake and the empty slip across from Tommy's thus lay to the east. He turned to Conklin.

"Terry, the presumed murderer would have to motor into the lake and then the marina and then he would have to back into the slip. Bow first might mean taking more time to get out and away, a lot of maneuvering." He then turned to Dempsey, "I'm not a sailor, but assuming a calm night, no wind, and normal tides, would he have to tie-up or could he just stay under low throttle in reverse and leave his boat there?"

"Depends on the boat, but probably, because minor movements would be buffered by the mooring poles. The broader in beam his boat, the more stable in place. Less swing and sway. So, yes, but I'd not want to do it for too long."

"Five or ten minutes?"

"I should think so, in good conditions."

The boats on either side of the vacant slip were sizable craft with spacious enclosed cabins and generous room for below deck bedrooms. They were motor yachts, not sport fishermen. All four neighboring boats could easily provide space for police officers to hunker down, to listen, to hear any conversation and then to make themselves known and apprehend the murderer.

"Terry, we know almost for certain that the gaffs on board were the murder weapons and they were never recovered, at least not in the waters near the boat. So, if we let this guy get onto Tommy's boat and he sees no gaff what does he do then?"

"I think he'd have three options. First's a knife. Many fishermen have one on their belt all the time. Hard to defend against a knife. Second is a gun, but that announces to the world what's going on. His third is to be carrying a gaff as back up, or go back and get his. I guess that's four options."

"OK, I agree no gun. So, we have to be prepared for a knife or his own gaff and we have to be able to stop him, shoot if needed, and have a way to protect Tommy, give him a means of defense until we can subdue his attacker. Your thoughts, gentlemen?" McKeon looked at both men.

Dempsey spoke first, "A spray can of Mace and then head for the drink." McKeon looked at Conklin.

"Not sure. IF we see the guy pull a knife and we announce our presence, what's to make him stop? Just our shouting 'POLICE!'?" I don't think so. We have to disarm or immobilize him or blind him so Tommy can get away. One of the newer tasers could be shot from the next boat. But if you miss? And answer this for me. How do we know it's him and not one of a group who have a vendetta? We have to hear the conversation between the two of them and if we hear enough, we don't have to put Tommy at risk. Don't wait for him to show a weapon. If we hear what we want to hear, Tom, why wait?"

McKeon turned toward Dempsey, "Chris, you never heard this part of the conversation, did you?"

Dempsey shook his head, "Guys, I wasn't even here. You were on your own. But, truthfully, I was a marksman in the Guard and I'd be happy to have a shot at him for you."

McKeon's cell rang and the text read "All phone data is in". "Gentlemen, I have to go back. Terry, we'll chat. Chris, just make sure all your staff keep eyes and ears open and report all strange boats and nosey strangers. Thanks." The three men headed back to the marina.

The incoming call to Sayger's hard line and cell both had calls from the New Bedford area but—the big but—all were placed from different public phones in the city. Only one was of any duration, about seven minutes, and none of the others were apparently answered. Storz had only a hard line, but the story was the same. A week before his murder he'd spoken to someone in New Bedford for ten minutes. Whatever the conversations had been they'd had to have been compelling enough to get two men to their boats at night to meet who McKeon was sure was the, same man, their murderer.

11

Day 9: Thursday, July 31st

He awoke rested but agitated. The money from the swordfish would keep him solvent for a few more days but soon he'd need to fish for profit. After a shower and a cup of coffee he went to the desk and as he picked up the framed picture of the young man, tears began to form in his eyes.

"Soon, very soon, another of those bastards will rot in the hell they made for you. I didn't see or wouldn't see that hell. But if I had, you'd be alive. I can't make them drown in their own puke but I can make them drown in their own blood. That I can do." He picked up the red marker and drew one line, half of an 'X' through the photo of Tommy Van Winkle. ""Rest of the 'X' soon, very soon!"

Rumors had filtered in over the last few days about large pods of bluefin feeding off the banks of Block Island. Those fish had been off Cape Cod, in easy reach for him, but had moved well north into waters off

Nova Scotia. They were safe from him because those seas were usually too rough and unpredictable for a solo angler, even one as skilled as he. It was unthinkable to try to handle, gaff, and boat a giant tuna that could weigh 700 pounds. So, after some hesitancy and debate he'd concluded that the aspect of several thousand dollars in his pocket outweighed the risk of traveling south. And what risk could there possibly be? No one knew him, no one had seen him and no one would be suspicious of an old boat trolling around in the sound. The approximately forty-five-mile trip to Block, without push and wasting fuel, would take only about three hours. He'd planned to set his troll northeast of the island and continue south along the Atlantic coast and then, finally, westward along the southern coast of Block. He would troll four lines all baited with ballyhoo rather than trying to fish in the standard fashion of tossing chunks of bait and hoping some fish would get interested. Instead his whole fish, threaded onto the end of the line complete with treacherous hooks, would be floating with the tide. They always said he was nuts to fish giants this way but over the years he'd out fished all of those brainless pricks.

He had fueled his boat, packed beer and sandwiches and packages of ballyhoo in the same cooler, and after boarding, stowing and feeling he was ready, he motored slowly past the breakwater which had been built to protect the harbor from the seas of a Nor'easter. Unfortunately, all the structure did was decrease the ebb and flow of cleansing water into and out of the harbor and create a stagnant, lifeless pond barren of life.

Outside the harbor he turned south along the breakwater. As he passed the Coast Guard vessel perennially stationed there, he waved. It never hurt to be friendly, did it? An hour into the trip he placed one of the packages of frozen ballyhoo into a five-gallon bucket of sea water to slowly defrost it. This bizarre baitfish from the subtropical waters looked like a miniature, one-foot long swordfish. But a closer look reveals that their "sword" was their mandible, the lower jaw, and not at all like other billfish. Rigging them so that they swam straight in the water and did not rotate was a skill that had a long, sloped learning curve.

Half an hour from his destination he rigged and set his troll. The two riggers set well back from the boat, at least one hundred yards. The other two lines trailing from the stern he set at fifty and seventy-five yards. Tuna generally don't like boats so separating the bait from the boat made sense. He kept a steady eight knots on a zigzag course down the eastern coast of Block, heading southwest until he was forced to turn west along the south coast of the island and into Block Island Sound. A few minutes later he noticed a distant belch of black smoke, most likely a trawler backing down on a haul. Half an hour later the trawler was much closer, only a mile or so off his port side. He picked up binoculars and was shocked to see someone glassing his boat. "What the fuck?" he exploded and quickly he moved to drop his canvas hull covers and turn away from the trawler.

<<<>>>

Ten minutes earlier aboard the *Suzie-Q*, Mike Michaels had spotted the Down Easter. At first, he thought nothing of it but when they were closer to it, he called Fred Wakeland over.

"Wakie, off the starboard a mile or so. What do you see?"

Wakefield paused in his sorting and went to the rail.

"Damned if that doesn't look like an old Bedford boat. But whose?" He turned to the bridge and called out, "Cappie, can you glass that boat for us and see if you can get her name?"

As the captain focused on the Down Easter, parts of the image, the name and registration, seemed to vanish. He called down to his crew, "Looks like he doesn't want to be ID'd. He covered all the writing."

The two deck hands looked at each other and almost simultaneously muttered echoing expletives, "Fuck. Mother of all Fucks!" and Michaels turned toward the bridge.

"Cappie, Can I come up?" He was motioned to the ladder. "Cappie, call this number for me, it's the South Hampton Police."

Soon he was talking to McKeon but when he turned around, the Down Easter was already out of sight behind the bluffs of Block Island.

Conklin was waiting for them where they temporarily moored the *Suzie-Q*, at the local wholesaler's wharf. He stepped aboard and talked to the two men as they prepared to offload their very generous haul of squid at Goswell's. Michaels did most of the talking and answering.

"Basically, sir, it could have been any one of at least half a dozen boats based on two things, her age of about twenty years and his size. His head was nearly at the cabin's roof. He's what, Fred, six-foot three?"

Wakeland nodded assent.

Conklin turned to the captain, "Cappie, you say he covered his ID? Dropped a sheet or the like?"

"Had to be. It was gone when I got into focus. Had to be so."

"But you say he was trolling?"

"You bet, four lines with two in riggers. Odd way to try for a giant, I'd say."

Conklin thanked them and looking back and forth at Michaels and Wakeland,

"Boys, do I need to say anything?"

"Nope," Michaels replied, "read you loud and ALL too clear." Wakeland simply gave two thumbs up.

Cappie moved in to give a hand. "Let's offload and get a beer. You boys need to give me some detail."

Back to the Barracks Conklin called McKeon, went over the meeting on the *Susie-Q*, and then came to the point.

"It could be him. Yes, or it might have been some druggie set to make a drop of a few bales and trying to look like a fisherman. Hell, Tom, he was fishing and if he'd picked up a giant on the way to the drop he'd been doubly well off. Maybe, just maybe, it wasn't him. Should we have jumped the gun and called the Coasties? If it wasn't him and they simply busted a druggie, our real guy would get wind and get nervous. And maybe more dangerous. I'm talking too much! But, Tom, I don't know."

"I thought the same thing, that we don't want to hop on the wrong person. But now? It's too late, I think we should have had the Coasties grab him. It was probably the right guy and I have enough evidence to indict him. And Lord knows what we'd find at his house. But he's tucked in nice and tight now and we can't go up there and snoop. And from what I hear about their constabulary, those guys won't even go near the docks. Conditions in New Bedford have gotten so bad." He paused. "Terry, your point of what might happen if it was not him is a valid one and I can't argue with you. We just have to go back to our plan to wait and be prepared, fully prepared for his return here."

<<<>>>

He cursed himself continually on the way home, realizing he'd almost blown any cover he had around Block and Montauk. Greed, he decided, was to blame. Yes, a giant was worth three or four times a big sword but he should have played it safe and gone sword fishing again. He sensed that even though no one could ID the boat, everyone on the trawler knew he was not a local, a stranger to the Block Island Sound, and as a result he would have to think carefully about revising his schedule.

Back at home he happened to glance at the fourth and fifth pictures and under each was written 'hand on the *Suzie-Q'*. He suddenly felt queasy and leaned forward, his head in his hands, and let out a crescendo of F-bombs, the loudest of which resonated through the house. But an hour later he had calmed down and that small portion of his brain capable of rational thought took over and said to him,

"THEY DON'T KNOW WHO OR WHY."

12

Day 10: Friday, August 1st

As if Thursday's drama had not been enough, it was Friday morning of another summer weekend and everyone was braced for another influx of party goers, sun worshippers and jerks in muscle cars. The latter would be a real problem if any of the drivers chose to show off inappropriately because not even the police's Ford SHOs could catch them if they had to. Last summer there had been two such episodes, both culminating with the dork behind the wheel not knowing the back roads and ending up sunk above his expensive hubcaps in sand. No one was hurt but the vehicles were impounded until a judge could decide on confiscation or just a fine.

McKeon spent most of the day trying not to flagellate himself any further over the decision not to pursue the Down Easter the day before. He toyed with his flow sheet, bracketed in what had happened, and added an asterisk. But he knew that the decision had been made and there was no point in retrospective moldering. He just had to wait.

The family had made the unanimous decision to stay close to home and not venture out into the mayhem on the roads and in every shop in town. Gaby's early Friday visit to the farm stand provided them with all they would need for the weekend's meals. Relaxing, reading, and a Sunday afternoon beach outing, were all that the family had on their calendar for the weekend.

Through Saturday night the only event that required police intervention had been an empty Dos Equis beer bottle brawl at Quito-Quito, the Ecuadorian bar outside of Amagansett. Some bumps, a couple of lacerations but no weapons in evidence so no arrests, only a resultant ride to the ER.

Bishop Keenan's homily that Sunday morning returned to his normal concerns which he addressed to the assembled, fully realizing he was preaching to the choir. Each year he saw fewer and fewer communicants, and even fewer young people. He was not a hermit, "As many of you know, you see me out and around town. Our wonderful school is filled with youth and I see baby carriages everywhere. Have I lost my ability to draw them into this tabernacle? Is the Mother Church failing to meet your needs? My confessional lies empty week upon week and I hope it is because you are all behaving and not because you are just derelict or believe your transgression too petty for my ears. Pope Francis, His Holiness, sees much of what I see and he, as am I his humblest of servants, is concerned. This is your church, my friends, and I am here to serve you. Come and talk to me. Help me to inspire more of you to join us beneath this roof." He paused and gazed quite beneficently over his parishioners and then said, "Let us pray."

As the McKeon family passed from the church, Keenan took Tom's hand warmly in both of his own, "I pray daily that you might apprehend the villain. But I must admit that I also pray that he sees the error of his ways and seeks redemption. Is that wrong of me, Thomas?"

McKeon paused thoughtfully and then spoke softly to the man still holding his hand. "Do you want the truth from me, Father, or just a platitude?"

"The truth of course, Thomas."

"In your eyes I may be wrong but I do not and cannot care a…" he paused and smiled, "about him or his soul. I only want to prevent another murder and to put him away for the rest of his life. I'm sorry, Father, but that's the truth."

"That's all right, Thomas. I suppose that is why people such as I are still necessary, so we can hope to help those who all others would cast aside." He patted McKeon on the shoulder and actually winked at Gaby.

As they walked toward home, McKeon took his wife's hand, "Well, the good pastor still has an eye for beauty."

At almost three-thirty in the afternoon when the air began to cool and the sun fell behind the low hills of the sand spit known as Long Island, the McKeon family donned swimwear, picked up the Torkelson kids from next door, and went to the nearly deserted beach. It was a full low tide so an almost endless and uninhabited expanse of smooth sand spread before them.

13

Day 13: Monday, August 4th

When and how did the term "cheese" become the slang meaning for both money and drugs? Initially it was because in the early 20th century welfare lines handed out both money and blocks of cheese. Later on, money was needed to buy drugs which were more harmlessly named cheese. Today in New Bedford you had to know the context depending on whom you were talking to, your dealer or someone you were trying to mooch. He knew now only really one meaning for the word and that was money. He was clean, over ten years clean, so his cheese was cheddar or cash, and at the moment he was getting short on both.

Mechanically he reached for the two pill bottles which were nearly empty and realized he'd have to refill them very soon. He hated them as they represented an addiction, but he knew they were what kept him out of the hospital and living a decent life in his home. Anything that kept him out and away from those crazies he'd accept. Anything.

After his aborted Block Island near-disaster, word was that those fish were now in the Gulf of Maine on their way to Nova Scotia but not yet there. So, he decided he had to travel north into that area. Instead of sailing into Nantucket Sound, around Monomoy, and then northeast to Scotia, he chose once again to go through the canal and save fuel. Finally, he'd push north-northeast through the Gulf of Maine toward the southwest tip of Nova Scotia. He checked his freezer and found two packages of horse ballyhoo, the largest and best ones, and put one pack into a five-gallon bucket to slowly defrost. He looked at the clock above the sink and saw it was almost ten p.m. He tossed a few new lures with feathered skirts into the bucket and set the alarm for four-thirty a.m. He took three ibuprofen from a container and washed them down with the last of his beer and then stripped and went to bed. He'd get more than enough sleep.

He awoke at four-twenty a.m., just ahead of the alarm. His biologic clock rarely failed him, so he dressed, picked up the bucket, added the second pack of bait, and went to his truck. Taking the thermos from the front seat, he emptied it of stale coffee and using the hose at his garage he made the container acceptably clean enough to receive the coffee from the donut place. When he fished early, he ran, as the ad says, on coffee and sugar, preferably half a dozen glazed.

The reason that he was risking a solo trip up north was not just the money but rather the reports heard on NOAA, the National Oceanic Atmospheric Association. They had been predicting almost balmy weather and almost no sea. Of course, that could change but the forecast had held the last twenty-four hours so he felt safe. Half an hour after leaving his mooring it was becoming light and he was well into the canal. Entering Cape Cod Bay, he set the autopilot to keep him twenty miles off Provincetown heading into the Gulf of Maine. He'd added salt water to the bucket holding the ballyhoo and when he checked them now, they were ready to rig. On half of them he broke the spine in two or three places so they'd wiggle more when trolled but the others he left unfractured. Slowly and carefully he rigged four of the baits for his initial troll. Two had skirts and looked like hula dancers when he held them up and shook them. The other two were free of adornments. Two hours later he was well into the Gulf and he decided to set course toward Shelbourn on the Scotia coast.

Entering the Gulf, he saw only the occasional trawler headed toward George's Bank but very little other boat traffic and that pleased him. He hated company on the water because most people were busy bodies, always crowding because they thought you had a better line of troll. When he was still about forty miles off of the Scotia coast, he dropped his outriggers and sent two lines back about 150 feet. Before setting the other two lines he adjusted his course to follow the coast but stayed about twenty miles off shore. When the two stern baits, the naked "hoos", were in his last wake he rechecked drag on the reels and set his speed at four knots. Again, he was breaking all the traditional rules for catching giant bluefin tuna but it always worked for him.

Moving to the helm he came off auto pilot and began a zigzag course dictated by whim. When he felt the baits were better swum in one direction, he held it longer. About an hour later the line in the port outrigger popped but the rod stood unbent. He quickly free spooled about ten yards of the eighty-pound monofilament line off of the reel and began to work the bait. Nothing. He swung the boat ninety degrees to the starboard and watched the lines slack and the baits settle into the water. As the lines straightened behind the boat, he knew the baits would rise rapidly in the water column headed toward the surface, as if fleeing from someone or something. Actually, this was the entire basis of the zigzag movement resulting in an artificial up and down movement of the baits meant to excite an otherwise uninterested predator.

Then the starboard rigger popped and almost at once one of the stern rods bent sharply. He picked up and set on the outrigger rod and watched as both reels were being stripped of line. He edged into the cabin and put the boat's speed at almost half of what it had been and then he took a gamble. He knew he couldn't really hope to land two fish alone without a tangle, but he could certainly give himself a shot. He put down the rigger rod in a holder and quickly brought in the other two lines and stowed the rods, fully aware that any slack given to a hooked fish would almost guarantee it would shake the hook. He picked up the stern rod and began to fight whatever had taken the bait. He rapidly gained line and soon saw the small tuna. He carefully reached for his long gaff and when the fish was close enough, he slipped the gaff into the bend of the hook and yanked upward, pulling the hook out.

He stowed that rod and turned to the rod still straining mightily against the fish that had sounded almost straight down only about fifty yards behind the boat. Thirty minutes later he opened the tuna door, put his gaff under the gill plate, and slid at least 400 pounds of giant bluefin onto his deck. One blow of his hammer quieted the fish, then he cut the gills and watched as warm blood pumped onto the deck. Opening his forward hatch, he took out an insulated fish bag and after hosing down the fish and boat he somehow managed to get his prize into the bag. He covered the bag with wet towels and turned the boat toward home with full knowledge that he'd have cheese aplenty. He picked up his radio and called the Japanese buyer.

<<<>>>

Summer heat, more typical of mid-August, had returned to the East End, and the beaches were crowded earlier each morning and stayed so until past what ordinarily would have been dinner time. Those who had AC then dined at home, but those who didn't lined up to get into cool restaurants. Midday the shops in most towns were so empty that merchants were closing from noon to three, in European fashion, then reopening until nine at night, hoping that the cooler temperatures would bring the shoppers and the strollers, those impulsive buyers, back onto the streets and into their stores.

On Monday McKeon spent the morning reviewing his graphic flowsheet and re-shuffling his pile of printouts. Tapping a pen on the blank space of the last couple of days, he tried to insert himself for the first time into this "dead end" as he now was beginning to think of it. What was going on in New Bedford? In the head of the person so seemingly remote from them?

"The Criminal Mind" was a subject about which so many books had been written and many had been required reading in college and then in the Academy. Some people were born that way, with a brain labeled "abnormal", clearly crazy or disturbed. Or others were "sociopaths." McKeon remembered Cleckley's book, *The Mask of Sanity*, and the impression it made on him. The "mask" made one seem normal while hiding the face of psychopathology, some madness or deviant behavior.

McKeon was sure that the murderer was living his day-to-day existence in some sort of community, perhaps among similar fishermen and not part of a family. God, he hoped that the community were not similar souls and that the murderer was alone in his madness. He pushed back in his chair and tried to distance himself from the flow sheet and its seeming dead end. What had been the lessons in those many books? One was that you could not easily get behind that mask and into the mind of the criminal—not unless he made a mistake and, as it were, lowered his mask. Freud spent his life trying to find a way into the mind. That everyone knew. But, how many thousands of modern-day Freuds were trying to do the same thing? Freud didn't have today's pharmacopeia to supposedly help those patients and yet what progress had been made? McKeon did not have a hotline to call to which he could give data about a given criminal and automatically get an answer. He still had to rely on footwork, desk work and luck. So, his Monday passed in frustration, and so did Tuesday.

<<<>>>

Day 15: Wednesday, August 6th

On Wednesday morning, McKeon met Tommy V. at his boat. The evening before he'd called Tommy and asked him about traveling by boat from New Bedford to Montauk via the route past Block Island. Van Winkle had offered him a ride out to see Block and the sound and, his curiosity peaked, he'd accepted. The weather was perfect with wind from the southwest at five knots and there was no appreciable swell. Tommy tossed a vial of Meclizine to McKeon.

"It can't hurt, especially in the sound west of Block Tide it can run pretty good through there. Please have a seat in the bow until we get outside. Lets me have a full view and more room back here when I need it. Later come back and we can chat."

As they eased out of the Club marina McKeon saw the Coast Guard station on his right. To his left he saw several other marinas. They were just now entering the inlet and he saw that the western shoreline was occupied almost exclusively by Goswell's. On the end of the protective jetties he saw about a dozen fishermen with lines well out into the current. He felt the boat accelerate and head NE, paralleling the shoreline.

"Come back here now, sir."

Holding onto the railing on the starboard side of the center console McKeon worked his way back until he stood beside Tommy.

"If I kept this bearing," Tommy said, pointing to the compass, "we'd hit Block almost dead center. Here, look." He uncovered the display for his onboard electronics and brought the map including Block Island to scale.

"Here we are, that little boat-like thing, and that's Montauk Point. And there's Block, not fifteen miles from the point. I'll run us up and into the sound. You can either stand or sit."

McKeon chose to stand. "Tommy, how fast are we going?"

Pointing to the left side of the display, Tommy showed McKeon their speed, RPMs, and some other data.

"So, at this speed we'd be at Block, fishing, in about ten minutes?"

"From here? Call it fifteen, Yes."

"But the Down Easter wouldn't run at thirty knots, would it?"

"No, sir, not unless someone's got some souped-up diesel. Not only that, but those boats aren't fun at any speed. Much too much swing and sway for this boy. Shut her down and she takes forever to stop, wallowing in her own wake all the time. But they have their place, especially in a big sea. There, you can just see Block, that grey bump on the horizon."

"So, getting down here, to Montauk, in that boat—how would you do it and how long a trip?"

"As the crow flies it's about forty-five miles and comfortably at twelve to fifteen knots, it's easy math. But wind and tide are always a factor and can add another hour or more to what should be a three-hour trip. And doing it at night? It's no piece of cake getting through the sound even with good electronics."

They watched the bump become an island with contour and color, and as Tommy turned toward the Sound he throttled down and turned to McKeon.

"Sir, look at Block. That boat Wakie and I saw, the Down Easter, had come down the ocean and not through the sound. It left the same way. He was fishing and probably didn't have local permits to take a giant. He was looking for a 'speak easy' fish as we'd call it. He was taking a chance at not being caught for the prospect of thousands of bucks. So, I'm not sure who we saw, but if it was your guy, he's pretty stupid. Or, sir, f-ing crazy!" He slowly increased his speed and headed in to Block Island Sound.

They were well into an outgoing tide and as they proceeded into the sound, McKeon could see the tide pouring out of the narrow body of water as it sped to the Atlantic. He thought he could even hear it and if Tommy had shut down, he would have heard it.

"Is this as bad as Plum Gut? They say that can be pretty bad."

"Every bit, and probably worse at times. I wouldn't want to be in either place in bad weather. OK, we have Block on our right, Rhode Island proper on our left, and New Bedford a couple of hours dead ahead. Want to see more?"

Tommy saw McKeon look under the gunwales and up at the rocket launcher full of rods and laugh guiltily.

"Tommy, since no one has called me, I have some time. How about we do a little fishing?"

Back at the marina Tommy quickly scaled and cleaned the bass they had just caught, put some ice in a bag and then double bagged the fish. His own fish could wait in the well until later. McKeon thanked Tommy warmly and started off the dock toward the mainland. He spotted Chris Dempsey, hands on hips and shaking his head. "Fishing on the job, is it?"

<<<>>>

Day 16: Thursday, August 7th

Thursday began as had the rest of the week except it was more humid. To his amazement one of the staff had found a copy of *The Mask of Sanity* in a down-county library and had just delivered it to him. Refilling his coffee cup, he kicked off his shoes, loosened his tie, and went back to college and a Crime 101 course. The further into the book he read the more he realized the difficulty he faced in trying to understand the man in New Bedford. But he spent most of the day doing his best at the attempt.

That evening the weather began to change. The forecast was not exciting but weather on the East End was often unpredictable. By eight p.m. it was raining and by midnight a squall swept across the island. But on Friday morning the air was fresh and once again cool. Plants and people, especially the farmers, were happy for having had the rain without any punishing winds. As the month would wind towards autumn and the first Nor'easter, any dark clouds or a drop in the barometer made people, especially fishermen, worry.

At the Barracks in South Hampton, McKeon was still moldering over how to handle things when and if Van Winkle received that phone call. He knew that once the man was in Lake Montauk he couldn't get out. They would not let him get out. But he wanted to hear that man tell someone why he'd acted as he had. He wanted, as it were, to hear a confession.

His intercom buzzed. It was the officer watching the tap on Tommy's line. A call had come in from New Bedford less than an hour ago but had not been answered, no message was left, and it came from a pay phone. McKeon opened a drawer in his desk and put his feet on the edge of the open drawer. "I used to be comfortable with them on top of the desk but not anymore," he said to no one and then he continued. "What is his lure? How does he get them to their boats after dark? What does he have to offer them or have to hold over them? That would right now only be Tommy, the only boat owner. Something has a draw strong enough, but what could pull a man that hard?"

He sat up, took out his flowsheet, and reached for a pen. Several times he started to write only to pause and re-consider. He looked at his graphics of "who" and "why" and "where are we" and finally added a new entry, "why did they come?" Under it he began to enumerate plausible reasons: One: money; two: a bargaining chip; three: intrigue or blackmail; four: drugs-doubt; five: evidence of something from past life (money, drugs, a crime).

Theorizing was getting him nowhere. Time to pick up the phone and get Tommy on his cell.

McKeon dialed Van Winkle's cell and was greeted by the now familiar, "Yaa-low, Tommy here."

He told him about the call and asked when he'd be docking. Then he called Chris Dempsey at the Yacht Club and told him that a Montauk squad car would be at the marina when Tommy V. planned to be mooring.

"Same old song, Chris, just keep an eye open for anything strange. He won't show in daylight but be careful."

McKeon had almost ruled out that the murderer would try to arrive by land because to get to Montauk from New Bedford was at least a five-hour journey. Counting summer traffic on the roads and ferry it could even be longer. But just in case he had the desk call to see if any ferry reservations had been made from Massachusetts and at least by area code none had.

Dempsey met the Montauk officer and they sat on the upper veranda where they could glass the approaching boat traffic and see that the slip opposite Van Winkle's was vacant. He pointed out into the lake,

"There, that's Tommy's boat. He should be docking by the time we get out to his slip."

They were there in time to toss him the stern lines as he put his motors on idle.

"See anything on your way in?" Dempsey queried.

"Nothing of interest except this guy,"

Tommy pointed into his boat and unzipped and flipped open the insulated fish bag,

"About a three-hundred-pound bigeye. In friggin' daylight! No one's gonna believe it."

As bigeye tuna were notoriously night-time feeders it was almost exclusively yellow and bluefin that were day caught. But Dempsey knew it wasn't all luck. Tommy V. was a skilled angler.

"Do you want to go to Goswell's and then come back? If so, I'll ride with you, because it will be fun to watch them when you open the bag."

Tommy nodded "yes" and offered Dempsey, who asked the officer to tell his office what he was doing, a hand into the stern. Then he cast off and headed back into Lake Montauk.

More generations of Gosmans than can be counted on one hand have populated the East End, most of them in Montauk. Every branch of the family will claim that their line stems directly from the Gosmans of Cork, Ireland. Now the only thing that really mattered was that the family essentially controlled the wholesale flow of fish and shellfish out of Montauk. At any hour of the day or night trawlers could be found unloading boxes of fish, shellfish or crustaceans. Trucks were always there off- and onloading more boxes. Even sport fishers and solo anglers could be found delivering a single prize fish to the ice rooms and cooled warehouses. Goswell's was always bustling. In addition to the wholesale market, there was a retail fish market and grocery, a large restaurant, and several gift shops. Located on the western mouth of the lake, it was a magnet for tourists, towns people, and fishermen alike. It was into this maelstrom of boats and people that Tommy V. took his bigeye.

Dempsey held the boat steady as Van Winkle pulled himself up and onto the dock, his boat dwarfed by the trawlers moored temporarily next to him. He shouted up at an open window on the warehouse's second floor, and a fair-haired man who looked to be in his mid-thirties came to the window.

"What do you have in the envelope, Tommy?"

"Three-hundred plus bigeye"

"From last night?" came a reply and it had a frown attached to it.

"Breen, would I do that to you? Not even three hours old. Pop down."

Half an hour later Tommy was taking his passenger back to the Club, knowing that he had established a fat credit that he could collect at any time. Dempsey tried to assure the young man that everyone had his back and if he ever saw anything at his mooring he should just motor up to the main building and call him. That was exactly what Tommy intended.

He dropped Dempsey at his office's dock step. After he had finally tied up, Tommy took his gaff, billy club, and rods onto the dock, washed them, and then took them to his truck. Instead of going home he called Fred Wakeland and asked if they could have a beer together and to bring Michaels along if possible. They'd meet in half an hour at the Shagwong Bar and Grill.

Tommy arrived first, asked Bridget for three IPAs, and went to an empty table in the rear of the still reasonably quiet bar. As he sipped his beer, he thought that more noise might be better because no one needed to hear the conversation. When the others walked in, Tommy rose and waved. As they sat down, he pushed a bottle toward each of them and raised his in a gesture of friendship.

"I had a call this morning. Just after I'd left." He took a pull at the beer. "No voice, no message, not traceable, but from a public phone. Not sure I want to bunk there tonight. Police said they'd cover me but, jeez, I don't know."

Both of his friends offered a crash pad but Tommy shook his head.

"That's not why I called you guys. We must have a common ex-friend." Seeing them shrug he went on. "I know. No matter what I can remember of those years before I cleaned up my act, I didn't leave any debts or angry people behind. I had no one to leave behind. No wife, no family, nothing. Never ratted on any of the dealers as I figured I was my own worst enemy and didn't need another one. If anyone would have killed me, I'd have done it myself."

Michaels and Wakeland both had similar stories and could come up with nothing of help. After he'd waved to Bridget and held up three fingers, Tommy resumed.

"Guys, I've had one call today and that scares me. There must be some names we can put on a list for the police. People who even though we don't think we crossed might have been able to do this. Crazies, or nut cases with no brain left after drugs."

Fred looked at Tommy and shook his head. "Tommy, I could name twenty such nut jobs. We *were* those nut jobs. But kill two people and travel all that way to do it and to have three more on your list? Un-uh. You're talking no brains, but talking about a—I don't know—vengeful, plotting madman?"

Van Winkle pulled on his bottle, wiped his mouth, and began again.

"OK, how about some not crazy, non-druggie? A clean, honorable, and upstanding New Bedford SOB who you pissed off. Made his daughter preggers, boinked his wife, killed his dog when it wouldn't stop barking. For Christ's sake there's got to be someone.

Got to be! Fuck, there is someone! Who, guys, who? I don't plan to be number three and he already rents the slot across from me. I'm ready to borrow some cappie's pistol to carry around and have under my pillow. Probably pull the trigger during a nightmare and blow my own brains out. You two better think about how he's going to get at you. You don't solo. And meanwhile you mean to tell me that we leave without one name out of all those guys still up there?"

When neither answered, Tommy began to get up but Michaels pushed him back into his chair.

"Listen, how about we round robin, always two at your place whenever you need to stay there? Other times you bunk with one of us. Daylight you should be able to see trouble coming and fend until you call McKeon or 911. 911's better, and right here in town. I'll run it by McKeon. Do you need anything to bring to bunk with me tonight? If so, we'll go over together to get it. Then I'll call McKeon from my place and he can advise us or whatever. But, Tommy, for now we've come up blank."

After tuna burgers, Michaels followed Tommy to his house and waited for him to get what he needed and to close up before they headed to Mike's apartment. It was almost eight when Michaels finally called McKeon but he apologized and summarized the Shagwong conversation.

When asked what he thought McKeon replied, "A good idea because it will make you all feel safer. Keep thinking about names and maybe one will pop up.

Mike, I don't have a firm idea about how he could target you and Fred but it's always on my mind. And in Chief Conklin's as well. He, our guy, would have to come up with an entirely new scheme for you two, and based on this morning's call I think he has a one-track mind. Just keep in touch."

Tommy V. sat at his friend's built-in, drop down kitchen table and shoved a slice of lime into a Corona. Tapping the bottle rhythmically with a fork he looked across the small kitchen toward the pullout sofa bed, and then turned to his host.

"Mike, how well did you know Sean Storz? Not just here but at home. Hah, some home! But I mean really know him. I don't recall much from New Bedford. He was just a face, a fisherman, you sometimes saw. Occasionally."

Michaels, who had been at the fridge to get two more beers, closed its door and leaned back against it.

"I crewed with him early on. A scallop boat with a mixed crew: a couple of crazy Portuguese, Sean, and me. It was good money for a while until the Feds started restricting everything. Sean didn't like the other two, the Portuguese. Said they were slacking, not shucking their share. They even had a couple of brawls on shore. Then one night one of them was stabbed, knifed, and almost died. People thought it might have been Sean but no one knew anything. Sean became a no-show on the boat and Cappie had to find two new crew members. Rumor was that Sean had holed up, gone cold turkey, and when he was finally up and around, he left town. A year or so later I got a note from him. He was clean and fishing in Montauk. He invited me down for a visit and I'm still here. It's funny because I had weaned myself a short time before that. That stuff, that shit, is still around here but not like home. Other than the cappies there were not many who were shit, Tommy, you know as well as I do. Sayger came down here even before Storz. I didn't know much about him though. Like with you and Sean, he was just a face you knew."

Tommy set down his bottle. "Sayger I knew. Good guy. A ladies' man. Mostly wrong ladies, and always getting antibiotics for one thing or another. You think he'd have worried about AIDS. He was clean, that I know. We'd sometimes fish together if we didn't need to work. But I know for a fact that once in a while he'd move bales of weed for someone there. He told me it was easy money but I couldn't see the risk was worth it at all. I guess he did and I wondered about it when he was killed. But now with Storz, and us on a list, I've sorta stopped considering that angle. Probably this is the kind of chatter the police should know about. Just in case. But Mike, what do we do when and if we see this guy, other than call the police, I mean. McKeon's told me my boat would be wired and that they'd have men in the boats on either side of mine. At that point we'll all know who he is and perhaps I should feel confident but I can't. I just can't sit there as bait waiting to be hooked, or knifed, or clubbed when he doesn't find a gaff on my boat. Crap, minute he gets on board and starts to talk I'm in the drink, headed down and away."

"Didn't think you could swim."

"Don't have to swim. I'll just crawl away on the bottom. It's only four foot or so there."

Michaels looked at his watch, got up, went to a cabinet, took out a sheet, and tossed it to Tommy.

"At least you won't have to sleep on year-old dry jizz. Goodnight. Need a wake up and are you fishing?"

"Yes to both. Four-thirty please, and Mike, thanks. Thanks a lot."

14

Day 20: Monday, August 11th

MONDAY DAWNED CLEAR and warm but an onshore breeze meant few bugs to bother the vacationers. McKeon cleared his desk of the weekend's accumulated but minimal paperwork and looked toward the coffee pot which still held the residue of Friday's last brewing. As he started to get up to clean it, Audrey entered with a fresh, full pot.

"Sorry, Boss, I overslept. Too much of a quiet week-end, I guess. How was yours?"

And after a pleasant exchange she handed him his refilled travel cup and went back into the day room.

McKeon took out his flow sheet and looked at the time line which ran across the bottom of the page. Since Day 9, the eventful Thursday almost two weeks ago when that boat appeared off Block Island, the only additional entry was the phone call to Tommy's house this past Friday, Day 17. His conclusion was that who-ever "he" was, he'd been too sufficiently rattled by his

Block trip to set up a plan of action that would bring him to Montauk.

On this last rainy Saturday McKeon had called a young psychiatrist whose acumen he admired and they met for lunch at an oyster bar in Riverhead. They chatted through three dozen oysters and two braces of IPSs and finally McKeon asked the question which he himself could not answer. Not even after he'd struggled through Cleckley.

"Who the hell is this guy and what is he waiting for?"

The answer came slowly and in fragments but cogently. He was clearly a man on a mission. But that mission was clouded by so much rage and hatred, and probably self-hatred, that he could not be expected to be rational. He was probably someone who had chemically stabilized functional mental illness and some event had destabilized him, starting him on a course of action which he could not, and clearly chose not to alter. Yet he was capable of recognizing when he has made a mistake; the Block Island encounter and his subsequent almost complete silence. This made him even less predictable, more elusive, and probably more dangerous. He had given in to making one call but only that one. Again, he was silent and what he did in that silence was anyone's guess. Maybe he could function, presumably fishing, and control the urge, whatever it was, to target five people and to try to kill all of them. He was probably schizophrenic and on medication. This was not really sociopathic behavior and explained why McKeon had not found an answer in Cleckley. This was the behavior of someone who could decompensate totally into a vindictive, brutal rage, and then disappear into what seemed to be a fairly normal life.

Did this help? Did it do more than reiterate the facts? Did those facts give an understanding which might help McKeon find who he was looking for? Probably not, but it might explain lag time, delay, hesitancy. It had been, after all, a month between the first two murders and they were now where? Barely three weeks since Storz's death. Eventually "he" would call and he'd have a reason for Van Winkle to meet him. Of that McKeon was sure. But of the rest, who but "he" could really say?

The two friends parted, each wishing the other a less disruptive rest of the weekend. McKeon was left with his ever-increasing disquietude and feelings of frustration. He still thought back to Day 10 and Block but after this mid-day discussion he began to feel that Conklin may have been right, and interdiction of the wrong person, a statistically reasonably probable event, might well have put off "his" surfacing for a very long time, long enough that complacent constabulary might lose interest.

So, with all of this conversation fresh in mind, McKeon stopped pushing around his pen and began once again to try to put himself into the head of the man in New Bedford, not to strip him of a mask but to get an idea of where he lived, what he did day-to-day, and what drove him. Getting up from his desk he went into the day room, nodded to his crew and went out. He walked slowly from the Barracks toward his favorite secluded park bench, the one which the cat bird thought it owned.

"I'll bet your little guys have fledged and you will let me share the bench," he said to no one in particular. The Jamaican food truck was there and the ever-smiling face greeted him warmly,

"Aftahnoon, Offissuh. Ah see you in dat papah but you more hansom in puhson. Gingah bee-ah?" He nodded so she passed him a bottle.

"Mah treat, Offissuh!"

"But I can't," he began but she interrupted, "You can and will!"

He thanked her, picked a napkin from the pile under a large clam shell and walked into the park to think.

He had done this in the past when a particularly puzzling case had stagnated, seemingly becoming an insoluble dead end, and whether by serendipity or his mental maneuvers, something changed. He intuited a pathway to a solution, and an arrest. Not every time, but more than once.

But those criminals had not been like this one. They'd been clever and devious, but they were not irrational. Yes, they thought they could get away with their crimes, almost did, but they were not insane. And that was how McKeon thought of this man.

He sat down under the same obscure conifer and in front of what he now knew was a magnolia, but this time no bird scolded him. He began to pretend to actually be the man in New Bedford and have him talking while McKeon was listening,

"I fish for a living and you saw me doing that off Block Island. I really goofed that one, didn't I? My actions are revenge. Revenge for a transgression of Biblical proportions. Someone needed to damn those men and I was forced to do it myself. No one could or should help me!"

McKeon stood up and began to pace. "But why? What did you lose? Who did you lose?" He walked to the recycle bin and deposited his bottle. "That's it, it has to be! You lost someone and blame them! I don't need to unmask this lone avenger; I just need him to come to me."

He looked at his watch and saw it was almost four-thirty. Time enough to make some notes and get home for a pre-dinner Prosecco backyard walk with Gaby around their now very productive veggie garden. With the warmer weather, even the eggplants were ready to pick and add to French beans, tomatoes, zucchini, cucumbers, lettuce and herbs. What a beautiful harvest!

<<<>>>

Day 21: Tuesday, August 12th

On Tuesday morning, after clearing his desk, McKeon called Terry Conklin and told him about yesterday's out of body musings and his conclusion: that loss, which he apparently blamed on five men, of someone near and dear had caused the suspect to seek revenge. Conklin agreed that it made a lot of sense but he wasn't sure it brought them any closer to knowing who the murderer was or to apprehending him.

"But, Tom, just perhaps such a compelling reason for his behavior assures us that he will not quit his quest and will show up here in Montauk."

Later in the day Conklin called Tommy V., told him about McKeon's idea, and pointedly asked him if he could remember any situation that had occurred in New Bedford, namely a death, that in any fashion, no matter how tangentially, might have involved Tommy and his friends. When he didn't get an immediate answer, Conklin prodded, "Tommy, you still with me?"

"Yes, sir, I am, but I'm trying. Firstly, no I can't think of anything. But I'm trying to understand how someone could think five people who really were not close friends, although some did fish together, all warranted killing. And all for the same reason? Sir, I just don't get it, but I'll talk to Michaels and Wakeland tonight."

Tommy called Michaels late in the afternoon and Mike felt much the same as Van Winkle. He could not think of an event or even understand why they were targeted. Since Tommy was bunking that night with Wakeland, he waited until they were together to have any discussion. Through dinner and for several hours later the two discussed their past lives and Tommy related his long chat with Michaels from a few evenings ago about their relationships with the two deceased. As regards McKeon's theorem of cause, Wakie could add nothing. Neither thought that they had precipitated this vengeful activity, and, therefore, there must be some other reason for the murders. At eleven p.m., emotionally drained, they went to bed, ready to be awakened at four-thirty in the morning.

Wednesday passed the way any other late summer day had for who knew how many years. The day room busied itself with paperwork that had been generated by fender benders, two bicycles stolen from the bike rack outside of the IGA, another person was bitten by his own dog, and someone who'd been arrested trying to sell untaxed cigarettes to the Barracks's only undercover officer.

McKeon lived with his angst and tried to find something to do other than clip his fingernails for the second time that week. And he tried very hard not to carry his disquietude home with him in the evening and to leave it on his desk. But the family knew that the man who'd dined with them the last couple of evenings was not "the real Dad," and they coped.

15

Day 23: Thursday, August

He spent the morning doing needed chores, dropping off laundry, paying several bills, buying beer, and going to CVS, and when he was ready to return home it was almost noon and he was hungry. Bored with pizza he drove to one of the last remaining true and old-fashioned Italian pork stores. It was out of the way, not near the docks or his home but he knew they made the best hot sandwiches on a large wedge roll. He had to park half a block away and the scene, the glimpses of the life on the block, screamed that this place was doomed. No one he passed on the street looked as if they knew what an Italian was still doing in the 'hood.

The door was held open by a stop. Half a dozen people were sitting and eating and another four were being served. The well-armed owner sat on a stool by the register, an obvious bulge under the left side of his tomato-stained apron. Behind the glass of the steam table were four trays: veal and peppers, chicken and peppers, sausage and peppers, and some fish thing, a nod to the Portuguese clients. Stacked on the work bench behind the hot food were the classic sixteen-inch long Italian bread wedge rolls. A whole sandwich was fourteen dollars and a half was eight. Two people could easily share a half but he had the hunger of at least two people so he bought a whole sausage and peppers. Cut in half, with each half separately wrapped and bagged, he estimated it weighed almost three pounds.

Home, he took out one half and put the other into his fridge, but before closing the door he took out two beers. He avoided looking at his desk and the photos because he didn't want to feel pushed into mania. The trip to Block still hung like a pall over him. He looked around the living room for something to occupy his time. In one corner, almost hidden behind several fishing rods, he saw his harpoon. He took the last bites of the sandwich, walked over, and picked it up. It still felt light and balanced so easily in his hand, even when he brought his arm up so his hand was behind his head and above his shoulder. It was clear that the blade would need some work to have it gleaming and razor sharp once again, but he had the time to devote to it.

He remembered how as a teenager he'd honed his skills by hitting lobster pot floats, severing them in half from a distance of over twenty yards. But it had been years since he'd hunted swordfish with it, the days when they were plentiful and everyone harpooned them. He'd planned another trip to Stillwagon on the next day because he'd seen other swords when he'd recently caught his big fish. So why not? He was confident that he had the eye and the arm, so why not plan to harpoon a sword? And if he failed, he could always bait one up. The weather report was perfect for a try: light winds and almost no sea. And, of course, he'd have sunshine, the essential element for basking swords. He knew if he spotted one, and could drift down onto it, he wouldn't miss.

Today fishermen attached heavy monofilament, perhaps 150-pound strength, to the harpoon line. The monofilament was light and offered no resistance or friction when the harpoon was thrown. It was nothing like the quarter inch-thick rope that lay coiled in a barrel, line that made even a short throw much more likely to go off target. The added incentive was the much higher price he would get for a freshly harpooned sword as compared to those hooked and drowned on the long line of a trawler. Those fish were in the water, dead, for many hours. He'd get big cheese for this fresh fish. After he'd made all the other preparations for the trip, he spent the late afternoon and evening sharpening the harpoon. Toward dusk he took out the other half of his sandwich and two more beers. After taking one bite he decided it needed to be warmed so he opened it and put it on a tray that just fit into the toaster oven.

Between bites he put finishing touches on his honing and when he was satisfied, he stood and gripped the steel shaft just above the blade and ran the blade over the back of his left hand, shaving it clean. Smiling, he stood the harpoon next to the door and went back to the kitchen table. He picked up the CVS bag, tore it open, and removed the two vials. He took one tablet out of each and washed them down with his beer. Looking over his shoulder at the clock, he saw that it was nine-thirty and if he was getting up very early, he wanted to try for six hours of sleep. Opening the second beer he tried to remember the last sword he'd harpooned but it was certainly ten or more years ago and his memory of those days, when his cheese was heroin, were not at all clear. He walked into the bedroom, took three ibuprofen, showered for a long ten minutes, and then went to bed.

By ten a.m. on Friday morning he was on the edge of Stillwagon and with his boat on autopilot plot to stay a quarter mile outside the preserve, binoculars hanging from his neck, he climbed atop the cabin, sat down, and began glassing the sea. As NOAA had forecast, the weather was perfect and the boat was barely rolling under him. In an hour he'd seen only two small swords, hardly legal fish, and not worth killing. He dropped down, went to and opened his cooler, extracting a sandwich and a beer, and climbed back up. The sun glare on the glassy sea assured him that in time he'd find what he was looking for. This was what down on the cape they called a tuna sea, one on which you could see birds further away than usual and even the turmoil the tuna would create under them. Then off the port side, about one hundred yards away, he spotted his fish. He estimated it was as large as the one he'd caught a couple of weeks back. He was drifting on a parallel course with the fish and knew he'd have to get closer without spooking it. He dropped into the cabin, pointed the bow a few degrees more toward the fish, revved the big diesel only long enough to push him ahead, and then cut the motor. He could steer the drifting boat just enough so he'd not intercept but wind up almost parallel and about twenty-five yards away from the fish. He went up into the bow wishing he had more of a bowsprit, an old-fashioned harpooning pulpit sticking out almost six feet. But he could deal with what he had, just so he was close enough. His fish had not moved and was about thirty yards away. Just so that big eye closest to him wasn't on high alert the fish would be his.

At twenty-five yards he slowly raised his harpoon and five seconds later hurled it toward the fish. It hit just behind the huge eye with such force that it went through the fish up to the hickory of the shaft. The fish quivered a couple of times and lay dead on the water. Quickly and carefully he drew it toward the boat and along the port side to the stern. He bent and opened the tuna door and, to add security while bringing it into the boat, he reached for his long-handled gaff and deftly brought the point through the eyes. Then, with one hand on the gaff and the other on the sword, he pulled it onto his boat. He quickly bled the fish and then sat down, in awe of the creature. It was clearly larger than his last fish and he guessed mid-400s. He curved the tail end across the stern, covered the entire fish with wet towels, and turned the boat toward New Bedford.

16

Day 27: Monday, August 18

Everyone in the day room was busy at work when McKeon arrived at the Barracks. The weekend had been a busy one for the East End. First there was the bungled burglary in a Watermill boutique when the numb nuts tripped over a rug and fell into an alarmed glass showcase, most of it falling on his head and knocking him unconscious. Add to that the usual DWIs and another underage drinking party in a McMansion that would have gone unnoticed except for the loud music at two a.m. But the real excitement occurred at the IGA in Amagansett when at five p.m. on Sunday evening two shoppers put on ski masks, pulled guns, and headed toward the registers in the front of the store. Each held a cloth shopping bag and demanded the money in all the registers. As she opened her cash drawer, Maritza pushed the panic button next to her register. Immediately a loud claxon sounded, lights flashed on and off and the two men dropped their bags and ran toward the front doors which had just automatically locked. The two cashiers hurried toward the rear of the store, herding the few terrified shoppers with them. The owner, ex-NYC cop Lloyd Carver, directed them into his office and closed the door behind them.

When the two burglars reached the doors and found they were unable to exit the store, they looked at each other in alarm and tried to pry the doors open. The taller man pushed his partner away and fired at the right-hand door but the glass only cracked, giving it a shower door appearance. He fired again and a two-foot hole appeared where the bullet had hit. Coming through the hole was the ever-increasing wail of siren sound cutting through the otherwise quiet evening air. Firing a third time, the burglar enlarged the hole enough to let him try to belly his way through to the outside.

His accomplice, meanwhile, leaned down to begin his exit, but saw a movement behind him and then felt a searing, paralyzing impact to his shoulder. His gun fell to the floor and in short order he followed it. As he was being dragged away from his escape route, he saw his colleague prostrating himself and tossing his gun far from his body as patrolmen surrounded him. Carver cuffed the accomplice then called to one of the girls in his office to shut off the alarm and let the doors resume operation.

One of the patrolmen greeted Carver warmly as he helped lift the inside perp to his feet and said,

"These two certainly aren't state of the art. Guess they expected a good old easy in and easy out job. Well, they'll certainly be 'in' for quite a while."

With both men, who were now felons, safely inside the back of the patrol car, Carver turned to the now freed shoppers, all of whom were anxious to leave.

"Maritza, help them bag whatever they had and let them go. My treat for spoiling their evening."

And he went to get a broom to clean up and a piece of plywood to cover the door.

So that was what McKeon walked into that morning. He'd not had a call on his cell for the entire weekend. All had been managed without him and for that he was grateful. Tommy's tap had been silent and neither Mike nor Wakeland had any unusual contacts. He cleared his desk of annoyances and turned around to face his nemesis, The Crappy Computer. Half an hour later when he saw his coffee pot empty, he walked into the day room where everyone suddenly seemed busy at work.

"Did I miss something on my desk? Just what is everyone working on so diligently? Pierce?"

"Boss, we just want clear desks by noon. It's pizza Monday, remember? Will you join us?"

McKeon heard someone suppress a laugh.

"Pizza Monday? News to me, but sure. Margherita, please, nothing heavier. And, thanks."

He filled his coffee cup, went out into the bright summer morning, and sat on the steps of the Barracks in the shade of a still healthy hundred-year old elm.

"Pizza Munday, malarkey!"

After McKeon had left, Pierce resumed the conversation in the day room,

"His wife knew he'd forget his birthday, he always does. No mention at home because they plan a party tonight. So, we look good to go. The caterer will be here at noon sharp. Nothing brewing out there in the world so just maybe it will stay that way and he'll have a good surprise."

But from the next room came an ominous warning. "Call coming in on Tommy V.'s line, not local, no voice and just hung up on the machine. Umm, just a moment, not traceable beyond New Bedford. Let the boss know."

Pierce stood and went to the front door. "Close one, guys."

A minute later Pierce was back at his desk. "He just said, 'Thanks', that's it, but you can see he's on edge. I hope he can enjoy this."

At noon the boss was at his desk with his flowsheet spread in front of him. Except for the two phone calls it looked much like it had two weeks ago and that bothered him. Nothing else since Block Island. What was it? He wouldn't call it an interlude, but it needed some name. He was sure that it was a fiasco for whoever was on "that boat", as he referred to it.

His cell rang and he recognized Gaby's number and he knew just hearing her voice would cheer him.

"Hi, dear, where are you?"

"I'm in the day room, Detective."

"Come in, I'll get the door."

He opened the door for her and stared into the day room. A table was spread with a lovely lunch buffet and above it hung a birthday banner. He kissed his wife and at looked around at his very happy team and then asked:

"And just where is my pizza?"

Fortunately, the phone did not ring for an hour and when it did it was just a nuisance call, a cat stuck up a tree, afraid to climb down, and the owner without a ladder. At one-thirty they cleaned up and attempted to get back to work. The rest of the day was relaxed and everyone was pleased that their boss had enjoyed his party.

That night at home the family sat on the veranda and gave McKeon several wonderful gifts. Gaby gave him a new iPhone and showed him how to take selfie videos so at a crime scene he could beat the TV people and be sure they had his better profile. With their mother's help they had arranged an outing for fall fly fishing with Tommy V. during the blitz, and they also presented him with a neck tie. But what a tie! From Hermes no less, pale blue with little pink bunnies on it. "Dear, it's to go with the new suit you're going to buy yourself," and "Nice for next Easter," she told him when he looked at his wife with a frown, "but right now the chef needs a few minutes alone in the kitchen. Birthday boy, would you open a bottle of white?"

His celebratory dinner was really quite wonderful. It began with their favorite Vermentino to accompany sumptuous shellfish pasta in a white wine sauce with lots of garlic and some fresh parsley from the garden. Then the sous chef was allowed to grill his own rib eyes on the barbie and plate them next to the faux frites and garden salad and pour them each a glass of a splurge, a rare Cab Franc from the North Fork. Dessert came from a small bakery, another hidden gem on the back roads of South Hampton. After he had Vacu Vined the two wines and as they slowly cleaned up the table and then the kitchen, McKeon thanked his family once again for a very special day and dinner.

This week had marked the start of the fall sports camps for the McKeon teens, football for Giovanni and track for his sister Deirdre, so that soon after dinner they were all very happy to say good night and head to bed. But McKeon's cell rang just after eight.

It was Tommy. "I'm sure you know there was a call. No voice or message, just hung up on the machine."

"Tommy, it was just that, another non-traceable call. Do you have company at home or are you bunking out?"

"Company, and we're both armed. Legally, sir, but adequately, except against a machine gun."

McKeon chuckled, "I can just imagine. Tommy, there's been nothing at the marina. Chris even has the night watchmen spending more time out on the moorings. Anyone moving would be seen unless they tried to come in dark, and I doubt anyone not very familiar with the lake would try that. And, of course, why should he come in if you are not on your boat? Go to sleep. Are you fishing tomorrow?"

"Dunno. Mike and Wakie are. It looks to be a nice day on the water and the albies and skipjack are starting to show. Would you like a couple of morning hours on the water? Bring the missus. My treat!"

McKeon had nothing pressing on the docket for the a.m. and the kids biked to camp, so he said, "Let me buzz you in five."

After an enthusiastic "yes" from his wife, he called Van Winkle and arranged to meet at Tommy's boat at six the next morning. The proviso was that they'd be back dockside by ten-thirty.

He and Gaby set out appropriate boat wear, hers perhaps a little less so than his because when he looked at her planned wardrobe, he just shook his head.

"You're not going to see much sun at that hour, dear, and it will probably be chilly on the water."

"I'll be fine," was her retort, "you worry about getting seasick and I'll worry about being cold. Good night."

After calling the Barracks, talking to the Night Sarge, and giving them a head's up, McKeon set the alarm for four-thirty, brushed his teeth and took a last look at Gaby's selection of boat wear.

17

Day 28: Tuesday, August 19th

Tommy V. was on board the *Nibble This* rigging two lightweight spinning rods with very small, dime bright lures—appropriate enticement for most smaller predator species. When he saw the McKeons on the mooring, he set the rod down and went to the stern to offer a hand down into the boat. After intros Tommy asked if McKeon had ever used a fly rod.

"Yes, years ago I was a decent caster. But that was trout fishing, not this."

"It's no different and if we find albies on top and you hook up on the fly you will be in for a shock." Tommy pointed to the cushioned seating in front of the console. "Have a seat, folks, and we'll get underway."

The morning was cool and the flags at the marina hung limp on the poles. A pale hint of dawn lit the eastern sky but sunrise was still half an hour away. As he zipped his jacket McKeon looked at his lightly clothed wife, but she seemed comfy and content. She hooked her arm in his and smiled.

As they approached the inlet McKeon noticed a strong outgoing tide and a small wave break about one hundred yards out in Peconic Bay.

"Perfect tide," came the word from the helm. "Now please stay seated until I slow down again. I'm going to run east toward the lighthouse and won't stop unless I see birds."

The boat came quickly to plane and they sped past Gin Beach and then Shag. The Montauk lighthouse came into view just as Tommy said, 'Hang on, a sharp turn coming." And he swung quickly to the port and out into the bay.

"See that gray mass just above the water? Those are birds and you'll see them in just a few seconds. Might be over bluefish as it's still too early for bass blitzing. I'm hoping."

Before he finished talking, the gray mass had split in two, each half moving away from the other.

"Perfect, guys, a dollar says albies. I'm going to go past them, shut down, and drift towards them. Ma'am, can you use a spinning rod?"

"Yes, Tommy, I can."

"Good. When I start to idle, I want you in the bow. You'll cast to the edge of the pod and start to reel as soon as your lure hits the water. Fast as you can, and don't worry about setting the hook, they'll hook themselves."

They felt the boat suddenly slow and rock gently on the water. Tommy took down a rod from the rocket launcher, checked the drag, and escorted Gaby to the bow.

"Knees right against the gunwale. Keep your balance and when I holler, you cast. Remember, to the edge."

She could see the water boiling under the swirling and screeching gulls terns, and a few pelagics tossed into the mix.

"Detective, come with me." Tommy took a fly rod from under the gunwale and went to the stern. "As I recall, you are a righty, yes?" McKeon nodded assent. "Good you're positioned so you can cast over the motor. The fly is small so don't worry about dings on the cowling. I'll set you up for a short cast."

He worked out about forty feet of the line and handed the rod to McKeon. "Same as trout fishing but it's easier from a platform. That rod balances with about half of the line on the deck and the other half in the air. Here, watch." He took the rod and sent half of the line out onto the water and then, lifting the rod, brought the line arcing back over his head. Then he drove the rod forward, the remaining line shooting out of the rod.

"Just be SLOW! Nothing should be fast. Test cast for me." McKeon took the rod and after two or three casts the muscle memory and motion came back to him. "Good, now just wait. If they don't dive, you'll be able to reach them in thirty seconds. When the fly hits the water, strip it in as fast as you can. If one hits, just pull back once and then don't touch a thing. Everyone ready? OK, cast!"

McKeon heard Gaby let out a squeal and saw Tommy move to the bow and then he remembered to strip in the fly. On the third strip the line was suddenly pulled from his hand and the reel began to sound like a dentist's drill. He heard Tommy shout, "Just don't touch the reel, and don't go near it! Hold the rod up high and wait until he stops."

In the bow, Gaby had the advantage of more drag on her reel, and soon Tommy reached over and caught the little tuna-like fish by the tail, removed the single hook, and after giving the fish a little kiss he shot it head first back into the water. He put Gaby's rod into a holder and then said, "Let's go see what the boss is doing."

In the stern, McKeon looked in awe at the line still running off of the reel, and with one eyebrow raised he turned to Tommy.

"He'll stop any second now," Tommy said. "Must be a very big albie or maybe a skipjack. There have been some fifteen-pound skippies around. He's stopping. See if you can regain some line, but if he wants to go just let him. We have nothing but time."

Fifteen minutes later their captain tailed what he'd predicted, a gleaming, multihued skipjack.

"People do eat them but I don't think they are table fare. Not when we have better. In you go, Skippy." He turned to his guests and smiled. "Just how many more times do you think you can do this? Take a seat and we'll find some more birds. What we call albies are False Albacore. They taste like liver but fight like hell. Down south, in the Carolinas, they grow to twice the size of yours, Mrs. Mc."

"Please call me Gaby, Tommy."

"Sure." Tommy pointed. "Look dead ahead, about two hundred yards. See the birds?"

McKeon saw them but he also saw two other boats, recent arrivals, bearing down on the flock of birds.

Tommy frowned. "You are about to see two boats full of idiots. Dollar says they'll run right into the school of fish. Those two always do that."

"You know if they are from here?"

"Yup, only one blue hulled flats boat out here. He's on the left. On the right, the Parker, a big shot from the Club. Watch."

Both boats did run towards each other, neither willing to yield until the last second. The fish sounded and neither boat managed a cast.

"Sit down, guys, we are out of here. We're going to the south side. We prefer here, on the north, on an outgoing tide. Usually fishes better. Opposite on the south, it fishes better on incoming. But not always. I just hope those two don't follow us."

They didn't, and the McKeons each caught two more fish. Tommy then said, "OK, take a look around. Twenty-plus boats over here and many more to come. Time for us to head home, but first we get you some supper. Come back here, sir, if you would."

Working his way along the console, McKeon stood next to Tommy.

"Take out that fly rod, the lower one, yes, and free up the fly from the reel."

The rod was much stouter and the fly was almost six inches long and seemed to weigh at least half an ounce.

"See the choppy water north of the lighthouse? That's called a rip. It's the result of an abrupt change in depth from shallow to deep, and as the flow drops down and under the deeper water it pushes up a wave of resistance the faster shallow flow hitting the slower and deeper. Anyway, the water does funny things but what it does do is wash bait and stuff over that edge and pushes it down to fish waiting for it. It's sorta like a cafeteria down there. I'm going to go above the rip fifty feet or so, into the shallower water, and keep the boat up there. I want you to strip off all the pale line and when you see the color of the line change to orange just stop. That long line is weighted and when it and that heavy fly get behind the boat, they will sink maybe fifteen feet as it heads into the rip. I'll hold the boat in the water above the rip and move slowly along the edge. When I give you the nod, I want you to start stripping in the line and when you think you're are about half way in let it all go out again. Let it run slowly through your left hand."

When they were moving slowly along above the rip, Tommy said, "OK, let it all out and keep repeating the process. If a fish hits or the line has resistance to a strip, pull hard on the line. Three times! Then let the line in the boat go out slowly, keeping resistance on it with your hand until it reaches the reel. OK, go!"

On the third session of retrieving the fly over the rip, the line seemed to stop and McKeon's natural reflex lifted the rod.

"No, no, no! Hit with the left hand! The rod is useless, it has too much bend. That WAS a fish. Back in and keep going."

Almost at once another fish hit the fly and McKeon strip set vigorously.

"Hang on, we're going over the rip to fight in deeper and slower water."

Ten minutes later, his instructor at his side, McKeon saw the striper come to the surface and turn on its side. Tommy reached down and lifted a thirty-four-inch striped bass onto the boat, unhooked it and put it in the live well.

"Guys, there must be a pod of fish there, as you had two hits within seconds. We won't keep more but, Gaby, it's your turn. Stay seated until I set up again and then the same routine. And remember, strip and hit hard with that left hand."

Tommy had marked the GPS when McKeon hit the two fish and after re-crossing the rip and positioning the boat, he called Gaby to the stern.

"Again, get your knees against the stern for balance and when we go over the rip with a fish don't be afraid to hang on. If he's hooked, he won't get off. OK, let out all that line."

The fish Gaby hooked repeatedly refused to come to the boat, sounding each time she was able to get it near. When it finally tired and came to the surface, Gaby gasped.

"My gosh, Tom look at this!"

Tommy took a picture as the fish lay on her side next to the stern, glistening violet on her flanks and turning darker up onto her shoulders and back. Tommy leaned over, grasped the lower lip and removed the fly. He held her upright until she was able to hold that position and when she finally bit down on his thumb, he let her go. With a flick of her tail she disappeared into the depths.

"That folks, is what we call an egg wagon, the gene pool we want to preserve. Gorgeous fish, huh? We could stay right here and catch fish after fish until slack tide, but just let me bleed your fish and then we head for home."

Back at the Club Tommy scaled and filleted the fish to Gaby's specs and then bagged it for them.

"Thanks for coming. I appreciate what you are doing and wanted you to know. So, back to work and enjoy the fish."

As they walked to their car, Chris Dempsey intercepted them and Tom made introductions.

Dempsey pointed to the bag of ice and bass fillets.

"Tommy got you a nice bass. On the fly?"

"Yes, fishing along the rip. Gaby landed, actually released one over forty inches, an absolutely gorgeous creature. Why the stop, Chris?"

"Well, just some radio chatter. As you know, we monitor VHF for safety reasons. A couple of hot heads were talking about forming a group. I don't know, sea going vigilantes, I guess. They want to patrol outside the lake every night in case some guy tries to sneak in. Well, Tom, the word has gotten around about the Down Easter off Block. Mike and Fred were not the only ones to see him. At first, they were just pissed at an outside boat trying to mooch a giant. But then someone else saw him go stealth and run. Also, unable to ID him. They are even asking why no Coasties were in pursuit. Lots of the locals have weapons and most are legal. I just don't like the idea of vigilantes. If you and Conklin wanted observers, wanted to set something up with them, maybe it could work. But they have decided that that boat belongs to the murderer and well, you know what some guys around here might do if stoked.

"Anyway, that's what's up. You can think about it. You or Conklin could even get on the VHF and 'chat room' with them to see if they'd work within the law. I guess more eyes and ears couldn't hurt. Enjoy that fish and make some ceviche with it. I'll tell you that as good as that fish will taste tonight it will be better tomorrow. The flesh relaxes and becomes flakier and tastier. Tom, Gaby, pleasure as always."

McKeon glanced at his watch and reached for his new phone.

He stopped at home to shower and dress and was at the Barracks just before noon. Nothing had disturbed his morning or that of his team. The tap line was quiet, no pets were stuck in trees, no one had run out of gas, and he'd made all the needed entries on his computer. So, when four-thirty rolled around, McKeon said good afternoon to the day room and headed home. En route he called Conklin and briefed him on the talk with Dempsey. McKeon's call didn't surprise him as one of Conklin's ears on the water had called him earlier in the day when he'd heard the same chatter. Conklin had already decided what he wanted to do and was sure that McKeon would approve. Tomorrow he'd talk to Dempsey but now he was listening to McKeon.

"Think about it, Terry. It's your gang out there and you know them. It's probably better to organize them than to let them do it themselves. Give them rules and regs. And just hearing YOU on their VHF might just sell you as 'one of us.' Just a thought. Oh, my wife and I spent three hours this morning on the water with Van Winkle. He's a good man and a very good fisherman."

"Yes, I heard, my 'eyes and ears' told me, Albies, skippy and stripers. All good! We'll chat."

<<<>>>

Day 29: Wednesday, August 20th

Wednesday began with a rose-colored sky on the eastern horizon. The Accuweather folks were watching a depression forming off the Carolinas, a not uncommon meteorological event for the end of August. If it evolved into a storm, the prediction was that it would head east-northeast and not involve the coastal US or the Maritimes. Six hours later they announced that the depression was turning into a "Sou'wester." This was all fine except that on the East End everyone relied on NOAA for their weather information and they were not as yet running up any warning flags. As a result, anyone who had planned to head out to sea did not change those plans.

At nine Chief Conklin called the Montauk Yacht Club, was switched to Chris Dempsey's office, and told him about the word from his "ear on the water".

"Terry, I've sat and listened to the chatter and it started again at six this morning. Oh, by the way, did you see the sunrise? Spectacular! And NOAA is poo-pooing it. I assume you're concerned about the fishermen organizing some kind of vigilante group."

"Yes, but I think we might make some use of their enthusiasm. What if I come over and sit with you and we cut in on a conversation? Can you do that?"

"Certainly. We just find a busy band we like, say 'Hi', and then you give them your spiel."

An hour later Conklin was sitting with Dempsey and they were trolling through the most commonly used VHF bands until they found the chatter they were looking for. Then, Dempsey cut in.

"Gentlemen, Chris at the Yacht Club. Can I have a word with you?"

There was silence for a moment and then a query, "Are you snooping, Dempsey?"

"No not snooping, just sharing what I've heard from some friends, your friends, about forming a patrol group. Someone with me likes the idea and wants to give you some advice on keeping it safe and legal. Are you interested?"

"Should I be?' came the reply.

"I think you'd better be if you want to be effective."

"OK, who else is listening?"

"Chief Conklin." There was silence again.

"You're kidding of course?"

"Nope, he's not kidding. This is Conklin and I think your idea might work and could be helpful and I'd like to give you some guidelines and organization. Even sanction it if you look at it as I do and see that I might have a valid point. My suggestion is that tomorrow we get some of you together and let me explain how to get you up and running. Talk to some other men and call me later. We can meet anywhere you like, but Chris will let us use the Club. Any questions?"

"You're for real on this, Chief?"

"Yes I am. My word on it."

"OK, I'll get back to you."

Conklin turned and looked at Dempsey. "I pre-empted use of the Club. Any issues?" Dempsey shook his head. "Good, I'll call McKeon and get him on board. He will be, as long as there are proper guidelines and they don't get in the way when and if 'HE' shows up."

McKeon did suggest strict rules. He wanted a schedule, on paper, with names and dates, and they would have to use a VHF channel that was essentially not used by fishermen. Talk kept to a minimum was a must and they should have some common password for transmissions, not a name. Dempsey said he could arrange it so all chatter would go to barracks as well as be heard at the Yacht Club. When they were satisfied with their morning's work Conklin left for his office.

<<<>>>

Day 30: Thursday, August 21st

McKeon spent the late morning re-editing what he felt needed to be the regulations and rules of conduct for the fishermen and their night time vigil. His greatest concern was that they might go beyond simple reporting and attempt an interdiction on their own. So his rules were: One: Report any unusual traffic with GPS coordinates,; Two: Keep vessel in sight but do not follow; Three: Stay on station; Four: Use only the designated VHF channel and only when essential; Five: Do not follow; Six: the Coasties would have to know all schedule data and be on board.

He moved to his flowsheet. A month had now passed since Storz's murder. What was going on in New Bedford? Were they ready if "he" did come back? Both nagging questions for him and only the latter had any answer.

Dempsey and Conklin had contacted the owners of the boats on either side of Tommy's slip and had permission to use them when and as needed. They had the Club keys and had examined how best to be concealed on those boats. Rigging Tommy's with a listening device was a simple matter and it would never be noticed.

18

Day 31: Friday, August 22nd

He sat at his desk looking at the five faces on the wall and wondered how he was going to kill Michaels and Wakeland. As yet a reasonable plan escaped him so he returned to Van Winkle. He'd hardly known him but had seen him sitting and chatting with his son so he was guilty by association.

The docks were still rife with drugs and addicted fishermen. The captains often had to hire those addicts to fill a crew but they were careful to select those who they felt could work while "wired", at a pace above normal. Those men could shuck more scallops in a day than 'clean' hands could. He'd seen other men around his son but these five he'd shipped with at one time or another and had considered them friends. Friends, he thought, shouldn't lead you to an inappropriate and greatly premature death. Only enemies did that.

Pushing back from his desk he went to the fridge, took the last beer from the door rack, set it on the counter, and then refilled the rack with eight bottles. The laundry pile caught his eye, and then the pile of mail. He pulled a trash bag from a box under the sink, sat on the floor by the front door, and began putting weeks of junk mail into it. The few bills he found he'd pay with cash. He had no bank account other than a coffee can on the shelf and therefore no checkbook. He lived as most fishermen did, in a cash economy. In many respects he didn't exist. Unfortunately. he received a small, undeserved disability check so the government knew who and where he was, and that meant filing a tax return. Usually he'd get money back, even if only a few bucks. Try as they might the Feds couldn't get a handle on the flow of cash around New Bedford but they were otherwise always occupied chasing drugs and regulating fishing. His only real expenses were his utilities, food, and fuel and he covered them easily enough. And then there was the cost of his medication, which was pricey but he realized it kept him on an even keel, able to fish and do the other things he had to do. So, except to deal with those items he rarely left home other than to fish. Going to a bar meant you might risk life or limb, and the whores were mostly older than he, so why bother. His home, as much as a mess as it was, had become his castle.

Getting up he moved to the laundry pile, bagged it, and then slipped his feet into barely intact Dockers and went to his truck.

<<<>>>

McKeon had cleared his desk and struggled almost an hour with Crummy Computer, summarizing the week's essentially non-events. On the large calendar on his office wall Labor Day Weekend loomed only a week away. It was the last big push, the last massive influx of weekenders before things quieted down on the East End. The ungovernable and rowdy lines outside breakfast nooks, lunch trucks and dinner restaurants would be mostly gone. Renters who never drove during the week and didn't recognize stop, pedestrian crossing, or yield signs would have largely gone the way of the dodo.

Parking lots would no longer be jammed and native East Enders would see the beach population drop by eighty percent from what it had been for the last three months. Sidewalks and curbsides would be litter and vomit free and dog poop would become only an occasional nuisance. And the clean beaches would be a wonder to behold.

The Halloween parade in Montauk would be the only busy day on their streets before the Thanksgiving holiday. And everyone was really already giving thanks, especially the men of the East End Barracks. But until the murderer was apprehended no police officer would rest easy.

At four-thirty McKeon headed east early enough before the meeting that he'd have time to talk to Conklin and Dempsey before the six p.m. meeting with the fishermen. Gaby knew that dinner might not be until eight or nine but after feeding the youngsters she'd have a quiet reading time until Tom returned home. And she was anxious to hear the results of that meeting.

A large room, one of the many open spaces in the Yacht Club, was set up with a dais and a dozen chairs in a semi-circle in front of it. A cloth covered table to one side held a coffee urn, real cups and bottles of water. Right before the meeting began, Franny Furlong came into the room. Unbeknownst to Conklin, he was that man he'd been talking to on the radio. He walked up to the chief and offered his hand.

"You were talking to me, Chief, and on your word, we have a bunch of the guys who promised to show. We'll see."

He went to the table, saw the cups with the Club logo, smiled, and filled one. By six-fifteen there were more fishermen than chairs but they seemed happy to stand against the far wall rather than sit near the constabulary. Edgy would best describe them. Dempsey welcomed them and thanked them for coming. He gave Furlong a nod and then introduced Chief Conklin.

Chief Conklin began. "I'll cut to the chase. What I'd like to do is satisfy your desire to do something and at the same time lessen your anger at losing two friends, and to this point without seeing justice served. I propose the following. You will become almost deputies and will, therefore, act within the confines of the law, laws of both land and sea. Under Franny's leadership I want you to set up a schedule." He continued for about fifteen minutes and then paused.

"I should have introduced Chief Detective McKeon before this and before I answer questions."

McKeon simply re-emphasized the need to stay within the guidelines and to stay out of harm's way. He listed his six priorities as emphasis. He ended by telling them they had to understand that someone who'd murdered two men so brutally would not hesitate to kill anyone who might get in his way. Then he nodded to Conklin.

Half an hour later, as the meeting broke up, Conklin motioned to Furlong,

"I need a schedule, names, cells, all of it, as soon as possible. Every little detail, and Franny, no one can do anything that might get them hurt." Dempsey moved toward his office. "Cervesas, señors?"

Having phoned home as he left Montauk, when McKeon entered the kitchen, he found that dinner was ready for him. He gave Gaby a hug and then went up to say goodnight to the kids. He unburdened himself of jacket, tie and shoes and went back down stairs.

The last of the bass fillet had been lightly sautéed, topped with a layer of buttery and garlicky mashed new potatoes, and then put in the oven under the broiler for just enough time to brown the potatoes. The addition of a garden salad to the plate resulted in a perfect summer dinner.

"So?" Gaby asked him. McKeon finished his mouthful, took a sip of wine and then wiped his lips.

"Must have been twenty who came, many more than we expected. They listened quietly and most left as a group. They were still in the parking lot when I called you." Taking another forkful of the bass he smiled, savoring his meal.

"Dempsey was right. The fish was great after a rest and is just as good if not better today. You have to live out here to understand what fresh fish really means. Dear, when this mess is over, we really need to spend more time on the water."

"We are not thinking of a boat, are we?" his wife asked, one eyebrow cocked, a sign that could be read as "don't even think of it!"

After taking another bite, he raised a calming hand.

"No boat. Just do the math and see how many charters you can have on the interest of the money you don't spend on a boat in one year. And there will be many grateful fishermen when this is all over."

He poured each of them another glass of the Channing Daughters' Tocai and looked to see if there was still another portion of the bass they might share.

"Conklin will get the actual working set up and also do most of the monitoring. I want to stop and talk to the commander at the Coast Guard station. He needs to be fully informed and on board, not only with what we are doing, but because he might ultimately need to interdict. It has been over a month and I expect something to happen, sooner rather than later. But we can't count on a mad man to follow our schedule."

He stood, cleared the dinner plates to the sink, and returned to the table, brushing his wife's hair as he passed. But before he could sit down his cell rang.

<<<>>>

That evening he decided it was time. He had to meet and kill Van Winkle, this weekend if he could arrange it. But he had to talk to him. There could be no leaving messages. It had to be one-on-one so he could sell the meeting. It had worked with the first two and he'd make it work again. He didn't have the supposed "information" that had lured Sayger so he'd have to get Van Winkle to mule a few bales for him. He'd offer 10K. That would be easy money, even better than having someone drop a giant tuna onto your boat. Greed. He'd appeal to that universal among fishermen.

He went out to his truck and drove to a phone. They were harder to find every day because someone would rip them out or just destroy them looking for what, a few dollars?

"Please deposit..." but he knew the routine and before the voice had finished, three quarters chimed through and then dropped sequentially into the coin box. After five rings he slammed down the receiver, "Fucking machine! That's the third time. Where is he?" He stormed back to his truck. "Later, I'll try again later."

It aggravated him and he didn't need that. He had a schedule to try to keep and he wasn't about to leave a message. Tomorrow he'd try again.

19

Day 32: Saturday, August 23rd

McKeon had been able to make an appointment with the commander of the Coast Guard Station in Montauk so on Saturday morning he and Gaby made sure the kids were off to camp on time and then they drove east. He used back roads to stay out of Route 27 traffic but still the trip was taking longer than he'd expected. As they passed The Milk Pail apple farm, Gaby turned to her husband. "Tom, the sign said they're open for apple picking. Doesn't it seem early?"

He glanced at his watch. "Yes, it's only the twenty-third, but we'll stop on the way back. How does an apple pie sound for dessert?"

"Deal," was her only reply.

As they left Amagansett and got on the Napeague Strip, the traffic slowed well below the speed limit of fifty-five mph, and even though it was only mid-morning the parking areas at The Lobster Pot and Cyril's verflowed onto 27.

"Tom, did you hear anything about an issue at Cyril's? Wetlands or something?"

"No, but I don't see all the East Hampton Court issues. Haven't heard a word. Busy enough now though, isn't he?"

McKeon veered to the right onto Old Montauk Highway, the lower, slower more scenic road into town. He stayed close to the speed limit, if just a bit above it, and had someone pushing him almost at once.

"I hope he doesn't pass me. I'd hate to ruin his day with a summons."

"Can you ticket someone here?"

"No, but I could relay his plate number to the Montauk Barracks. They would meet him somewhere soon enough."

Entering town, McKeon turned left onto Flamingo and away from the worst traffic. When he reached the marinas on the lake he turned right and wound his way onto Old West Lake Road and then turned into the Coast Guard station on Star Island Road.

In 1955 Station Montauk was established on Starr Island, consolidating service on the East End by replacing the two oceanside stations at Ditch Plains and Napeague. They could now have larger, modern ships instead of small surf-launched rescue boats. Station Montauk was now as capable a station as existed on Long Island.

Security at the entrance checked McKeon's ID and the visitor's list and, instructed on how to find the officer in charge, Nathan Bramley, they were then allowed to pass around barriers and onto the base. McKeon knew that Conklin had visited with the OIC so when they were admitted into his office and he had introduced Gaby, he did not have to go over basics, just his own concerns about the posse of fishermen.

Bramley was an affable man in his mid-fifties, handsome, fit, and soft spoken. McKeon was sure his demeanor could change rapidly as the occasion demanded.

"Tom, we can't be everywhere at the time but when and if you need us, we will be there. Having an early warning heads up of his calling, meeting time, and a peek from your 'posse' will all help to assure our being able to get to where we would be needed. Certainly, if anyone comes into Lake Montauk they won't get out, and there are few fishing boats we can't catch in a race. But now, let me take you and Mrs. McKeon on a tour of our station. I recall you were here on messy business years ago Tom, but that was not a fun visit."

The *Cutter Ridley* had been the pride of the Station for a number of years. Commissioned in 2001, the sleek eighty-seven-foot ship had a crew of ten men and women, a range of 900 miles, and a speed in excess of twenty-three knots. Her bow cannon and stern SO-caliber machine gun were ample armament for most problems she might have to deal with. The crew saluted smartly as the OIC and his guests walked by.

"Besides the smaller vessels you see across from Ridley, we have both helicopters and fixed-wing aircraft at the Montauk airport, so we can get up and out quickly. The last years, most of our work has been rescues and chasing foreign trawlers out of our waters. And, of course drug interdiction when we get a tip, which is not very often. A lot gets through."

Bramley walked the McKeons back to their vehicle and asked if they had planned to lunch in town and when McKeon said yes, Bramley said the sushi at Eddison Park was very special and that they should go there.

"Sounds wonderful," Gaby said enthusiastically.

"Then just a minute." Bramley took out his phone and moved a few feet away. A minute later he turned back smiling, "You're all set, a table is waiting for you."

McKeon frowned, "How did...?"

"Doesn't matter, does it? Just go!"

As they passed out through security at the gate, the young woman saluted and asked, "Going to Eddison Park for lunch?"

There were about a dozen cars parked in front of the restaurant and when they had entered and McKeon had identified himself to the young woman at the desk inside the door, she smiled, picked up two menus and motioned them to follow her.

"Right this way, sir, Uncle Nathan said to expect you."

They were shown to a quiet table away from the rest of the diners. Gaby looked around the bright dining room, its simple and understated decor saying "elegance, not extravagance".

"Red carpet treatment, Tom. Folks will think they should recognize us and wonder why they can't."

"They'll see you, my dear, and wonder why you're with such an old man!"

A waitress appeared with a water pitcher, glasses, and a list of the luncheon specials. McKeon asked her for the wine list which arrived promptly. It revealed a short but inclusive and very fairly priced selection. Gaby looked up from her menu and asked if he'd be happy with just a selection of sushi and sashimi.

"After half a dozen oysters, I would be, of course. How about a dozen pieces for each of us and we share a tuna roll, plain, no sauce? Then we can order more if we need to."

"Fine, what do they have in half bottles?"

"Here's a North Fork gewürztraminer that should be superb." He turned to the waitress,

"Please have the chef fix two plates, both the same with a dozen pieces, six nigiri and six ·sashimi. His choice, just no crab or shrimp, just fish. Also, we'll share a tuna roll and I'll start with a half dozen oysters, three of each of those on the menu. And, please, a half bottle of the gewurtz."

"Uncle Nathan? Well, Thomas McKeon we travel in good company today. Friends of the admiralty, we are."

The wine arrived, was opened and a taste poured. McKeon took a sniff and smiled and then he passed the glass to Gaby, "She is my *bec fin*, my sniffer and taster." And with Gaby's smile and nod of approval the golden liquid was poured and the bouquet was noticeable from the glasses as they sat on the table.

"Nice choice, fellow traveler. Cheers!"

Gaby managed to pilfer a pair of his oysters, both sweet and briny, and with no adornment except a light squeeze of lemon, and she slurped them directly from the shell. Everything was excellent and McKeon left an appropriately generous tip, in cash.

On the way home he pulled into the Milk Pail and Gaby found three varieties of apples, her minimum number for a proper pie.

<<<>>>

Saturday night Tommy V. was at home with Mike Michaels as his guest. They had just finished tuna steaks from a small yellowfin he had caught. Grilled outside on a hardwood fire all he added for a perfect meal were sliced tomatoes and homemade coleslaw. At nine p.m. his phone rang and the display read "unknown caller". He looked toward his friend who pointed at the phone and said, "Do it!"

"Yaa-low, Tommy here."

"Van Winkle?" The accent was New Bedford. Waterfront.

"That's me. Who's this?"

"Not sure we've met but you shipped with my son, Jamie Flynn. Remember him?"

Michaels had moved next to Tommy when he'd pointed to the phone and waved him over. Head to head, he could hear the conversation.

"I think so, it was on *The Half Shell*, a scalloper, wunnit?"

"That's right. Good memory. I called 'cause I need

some help and I remembered your name and found you there in Montauk."

"What do you need, Mr. Flynn?"

"Simon, to you, Tommy."

Mike pointed to the phone and mouthed "Flynn?" Tommy nodded yes.

"I need someone to deliver something for me. I can't get anywhere near the spot in my Down Easter. Are you interested?"

"What am I supposed to be interested in exactly?"

Michaels, knowing the police would be listening, made a "stretch it out" move with his hands.

"Let's say ten grand in cash. Does that interest you?"

"A gift, Simon?"

"For two hours work I'd call it that. Yes, a gift."

"What's the work?" and Tommy heard the ching-a-ching of a pay phone.

"Moving a couple of bales for me. Three to be exact."

"Bales mean weed, dunnit?"

"Yup. As I recall and hear tell you was quite familiar with it and other stuff."

"Was is the operative word there, Simon. Was. You mean risk my boat, arrest, and jail for ten grand? You must be kidding!"

"That was just a starting figure. Do you have a number in mind?"

Tommy looked at Michaels who mouthed, "Not right now." And pointed to his head, "Think about it."

"No number, Simon, I'd have to think about it. Give me a day or so."

"I don't have much time so I'll call you tomorrow same time..." And the line cut off.

The two friends sat down but Michaels was up almost at once and went to the fridge and came back with two beers.

"Jeez, Mike, there it is. Not a happy camper right now. Simon Flynn? Did you know him?"

"Unfortunately, I did, as a big, tough SOB. His kid, Jamie, was quiet. Good kid but a stone head."

"And who wasn't?"

When the phone rang again, they looked at each other and Michaels went over and checked the caller ID. "McKeon!"

After Tommy had finished talking to McKeon and had replaced the phone, Michaels called Wakeland, told him about the call and that they were meeting McKeon and Conklin in the a.m. in Montauk

"Did you say it was Simon Flynn who called?"

"Yup, do you remember him?"

"Sure do. His son Jamie ODd a couple of years ago. Heard it on the grape vine. He was crew with me on my last boat, just before I left town."

"The kid?"

"Yeah. Heard the old man went nuts over it. He confronted the captain and threatened him and the crew. Must have blamed him I guess."

"Did he know you were on the crew with Jamie?"

"Yeah, and when he wasn't fishing alone, he'd often meet us at the dock to meet Jamie and lend a hand.

"Fred, you need to join us in the morning with the police. Cappie's not working. Sunday is always family and church day for him."

After talking to Tommy and Conklin, McKeon called the Barracks and spoke to the sarge at the night desk and put him to work. He had a name now and that would let the office go to the computer and start digging. McKeon told him that he'd be there at the Barracks at eight a.m. and if by then nothing had turned up, he would be talking to the New Bedford Police. Grudgingly McKeon went to bed as for the moment there was nothing else to do. Slipping under the covers he muttered, "And visions of weed bales danced in his head."

"Honey?"

"Nothing, Mrs. McKeon, nothing at all."

<<<>>>

Day 33: Sunday, August 24th

McKeon reached for the computer printout the sleep-deprived sergeant held out for him. Nothing in the NY or CT records that they could search, and the only reason he could see that far was because the Montauk Coasties were responsible for portions of those states' waters.

He picked up his office phone and moments later Verizon information had connected him to the New Bedford Police.

"Good morning, Sergeant Shea speaking. How can I help you?"

After introduction and explanation Shea spoke again.

"I'd be glad to help you, sir, but we will need an official request. If you fax me on your stationary, I'll have someone get right on it."

McKeon jotted down the fax number and swiveled around to his computer, logged on and clicked on 'shortcut to TFM letterhead' and waited for Microsoft Word to open. He printed the completed letter and faxed it to Shea.

His phone rang 'Got it, sir, and we'll get right to it."

McKeon glanced at his watch, "Montauk, here I come," and told the day room where he'd be and to call him when they had anything from New Bedford.

At the Montauk Barracks, he greeted the three fishermen and handed Conklin a CD.

"Terry, could you play this for us?" He walked to the coffee pot, looked back and saw everyone with a cup, filled his own, and sat at the large table in the day room and watched as the desk sergeant. went to his computer. Moments later they were listening to Tommy V.'s conversation with Simon Flynn.

Michaels spoke first, pre-empting the policemen,

"I got Fred to come along because of what he told us last night. You need to hear this." And when no one objected he pointed to Wakeland.

When Wakeland had finished retelling his information, he saw McKeon and Conklin looking not at him but at each other. Finally, McKeon turned to him and began.

"Fred, you may have just given us his motive, the revenge of his son's death. But why blame you five alone?"

His cell rang.

"McKeon. Good, Fax it over." He turned to Conklin. "From New Bedford. Maybe it will add something. But as yet I don't understand Flynn, just what he's doing."

The fax rang and began to print. Two pages finally sat in the attached bin. Conklin looked at them briefly and handed them to McKeon. Page two held his interest.

"Well, no police record and no prints. Two years ago, he wound up in the ER with scalp lacerations and was banged up some. X-rays and CT were negative but he needed to be restrained and a psych consult was called. He was labeled 'schizoid/sociopathic' and was hospitalized. Apparently, he'd decompensated after his son's demise. Flynn was finally discharged on medications. They have had no contact or record other than this one. So, apparently he went bonkers and, it seems to me, he still is not right. Let's back track to Sayger and Storz. What was each one's connection to Simon or Jamie Flynn? Sayger first. Anyone?"

Van Winkle began. "At one point, Sayger, Storz, and I were on the *Half Shell* together. That was before Fred."

"Hold it!" McKeon interrupted. "Before Fred?"

"Yes, sir, I'll get to that. We were a man short on the boat and Cappie asked if we knew someone. Well, this kid, Jamie, had been hanging around and seemed nice. He said he could shuck fast. So, we told Cappie and he hired him."

"Was he on drugs then?"

"Dunno. Don't think so. Mike? Fred?"

Both men shrugged.

"So he worked out OK, and sometimes he'd share weed with us, you know, a beer or two and a joint. I don't think he knew we were stoneheads. After a year or so Sayger quit and Cappie replaced him."

"Hold it again! Did Simon ever mix with you guys, beer and a joint? Did he know Sayger and Storz?"

"Yes, once in a while. Rumor was he'd once been a crackhead but was clean. Made a point of saying 'nothing but weed is safe'. So, Cappie had to replace Sayger and then a few months later, Storz. Cappie couldn't get regulars and was relying on day workers until, I guess, Fred signed on. I left soon after. That about it, Fred?"

"Best as I know. I left the *Half Shell* six or so months later. Couldn't deal with the catch-up crews who didn't carry their load."

McKeon looked up from his notes. "Tommy, was Jamie on drugs when you left?"

"Probably."

"You are not sure?"

"Hard to tell on the boat. But he was always short of money and always mooching. So, I guess, yes."

"Fred, same question."

"When I left there was no question. Yes."

"So," McKeon began, "a kid who is probably clean starts to work on a scallop boat, recommended by three guys who are addicted, becomes an addict and ODs. And his father is pissed, pissed and psychotic. And now two men are dead. Jeez, Louise!"

The room was silent until Conklin stood and went to the coffee pot.

"Tom, can't we call New Bedford and ask them to pick him up? Don't we have adequate suspicion and evidence to do that?"

"In our own jurisdiction probably we would have, I'd say yes. We could get a warrant, search his place, and get prints and DNA."

His cell rang once again.

"McKeon. Christ! Sorry, He's called again but this time on a cell." A visibly disturbed Detective McKeon looked at Conklin. "Flynn says he's on the way down here. He left a message on Tommy's machine. He even left his cell number! He's upped the ante to twenty-five grand for six bales and he'll be off Block by dusk."

The three fishermen were silent and Tommy looked ill.

McKeon was up and pacing the room. "It doesn't make sense. None at all, without an answer from Tommy. We know there are no bales, and he knows because no one would wander around in daylight loaded with six bales. He wouldn't get out of Bedford with that on board. So, he has not budged. He's home. This is a ruse to get Tommy's interest and get him moving." He turned to Van Winkle.

"Tommy, call him. on your cell. Tell him you were checking your messages from the marina. You are working on your motor so no way you can get to Block today. Can you do this?"

Reaching into his shirt pocket he took out his iPhone, looked at McKeon, let out a deep breath and dialed. When Flynn answered, Tommy played him perfectly, no breaks or quaver in his voice.

"Yes, I'm stuck here for now."

McKeon prompted him to say a day or so, at least, probably Tuesday repairs will be done.

"Yes, Simon, I'll have parts in the a.m. and a tech to help. But it might be Tuesday. Can't you get in here?"

Tommy gave a "dunno" wobble with his hand and pointed to his phone. "Well, if you call, I'll be here."

He looked at McKeon. "You were right, he was trolling me. Even though he did not ask if the twenty-five grand was OK, he was assuming I'd call back. Now what, sir?"

Conklin gestured and tapped the table with his pen. "My guess is that we will hear back from him, either today or in the a.m. It's what? Noon, on Sunday? I think we need to prepare for his dropping in on us tonight. Get our assets in position now. And if it turns out to be a practice run, that's fine. Tomorrow we'll be wrinkle free. If he calls back, we'll be ready. Tom?"

McKeon had been walking toward the coffee but stopped. "We need the listening set up, an armed man on each of the two boats on either side of Tommy's, and he needs some protection. We can start with a light Kevlar vest and add whatever we think appropriate, something in his hands. There will be no gaff on Tommy's boat we're OK in that respect, but if we see Flynn head toward Tommy with a visible weapon, or if he goes back to his boat, aborts, it will be fine to take him down, before he can get back to Tommy. And we have to have someone cripple him if he shows a weapon from his boat. And, just as important, the

Coasties have to know he's around the moment we do. Can we do this Terry? Do you have the bodies for tonight?"

"I do and I'll get on it now." Conklin went into his office. McKeon called Chris Dempsey at the Yacht Club and told him to be ready for Conklin's crew. Then he spoke to Tommy.

"I am sure we can protect you but it would be smart to stay away from Flynn if you can. Also, we need you to ID him as soon as you can. Just say 'It's Flynn'. We don't want to make a mistake."

"I only saw him a couple of times when he met us unloading the *Half Shell*, but I'll certainly know if it's someone else."

"Good. We'll hear any and all conversation. All of us." He turned and went to Conklin's office.

"Terry, find a spot for me. Maybe next to Flynn's slip. If any mistake is made, I want it to be mine. Just clear it with Dempsey." McKeon went back out to Van Winkle,

"I'll be around whenever it happens, and tonight you'll have an armed guest, just in case. Gentlemen, find something to do and stay alert. Terry," he called toward Conklin's office, "do we have any eyes out on the water tonight?"

Conklin waved him into his office, "I have not heard as yet, but 'I'm sure Furlong can set something up with the radar. I'll call him in a moment."

<<<>>>

Flynn sat staring at the kitchen clock and moldering over his options. Not for Van Winkle, but for the next two men whose faces were on his wall. He'd almost concluded that he might not be able to get at them because the entire East End would be on alert. He felt that the chance of getting at these two was rapidly escaping him. "Not by boat and not now" was becoming his mantra and he did not like it.

The fact that his rented mooring at the Yacht Club was not next to Van Winkle also annoyed him, especially the seeming distance from Tommy's boat. Yes, stern to stern they would be about fifteen feet apart and what would it take? Ten seconds? To get out, walk across the dock and then hop down into the other boat? And when Van Winkle saw there were no bales visible? Tommy couldn't run away but he could go overboard. Then what? It was looking like too much time and too many chances for a mistake. Getting up for another beer he saw his harpoon standing next to the door. Picking it up the thought, my stern will be level with the dock so I'll be looking down at him and, at most, twenty feet away from me. Just tell him why I'm going to kill him and do it without getting out of my boat. And then just get out of there. He'll die quicker than if I gaffed him. Tomorrow night, not tonight, it's Sunday. Better tomorrow.

At nine he called Van Winkle.

"You got your motor fixed?"

"No, the tech is coming tomorrow or Tuesday."

There was a pause and then Flynn's voice again. "OK, I'll chance getting in and out in the dark. Ten or ten-thirty at your boat tomorrow night."

And the line went silent, but a minute later McKeon called.

"Is the officer with you?"

"Yes, and also Mike."

"Fine. I'm going home to get some sleep and I suggest all of you do the same."

20

Day 34: Monday, August 25th

THE NIGHT BEFORE all had gone smoothly in what had turned out to be the practice run. Men were in place, armed, and well-hidden but where, in a moment's notice, they could confront Flynn. Conklin had mounted several spotlights which could immediately light up Flynn's boat, blinding him, and hopefully freezing his movements long enough for the police to apprehend him. So, when McKeon called Conklin that Monday morning both men were sanguine about their ability to achieve a desirable outcome this evening: an arrest and Tommy unscathed.

McKeon was particularly pleased with his perch on the flying bridge of the big Hatteras next to Flynn's slip. He would be stationed well above Flynn with a clear view of him and his boat. The final piece they'd put in place tonight was one of the Coasties with night vision binoculars perched atop Goswell's, a location giving him a clear view of the entrance to Lake Montauk. His station would also have two craft manned and ready to intercept if Flynn managed to leave the Yacht Club marina.

As excruciatingly slowly the day seemed to pass for McKeon, it seemed to fly for Tommy. He and the Montauk trooper went to his boat, took the cowling off of his 225hp Yamaha engine, laid tarps on the stern and port gunwales, and laid tools in easy sight on the deck. He'd added a baseball bat and a pepper spray when he came back later that day.

In case Flynn arrived earlier than expected everyone was at the marina by seven-thirty and the Coastie was atop Goswell's. When at nine he was still not in sight, everyone took their positions. All weapons were checked and rounds would be chambered when Flynn was spotted approaching the inlet to the lake.

Furlong saw him first on radar, the only vessel moving toward them. They waited to hear from the Coastie spotter. It was twenty minutes later when the Coastie saw the boat and radioed to Conklin "Down Easter" and only a few minutes later "Inlet" and then "In the lake!"

Flynn's boat had its running lights on and as he approached the Yacht Club, they could hear the groan of the big diesel engine as he slowed down even further. McKeon watched him crawl past the empty slip and then reverse, turning the stern toward the dock. After two more adjustments of the Down Easter McKeon felt his boat rock slightly and then heard Flynn's boat touch the dock. His motor idling in reverse kept his stern pushed against the dock.

As Tommy watched, his left hand opened and closed on the bat and with his right hand he felt for the spray. He stayed leaning on the center console eight feet from his stern. The lights went on in Flynn's cabin and then he turned and walked to the stern of his boat. Pausing at the gunwale, he pointed at Tommy.

"As you can see there are no bales on my boat. Just me. Had to get you here some way and I counted on a greedy ex-druggie to jump at cash."

He put a hand on the gun rail, felt the moisture and then cautiously stepped up onto it and steadied himself with what looked like a pole.

"You have no idea why I'm here do you?"

Tommy shook his head "no".

"Sayger, Stortz, you, and the others killed my son. Got him on drugs and then he drowned in his own puke. Them two drowned in their own blood and you, Mr. Winkle, are next!"

The young Montauk police officer who was sequestered on the flying bridge of the huge vessel to Tommy's port side moved cautiously in his eyrie to obtain a better siting for his weapon. The Down Easter swayed slightly as its running motor held it against the dock and mooring poles. A gentle rocking of all the neighboring boats ensued and transmitted to the flying bridge a magnified motion just enough to unsettle the policeman up there. He moved his left foot in an effort to steady himself. It was just a couple of inches but suddenly he was off the narrow platform. An airborne "God damn!" was followed by a decrescendo "Noooooooo!" and a resonant thud on the deck below.

As Tommy turned and saw the young officer scrambling on the lower deck, Flynn jumped back into his cabin, threw his motor into forward, and accelerated out of the slip. Turning as sharply as he could, his boat bounced off the bow in the adjoining slip and then headed toward Lake Montauk. In the excitement and relative darkness, neither McKeon or the officer in the starboard boat could get off a shot. Conklin radioed the Coasties to intercept. Flynn was halfway to the inlet when a spotlight from the station's smaller but fastest vessel lit up his stern and cabin.

"Flynn, heave to," came over a loud speaker.

Flynn pushed the throttle to full speed and swerved toward the Coast Guard boat and then almost immediately turned back, causing a huge wake toward the Coastie vessel. Behind him he saw he was being chased by one of the inflatables used in rough water rescues, and his move had done nothing to slow it.

"Flynn, stop or we will fire."

He stepped out of his cabin and picked up the harpoon and hurled it at the inflatable closing in on him. His missile glanced tangentially off the boat and landed harmlessly in the water. The sharp stone jetties of the inlet were just ahead of him when he heard a short burst of a machine gun and felt the bullets hit the hull of his boat. Looking ahead he saw three or four well-lit boats blocking the inlet.

A second burst of fire raked his stern at the water line and then a third burst swept along his starboard, hitting his engine. Quickly his steering was lost and he headed toward the rock jetty. He was still traveling at twelve knots when his bow smashed into the rocks. He stumbled out of the bow and onto the rocks and headed for shore. Armed Coast Guard men stationed at the base of the jetty watched as Flynn fled towards them. Again, he heard the loud speaker, "Flynn, on the ground or we shoot!"

When Flynn kept running and bellowing with rage, one of the Coasties dropped to one knee, took aim at his legs, and fired a single shot. Flynn went tumbling down and then tried to crawl away. In seconds the two officers had subdued and cuffed him. The single shot had shattered his tibia and dislocated his knee. Not many minutes later McKeon and a still annoyed Conklin arrived to read Flynn his rights and wait for the ambulance.

Epilogue

It was as if a divine blessing had been bestowed on the East End, for the long Labor Day weekend had passed uneventfully for the people and constabulary living there.

On Tuesday, September 2nd, the New Bedford police contacted McKeon with the details of their search of Flynn's house and they faxed him a picture of the desk with the five photos on the wall above it. They also found two bloody gaffs hanging on the first two of five hooks in his garage. DNA samples from them were in the lab.

Simon Flynn was convicted of two counts of murder in the first degree and one count of attempted murder. His sentence was three consecutive life terms without parole. His boat had been impounded by the Coast Guard, its fate to be determined at a later date.

McKeon and Gabby celebrated the outcome with a bottle of fine Oregon pino noir.